Praise

"Varni delivers a solid debut focusing on the stories of ordinary Midwesterners. Readers will appreciate the small-town flavor and humorous anecdotes."

Library Journal

"This novel is a love letter to small towns and unlikely friendships, to the family you build around you and the faith you make your own."

Reading Is My Superpower

"The author has a way of describing people that really brings them to life. This book brings people closer to one another and encourages them to make connections."

Compass Book Ratings

"*On Moonberry Lake* is sure to sweep you up and away with characters who will reach into your soul and make you long for friends just like them."

Interviews & Reviews

"Delightful! Charming! Full of characters who take up residence in your heart. The best of 'News from Lake Wobegon' and Father Tim combined."

Lauraine Snelling, bestselling author
of the Red River of the North series

"An uplifting novel about the power of small-town community."

Suzanne Woods Fisher, bestselling author of *The Sweet Life*

The Blooming of Delphinium

The Blooming of Delphinium

A Moonberry Lake Novel

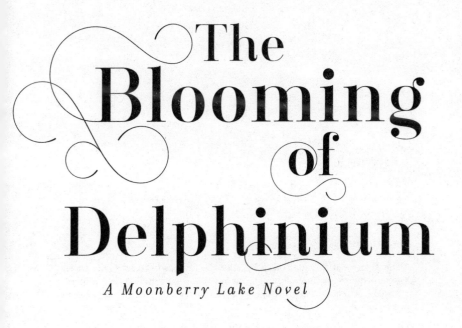

HOLLY VARNI

Revell

a division of Baker Publishing Group
Grand Rapids, Michigan

© 2024 by Holly C. Varni

Published by Revell
a division of Baker Publishing Group
Grand Rapids, Michigan
RevellBooks.com

Printed in the United States of America

Library of Congress Cataloging-in-Publication Data
Names: Varni, Holly, 1972– author.
Title: The blooming of Delphinium : / Holly Varni.
Description: Grand Rapids, Michigan : Revell, a division of Baker Publishing Group, 2024. | Series: A Moonberry Lake Novel
Identifiers: LCCN 2024005086 | ISBN 9780800744984 (paper) | ISBN 9780800746469 (casebound) | ISBN 9781493447268 (ebook)
Subjects: LCGFT: Romance fiction. | Novels.
Classification: LCC PS3622.A755 B58 2024 | DDC 813/.6—dc23/eng/20240205
LC record available at https://lccn.loc.gov/2024005086

Cover photo illustration: Anton Markous
Cover design: Laura Klynstra

The author is represented by Illuminate Literary Agency, www.illuminateliterary.com.

Baker Publishing Group publications use paper produced from sustainable forestry practices and postconsumer waste whenever possible.

24 25 26 27 28 29 30   7 6 5 4 3 2 1

To my James
There is nothing better than the sound of your voice
and your scent—other than your love.

*The most precious gift we can offer others is
 our presence.
When mindfulness embraces those we love,
 they will bloom like flowers.*

Thich Nhat Hanh

One

Delphinium Hayes could identify the goodness—or wicked-ness—of a person by their scent. With the slightest passing whiff, she immediately knew someone's most admirable or weediest characteristic.

Generosity had the full-bodied boldness of lilies. Kindness possessed the reserved yet intense fragrance of pink azaleas. Humility smelled of lilies of the valley. Those who had a great sense of humor or who were natural storytellers conspicuously reeked of poppies. And people who were good at keeping secrets were rose-scented.

When the smell of rhododendron wafted around a person, it was a dead giveaway that the individual was vain and selfish. Bullies who insisted on getting their way stank of onion weed, liars were always oleander, and wisteria sprang up from hypochondriacs.

Delphinium used her ability to her advantage. She knew which buyer at her flower shop would be good to work with and which would cheat her. She had the dearest and most trustworthy friends, and customers marveled at her knack for giving them exactly what they were seeking. Her acute sensitivity was her intuition and guide, telling her someone's true character before they even spoke. This perception never failed.

Until it did.

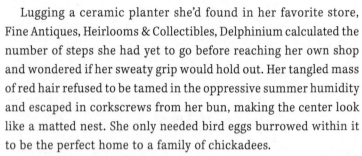

Lugging a ceramic planter she'd found in her favorite store, Fine Antiques, Heirlooms & Collectibles, Delphinium calculated the number of steps she had yet to go before reaching her own shop and wondered if her sweaty grip would hold out. Her tangled mass of red hair refused to be tamed in the oppressive summer humidity and escaped in corkscrews from her bun, making the center look like a matted nest. She only needed bird eggs burrowed within it to be the perfect home to a family of chickadees.

Though her namesake flower came from the azure shade of her eyes, her hair, compassion, and intuition came from her beloved grandmother, Annie. Delphinium could still picture the old woman's white hair springing out of her head like fusilli pasta, making a near-audible *boing* as she moved.

Delphinium smiled wistfully as she adjusted her grip. How her grandmother would have loved to go antique shopping and find such a treasure. She let out a heavy sigh. The lingering grief from the absence of her kindred spirit pressed on her chest. Annie was the only person who had truly understood her—she not only believed in Delphinium's ability but celebrated it.

Annie had known what it was like to be different, or at least to feel that way. She had lived with a form of synesthesia where she saw color and even tasted flavor for every letter and number. The letter *A* was red, *O* was white, *P* was orange, and *E* was teal. The number *5* was blue, and *2* was green. When her grandmother bit into a brownie, she tasted purple. All the mundane components within ordinary life were an assault on the senses, an exploding rainbow always in front of her eyes or on her tongue.

As a little girl, Delphinium had wanted to be just like Annie and was devastated when *K* didn't appear magenta or when she couldn't taste saffron when she saw *47*.

However, her consolation prize of genetics, or her "gifting," as Annie insisted on calling it, was her ability to smell fragrances that were nearly imperceptible to everyone else. Scents not created by perfume or soap but what a person emitted naturally.

In a small way, Delphinium felt like she had a superpower too, and that was her link to her grandmother. Instead of seeing colors, she smelled personality traits. No matter how faint, Delphinium was able to detect a fragrance linked to the person's most dominant characteristic. All she had to do was get a whiff for the insight.

Delphinium blew out a sharp breath to move a bouncing curl from her line of vision. The stagnant, muggy late-June air melted not only her eyeliner but her patience as well. Every passerby looked as wilted as she felt. The humidity made it hard to breathe. Her nose wrinkled as a puff of petunia wafted from a man who walked past her, appearing equally annoyed with the foul weather as she was. Petunia always indicated anger and resentment.

Feeling a trickle of sweat trail down the hollow of her back, she held the cumbersome planter in a protective cradle, determined not to let it slip from her grasp. The front of her shirt was going to be badly wrinkled from dampness.

Delphinium groaned. *Why couldn't I have waited for it to be delivered? Why can't I ever simply wait?*

She knew the answer, of course. When it came to her beloved store, she possessed the tolerance of a toddler. As soon as she had seen the beautiful hand-painted planter dreadfully misplaced and abandoned on the bottom shelf of the antique store, she envisioned the exact plant she was going to put in it—bird of paradise—and the price she'd get for the match. The three-block jaunt to her shop would pay off.

Surely it would turn a nice profit.

That's why she was heaving this monstrosity down Main Street, she told herself. She'd rather be more creative and come up with lucrative arrangements customers couldn't resist than hike up all her prices to pay the mortgage on her corner property. Her dire financial state only meant she needed to up her game in presentation and quality.

Giving herself little pep talks calmed her down when she was anxious and helped her lift her head proudly in these moments when she knew she looked like a hot mess.

Literally.

Main Street was the heart of the small Northwoods town of Moonberry Lake, Minnesota, and she knew she and the oversized planter made quite a spectacle. Having ogling eyes was known as perfect vision in the small town. Delphinium was accustomed to her family feeding the gossip mill.

Annie had been a regular topic among coffee shop discussions. Being quirky or, rather, having an "artistic flair," as Annie described it, attracted stares. "The price for not being ordinary," she'd say, waving a bit too enthusiastically toward scrutinizing eyes. "Be proud to be the *spectacle*, not the spectator, sweetheart."

Delphinium's shoulders relaxed a bit as she approached the shop. She pushed open the door, and it dragged, sticking halfway. With a grunt and a swift kick, she budged the door another inch, allowing her to escape the outside heat.

"Paavo! The door is sticking!"

Placing the planter down on the counter carefully, she shouted again, "Paavo, where are you?"

Wiping away the strands of hair stuck to her sweaty forehead, she headed to the storage area and back room. Paavo was standing at the worktable, pulling thorns out of a shipment of roses. Although he had his earbuds in, she could hear the distant clamor of music from ten feet away. She walked closer and waved her arms. He pulled out one of the earbuds.

"Oh hey, Miz D. I didn't hear you come in."

Between his earnest smile and the chilly air-conditioning, her annoyance dissipated quickly. "Paavo, didn't you notice that the front door sticks?"

The teen shook his head. "Nope. I came in through the back door. There's nothing wrong with that door."

"Well, the *front* door, which coincidentally is the entrance to the business, drags like it's being pushed through taffy."

An ornery voice spoke from behind her. "That's because this horrid weather is making the wood expand. Everything swells up. My fingers are like sausages!" Henry, her right hand in this business, must have been one minute behind her. He came in regularly to check that everything was running "shipshape."

"Good morning, Henry."

The elderly man tipped an imaginary hat at her in greeting. "That flowerpot out there is a pretty one. You'll get a good price with the right plant."

Delphinium smiled. Great minds think alike. "Checking on me this early?"

Tight-lipped, the man shook his head, his jowls hanging slightly below his jawline.

She didn't miss the quick glance between Henry and Paavo. "What?" she asked. "What are you guys not telling me?"

Paavo grinned at Henry. "They're in the refrigerator."

"What's in the refrigerator?" she asked.

But before either of them could respond, Delphinium strode over to the floor-to-ceiling cooler door. After pulling it open, she stared at the contents, turned around, and marched back to her two employees, hands on her hips.

"Does someone want to tell me why there are three *men* in my refrigerator?"

A huge smile spread across Paavo's face. "They're playing cards."

She felt her mouth open.

"Now, Delphi, hold on a second," Henry began, but she was already marching back to the oversized refrigerator.

Opening the door again, she studied the three elderly, half-dressed men sitting on upside-down tall, white buckets. "Excuse me, gentlemen, but why are you playing cards in my walk-in fridge?"

Hunched in concentration, two of the men didn't even look up from their hands, and the one who did answered her question with a question. "Why do you look like a raccoon?" His face contorted.

Henry stepped to her side, draping an arm around her shoulders.

"The answer to both questions is that it's blazing hot outside and we're all melting." He looked her in the eyes. "Your makeup runs clean down your face in this temperature, but for us, we're at risk of melting into a clump of wax. We needed a place to play poker where we wouldn't die doing it, and I suggested here. It's the coolest place in town."

Delphinium wasn't following his logic. "What's wrong with The Gardens?" Henry's typical hangout was the game room at the assisted living facility where all the men lived.

With a scowl etched into his face, man number two spoke up. "The air-conditioning is out everywhere except the dining hall, so they tried to herd us all in there like cattle. The room is a mass overcrowding of wheelchairs and sleepyheads. And the director only allows cards if we don't gamble. There's no fun if there ain't somethin' at stake."

"This is a free country and I'll gamble if I want to. It's my right!" barked one of the other men, still not looking up from his cards.

"We should know. We fought for this country. We fought to be able to gamble, and that director is unpatriotic for denying us that right!" the third man piped in with a fight in his tone. The other men grumbled in agreement.

"All right, boys, simmer down," Henry interjected. "Delphi is fine with us being here."

Delphinium whipped her head to the side to gawk at him. "I never said that!"

He patted her on the back. "We just need to give her time to get used to having the walking dead in her cooler."

All the men chuckled.

Poker Player Number One, the grumpy man who had pointed out what a mess she was, looked up at her again. "We're being *preserved* in here instead of turning into a liquefied mess like the others down at the home."

Delphinium scrutinized him. "So how long will this *preservation* take?"

"Forever!" he shouted.

"Anarchy!" Poker Player Number Two added, raising one fist in the air.

"Jump ship!" Poker Player Number Three yelled.

Delphinium turned to Henry, who smiled crookedly at the feisty behavior of his buddies. He shrugged as if to say he had no control over what was happening in her shop. "I guess that's your answer. Any other questions?" The goofy grin on his face indicated he was enjoying their rebellion.

Delphinium whispered in Henry's good ear. "Why must they all be in their undershirts?" She looked back at the men in their too-thin white tank tops. "Are you playing strip poker?"

"Oh no, it's just more comfortable this way." Henry winked, then stepped inside the giant cooler and began unbuttoning his own shirt. "The fact that this cooler only runs on half its cylinders makes it the ideal temp."

She frowned at the reminder of another expense. "It's on the list to fix."

"Don't. It's the perfect breeze in here." He smiled.

She sighed, her shoulders lowering in defeat, knowing this was no battle to fight. She felt totally drained, and it wasn't even ten o'clock. With a roll of her eyes, she turned and left the men to their game.

"Shut the door!" they yelled in unison.

She went back and closed the door, shaking her head. *What am I going to do with a refrigerator full of elderly men?*

She let out another long sigh. "I need to find a person who's a hydrangea," she muttered as she passed Paavo on her way to open the shop.

He paused in putting his earbud back in. "What's a hydrangea?"

"Hydrangeas are always team players. I need someone to take my side and agree that this place is out of control!" she said over her shoulder.

She reached the front counter, then absentmindedly opened

the drawer where Paavo always put the mail. The sight of three words stamped in red on the top envelope caused her to close the drawer just as fast.

Notice of Foreclosure.

The beating of her heart thumped loudly, and her head began to swim.

It's just the heat. She drew in a breath and focused on the expansion of her lungs.

Opening the drawer again, she glanced at the envelope, willing the printed red words to change.

They didn't.

They might as well have been stamped in blood by the way her heart ached.

The reality of eviction was getting dire. Things were going from bad to worse.

She slammed the drawer shut.

Breathe.

Just breathe.

Two

Reaching the front of the store, Delphinium turned over the quaint sign with *Open* painted in pretty scroll, flipped on the lights, and then paused for a moment to imagine the feeling customers would get at first sight of Delphinium's Flora Emporium. The charm of the flower shop always made her smile, and she hoped it made others happy upon entry also.

It was a place she'd enjoy browsing if she wasn't the owner. Beside the vast array of beautiful flowers and plants against the painted delphinium-blue walls, there were flower-related gifts scattered like little treasures to discover—napkins with big sunflowers printed on them, dish towels with embroidered lavender sprigs, stationery decorated with forget-me-nots, soy candles in rose, geranium, and hibiscus scents, and fairy houses to add whimsy to any garden.

The shop held an eclectic selection of vases and planters that accentuated a flower's or plant's beauty. Delphinium hunted for the most uncommon containers, ones that could be works of art if they stood empty. She hoped her artist's eye and slightly outlandish taste would draw customers back. Both she and the store had a reputation for being different.

And she loved it.

Delphinium wore her oddness proudly like an heirloom brooch. She was honored to be Annie's granddaughter. She only wished she had also inherited her grandmother's tenacious confidence. The woman was the brightest bloom in any gathering, while Delphinium was more shy. The only time she felt confident was when she was in her shop surrounded by her flowers. Annie had always consoled Delphinium's concern over her insecurities by declaring her an "old soul." Perhaps that was why she felt more comfortable with older people than those her age.

Unlocking the cash register, she opened and closed the drawer at the same moment the front door opened.

A man with perfect eyebrows and chestnut hair with just the right amount of wave eased open the door as if its hinges were buttered. Dressed in a starched white shirt, navy dress pants that still showed the crease, and expensive Italian leather shoes, he appeared untouched by the sweltering heat. Confidence radiated from him, and Delphinium found herself staring at his cool, self-assured walk. Appearing to be perhaps in his midthirties, he wore his age like most people do when they find their true skin in their fifties.

Delphinium gulped as he moved around the space with an air of ownership. She knew his type. He didn't take the spotlight—he *was* the spotlight in whatever room he entered.

She cleared her throat. "Good morning."

The gentleman glanced over at her and startled, his eyes widening. He stared at her for a moment and then looked away. Delphinium brushed off her paranoia as nervousness and straightened her shoulders. She would not repeat past mistakes. *Stay professional.*

"Please let me know if I can help you."

He nodded. "Thank you."

She watched him browse some displays and then lightly trace the petals of a hyacinth. "These are pretty," he commented.

"Are you apologizing to this person?"

"Excuse me?" he asked, turning to her.

"Purple hyacinth typically means you are asking for forgiveness."

One of his eyebrows lifted, and a small smile played at the corners of his mouth. "I see."

"What type of flowers are you looking for?"

"Something for a friend. How about these?" He pointed to a vase of white jasmine.

"It's a good choice if you're in love."

He retracted his hand as if something had stung him. "Oh, no, no. Like I said, she's a *friend*."

"Then you can't go wrong with chrysanthemums."

"Do you have any of those?"

Delphinium went over to a huge collection of raspberry-colored blooms.

The man took his time considering them. "Hmm. They're not that remarkable."

"They will be if I mix them with some dahlia, calla lilies, and hypericum berries. Then they would be glorious."

He stared at her unapologetically. His blue eyes were haunting in their paleness, and his nose was a bit crooked as if it had been badly broken in his youth.

She found his boldness unnerving. Just as she was about to break the uncomfortable silence, he spoke. "Would you like to use this?" He took a handkerchief from his pocket and offered it to her.

She looked at it, confused.

He brought his index finger up to his face and tapped the skin beneath his eyes.

His response dawned on her. She'd forgotten about her smeared makeup. She took the handkerchief. "Thank you."

The man suddenly seemed enamored with a grouping of bromeliad that were browning at the tips while she turned to a cabinet with a mirror backing. The frightening reflection made her gasp. She resembled a character straight out of a horror movie. Her eyeliner and mascara had liquefied in dramatic streaks down her reddened cheeks. She rubbed her face vigorously with the handkerchief.

"I would like that bouquet you spoke of with the chrysanthemums."

She turned, pasting on a smile. "Lovely. Just fill out the delivery information for me." She slid a pad of paper across the counter.

He cleared his throat. "Actually, I'd like to deliver these myself."

"Oh, that's great. Let me get started on the bouquet, then."

She gathered up the flowers she needed and went to the back, her arms full, and placed the bundle on the worktable.

Paavo's face lit up. "Haven't been open fifteen minutes and you already have your first customer. Things are definitely looking up. Maybe it's a sign that the shop will have a stellar day in sales."

She nodded and gave Paavo a small smile. She had hired the optimistic teenager as soon as he entered the store smelling like daisies. Trying to focus, she went to work. For some reason, she felt distracted. Putting together creative arrangements was the reason she got started in the flower business. It was her passion to work with flowers, combining complex colors and scents. She took a deep breath in an effort to calm her nerves and grabbed some twigs and a couple roses Paavo had just finished stripping. Six minutes later, she tied the arrangement with a satin bow and held it up.

"Whoa," Paavo said. "I don't know how you do it, Miz D."

Delphinium gave a small smile, satisfied with the end product too. She walked to the front of the store and placed the bouquet on the counter. The man stared at it, his eyes widening for the second time that morning.

She waited for a compliment or at least a comment, but nothing came.

"Is something wrong?" she asked. "You don't like it?"

He lifted one hand to stroke his jaw and studied the arrangement. "They are not what I was expecting. They're . . . magnificent."

"I'm glad you like them."

"I don't."

Her fingers froze on the cash register buttons.

He went on to explain. "You took something that was supposed to be simple and turned it into something extraordinary."

She stared at him.

"What I need"—he hesitated, looking a bit embarrassed—"is a *bad* bouquet."

She must not have heard him correctly.

"You see, I was hoping for something humble," he said hurriedly. "Something more . . . um, *mediocre*." He spoke the last word quieter, as if anticipating her reaction.

Delphinium flinched as though she'd been slapped. "Sir, I do not make *mediocre* bouquets. I wouldn't be able to stay in business if my arrangements were mediocre. Customers would not come here if they got some subpar, thrown-together, ordinary bunch of flowers. My standard is nothing close to a *bad* bouquet."

He put his hands on the edge of the counter and began to drum his fingers. "Maybe *mediocre* is the wrong word. How about *simple*? I'm giving this bouquet to a woman to wish her well as we part ways."

Delphinium's mouth dropped open. "You mean to tell me you're using my flowers to *break up* with someone?" She hoped the outrage in her voice didn't reach the back for Paavo and the men to hear.

The man stopped drumming his fingers. "Why do you look so offended? What does it matter what I do with them?"

"It matters a great deal because they're *my* flowers! I have a reputation to uphold. I put a lot of thought into my creations. I take pride in what I blend together. They're supposed to bring people closer together."

The man nodded. "Precisely. That's the problem. I want to get this woman *out* of my life. All these flowers will do is invite her back *in*. This is the kind of bouquet I would give a woman to celebrate something special."

Delphinium rolled her eyes. "You clearly know nothing about flowers."

He cocked his head and crossed his arms across his chest, matching her stance. "Hence the reason why I came into a *flower* shop for help." He spoke slowly as if she were mentally lagging and he was giving her time to catch up.

They glared at each other in a silent standoff.

"Do you want the sale or not?" he challenged.

"Not if it means selling my artistic soul to do it," she responded, narrowing her eyes.

She felt like a child participating in a staring contest. She was about to say something, but he beat her to it.

"Look, all I'm asking is that the flowers make less of a statement. Eliminate the wow factor. I'll still pay the price of the original bouquet. Just make it more ordinary."

Delphinium pressed her lips into a small frown. She couldn't let her stubbornness and pride get the best of her. She really did need the sale. *Who cares what he does with the flowers after they leave the store? He's doing the woman a favor by letting her go. No one deserves someone like him.* Letting out a heavy sigh, she untied the bow and opened the bouquet, then she began to remove the flowers as delicately as if she were performing surgery. "I need to take out the roses because they represent love. I'll include more chrysanthemums because they represent death and grief."

The man winced. "That's a bit harsh."

"It only means that in certain countries. Elsewhere, they mean joy and optimism. I'll leave the calla lilies, which represent beauty, so she'll at least feel pretty when you break things off." She extracted the flowers carefully so she'd be able to reuse them, then replaced them with something more subdued. After she was done, she held the bouquet up. "Smell."

Though he looked confused, he leaned forward and took a quick sniff.

"Do you feel anything?"

He shrugged. "No."

"Precisely. She'll be anesthetized from any pain or heartache."

A slow smile crossed his face. "You're good."

"I typically use my flower power for good and not evil, so don't you dare tell anyone where you picked these up. My flowers are not intended for *dumping* girlfriends."

He flashed a smile. "You've got my word." Taking out his wallet, he paid cash for the order.

"Would you like to include a note?" She passed him a small card.

"Sure." He scribbled in writing that was a combination of print and cursive, *Take care—M.* Then he slid the note across the counter.

Delphinium sucked in her cheeks and bit down on them to keep from saying anything. She didn't care how amused he looked at the fish face she made. She tucked the note into the bouquet center where it couldn't be missed. "I hope your friend likes the arrangement." She was sure her smile came across as more of a sneer.

One side of his mouth lifted high into a crooked smile, making him look younger. He was enjoying how torturous this was for her. "Thank you, but I'm hoping she *won't.* We'll see if your magic works." He winked.

The audacity of this man!

Delphinium didn't respond. Her expression remained frozen.

With a nod, he picked up the bouquet, now tied with plain brown raffia, and began to turn when something must have caught his eye.

He did a double take, then froze in place.

Delphinium followed his gaze to the back room. She'd left the door open, and now Henry and his buddies were in full view, strutting about in their thin undershirts. Their bottom halves were hidden by the huge worktable, so from the waist up, they looked nearly naked. She looked back at the man, who appeared mesmerized by the sight.

"Those are my . . . helpers."

The man coughed. "Those guys have to be in their eighties."

Delphinium nodded. "Yep. Good help is hard to find. When I find it, I like to hold on to it."

He seemed to be waiting for her to say more and when she didn't, he asked, "Do you have a policy that they can't wear clothes when working?"

She held her head high, jutting her chin out a bit. "I leave our store uniform up to the discretion of the employee."

The man studied her face, but Delphinium didn't blink. "Thank you for the bouquet," he said finally.

Delphinium watched him exit the store.

That's when it hit her.

That's when her world tilted ever so slightly.

She hadn't *smelled* him.

She reached for the crumpled handkerchief, which she'd stuffed into her pocket, and quickly held it to her nose. Inhaling deeply, she closed her eyes and concentrated.

Nothing.

She smelled absolutely nothing.

There wasn't even a whisper of cologne. And he definitely was the kind of man who would wear cologne. Her sweat and makeup had eliminated any lingering scent. She rubbed the soiled handkerchief between her fingers, noticing an embroidered *M* in the corner. White thread on white fabric. Classy and understated, supposedly a reflection of its owner. She felt bad for not remembering to return the handkerchief but equally relieved that he hadn't seen how she had ruined it.

Still feeling the uptick of her heartbeat from the fact that she couldn't smell him, she let out a shaky breath. Hopefully she would never see him again.

She inhaled and exhaled slowly to settle herself. What a strange encounter. Never had she not picked up a scent on a person.

Let it go. It doesn't matter.

There were more important things to focus on, like dealing with the half-naked senior runaways hiding out in the back of her shop.

Three

Delphinium stormed to the back room feeling embarrassed—no, *ridiculous*—that the gentleman had seen Henry
and his friends strut around half-dressed. She imagined
she knew exactly how they must have appeared to him because
she shared the utter astonishment. The worktable was covered in
packages wrapped in white deli paper. "What on earth are you all
doing now?"

The men were working an assembly line.

"What does it look like we're doing?" the grumpy man who had
compared her to a raccoon answered. "We got hungry, so we're
making sandwiches."

Delphinium rubbed her forehead to smooth the stress lines she
imagined were imprinted into her fair skin. "This can't be your
new hangout. This is a place of business."

Henry waved her off. "This is only temporary. We'll be out of
your hair as soon as the air-conditioning is fixed at the old folks'
home. Consider this an I-O-U." He wrote the imaginary letters in
the air with his index finger. "Plus, I'll start your taxes extra early
this year, Delphi." He crossed his heart with the same finger as a
solemn promise.

And just like that, all the argument in her was gone. It had
nothing to do with money, business, or men hanging out in her

shop. Delphinium could never say no to Henry. He was family to her. He was also her greatest asset and the secret to her staying afloat. Flowers she knew. Running the accounting side of a business, not so much.

"Well, can you at least put your shirts on when you're outside of the refrigerator?" she asked with a small pout.

One of the men chuckled, looking at her with a glimmer of mischief. "Honey, we're already doing you a favor by keeping on our *pants*. Charlie wanted to get down to his skivvies, but Henry put a stop to that idea."

Delphinium walked over to the gentleman and leaned in close.

The man leaned away skeptically. "What is she doing?" he asked Henry.

Henry grinned. "She's smelling you."

Delphinium shook her head. "I should have guessed. You're lilacs."

The man frowned. "What does that mean?"

"It means," Delphinium replied, "that you've held on to the joy of your youth. You're playful and always up to a little mischief. You've never quite grown up, which means you're a handful and won't make my life easy. In layperson's terms, you're a big baby."

The man gave a toothy smile. "I like that, and I think my girlfriends would agree. I'm young at heart!" He wiggled his hips a little. "I still got it after all these years."

Henry shook his head. "The only thing you've *got*, George, are long-winded stories of past shenanigans."

"Well, that's somethin'," George agreed before returning to his sandwich.

Henry put his hands on Delphinium's shoulders and turned her around and led her to the front of the store, grabbing the back room door and swinging it shut behind them. "Why don't you go splash some water on your face and then finish opening up. All the plants need watering, and I can't wait to see what you put in that new pot you brought in."

Delphinium spun around. "This whole morning has been off.

You wouldn't believe what happened with the customer that was just in here. I couldn't smell—"

Henry cut her off. "Let's start fresh, then. Go wash up and begin again. All is right with the world if you look at it the right way. As my pastor tells me every Sunday, 'This is the day the Lord has made; let us rejoice and be glad in it.' I think she's pretty smart, so let's take the sound advice and be thankful for the new day, Delphi."

As much as she wanted to argue that life wasn't that simple, she kept her mouth shut. The kind crescent curvature of Henry's eyes when he smiled, along with the crisscross of wrinkles making up the canvas of his face, softened her heart. She couldn't deny that his words calmed her. Wrapping her arms around his skinny waist, she gave him a gentle hug, frowning at how frail he felt. His worn belt pulled to nearly the last notch was the only thing holding up his baggy pants. She drew in his scent as he patted her back.

Honeysuckle.

Henry always smelled of honeysuckle. The flower that meant bonded with love. He cared about her and had her best interest at heart. She supposed they had adopted each other like two foster kids in need of a permanent home. He needed a purpose for getting out of bed and to keep on living, and she needed a grandfather figure and sense of family since her parents lived across the country in California. They were not involved in her life since they understood her about as much as they had understood her grandmother.

Henry gave her a pat on the arm and a little shove to get moving. "Begin again, sweetheart. The next moment can always be renewed with a smile."

Delphinium nodded and went to wash her face, feeling better from his affection. She had established a wonderful life in Moonberry Lake and was proud of her shop. Keeping any small, independent business open was an accomplishment. Delphinium was determined that her passion and perseverance would pay off. However, she had to admit that things felt steadier and more anchored with Henry around. There was no one she trusted more as her bookkeeper and closest confidant. Once an accountant for a Fortune 500 company, in retirement he took her under his wing as a hobby after Annie passed away. She was indebted to him for his wisdom and loyalty.

And there was no way the flower shop would have survived without his accounting wizardry and help in establishing a budget and marketing plan to end each month in the black. Well, in the dark gray, at least.

In the last couple months, she hadn't been entirely honest with him about how much the store was bringing in. She hid the fact that she had gotten into a bit of trouble not paying her mortgage in full. Henry came into her life after she had signed the mortgage and she hadn't told him yet about how she had fallen behind in payments. It was too embarrassing to admit she was failing as a florist, the thing she loved doing the most.

She kept praying for a miracle so she'd be able to keep her charming shop tucked on the corner of the block. She had purchased the flower shop two years ago from a couple who had run it for fifty years. The shop was a marker in the community representing a piece of history in the small town. It was also the ideal location for foot traffic and cars driving by on Main Street. The space would be gladly snatched up by another business.

And Delphinium knew she wouldn't be able to afford anything else in the heart of downtown. The only reason why she got the coveted spot was because she had promised in her contract that it would be maintained as a flower shop. The owners realized the historical significance and had waited for another florist to carry on the tradition.

The building was one of the originals in town, replete with brick in gingerbread brown and ornate trim that builders no longer took the time or expense to use. Her grandmother had rented the second-floor apartment for years. Now, living in Annie's apartment and working in the space below was a dream come true for Delphinium. Though renovation and repair on the old building kept money tight, it was worth it. There was no way she was leaving her home and shop. The community needed the store as a connection to the past as much as she did.

In the bathroom, she splashed cold water on her face until her freckles were the only decoration against her ruddy complexion. Taking the handkerchief out of her pocket, she ran cold water over the small square of fabric. Maybe she could prevent the stains from setting. She studied the embroidered *M* again as if it would give her a clue to the owner's name.

All it did was conjure up the stranger's image—the strength in his face, the poise in his stance. However, it was his imperfections that made him memorable. His slightly crooked nose and the thin scar underneath his left eyebrow that at the time was barely noticeable but now jarred her memory as very apparent.

Why was she thinking of him?

Why did she care?

He was a player.

Stop it.

Draping the wet handkerchief over the faucet to drip dry, she returned to the front to move the new planter to the worktable. Paavo could begin filling it with soil. As she lifted the planter, something caught her eye. A business card was face down near the bottom of the pot.

Delphinium set the pot back on the ground and picked up the small card, immediately detecting the thick, linen weight of the crisp, white paper. She turned it over and her breath caught as she read the elegant, bold script.

Mason McCormack
Attorney at Law

She liked the way his name rolled off her tongue as she whispered it. She had long been obsessed with names and their meanings and the way they sounded when spoken aloud. She whispered his name—*Mason McCormack*—smacking her lips a little at the end. It was solid and authoritative. Thinking about the confidence he exuded as he walked away from her, she concluded that his build and persona matched his name perfectly.

She believed that when her parents had chosen such an unusual floral name for her, it sealed her fate like an invisible insignia that she wore as a weight around her neck or as a tattoo emblazoned on her chest. She was predestined to be a bit strange and inevitably go into the flower business.

As the only kid named Delphinium in her big-city school, she'd been a wallflower. She had always been envious of the countless girls named Sophia, Olivia, and Grace. If her parents were dead set on a flower name, she would have preferred Lily, also quite common. A majestic flower in ancient mythology, lilies were revered by the Greeks who believed they had sprouted from the milk of Hera, the queen. When she was younger, Delphinium used to imagine how her hair would flow down in a wavy cascade if she had been named after a queen, rather than go every which way as though she played with electrical sockets.

She remembered the crushing feeling when she found out that Delphinium came from the Greek word *delphis*, which means dolphin. The flower was given the name because the buds resemble the nose of a dolphin. She was sure that her name influenced the shape of her nose, which was pronounced with a spray of freckles as numerous and random as a constellation in the night sky.

Tucking a rebellious lock of hair behind her ear, Delphinium thought about how long it had been since she last spoke to her parents. Everything had changed after Annie's funeral. The calls had gotten sparse on her end and desperate on theirs. She rarely spoke to them and hadn't bothered returning their calls in months. If they texted, she responded with as few words as possible.

The sting over their lack of emotion about her grandmother's death would return like a forgotten sunburn that's mistakenly pressed on. Then the heat of her anger would also return, and she'd dismiss the idea of talking to them. They had no clue what a tremendous loss it was for her. Losing Annie meant she lost her dearest friend—the person who had loved her the most.

As professors immersed in academia, they handled Annie's death with the same demeanor they presented to their students in class. The eulogy was a concise lecture lacking heartfelt sentiment. And they were flummoxed as to why Delphinium insisted on moving into Annie's apartment after her death.

Delphinium rented a house with two roommates the first year she owned the shop. There had been a lot of learning experiences that first year in Moonberry, but the best part was being able to see Annie every day. After closing, she'd go up and have dinner with her grandmother most nights. So when her parents wanted to give away all her grandmother's possessions like they were the belongings of some stranger, Delphinium lost it and told them not to touch a thing and to leave.

Henry came through the door, piercing her daydreaming like a pin to a balloon. She quickly tucked the business card in the drawer of the cash register and slammed it shut, then she turned to him as he spoke.

"Hey, Delphi. Word has gotten out and a couple ladies want to join the game. I was going to shut it down, but Gertrude promised to put on her flapper dress from Halloween. What do you say?"

Delphinium flinched. "A *flapper* dress?" She shook her head adamantly. "No way. Absolutely not, Henry. You're not turning my flower shop into some sort of brothel for people seventy-five and up."

"Aw, it won't be like that."

"Any activity that includes costumes or the clothes of your friends coming *off*, I say no."

He threw his arms up in the air. "There's nowhere we can go. The nursing home is making us old."

Delphinium rubbed out the stress lines on her forehead. The action was becoming a habit. "Well, first of all, you are residents there because you are indeed *old*. I mean, you do in fact meet the

31

age requirement to live there. Hence the title *senior* assisted living facility. And second, if the nursing home makes Charlie keep his pants and shirt on, I'm on their side." She moved around the counter, grabbed the spray bottle from a nearby stand, and began misting the plants.

Henry didn't let up. "This isn't about the dress code. There is a bigger issue at stake. We're being oppressed, I tell you! You wouldn't believe the rules, and the food is atrocious." Henry's voice reflected his genuine outrage.

Delphinium decided to humor him. "What's wrong with the food?"

"They feed us like a bunch of kindergarteners. Tiny cups of diced-up fruit, scrambled eggs, stewed prunes to keep us regular, chicken that's been beaten to a pulp so it doesn't even require chewing—and if the potatoes didn't come mashed, they mash them for you."

"So, it's not the quality of the food that bothers you but the *presentation* of it," she said with her back turned, giving every plant a generous spritz.

She glanced at him when he didn't respond right away. Henry seemed to be thinking about that. Then he shook his head. "Nope. It's both. There's no taste, and everything is cooked down to the point where it just slides through you, bypassing the stomach. We don't want food that could fit into a Dixie cup, we want a buffet like they have in Las Vegas."

Delphinium stopped watering and stared at him. "I don't think that's ever going to happen. You've got to be somewhat realistic in your expectations. Let's lower the bar a bit."

Henry straightened like a soldier called to attention. "Nope. We are fighting back. We're planning on staging a coup. Everyone has agreed to go on a hunger strike."

Her eyebrows shot up. "That's a terrible way to get your point across. You have to eat. Not eating would be dangerous for all of you. You haven't got two pounds to spare."

A corner of his mouth lifted, and his eyes were playful like he had the best secret ever. "Oh, we're going to eat, just not *there*." He winked. "Which reminds me, you need to stock up on snacks. This is going to be the headquarters of our fight." With that, he turned and began humming a happy tune as he walked away.

Delphinium stood by the open door to the back, speechless as she watched all the men march back into the cooler, giving her either a wink or a salute.

She groaned. *This isn't good.*

The rest of the day was filled with the sounds of men talking at a holler and laughing. Thankfully most of her orders were called in. Only one walk-in customer was curious about whether there was a party going on in the back room. When Delphinium went to the cooler and requested that they not speak so loudly, she was informed that the batteries in the hearing aids of two of the men had died and was asked if she could go and pick up a couple replacements at the drugstore along with some hard candy.

She must have looked as flabbergasted as she felt at the request, because one of the guys slipped her an extra five-dollar bill and told her to get a treat for herself while she was there. "Something nice," his rough voice crowed. "Not the store brand." Then he winked.

Delphinium stood blinking at the cash. *How did I go from florist to caretaker of four grandpas in one day?*

That evening, Delphinium released a heavy sigh and her shoulders dropped in relief as she reached the threshold to her apartment. Everything in her small space was a reminder of Annie. She loved it. Life was less lonely when shared with someone who also experienced the world differently. "You and I are the same," Annie would always say with a smile. "Your gift is special and should never be taken for granted. Allow it to reveal the truth about others and use it to bring joy to your life."

As an only child, and one who did not identify with her highly academic parents—linear thinkers who dismissed the "silliness" of Annie as "quirks"—Delphinium hoped her ability to pick up scents meant that she was different from them. It made her feel special and offered the possibility that her life was destined to be different than the household she grew up in. Her gifting allowed her to dream her life could be as wonderful and happy as Annie's had been in Moonberry Lake. That's why she moved to the small town tucked in between lakes and forest where the sense of community was as strong as the coffee and the beauty of the area was the balm to any problem.

Lifting her arm to put the key in the lock and then pushing the door open took the last remnants of her energy for the day. She let her keys and purse fall to the floor with a thud. Too weary to care about placing her tote on the narrow entryway table or her keys in the scratched-up pewter bowl, she walked past the kitchen without a glance.

Making or eating dinner would take too much effort. She wasn't hungry anyway. Between going to the grocery store for snack food, the bakery for donut holes the men couldn't drink their coffee without, and the drug store twice—the first time for hearing aid batteries and lemon drops, the second for the *correct* battery size and caramel nips—and then running her business, all she wanted to do was take a hot bath and go to bed.

Normally, her home was her safe haven with its outdated 1960s kitchen, funky furniture, knickknacks from thrift stores that her grandmother had scoured and collected over decades, and the soft blankets and decorative pillows at every arm's reach to snuggle up with on lazy weekends. But tonight, Delphinium headed straight for the master bath. She turned on the hot water and peeled off her clothes, pitching them into the hamper. Adding some lavender salts to the bath, she didn't even wait for the tub to fill up before getting in.

Lying there with a washcloth folded over her forehead, she attempted to figure out how she could get out of the mess she'd created. When she originally signed the property loan, the payments seemed doable. She had been so sure that profit from her flower shop would be able to cover everything.

Her choices were to come up with the money to pay off the loan, refinance, or lose the property in one swoop. Paying the total loan off wasn't possible, and asking her parents for money wasn't an option. They kept themselves on a tight and sensible budget, and she wouldn't ask them to dip into their retirement savings. Refinancing would cost her dearly because her credit rating had dropped. On the slim chance the bank did allow her to refinance, she wasn't sure she'd ever recover. She wouldn't stay afloat with no equity, and she'd eventually be forced to sell. She also couldn't afford to relocate the shop anywhere near the coveted downtown space she had currently.

The thought of losing both the shop and her home made her feel like she was losing two of her limbs. She placed her hand at her throat and rubbed her skin to soothe the constriction.

She breathed in and out slowly, trying to calm down the rising panic.

I'll come up with something. I'll figure it out.

She had to.

Four

There were still old men playing poker in her fridge one week later.

Though the air-conditioning had been fixed at the nursing home, Henry explained that poker was still banned, and they needed a place to formulate their food retaliation strategy. Gertrude did tag along to the shop to see what all the fuss was about.

Gurdy, as she preferred to be called, was a spry little bundle of energy, standing at four feet and eleven inches tall. She maintained her ninety-pound frame with coffee and donut holes. As soon as she walked in smelling of goldenrod, Delphinium knew she was an encourager.

Gurdy didn't play poker, but instead put on an apron and stood next to Paavo as his assistant. The two looked mismatched side by side, like a boy with his sister's doll. When Gurdy wasn't helping with flowers, she chatted away on a stool that Paavo had pulled up for her. As a retired middle-school teacher and grandmother of six, she listened and showed animated interest in his life. She encouraged Paavo on every school subject, and he soaked up the attention like a succulent. It was obvious how they uplifted each other, so Delphinium kept her mouth shut about the growing number of seniors in the back room.

To get some space from them, Delphinium spent time in the

front of the store putting tiny twinkle lights around the plants to spiff up the display shelves. She thought it added to the ambience of the fairy houses that were now numerous enough to be called a village. She knelt on the floor between two display tables and tried to connect all the plugs to one long power strip. Crammed into the tight space with her fanny high in the air, she worked to untangle the cords. She was hunkered in that position for a while before she heard someone clear their throat from behind her.

She froze.

She hadn't heard the door scrape against the floor.

The person cleared their throat again. "Excuse me, are you, um . . . okay?"

She knew that voice. *No. Please no. This can't be happening to me again.*

Dropping her head and squeezing her eyes shut, she silently cursed the stupid fairy lights and then began to shimmy out of the hole she'd burrowed herself into. Her face grew warm as she imagined what she must look like with her rear end swaying from side to side as she backed out. The image of the bulbous behind of Winnie the Pooh stuck in a tree trunk came to mind.

"Are you all right?"

"Yep."

"Do you need help?"

"No thanks, I'm making my way out." *Just call me Pooh.*

Finally to the point where she could stand, she felt a hand circle her upper arm to help her up. Mason McCormack stood inches from her. His lopsided smile only made her stare. First his crooked nose and scar on his eyebrow, and now an irresistible smile.

His grin broadened. There was a boyish glimmer in his eyes, making it clear how funny he found her situation. "Hello again."

"H-Hi." She brushed some hair out of her face.

His hand was still on her arm. When her gaze went to it, he released his grip immediately.

"Looks like you're hard at work with something behind there."

Delphinium tried to smooth back more hair from her face. "Yeah, I was trying to connect twinkle lights." She blew away a curl in front of her right eye, wishing she had tamed all the wild tresses in a clip that morning after getting out of the shower.

Standing in such close proximity to him made her feel awkward. She didn't know what to do with herself, so she turned and picked up a random container of flowers and walked over to the counter.

She noticed him scan the shop from the ceiling to the floor. "I think the lighting in here is already very nice between the natural sunlight coming in through the big glass windows and the fixtures overhead. But I suppose some twinkle lights could add to the ambience if you're trying to sell those doll houses."

"They're not *doll* houses," she tersely corrected. "They're fairy houses."

He held both hands up. "My mistake."

She wasn't sure if he was making fun of her or not, but it irritated her nonetheless. "How did the flowers work in breaking up with the woman you were dating?" She was glad the directness of her question came out sounding strong.

Mason let out a small chuckle. He wiped his hand over his mouth, trying to make the smile forming less pronounced.

He failed.

"They worked just as you said they would. She didn't feel a thing. I don't think she even cared when I suggested we stop seeing one another. Your bouquet worked like magic." He looked like a fox with chicken feathers sticking out of his teeth, proud that he got away with the kill.

Delphinium didn't know how to respond, so she grunted under her breath as she grabbed a rag from underneath the counter and walked over to dust the leaves of a fiddle leaf fig tree. It was her most expensive indoor plant and she babied it.

"Did you come to thank me, or do you have another girlfriend to break up with?"

"Well, actually . . ." His pause felt ominous. "I need you to make me another bouquet."

Delphinium spun around. "You've got to be kidding me! You're dumping another woman *already*?"

"No, no. This time it's different." He paused, looking down as he rubbed the back of his neck.

She couldn't figure out why he suddenly appeared uncomfortable. This man really was a player. The pickup lines he used on women were probably delivered smooth as silk.

Still not saying anything, Mason began to walk around the shop and study the containers of flowers. He was wearing a navy polo and perfectly distressed jeans. No question that they were designer. Shabby chic looked stunning on him. He carried off the casual elegance of a movie star. *Ugh.* He was becoming more annoying by the minute. She could see how he would make women swoon.

But not her. Nope. She wasn't going to make that mistake again.

"I'd like a bouquet that will help me introduce myself to a woman. What flowers would you mix together so that I make a good impression and come across as a nice guy?"

"You're asking for a miracle?"

"Ouch," he responded, but he grinned as he said it, placing one hand over his heart to feign pain.

She scowled.

He gave her a killer smile. "I think you and I should become friends."

She choked on nothing and coughed. That was the last thing she expected him to say. And from the way his smile brightened, she could tell he was enjoying the shock value of his statement.

"What?" he asked with such innocence that it mocked her. "You're a talented individual. I'm a talented individual. And it has been my experience that great things come from talented people aligning together."

Delphinium cleared her throat but couldn't hide her suspicion. "I don't think so. I have enough friends."

"What? You don't like me?"

She rolled her eyes. "Give me a break. I know your type. You're like a piranha. You devour your victims, which happen to be any woman you find desirable, and then leave little bits of them spit out after you're finished."

He went over to the counter and leaned against it in a relaxed pose, like he had all the time in the world and was settling in for a nice discussion. "I am a nice guy, you know. I'm not sure why I have to prove it to you."

Delphinium scoffed. "Oh, I'm pretty good at reading people."

"You might be wrong on this hunch. All I've ever done is purchase flowers from you, an expensive bouquet I might add."

"I only sell to you because the shop needs the money," she grumbled.

"Oh, is the business in trouble?" Even though he asked casually, she didn't miss the interest in his stare. Which was odd.

"That's none of your concern." Then she added quickly, "It's been a slow day."

"Well then, I could become your favorite customer."

"That's not going to happen."

He leaned in with a coy smile. "What is it about me that you don't like?"

"The way you obviously go through women. One bouquet after another."

He couldn't hold back a smile. He really looked like he was enjoying her response. "I happen to treat women very nicely. No one complains. None but *you*—apparently." He narrowed his eyes.

Delphinium shrugged. "Guess I've had the appropriate vaccinations. Insincerity makes me break out in a rash."

He barked out a big laugh. "I give up. Are you going to help me or not?"

She hated how much she liked his laugh. And every second of this absurd conversation. He clearly didn't mind the insults. In fact, he seemed to delight in the sparring and teasing as much as she did. The tit for tat was the best entertainment she'd had all week. Never in her life would she talk so unrestrained to a customer, with such sarcasm and downright rudeness. But this guy brought out the worst in her.

She gave a frustrated shake of the head. She was learning that charming men were nothing but trouble and heartache. Bad guys were given that name for a reason. They couldn't be trusted. Whenever she felt herself falter, she had to remember the lies her last boyfriend, Colin, had told her—and how she had believed them. Pangs of humiliation and anger over his infidelity still pricked her when she thought of him. Trying to find an eligible guy in Moonberry Lake who was honest, hardworking, and sweet—not to mention able to find her *quirkiness*, as her parents put it, endearing—was proving nearly impossible. Colin had been a lesson and warning against online dating. When a guy's profile seems too good to be true, it *is* too good to be true.

She let out a deep breath. "Daffodils."

A smile that reached his eyes greeted her. "And what do they mean?"

"New beginnings."

"That's perfect."

With a dramatic huff, she surrendered and went over to the container of daffodils and grabbed a bunch, in addition to some other flowers. She began putting together a bouquet in short order, deciding to work at the front counter rather than go to the back. She gently laid the yellow daffodils in between sprigs of periwinkle hyacinths, yellow wax flowers, and purple irises for contrast.

Gurdy pushed open the door while holding a tall black bucket of fresh white roses. It looked half her size. Mason immediately sprang into action by reaching out and taking the bucket from her and then allowing her to lead him to where she wanted it put down. Gurdy nodded her thanks and then toddled back with her little shuffling feet.

Mason raised an eyebrow in question to Delphinium.

She simply shrugged, loving the fact that she was now the one giving him the shock factor. "Another helper."

Mason balked. "What are you running here? Some sort of elderly sweatshop?"

Delphinium pressed her lips together.

Wrapping up the beautiful floral creation, she brought them to her nose before handing them to him. She was a sucker for daffodils. They were such a bright and happy flower, and so unexpected. She favored flowers that people would normally not receive. She noticed him watching her every move.

"They're perfect," he complimented.

She nodded in agreement and rung him up without saying anything.

He handed over his credit card, not even glancing at the price. "Thank you . . ." he said, obviously pausing so she'd share her name.

"Delphinium."

His face lit up. "As in Delphinium's Flora Emporium?" It was clear he was holding back a chuckle. "Is that your real name or a gimmick for the shop? It's a kind of flower, right?"

Delphinium was accustomed to this response. "Yes, it is. And yes, my real name is actually Delphinium, and I'm the *owner* of this shop. Flowers have always been my passion." She said it with a deadpan expression, waiting for him to respond with laughter like most people.

"Well, *Delphinium*, it's nice to meet you. I'm Mason McCormack." He stuck out his hand for her to shake and she did.

She gave a judgmental grunt as she took back her hand.

Mason seemed amused by her lack of enthusiasm. "Thank you for the flowers. I have a sneaking suspicion the benefactress of these beauties is going to love them—and me hopefully." He waggled his eyebrows before turning and walking to the door. He was having too much fun at her expense. Just as he had a foot out, he paused and looked back. "Good luck with your sweatshop," he said, flashing a smile.

"It's not a sweat—" But he was already gone.

She couldn't wipe the annoyance off her face. *Just how many women does he date and dump?* His statement confirmed her opinion that he did nothing but break the hearts of countless women. *And he uses my flowers to do it! Why can't any nice men come into the shop?*

At that precise moment, George, the playboy of the men's group, stuck his head out the door from the back room. "Hey, Delphi, do you think you could run to the store and get some more chocolate pudding cups? They're my favorite. And not the generic—go for the good stuff." He winked. "Thanks, you're a doll."

She closed her eyes and took a deep breath. *Correction. Why can't any nice men my age come into the store?*

At that precise moment, the force of the door opening with such strength shook a nearby table holding a couple plants and made her eyes snap open.

Widgy McQuire entered.

Delphinium gulped.

The town handywoman was a force to be reckoned with and had always made her nervous. Although Widgy was nearing retirement age, it was agreed in the community that when it came to fixing things, the woman knew the most about, well, everything. She was a jack-of-all-trades and always gave the best price in town. Rumor was that Widgy didn't need to work since she had the retirement and life insurance money of five past husbands. The fact that the woman had been married five times was a whole other story that Delphinium didn't have time to think about.

As usual, the burly woman was dressed in overalls that pulled across her belly. Today the denim happened to be speckled in white paint splotches. Underneath them, she wore a long-sleeve T-shirt with a neckline that was stretched out and frayed, dirty work boots, and an old baseball cap. She stomped toward the counter with her signature no-nonsense scowl.

Widgy did not possess a floral scent but one of an herb. Thyme.

She emitted it as strongly as if she rubbed it all over her body. Thyme meant courage and strength. There was no question the woman possessed both traits. Everything about her indicated she was not only up for a challenge but would look for any opportunity to prove her brawn.

"I hear your refrigerator needs fixin.'"

"Where did you hear that?"

"That's none of your business," Widgy responded with her mouth in a flat line.

Delphinium wanted to point out that it was *indeed* her business since this was her shop, but she wasn't about to correct Widgy. "Um, it's running on half its cylinders, but it's okay." Whatever it cost to fix the refrigerator, she knew she couldn't afford it.

Widgy shook her head. "I'll take a look." Without asking, she clomped to the back room.

Delphinium was about to run after her but decided to stay put at the front of the store. There was nothing she could do to stop Widgy anyway.

A few minutes later, Widgy came out and stood before her with her arms crossed over her chest. She let out a big sigh that sounded more like an irritated huff. "I gotta say, this is the first time I've found men in the fridge. At least alive, that is. I knew a woman who kept her husband's hand in the freezer after he lost it in a chainsaw accident. But never a whole body. The guys explained to me that you're not keepin' them there against their will, that they willingly stepped inside."

"That's correct." She nodded. "They come here to hang out and like the coolness of the refrigerator."

Widgy considered this, squinting her eyes at Delphinium.

"Ya know, those men are too old for ya. You really should come down a few decades if you're lookin' for a husband. Two of mine were a bit older, but not that much older. I don't know why you'd want to hitch your wagon to one of them when they practically have one foot in the grave. Or maybe"—she rubbed her fingers together like a miser—"you're one of those gold diggers who go after money."

Delphinium blanched. "What? No!" She made a face. "Those are Henry's friends. I'm not going after those grandpas. I'm not going after anyone. Henry brought them here."

Widgy didn't look as if she fully believed her. "Well, either way, you better not be tryin' to kill 'em off by fixin' the refrigerator and freezin' 'em solid like the walleye I have at home."

Delphinium's mouth dropped open. This conversation was taking a dark turn.

Widgy shook her head. "In good conscience, I can't fix the thermostat knowin' you might lock them in there."

Delphinium gasped. "I would never *lock* them in there!"

"That's good, because otherwise I'd have to tell the police that you're gettin' rid of the elderly in Moonberry Lake in a real sneaky way."

Delphinium put her hands up. "They play poker and eat donuts—that's all."

Widgy gave a hard nod and pointed her index finger at Delphinium. "Stick to that story. It's very believable. Nobody would peg you as a murderer because of the hippie-dippie thing you've got goin' on here." Widgy scanned the shop. "This place is a little too flowery for my taste."

Delphinium gawked at her. "It's a *flower* shop."

Widgy didn't appear to hear her and went on. "The place would look better with a deer head mounted on the wall. You might draw in some more people if you had some stuffed animals. Give the place a nature feel. I've got a couple skunks and a gopher I could lend ya until ya git your own."

Delphinium's eyes widened in horror at the thought.

"Maybe add a vending machine." She pointed to Delphinium's head. "And I'd cut off all those curls. You look like ya got electrocuted. My fifth husband, Harry number two, had that problem from electrical mishaps. His hair was more singed than curly. But it was kinky and stuck out like yours. We solved it by shavin' it all off."

"Um . . . ah . . ." The woman rendered her speechless. She finally uttered, "I'll think about it."

Widgy gave a hard rap of her knuckles on the counter. "I can't fix the refrigerator now. Give me a call when you get rid of the old folks the *natural* way," she emphasized with an accusatory look. "Until then, I'll be readin' the obits to see if there's any funny business goin' on."

Delphinium could only stare as the woman exited as loud and thunderous as she appeared. The door shook as she slammed it shut.

Delphinium stood there for a minute not moving. *I live a very unusual life.*

Wanting a quick break, she opened *The Town Times* newspaper, which she hadn't gotten to that morning, and took a peek at the column "Sightings and Satire." She was a devoted reader of the gossip section.

SIGHTINGS AND SATIRE

Does your pooch need to be prayed over? Is your kitty cleansed of sin? It's time for the annual Animal Blessing put on by Our Last Saving Grace Lutheran Church. All furry, four-legged friends and otherwise are invited to come and receive a blessing from the pastor.

*Word of warning: the church will strictly enforce the leash law after the unsightly hanky-panky between two poodles last year.

To enhance the musical and eclectic mood of Moonberry Lake, auditions for a melodic town troubadour are happening Friday night at the park. Individuals who wish to apply must have at least an intermediate ability with the guitar, mediocre singing skills, general ability to memorize folk music, be open to wearing seasonal costumes, clear a police background check, and be committed to working all holidays and weekends. Payments come in tips, compliments, a bottle of local maple syrup, wooden bearpaw salad servers, and a membership to the monthly casserole club.

Jon Jorgenson has lost his dark green fishing jacket. He says he's worn it every time he's been out on the boat for the last twenty years, and it's become kind of a good luck charm. He's offering $10 to whoever finds the lucky jacket. He thinks it might be somewhere between the barber shop and Perfectly Pie Bakery & Bookstore.

Mia Jorgenson is offering $25 to whoever finds the jacket and doesn't give "that old rag" back to her husband. She assures discretion so that her husband will never find out. Note from Mia: "Burn it or bury it, and I'll get you the money!"

Apparently, there is a method behind the madness to the obscure messaging on the front lawn sign of the library. Head librarian Helen Arnold is trying reverse psychology to get people to come in. The signage now reads "Don't come in—we're hiding something" and "Stay away. Secret membership required." Based on the assumption that people want what they cannot have, the mental trickery has worked. Curiosity and the urge to break the rules has caused a surge of patrons. Helen states, "Our readers may have suspicious intentions, but we are thrilled with all the foot traffic!" She is trying out signs inside as well that say "These books contain nothing," "Precious resource, do not touch," and "Banned."

Town Council news: Moonberry Lake is going green! A recycling program has been deemed too costly, so to help the environment, townsfolk are being encouraged to stop using plastic water bottles and to simply drink from the hose like their parents did. Become an eco-friendly hero and leave your hose on your front lawn for people passing by.

Correction, Delphinium thought, *I live in a very unusual town.*

Five

Delphinium was putting the final touches on an anniversary party centerpiece when she looked up at the sound of the door scraping and saw her friend Lindsey. The scent of freesia enveloped her, reaffirming the sweetness and devotion of her personality. Lindsey was her closest friend and the absolute antithesis of Delphinium.

It was no exaggeration her friend had the opposite physical characteristics. Lindsey had stick-straight, dark hair that did nothing but hang obediently or stay in a neat ponytail. She had an athletic figure that was strong and muscular, not soft and curvy like Delphinium's. Her skin easily tanned and was clear of freckles. She was a couple inches shorter, was much more energetic and exuberant, and had a bounce to her walk that made her appear the same height as Delphinium. If Delphinium embodied Pooh Bear, Lindsey was her faithful Tigger.

Her friend also possessed the stamina of Tigger as a personal trainer, running a fitness boot camp in the mornings and evenings. She was a health fanatic who was always trying to get Delphinium to try turmeric-ginger shots and gut-cleansing smoothies. Delphinium would have never considered this young woman who strutted around in athletic wear like a runway model a potential friend had it not been for her strong scent of freesia—an absolute giveaway for a great friend.

Lindsey was a total sweetheart and the most thoughtful friend.

"Hey, how's it going?" She pranced up to the counter with a happy smile.

Delphinium shrugged.

"Do you still have a refrigerator full of men?"

Delphinium groaned. She regretted staying on the phone late into the night and telling Lindsey all the torrid details of Henry and the casino he'd been running out of the cooler all week. "Congratulations on making that question sound both dirty and disgusting. I'm not hoarding overheated grandpas in the back room, and I'm not killing them off and storing their bodies there either. The answer is the problem—I have a bunch of half-dressed men hanging out in my cooler."

Lindsey giggled and gave a little clap. "I want to go see!"

Delphinium waved her hand. "Be my guest."

Her friend ran back to the refrigerator eagerly. A couple minutes later, she returned looking deflated.

Delphinium bit her lip to keep from laughing. "So?"

Lindsey made a sour face. "You're right. There's a group of half-dressed men playing cards in your refrigerator. One of them even has his pants off. It was like catching my grandpa in his underwear."

Delphinium pushed open the swinging door and yelled, "Charlie, put your pants on! You guys can forget about getting any cookies or treats if your bottom halves aren't covered!"

Lindsey made a face. "I guess I don't have to ask why you're working out here."

Delphinium watched her friend pop something in her mouth. "What are you eating?"

"Gurdy gave me a couple donut holes." Lindsey gave a closed-lipped smile with round cheeks.

Delphinium stared at her.

"What? She has a whole apron pocket full of them."

"I know. I bought them!" Delphinium began tidying the area around the centerpiece, cleaning up bits of flowers.

"Do you know how long they'll be here?"

"Nope."

"Why don't you tell them that they all have to go back to The Gardens?"

Delphinium sighed. "Because it's *Henry*. He's fine. It's the others I don't know how to handle."

Lindsey leaned against the counter. "They all look happy to be here."

"Of course they do. I give them free rein to do what they want. I'm a florist, not the activities coordinator on a cruise ship."

"Maybe you're both," Lindsey responded with a grin.

Delphinium shook her head. "This has gotten more out of control than I thought it would. I didn't expect them to keep coming back. It's like they've claimed this territory as their new playground."

Lindsey covered her mouth but a snicker still escaped.

Delphinium stopped cleaning up and stared at her friend. "There's something different about you. What is it? You look extra happy today."

Her friend began to bounce like she did when she was excited. Delphinium wasn't sure she was even aware that she did it. It was like joy literally bubbled up inside her.

"I got an answer to my question!" she announced.

"What are you talking about?"

"I wrote to Dear Tabby in *The Town Times*, and she responded to me!" Lindsey took the newspaper out of her bag and laid it open on the counter, pointing to the advice column. Delphinium read it.

Dear Tabby,

I can't seem to find the right guy. It seems especially hard because this town is so small. I feel like it's slim pickings at this point.

What do you suggest?

Hope to hear from you,

Unsuccessful in Love

"Unsuccessful in Love?" Delphinium asked, raising one eyebrow.

"Hey, no judgment. I didn't want to reveal myself," Lindsey defended. "Read on."

Dear Unsuccessful in Love,

There might be slim pickings in my fridge, yet I always manage to find something to eat. Sometimes all it takes is a little imagination and opening your eyes to what's right in front of you for the makings of a wonderful surprise. When I give up my rigid expectation of what things should look like, embrace an adventurous spirit, and mix things I never would've put together, I often come up with something entirely new and delicious.

Don't dismiss what's already in your fridge or turn something (or someone) down because it's familiar. When warmed up, leftovers are often even better than when first served. Or be brave and try a new takeout that you were afraid to explore before.

Good luck!

Tabby

"So, you're supposed to reimagine the leftovers in your fridge for your future husband?" Delphinium teased.

"I'm supposed to be *open* to leftovers and make something new out of them. Or go to an entirely new restaurant. I'm going to be open to—"

The phone rang, interrupting her. Delphinium picked it up after the first ring. "Delphinium's Flora Emporium. How can I help you?"

"May I please speak with Ms. Hayes?" a man's voice on the other end of the line asked sternly.

"This is she."

"Hello, my name is Elliot Sturgis. I'm the director of The Gardens Assisted Living and Senior Care Facility."

Delphinium felt her voice and posture shrink. She should have anticipated this call. "Oh, hello."

"I wanted to talk to you about the current activity of some of our residents."

"Uh-huh."

"The situation seems to be getting out of hand."

A sharp laugh erupted from her. "Oh, you don't have to tell me that! I completely agree. I wish you'd just give them what they're asking for and make this all go away. Do you think I like having my shop overrun by a bunch of half-naked old men? I mean, is banning them from playing poker really worth this?"

His answer came in a very controlled, measured tone. "Are you aware that one of those men got into debt he could not afford to pay so he asked his children to help bail him out? Who then, in turn, called me and asked how I could allow elderly people who are on a very tight fixed income, some suffering from signs of dementia, to play with actual money?"

"Um, no. I didn't know that." Delphinium could swear she shrank another inch as her plea to defend Henry's poker club deflated like a hot air balloon on the ground.

"Are you also aware, Ms. Hayes, that there's a huge liability issue to what you're doing?"

She balked. "I'm sorry, what? There's a liability in letting some old men hang out here?"

"No, there's liability in *transporting* our residents in an unapproved vehicle."

She was getting more confused by the minute. "I'm sorry, I don't know what you're talking about. What vehicle?"

"A van with your business logo comes and picks up our residents each day. The driver is a teenage boy. Do you have the proper insurance if something should happen? Is the van handicap accessible?"

Delphinium was speechless. She tried to talk but nothing came out.

"Ms. Hayes?"

She cleared her throat. "Just one moment, please." She put the phone down.

"PAAVO!" she screamed at the top of her lungs.

"What's the problem?" Lindsey asked, alarmed, following her to the back room.

"The problem is that my problems just keep growing," Delphinium said over her shoulder as she stomped into the back with such force that everyone froze. The men stopped talking midsentence.

"Paavo, have you been driving Henry and his pals back and forth to the nursing home in the delivery van?"

The Adam's apple in Paavo's throat bobbed up and down as he swallowed hard.

"We asked the kid to do it," confessed George before Paavo could speak, which, by the color of his face, wasn't going to be anytime soon. "Half of us let our driver's licenses expire and the other half, well, they were taken by the state."

Delphinium felt hysteria rising within her, and she wondered how they all appeared so calm. "How are you transporting them? The van doesn't even have a back seat!"

A mountain of a man named Bob, who always wore an Air Force hat and a flag pin on his collar, answered this time. "We pile in and hang on tight like we did in the military planes before we jumped out. It's quite a ride."

"I've got a bad hip so I just lie down," Charlie added.

Delphinium closed her eyes and began massaging her temples. "I think I can actually feel the blood vessels in my head exploding. This must be what an aneurysm feels like."

"What's the problem?" George asked innocently.

"The problem, George"—she punctuated each word with a snap—"is that you all could get seriously hurt and it would be in *my* van. My van that has no seats or seat belts in the back because it is only supposed to be used for transporting floral arrangements, not human beings! I have no liability insurance for stacking people who are at a certain frail age like sardines. What you all are doing is illegal. The director of The Gardens is on the phone right now reminding me of the danger that *I'm* apparently putting you all in!"

She looked to Henry, who had his gaze fixed on the floor. Nobody said a word.

As the silence dragged on, she watched as all their shoulders slumped, making them resemble kids being called to the principal's office. Her outrage began to lose its fire. Glancing from face to face, she felt awful for yelling. They were at her shop because they believed they weren't being heard at The Gardens. It was not her place to discount their feelings now. She took a loud, audible intake of breath.

More composed, she began again. "Okay. Let's start over. From now on, I will drive you back and forth from The Gardens, three people at a time in my car. One up front with me and two in the back seat. Everyone will be buckled."

"I'm also happy to pick up whoever and drive them," Lindsey added, with her hand raised to volunteer. "My morning boot camp is over by ten."

"Thank you," Delphinium said, and all the other adults murmured the same response.

"We will figure out letting your food demands be known later. For now, let me talk to the director and reassure him that we plan on doing things in a lawful way and not putting any of your lives in danger."

Everyone nodded. Henry gave her a thankful smile.

Delphinium went back to the phone and after apologizing profusely, reassured Mr. Sturgis that things would change. She promised to transport everyone safely. Before hanging up, she asked out of curiosity how he had gotten her name.

"You are listed as the emergency contact for Henry."

Of course. It made sense. He would be her emergency contact too.

"Also, as the residents check out, each one of them writes your name on the form as the person responsible for them."

Her heart sank. *The person responsible for them.* She was as sad as she was touched. They put her in charge. What was she going to do now?

Mr. Sturgis's voice interrupted her thoughts. "That's a tremendous responsibility, Ms. Hayes, to be in charge of so many residents."

"It is," she said with a heavy heart.

"I take it you didn't expect any of this."

"No, I did not."

There was nothing more to say. After a few moments of silence, they both said goodbye and hung up.

She was the person responsible for them.

Why did that feel like so much more than just her name on a piece of paper?

For the next week, the carpool system worked well. Well enough that Arlene and Patsy, George's two "sweethearts," as he called them, started to tag along for the adventure. The two ladies were best friends and didn't mind sharing George since they both admitted he could be rather high maintenance. Delphinium was tickled to learn that, instead of George playing Don Juan with them, the two women were actually taking advantage of *him.*

"We are each other's best friend, but when one of us is tired and doesn't want to go out, we take George," Arlene explained. "Having him as our backup companion comes in handy when one of us isn't feeling up to snuff." She took a loose purple ribbon from a pile in front of her and began rolling it up. She was nearly finished organizing an entire drawer and lining up the ribbons by color. "Neither one of us wants a man at our age, but a dinner companion or someone to sit next to on the bus is nice. It cushions George's ego while filling a space in our lives."

Patsy edged closer to whisper in her raspy smoker voice. "I was married for nearly fifty years before my husband passed. I'm not Widgy McQuire, looking for a replacement." Delphinium was well aware of the handywoman's infamous nickname, Marry-Em-and-Bury-Em Widgy. Patsy eyed Delphinium. "What you have to remember is that male companionship at our age is like dessert— good in small quantities."

Delphinium wasn't about to question the women's logic. She

felt as though she'd lost all control over what was going on in her back room, so kudos to Patsy and Arlene for figuring out how to keep George or any of the men in line. Along with the women's philosophy, Delphinium admired how smart and sassy they both were.

Patsy was a card shark who smelled like begonias from six feet away. Begonia-scented people were natural talkers who thrived on interaction with friends. Patsy immediately joined in on the poker matches and was as rowdy as the guys. Arlene liked to fiddle around the shop, cleaning and sprucing up the displays. She embodied the scent of foxglove, which showed in her productivity and cooperation. She had worked in retail for years and had creative ideas on how to draw more attention to the front windows. Arlene's contribution actually made up for the inconvenience of having the back room turned into a gambling hall.

Gurdy remained at Paavo's side as he worked but now sat reading and discussing *Of Mice and Men* with him for his summer school class. Delphinium couldn't complain about the free tutoring for him and the free help in the shop. She was working on an order when Lindsey popped in for a visit. Her best friend had started to stop by more often to watch the senior commotion, which was becoming similar to a reality show.

"Hey!" Lindsey said in greeting. "Do you have lunch plans?"

Delphinium shook her head. "I was just going to order pizza."

"How about if I get some sandwiches, kale chips, and smoothies for everyone?"

"You don't have to do that."

"I don't have to, but I'd like to." She smiled.

"You know, feeding them will only encourage them. It's like placing cans of tuna outside for stray cats. Soon they'll make this their permanent residence. I've gone from having only one senior here to seven because I provide food."

"Are they still in the cooler?"

Delphinium shook her head again. "Only in the afternoon when it's hot. They've moved to my worktable, which is why I'm making all my bouquets out here."

"Are they still on their food strike at the nursing home?"

"Yep."

"I'll run home and get some of my homemade energy balls out of the freezer to send with them in small baggies. They can sneak them into the nursing home in their pockets."

Delphinium couldn't hold back a grin. "That's very sweet of you."

"My pleasure."

The door opened and they both turned.

Mason McCormack walked in with a gleaming smile. He mis-stepped when he caught sight of Lindsey but quickly corrected it so that his glide still came off as seamless.

Delphinium frowned. "If you're here for another breakup bouquet, you can go to the grocery store. I'm not making you one. I'm pretty sure you're the reason my sales are down."

Her response seemed to amuse him. "It's nice to see you too, Delphinium. Is it customary to reject customers right upon their entry?"

Delphinium ignored him and kept working.

"There's an elderly woman outside who greeted me very nicely. She's *washing* your windows." His voice held an edge she hadn't heard him use before.

"And?" Delphinium asked, feigning innocence.

Mason's agitation was shadowed with a piercing stare. "Is she even getting minimum wage, or do I have to report you to the authorities?"

His and Delphinium's eyes were locked on each other. The corners of his mouth turned up, and the corners of her mouth turned down. Lindsey's head turned from one to the other so quickly that she resembled a bobbing doll on a car dashboard.

When no one spoke, she jumped in. "Hi, I'm Lindsey, Delphi's best friend."

Mason lost the battle and a lopsided smile crawled up his face.

"*Delphi?*" He looked at Delphinium. "I like that." His attention went back to Lindsey. "Hi, Lindsey. I'm Mason McCormack. I've come in here a couple times for flowers"—he cast a purposeful look at Delphinium—"much to the disappointment of the owner."

Lindsey watched the silent interaction between the two before speaking. "Well, I was just leaving to go get started on lunch for everyone. It was nice to meet you, Mr. McCormack."

"Please, call me Mason. It was lovely to meet you, Lindsey. I really hope we'll run into each other again. You seem to have a much brighter disposition than the owner here."

Lindsey turned her whole body to Delphinium so that only she could see her expression. "I'll see you in a little bit with the food we discussed." Then she mouthed "*Wow.*"

Delphinium watched Lindsey nearly bounce out of the shop before she straightened her shoulders.

Mason watched her leave also. "She's nice. *Really* nice."

Delphinium scowled. "She's off-limits."

"What?" he asked, putting on an innocent look.

"Your tongue started hanging out like a dog panting. She's too good for you."

He laughed. "My admiration is sincere, I assure you. I am capable of giving a genuine compliment, you know."

Delphinium glared at him, lips in a flat line. "I doubt it."

He shook his head, chuckling. "How do you have any business when you talk to your best customers like that?" His eyes shone with entertainment.

Delphinium's stomach growled, a reflection of her midday slump. "What can I do for you? Is your 'new beginnings' bouquet girl ready for her 'parting is such sweet sorrow' bouquet?"

"Actually, I'm not here for flowers. I received a call to come here."

Her brows knit together. "I-I didn't call you."

"I did," Henry said from behind her. "I found his card in the register when I was tallying up the receipts and took it as a sign." He reached out his hand to shake Mason's. "My name is Henry Folden and there's a group of us geezers who want to retain your services to sue The Gardens Assisted Living and Senior Care Facility."

Mason's face revealed nothing. "What for?"

Henry stood with a grave expression. "Charges in aiding and abetting first-degree murder."

Six

Mason's eyebrows shot up, his eyes widening. "Murder?"

"*Murder?!*" Delphinium repeated, nearly choking.

Henry nodded, completely serious. "Yep. Their food and rules are speeding up the dying process for us. A person checks into The Gardens at a ripe old age but inevitably checks out in a body bag."

To his credit, Mason listened with a straight face. "Well . . ." He cleared his throat. "And I'm just playing devil's advocate here, sir, but if we were to bring this to court, wouldn't the argument be that what you're saying happens in *all* nursing homes and assisted living facilities?" He put his hands up as if in a sign of surrender. "Isn't it the purpose of these establishments to take care of folks in their . . . final season of life?"

Henry shrugged. "Sure. But living at The Gardens is making us cross the finish line a lot *sooner*, if you catch my drift." He gave Mason a pointed look. "The fact that the staff is aiding and abetting in our death is against the law."

"You have *got* to be kidding me," Delphinium said with her hands on her hips.

Mason crossed his arms and appeared thoughtful. "Tell me more."

Henry didn't need encouragement. "They lure us there under

false advertisement. They promise delicious, catered meals, field trips, and entertainment. But it's all a ruse—the happy retirement home is really a hospital ward in disguise. The food is subpar, the field trips are to the dollar store or to church, and the entertainment is putting together jigsaw puzzles. They are committing flat-out, premeditated murder."

Mason glanced at Delphinium who gave a slight shake of her head.

"Have you brought your complaints to the administration?" he asked, still acting professional.

Henry let out a disgruntled shout. "Ha! They won't listen. It's all green Jell-O, bite-size muffins, and sparkling apple cider when they get someone's grandkid to come and put on a piano recital."

Mason nodded, taking it all in. "Well, why don't we sit down, and I can begin writing down all your complaints."

Delphinium flinched. "Excuse me?" Her voice revealed both shock and horror. "You can't be serious!"

"Well—" Mason began, but she interrupted him.

"Please excuse us for a minute." She wrapped her hand around Henry's upper arm. Not letting him go, she guided him to the back room where they'd have privacy. She ignored all the stares in the back as she directed Henry to the refrigerator and shut the door.

Once it was shut, she began her tirade. "What are you doing? *Murder?* How can you be serious? What are you up to?"

Henry looked away and began whistling.

"Come on, fess up. We both know there is more to this absurd act you're putting on. You're not going to accuse The Gardens of murder."

"Who knows what will happen." Henry shrugged. "I've got a good feeling about this guy. I like him, and if he represents us, he'd be around a lot more."

Delphinium narrowed her gaze, studying him. "Why would you want him around more?"

Henry stared at her with a sly gleam in his eyes.

She groaned. "Oh. My. Gosh." The sensation of being both horrified and outraged washed over her. "I cannot believe this. You're trying to set me up! You're actually trying to take charge of my love life by making this guy keep coming back to the shop." She rubbed her forehead. "This is what my life has come to. I'm so pathetic romantically that you're conning strangers into spending time with me."

"He looks to be in his early thirties. He's handsome and dresses as if he's successful."

"No." She shook her head. "No way."

"And when I called his office, I confirmed with his secretary that he's not married."

She scoffed. "I know! I'm the one that helps him break up with and pick up new women with my bouquets."

"You never date."

"That's because I have a knack for picking liars like a built-in homing device. Any man that fabricates the truth within a certain-mile radius, I manage to find. I should wear a sign on my back that reads 'Fakes, frauds, and fibbers, here I am!'"

"So you've gotten burned once or twice."

"*Scorched*, Henry," she corrected. "I was put on a skewer over a fire by the last two guys. One had withheld the small bit of information that he was still married."

Henry put a hand on her shoulder. "You can't let those disappointing trials keep you from putting yourself out there. The right person is waiting for you. You just have to be open to something that maybe looks a bit different than you envisioned."

"You sound like Dear Tabby. I'm comfortable being alone. I have the shop, I have my friends, and I have you!"

A brief flash of what looked like deep sadness crossed over his face. But then he took a breath and crossed his arms over his chest. "Well, I'm flattered, but you need a companion that's under seventy-nine years old! I won't be around forever. You need more friends your own age. *Male* friends."

Delphinium's posture hunched in defeat. Reasoning with him

was like coming up against a brick wall. "I'm not into this guy. I don't like him."

Henry smirked. "I've watched you two. I disagree."

"We spar."

"That's something."

"A relationship needs sparks, not grenades."

"Both make an impact and can start a fire." He smiled mischievously.

Delphinium sighed. His arguing and debating skills rivaled someone a quarter his age. "Trust me, your radar is off about this one. Please believe me when I say I don't have that kind of romantic chemistry with him."

"*Yet*," he added with emphasis, raising his index finger. "You don't have any romantic chemistry *yet*. Betty and I argued every day, God rest her soul. It made life less boring and the nights—well, they were anything but dull, if you get my drift. Even your grandma took pleasure in putting me in my place." He winked. "Annie was a firecracker like you."

Delphinium made a face. "I don't want to hear about you and my grandmother. And I'm not a firecracker. You're only making that comparison because of the color of my hair."

"I took the fact that you put Mason's card in the cash register as a sign," he continued.

"Yeah, and the fact that you took it as a sign is an indicator that you're searching for anything. A move made completely out of desperation. You're not playing cupid. You don't know anything about this guy."

Henry's eyes lit up. "Exactly! What better way to find out than have a bunch of old folks put him through the wringer? We don't beat around the bush. We'll get the truth out of him."

"What *truth*? The only truth you'll find is that he goes through women like water!"

Henry offered a sly grin. "Well, you, my dear, are a fine wine. Perhaps he needs to adjust his choice of beverage."

Delphinium couldn't hide her smile from the sweet sentiment. He did mean well.

"A fine wine that is aging by the minute," Henry quickly added, making her smile fall, "so leave me to my master plan." He turned and left the fridge before she could argue.

Nearly jogging back to the front of the shop, Henry returned to Mason with a wide grin. "So, you'll take us on as clients?"

"I can't promise you the revolution you are envisioning," Mason said, "but I'm willing to gather more information to see if there's a case or not."

Henry clapped his hands together. "Perfect! I had a feeling you were the man for us. It was too convenient and coincidental that your card was tucked safely in the register."

Delphinium could feel the hot blush in her face extend to the tips of her ears.

Mason cast a glance at her with a raised brow, looking devilishly pleased. "I'd say our meeting was providential, then."

Henry nodded. "Precisely."

"You know, Henry," Mason went on, "I have a feeling this is going to take a while, so why don't I go and get some cinnamon rolls and bear claws from the bakery a couple doors down before we start. Is there a coffee maker in the back?"

"Yep, I brought one in yesterday."

Delphinium, who couldn't believe this conversation was even happening, whipped her head around to stare at Henry. "You brought in a coffee maker?"

Henry shrugged. "Of course. We can't afford to keep buying froufrou coffee. We're on a budget, you know."

"You guys get your coffee from the gas station," Delphinium argued.

"Exactly! We need to start saving our pennies for our upcoming legal services. It's also easier to make it here since we're never sure how many folks are going to show up. Our gang is growing."

Delphinium's mouth dropped open.

Mason nodded. "Smart thinking, Henry. Why don't you go put on a fresh pot. I'll be back in five minutes, then we can sit in the back and have a roundtable discussion."

"That's my worktable!" Delphinium protested.

"Are you using it right now?" Henry asked.

She gaped at him. "You know I can't because you're using it for poker!"

He shrugged. "So it won't matter if we use it, then." Henry looked to Mason. "I'll go tell the guys you're onboard."

Henry turned to leave but then peered back. "I don't know what your retainer fee is, but we can't afford much. We're all on the scrapings of retirement, and Medicare won't cover this even though it's affecting our mental, emotional, and physical health."

Delphinium scoffed. "And how is gambling and inflicting a fake self-imposed hunger strike when you're not really going hungry affecting your mental and physical health?"

Henry was quick to respond. "The thought of the fancy buffet food we're missing out on is causing emotional duress, which creates stress my old heart can't take." He did a couple taps over his chest.

Delphinium rolled her eyes. "Oh, gimme a break. The Gardens is never going to agree to prime rib or a seafood bar."

"Do you see what I'm up against?" Henry said to Mason, nodding his head toward her.

Mason waved him off. "Don't worry about the retainer fee. I'll do this one pro bono. Our firm takes on the occasional human-interest case if we feel passionate about it. And I feel passionate about this one. It's a real humanitarian cause." He smiled at Henry but snuck a wink at her.

Delphinium couldn't believe it. One player was playing the other.

Henry seemed jubilant, clapping his hands together. "Wonderful! The guys and gals will be thrilled." He disappeared into the back.

As Mason headed to the front door with his own spring in his step, Delphinium followed him.

"Why are you doing this? You can't really think they have a case in suing the nursing home."

Mason glanced back at her. "I haven't come across anything this unusual in a long time. It sounds interesting, to say the least, and I'd like to help them. Their accusations intrigue me, and I'm rarely intrigued by my work. As a matter of fact, I was feeling pretty bored with life until I walked into your shop. There's a lot of monotony in most of what I do."

He stopped at the door to allow Arlene, who had finished the windows, to come through. He gave her a nod. "Hello, I'm Mason."

She nodded back. "I'm Arlene. Did you find what you were looking for?"

"Yes, ma'am. And I'll be returning after I go to the bakery to bring you all some pastries."

Arlene's face lit up. "Wonderful." Then she walked to the back, carrying her dirty rags and cleaner.

Delphinium followed Mason out the door and then jumped in front of him, blocking him from taking another step. He stared at her incredulously.

Leaning in closer, she took a big whiff.

He arched back, clearly taken by surprise. "What are you doing?"

She scrunched her face. "Why don't you smell?"

"What?"

"I smell sandalwood from your cologne or deodorant today, but that doesn't count. Why don't *you* smell? You have no personal scent," she mumbled frustratedly, talking to herself more than to him.

"Um, I like to take showers. Maybe you're not accustomed to people with good hygiene."

She glared at him.

"*Should* I smell?" His expression was both confused and somehow bemused.

She gave a frustrated shake of her head. "Never mind. Just promise me that you're not going to encourage Henry and his gang to take legal action against The Gardens."

He didn't hide his smirk. "This will never go to court."

"How do you know that?"

Mason gave her a wicked smile. "Because I'm a real estate at-torney."

Mason and the seniors chatted their way through all the pastries and three pots of coffee. Mason had rolled the sleeves of his dress shirt up to his elbows and was taking notes on one of *her* yellow legal pads. *The nerve.* Henry had given it to him when they first started listing their complaints.

Delphinium pretended not to pay attention to their discussion while getting unnecessary things from the back and bringing them to the front of the store, all of which she would have to return later.

When Lindsey arrived with lunch, the additional sustenance fueled the seniors' hunger for justice. Mason invited the two women to stay and listen. Lindsey eagerly accepted. She had hours to kill before her evening boot camp, and she told Delphinium this was the best entertainment she'd had all week.

Delphinium also didn't miss how Mason took every opportunity to ask Lindsey's opinion or to involve her in the discussion when she had nothing to do with the issue at hand. *Some lawyer.*

After an hour and a half, Mason got up off his stool. "Okay, guys, you've given me a long list of what you want changed. If you think of anything we may have missed, just write it down. I'm going to run what I have by a couple of my partners and then I'll get back to you." He said his goodbyes to the gang and walked to the front of the shop, with Delphinium following him out.

As he reached the door, he turned to her. "I've changed my mind," he said. "I would like to order a bouquet."

Delphinium let out a low growl. "I told you, I won't—"

"It's for someone different. Someone new."

She turned. "What a shocker. There's always someone new."

Her disgust seemed to amuse Mason greatly. "I want to get to know this person for *real* this time."

"That's what you said about your last victim."

A dimple appeared on his left cheek that she hadn't seen before. It looked like he was trying not to grin. "I'm being sincere."

"I'm not sure you know what that word means."

Now he couldn't wipe the silly grin off his face. "What would you suggest? Give me something that would make my offering stand out."

Delphinium didn't even need to think about it. "Snapdragons. They represent a new journey. It would make your intention to get to know them open and innocent."

"Perfect."

"I don't have any in stock, so I'll need to place a special order, which will cost you more." She got out an order sheet.

Mason rubbed his jaw. "Which I have no doubt you'll gouge me for."

"Quality and expertise cost money," she said, smiling sweetly.

He narrowed his eyes. "That I am happy to pay for as long as this bouquet takes her breath away to represent our new journey together."

"Which may be a false assumption, considering your past history," she added under her breath.

He cocked one eyebrow. "You don't think my intentions are innocent?"

She shrugged. "I think you're the kind of guy that goes through a lot of women. I don't even know who this woman is, and I feel sorry for her."

He stared at her with mock offense. "I think you have the wrong idea about me."

She peered at him. "I know that you're falsely leading on a bunch of elderly people. That gives me a pretty good idea."

His playful smile disappeared. "I am going to help them," he said, glaring at her with no humor in his voice. "I have connections all over Moonberry. I can give them my time and advice for *free*, and if I think these respected members of our community genuinely have a case, I'll call a friend who could shake things up or at least scare the nursing home with some legal threats." His face was like stone and his tone caught her breath. If she had meant to upset or insult him, she had succeeded.

He leaned in and she instinctively leaned away. "I always walk a straight line when it comes to older generations. My grandparents meant the world to me growing up. I would never hurt any of those people in your back room."

Delphinium gulped at his firmness, not sure what to say.

"I'll pick up the snapdragon bouquet on Friday when I come back to talk to Henry." Mason turned briskly and left without saying another word.

Delphinium stood staring at the door that had swung shut. She wasn't sure what had just happened, but she knew she had gone too far.

Seven

T he next few days were a blur of activity as Delphinium got ready for the Fourth of July at the end of the week. There was a huge bump in sales from the vast quantity of red, white, and blue carnations sold to people decorating floats, cars, wagons, and bicycles for the parade down Main Street. This week would hopefully make up for any deficit the rest of the month, even with the discount she gave to veterans.

Moonberry Lake was a gem of a town that took pride in its big parade showcasing veterans, small businesses, school clubs, fire and police departments, and local officials who waved and shook hands with their neighbors. People crowded the sidewalks of Main Street, watching and cheering for the people they went to church with and whose driveways they helped shovel in the winter. Moonberry's Independence Day parade highlighted the everyday lives of everyday stars who made the town shine.

This morning she had just finished a huge bouquet for the parents of Luke Wilson, a Moonberry Lake native who was killed serving overseas. When the grief-stricken mother, Elise, came in to order it, the shattered look on her face broke Delphinium's heart. She went way above what the woman had ordered and then didn't charge her for it, figuring it was the least she could do to pay her respects. Luke was twenty-two, just a few years younger than she was. No matter the dire circumstance of her finances, she would not compromise on doing what she felt was the right thing.

The heat had driven the guys into the cooler instead of the back room, which made things quieter. As much as she enjoyed the sense of normality in her shop—even if it was fleeting—Delphinium was surprised that she actually missed the extra chaos. She was relieved for the distraction when she heard the tiny bell above the door announcing a customer's arrival. Before she could offer a greeting, she was accosted by their scent. It was like a wall of fragrance coming down on her. The heavenly aroma enveloped Delphinium, nearly sweeping her off her feet.

Violets.

One of the most difficult flowers to pick up any scent because of its delicacy. The aroma of violets was usually so faint that it typically went unnoticed. Most people chose violets for their color, but Delphinium believed that the virtue associated with the flower matched the shy gracefulness of its perfume. Individuals with a high standard of loyalty and love exuded a heavy essence of violets. At the strong scent wafting off her new customer, she felt as if she were in some sort of a trance or at least falling under the most heavenly spell.

A tall, studious-looking man who looked about ten years her senior was the unlikely source of her enchantment. He was wearing wire-rimmed glasses, tan dress pants, a beautiful medium-blue dress shirt, a complementary tie knotted so high at the neck it looked as if it was choking him, and polished dress shoes that practically gleamed. *Hmmm. Interesting.* She wouldn't have expected such heavy violet to emanate from someone who appeared uptight and all business. The gentleman could be a younger version of her father or even a more suitable combination of her parents rather than the mishap in DNA that resulted in her.

Delphinium did a quick shake of her head to clear her thoughts, remembering that it was the subtler nature of a person that captured her sense of smell—not the obvious facade with which the world made its judgment. The scent and physical appearance of someone could be surprisingly contradicting. The tincture of irises in full bloom always arose out of dreamers and artists, and they could look like anyone. The same with the introvert who hid tucked away in the corner at parties, inevitably infusing the air with gardenias. And the most passive-aggressive people emitted the aroma of peonies like they bathed in them. That one was truly a wolf in sheep's clothing.

She needed to focus and not be so distracted by this man's divine scent.

Pull it together.

He glanced at her and then busied himself by staring at her displays, or rather *analyzing* them. He didn't reach out and touch the flowers like most people but kept his hands tucked in his pockets. He stood examining them like they were math problems to be solved.

She cleared her throat. "Please let me know if I can help you."

He looked at her again and nodded before going back to studying the merchandise. She noticed him pause and stare at the fairy houses and miniature statues that most people skipped over. Delphinium tried to busy herself with the patriotic bouquets she was working on but found him incredibly distracting.

Just when she couldn't stand the silent inspection and was going to say something, Paavo came bustling through the swinging door from the back.

"I finished unloading the truck, Miz D. I couldn't get everything in the cooler because of Hen—" He stopped as soon as he noticed the customer.

Delphinium frowned. "What is it, Paavo?"

The teen didn't answer or make eye contact with her but instead turned and bolted to the back room.

Delphinium got up from her stool and stopped the door mid-swing. "Paavo, what's wrong?" she called after him.

The man surprised her by speaking up. "He recognized me."

Delphinium looked at him, confused.

"I'm Elliot Sturgis from The Gardens Assisted Living and Senior Care Facility."

Silence.

Delphinium stared at him with wide, unblinking owl eyes. After an awkward silence she finally managed to mutter an "Oh."

To her relief, Elliot seemed equally uncomfortable. Though she wasn't sure why, when he *did* have the upper hand in this situation. She was the one running her shop like a circus. As they continued to stare at each other, noises from the back room amplified. Neither broke eye contact as a couple whoops and roars of laughter erupted. Delphinium recognized Charlie's and Bob's voices.

Elliot reached up to straighten his glasses while discreetly clearing his throat. "I came to see what the draw of this place was for my residents. You seem to have a gift in dealing with seniors."

"Oh, I wouldn't say that. They're an unruly bunch. I really have no control of them. They've kind of taken over my shop."

"Which you've allowed."

She wasn't sure if he meant it as a statement or an accusation. "More like surrendered," she admitted.

Elliot pressed his lips together as if stifling a smile. "You make them sound like rowdy pirates."

"There are definite similarities."

His powerful stare made heat rise up her neck. His gaze went from her curly hair to her dangly earrings made of colorful beads and hammered brass. He was obviously trying to figure her out, studying her as if memorizing every detail for a test. The intense scrutiny made her feel exposed and sweaty. She thought the juxtaposition between the two of them was laughable. While she wore a vine and leaf print tunic-style dress with a stack of oversized bracelets on each wrist that matched her long earrings and necklace, he was dressed like her accountant, ready to go over taxes.

She opened her mouth to say something when Bob came through

the door. "Hey, Delphi—" he began but then stopped and sneered at the sight of Elliot. "What are you doing here?"

Delphinium was taken aback at the curtness in Bob's voice.

To his credit, Elliot smiled politely and greeted Bob as though he had gotten a warm hug. "Hi, Bob. It's nice to see you. I was out on an errand and passed this shop when I realized that I've never been inside, which I can see is my loss." He turned his head and scanned the room with his investigative gaze. "It's very nice. I was just introducing myself to Ms. Hayes."

Bob maintained his scorn. "You came to spy on us by crossing over into enemy territory!" He opened the door to the back and yelled to the others, "Hey, guys, we've got company. They've hunted us down. The enemy has infiltrated our camp."

Henry, Charlie, George, and the rest of the elderly mob came out to see what the fuss was. Mumblings of "What's he doing here?" came from all of them. They stood in a unified cluster staring down Elliot and giving the stink eye.

Delphinium actually felt sorry for the man. If she had learned anything in the past couple weeks, it was what a handful all the seniors could be.

She cleared her throat. "I was actually discussing an order that I was putting together for Mr. Sturgis before you all rudely interrupted us. Now, if you don't mind, I'd like to finish conducting my *business*. That is, after all, the intention of this establishment—to sell flowers." Putting one fist on her hip, she gave them all her most severe motherly glare. "You have all promised me that your presence wouldn't affect my business, or am I mistaken?"

They looked as if they were confused about who the traitor was now. With frowning disapproval and a few grumblings, they disappeared into the back in a single-file line. When they were gone, Delphinium noticed the slightest descent of Mr. Sturgis's shoulders.

"Thank you," he said in a quiet voice.

"I know they can be a force."

He stepped forward. "Please tell me your secret, Ms. Hayes. How do you do it?"

Delphinium gave a shrug. "I've learned that it's all about give-and-take with them. When I let them win on some issues, they let me win on things I want. There's a lot of compromise on each side."

"Such as?"

"Such as . . ." She paused, searching her brain for examples. "When it's hot, I let them take off their shirts and play cards in my cooler, and in exchange, Charlie keeps his pants on."

Elliot's business face faltered, and he let out a small chuckle that came out sounding like he was clearing his throat. "I don't know what it is about that man and clothes." He shook his head, grinning.

"I also listen to them and take their opinions to heart. Even the ones that seem insignificant to me, like the kind of donuts I buy or the type of bread they want for their sandwiches."

"And what are those?"

"What?"

"The kinds of donuts they like."

Delphinium couldn't believe he actually wanted to know, but she indulged his curiosity. "The women are split between cinnamon sugar donuts and cinnamon frosted buns. They cut theirs into pieces and eat them with a fork. The men like plain donut holes that they can just pop into their mouths so their fingers don't get sticky and interfere with the card playing.

"With their afternoon coffee, they all prefer a slice of vanilla pound cake. If they need cheering up, I'll treat them with apple turnovers. Then they view the day as something special."

"That's a lot of sugar."

"They don't get turnovers if they've had pound cake and donuts. It's one treat a day. I also make sure that they drink just as much water as coffee so they don't get dehydrated." Now that she got going, she couldn't stop herself from listing all the seniors' dietary preferences. She'd learned a lot about them in such a short time.

"For sandwiches, sourdough bread is everyone's favorite but

mine, so I buy a loaf for them and a single bagel with seeds for me. I make sure they get protein in their sandwiches through sliced turkey or peanut butter. If they're not in the mood for a sandwich, I offer energy balls that are made with almond flour, peanut butter, and protein powder. I serve chocolate milk with a little protein powder mixed in or offer water with some electrolyte powder added."

He stared at her so intently that she looked away feeling uncomfortable, and she tried in vain to press her hair behind her ears. This guy was too intense.

"These seem like very small things, but they give them a sense of power and choice," she added.

"You know, I'm not really the bad guy here."

She scoffed. "Well, I certainly hope you don't think *I* am the bad guy, because I never asked for any of this."

"Then what do you propose the solution to be?"

Delphinium hesitated before speaking. She had the feeling he was hoping for a quick and easy answer that he wasn't going to get. "Maybe you could start by listening to their requests and granting some of their wishes. What I hear them complain about may seem trivial to you, but it's important to them. It may actually improve your facility." She shrugged. "Make a few changes to the menu, give them some of the simple desserts they request, like extra whipped cream. You could bring in different entertainment too. Let them feel as though they have a say in what is supposed to be their *home*. If they are happier at The Gardens, it will have a ripple effect. They'll be easier for the staff to handle, which will ultimately make your job easier."

He turned his head, once again looking around the store while he took in her words. "I want to know exactly why they come *here*. I want to understand what the draw is. It's more than donuts and apple turnovers. Please explain the charm of sitting in the back room of a flower shop."

Delphinium didn't take offense at his confusion or clipped tone.

She was familiar with his type of personality. She grew up with it. Elliot's kind of thinking was methodical, strategic, and concise. Of course, he was clueless. She gave a little shake of her head. "I guess they love coming here because I make it inviting. Even though they are simply sitting on stools in the back, they get to hang out like they want. There's coffee, pastries, laughter, poker . . . even small projects when they feel like it. The one constant companion of old age is loss. Loss of people, familiarity, and ultimately loss of control. Here, they feel powerful rebelling against you. I simply give them a safe environment to do it."

His brow crinkled. He shook his head, frustration playing out on his face. It was obvious he was thinking about everything she said, but instead of asking more questions, he went back to staring at her like she was some sort of exotic animal he'd never seen. He clearly needed more details and explanation.

"For example," she continued, "Arlene was a homemaker for most of her life, so she likes to dust and putter around the shop making it shine. Tidying up helps her remember the pride she took in keeping her home beautiful. She likes to be active and move about.

"Gurdy was a teacher for thirty-two years and is now helping my worker, Paavo, not only pass his summer class but raise his grade to an A. Gurdy is an outstanding tutor, and interacting with a kid puts spunk back in her step.

"Patsy is a talented card player that can hold her own with the guys, but I've also noticed that they are all better behaved when she's around, and Bob only tells clean jokes and stories of when he was in the military. She keeps them in line because she's no delicate flower. She's tough and can stand her ground."

Elliot's brow still hadn't smoothed, and his stare made her shift in place. The man hardly blinked. It was no wonder the seniors formed a cohesive coup. No one person had a chance against the authority this man emanated.

"Charlie hardly spoke when he first came here, but now he is one of the chattiest in the group. Speech is a motor skill, and if you don't use it, you lose it. He has benefited from being immersed in the commotion. It's brought him to life."

Delphinium took a deep breath. She wasn't sure she was getting through to him. Elliot's gaze finally left her and went to the floor.

"Perhaps if you thought about where you like to spend time when you're not working and what draws you there, you'd under-stand why they come here," she added. "No matter a person's age, they want community. The deepest longing in all of us is a sense of belonging. Without community to give the feeling of home, a person feels only displacement and loneliness."

Elliot appeared to consider her words and gave her a sharp nod. "Thank you for your time, Ms. Hayes. I'm glad we met." He turned toward the door abruptly.

Delphinium was so jolted by the sudden ending and incom-plete conversation on his part that she went into action mode. "Mr. Sturgis," she called out, stopping him from walking out of the store. She moved over to one of her displays and picked up a small clear glass vase that displayed a giant bulb nestled inside the dirt with moss on top, then she walked over to where he had paused and handed the vase to him. "I'd like you to have this. It's my gift to you."

If he was confused before, he seemed totally bewildered now as he stared at the unimpressive planter.

"It's an amaryllis flower. It's in its resting period now. There is a bulb beneath the moss. Amaryllis flowers typically bloom in the winter, around Christmas. I know it's months away and may seem silly to have it out now, but I like to keep it in the shop to remind me that beautiful things sometimes take time. That the hope of something new will come at the moment it was intended. We just have to be patient and believe that hidden miracles will rise up in the next season." She nodded toward the vase. "Think of it as buried potential. The amaryllis is unusual, and when it blooms, it's quite magnificent. After its hibernation, a strong stem emerges out of the bulb, revealing a bright red flower." As she spoke, she couldn't help but smile. Looking up briefly, she saw he was studying her and not the plant, so she hurried on.

"The amaryllis symbolizes building harmony with yourself and others. Specifically, it represents allowing your spirit and soul to see the beauty and uniqueness of others. You can keep it indoors in a warm, sunny spot and wait to be amazed. The sight of it in full bloom will take your breath away. The flower is unique and strong but requires patience for the gift to be revealed to you."

Delphinium knew she was getting carried away, but she couldn't help herself. This typically happened when she began talking about the meaning behind flowers and plants. She looked up to meet his strong gaze. The way he stared at her made her self-conscious. He was definitely a man of few words.

She swallowed. "If you have any questions, you can contact me. That is, if you want to discuss the seniors again."

Without breaking their gaze, he thanked her in a quiet voice.

Feeling spellbound, Delphinium could give only a small nod. A waft of violet left with him. She sucked in the last of the aroma before the door shut, then stood there contemplating how odd the visit was and, even more, how strangely it had ended.

She wasn't sure if she had helped things or made them worse.

Eight

I t wasn't until the afternoon that the emporium got more foot traffic. As a woman entered the shop, the fragrance of rosemary hit Delphinium. She deeply inhaled one of her favorite scents. *Mmm, persistence.* She greeted the friendly-looking woman who had shoulder-length salt-and-pepper hair pulled back on one side with a simple barrette. She was dressed in bright colors and wearing red-framed glasses.

"Hello," she said, her big smile genuine and disarming. "I was hoping to talk to the owner of the shop."

"That's me, Delphinium Hayes."

"Hi." She put her hand out to shake. "I'm Kathryn Hughes and I write for *The Town Times*. I'm doing an article on the idea presented at the town council meeting that the old buildings on this block should be developed into something bigger and more modern. There is a proposal for Main Street to go through an expensive update and renovation."

Delphinium frowned. She hadn't heard about that possibility.

"I was wondering if you have time for an interview? I'd love your thoughts and reaction." The woman took her phone out of her pocket and her finger hovered over the record button.

Delphinium eyed the phone. "The only thing I have to say is that this flower shop has been on Main Street for over fifty years. The building is over a hundred years old. It's a valuable part of the town's history and community. It should be respected as a landmark."

Kathryn opened her mouth to say more when the bell on the door rang, and two elderly women came in.

A frail woman slowly scooted her walker forward inch by inch. She was slightly bent over with a little hump in her upper back. With her head tilted down but her eyes focused on Delphinium, she made her way to the register. "I hear you're the one in charge of casino night."

Delphinium blinked hard. How had this become her life? "Um, that would be a hard no. As in, definitely not."

The woman gave her a cold, hard stare. "That's not the right answer."

Her friend, looking close in age but walking erect, stepped closer with a pleasant smile. She was wearing gaudy rhinestone earrings with a collection of thick matching necklaces that typically only rap stars could pull off. "Hi, I'm Joanna. We're here to see the guys." She gave an obvious hard wink after drawing out the word *guys*, as if divulging the secret password.

Delphinium released an exasperated sigh and motioned to the door behind her. "They're all in back. You can go see them."

As the women shuffled through the swinging door, the reporter craned her neck to get a look at the commotion. Lively music was playing, and George was dancing with Arlene, putting an extra wiggle in his hips that was making all the other seniors laugh.

"What's going on back there?" Kathryn asked as soon as the door swung shut.

Delphinium held in a moan. "Some nursing home residents like to hang out here."

Kathryn considered that. "How many come here? How often? How long has this been happening? What do they do back there?"

Delphinium recoiled at the barrage of questions and didn't want to even try to explain the recent ridiculousness of her life. She simply gawked at the woman, not knowing how to answer.

"Sorry, it's the reporter in me. I have a bad habit of unloading all the questions swirling around in my head and don't give the person a chance to respond." She took a breath and waited for Delphinium to jump in.

"It's complicated," was all Delphinium could come up with. She watched as the eagerness in Kathryn's expression turned to skepticism like a radar detector switched on.

"I can see that."

The reporter maintained eye contact, which made Delphinium squirm. She already had a lawyer and the director of The Gardens interfering in her life. There was no way she was going to welcome a reporter into the mayhem.

Kathryn, true to her rosemary scent, didn't give up. "If you're not able to talk, would it be possible for me to go and introduce myself to the people in your back room and talk to them?"

"I'm sorry, no. I don't think that's a good idea."

Delphinium could only imagine the terrible things the uncensored bunch would say about the nursing home, adding fuel to the fire, and getting her in more trouble with Elliot Sturgis. She'd never get Henry and the growing-by-the-day senior menagerie back to The Gardens.

Kathryn, who had entered the shop appearing carefree, now pinched her face in concentration. "Thank you for your time today. I think there's a bigger story happening here than with talk of downtown development. I will definitely be back." She turned to leave.

Oh no.

"Can I interest you in some flowers?" Delphinium asked.

Kathryn lifted one eyebrow. "Will you tell me what's going on here if I buy some?"

Delphinium crossed her arms over her chest as she scrutinized her. She liked this woman. Although a story about the seniors would definitely be bad, Delphinium admired how Kathryn was true to her scent. As natural looking and sweet as she appeared to be, she was a bulldog with a chew toy when she wanted something.

The woman was driven. Her persistence in getting the job done was admirable.

"Maybe another time."

Kathryn gave a nod. "Then I'll definitely be back for some flowers."

As soon as she was gone, Delphinium pushed open the door to the back where all four men now had dancing partners. Paavo had put on some salsa music, and they all appeared to be having the time of their lives. The women giggled as the men tried to dip them, which was less of a body bend and more like the women tilting their heads back.

The sour-looking woman with the walker sat on the seat of her walker in the corner and continued to glare at Delphinium as if she were a cruel warden who came to shut down their party.

"Hey, Delphi!" Henry greeted, waving as he twirled Joanna around. "We just got off the phone with Mason. We're adding dancing to our list of demands. Who knew salsa dancing could be so fun?"

No one else even noticed her. Delphinium felt like an intruder in her own shop. Things had gotten completely out of hand. Though she was happy to see the light and laughter in Henry's eyes, the place was too crowded. As in, she could be served a hefty fine from the fire marshal for being so crowded. She couldn't access her refrigerator or the back door easily. Paavo didn't dare move from his little spot to work or he'd bump into someone. The place was not designed for nine people to be whooping it up.

Delphinium was through with it all.

She couldn't wait on Mason McCormack humoring them by listening to their endless ranting or Elliot Sturgis trying to figure out how to make the residents happy. If these people had the energy to dance, they had the strength to help her. She was tired of feeling as if *they* ran the place and she had no say. This was her shop, and she was taking it back.

Starting now.

She motioned Paavo to turn off the music. He nodded and everything went silent. They all turned to see what was happening.

"Listen up, everyone," she said, "there are new rules for you to hear. Rule number one, this is my shop. I think some of you may have forgotten that. It's a place of business, not a playroom. If you want to hang out here for a break from The Gardens, that's fine, but you're going to start to work for me beginning immediately. Fifty percent of your time here has to be spent either helping me with the flowers, cleaning up, or promoting the shop throughout town."

Everyone exchanged glances.

"What will our salary be?" Patsy asked.

Delphinium crossed her arms over her chest. "Nothing. Zero. Zilch. Nada. You work in exchange for the privilege of hanging out here."

More glances were exchanged.

"We would be your volunteers?" Gurdy asked.

"More like your platoon of soldiers," Bob added.

Delphinium nodded. "That's correct. Everyone would have a job. Gurdy, you are going to continue tutoring Paavo. Arlene, you can keep tidying up the displays because they've never looked so clean. Henry will continue doing the books. But the rest of you will be assigned different tasks. If you're not up for it, you can go back to The Gardens or to the coffee shop down the street, but you will not stay here." She was proud of the finality in her voice.

"I think we need to discuss our options," Charlie said.

She shook her head. "No. There's nothing to discuss. You're either in or out. I don't know how long I can keep this place afloat. Sales are down." She swallowed the lump in her throat. "I don't need the stress of having you guys play all day while I'm barely surviving. I'm going to lose my home and shop if I don't bring in more customers."

"We didn't know things were so bad, honey. Of course I'll help," Gurdy offered.

"Me too," added the guys.

"And me as well," Joanna said brightly. She had only been at the shop for fifteen minutes and was already onboard.

Every person either raised their hand to help or nodded in agreement. Everyone except the grumpy granny in the corner with a permanent scowl.

Henry clapped his hands together. "Great. We will be the team that helps keep this place from going under. Let's get to it!"

To Delphinium's surprise, they all seemed energized by the idea of a project and were working on it collectively. The legal pad came out, but instead of filling the pages with complaints and changes they wanted implemented at The Gardens, they turned to a fresh page and began brainstorming ways to help the emporium and were already assigning duties.

Within a half hour, Delphinium had a cleaning crew, a team to help with the care of the flowers and plants, and a list of volunteers who agreed to go up and down the street handing out business cards and putting flyers in other shop windows. The design on the flyer was what Delphinium had used when she first opened the shop. All the information was the same, so she decided to use the remaining ones simply to get rid of them.

"You know, my grandson could really spiff this up for you," Joanna said, studying the old ad. "He could make the information really jump off the page. He's great with computer graphics."

Delphinium smiled. "That would be wonderful."

"And wouldn't it be lovely if we walked around giving people some of your cheaper flowers that only have a couple days left in them. We could tie your business card to it with a pretty little ribbon."

Delphinium was gobsmacked by such a simple, brilliant idea she'd somehow not thought of before. "That's a really good marketing plan, Joanna."

"I know I'd like it if someone were to come up and hand me a free flower," the sourpuss in the corner interjected.

Delphinium went over to a bucket of chrysanthemums that

hadn't been put out front. She plucked out a bright orange one, then walked over and handed it to the woman.

In that fraction of time, the woman's demeanor completely changed. The hardness in her face softened, and the smallest smile formed on her pursed lips. She looked up at Delphinium.

"My name's Helen. My hands may be too gnarled to cut flowers, and my body can't take walking up and down the street, but I like to fold dish towels and napkins."

"Well then, there's definitely a job for you here, Helen."

The woman's face brightened at the idea, and Delphinium felt as though her heart expanded at the sight of it. Wasn't that what everyone wanted? Until the doors were locked and she lost ownership of the shop, she was going to give people a place to belong.

A few days later, Mason McCormack walked in waving one of the new flyers that Joanna's grandson had designed for the shop. Flowers decorated the border and the page featured a picture of Delphinium at the bottom, smiling, wearing her apron, and holding a bouquet of bright flowers. At first, Delphinium wasn't sure about having her picture on the flyer until the others convinced her that it added to the plight of supporting local shop owners.

Mason didn't stroll in smoothly like he typically did but at a clipped, irritated pace. "What is this?" he asked, waving the piece of paper.

"It's my new flyer."

"Yeah, I can see that. It was handed to me by one of the grannies who are typically in the back. And then I saw three other seniors on the main drive handing out flowers to people walking by. What's going on? Are you kidnapping these people from the nursing home?"

Delphinium couldn't hold back her sarcasm. "Yeah. You got me. I sneak into the nursing home after they've had their breakfast and grab whoever I can heave into my van. Then I bring them here and force them to hand out flowers." She shot him an annoyed look.

"Relax. They are just doing a little work to promote the shop. And then they go back to cards and conversation."

Mason was about to say something when Bob came through the swinging door with a hunter green apron tied around his waist with the shop's name embroidered on it. He was carrying a tall bucket of fresh pink roses and whistling a familiar tune. He nodded to Mason as he passed, placed the roses on the floor, and returned to the back room without breaking his song.

Mason's mouth hung open. "You're seriously using these people as your work staff."

"I've already told you that," Delphinium answered. "At their own will, I might add."

He stared at her. "They're . . . *elderly*."

"Yes. And they have a lot of spirit and plenty of energy to help me out. Why are you so quick to write them off because of their age? You know doing a certain amount of activity is good for them. They need to move around. Walking outside in the fresh air and sunshine is therapeutic."

"Are you paying them?"

"No. They're doing it in exchange for hanging out here."

Mason rubbed the back of his neck with one hand. "This is not good," he muttered to himself more than to her.

But Delphinium heard. "Why not? What does it matter to you?"

He looked at a loss for words. "Um, it shouldn't. I mean, it doesn't. I already told you that I have a soft spot for the elderly. But you're right, I shouldn't care if you're taking advantage of all the grandmas and grandpas."

"I'm not taking advantage of them—they're choosing to do this. They like doing some work. It gives them a purpose to their day. It's a short activity that keeps them moving. They like feeling that they're making a difference. I have given Arlene complete artistic control of the outside plants and display, and she couldn't be more excited. George has offered to help her water and add soil to whatever containers need it, and I think it's strengthened their friendship. Pairing Charlie up with Joanna has significantly helped the clarity of his speech because she has him talk to people constantly. They make a great sales team. And you see the strength Bob possesses. Picking up the buckets of flowers helps build the muscles in his lower body and back."

Mason raked his hand through his hair, which only made him look more like a movie star. "Do you hear yourself?"

Delphinium huffed an exhausted sigh. "Did you come in to buy flowers or simply to give me a hard time?"

Her words brought him out of whatever dialogue was happening inside his head. "Yeah. I need some more flowers."

"That didn't last long," she muttered under her breath. "What was it this time? A week before you broke the poor woman's heart? Perhaps you want me to put together a bouquet that evokes a kind of amnesia so she can't tell her girlfriends since you're developing quite a trail of victims."

He narrowed his eyes. "You think you're so funny and that you've got me all figured out."

"Oh, I think I have you sized up right."

He arched his brows and gave a smug smile. "Then it delights me to no end to prove you wrong. I want flowers for the same woman. She liked the uniqueness of the snapdragons. She called them *unconventional*. It made me look different, which I'm pretty sure got me a few brownie points."

"Hmm." Delphinium frowned. She wasn't sure how she felt about helping him snare this unsuspecting woman. However, she couldn't wait to tell Henry that his dating strategy for her wasn't working. For a moment she imagined Henry handing out the new shop flyers with her picture and adding "And she's single!" to any male recipient.

Mason's words stopped her internal monologue. "I want something that is going to surprise her again. Something that really brightens her day and, of course," he added with a haughty grin, "makes me look good."

Delphinium raised her eyebrows. "That special, huh?"

"Definitely."

"Are you ready to profess your undying love yet?"

He narrowed his eyes. "No, and I don't appreciate the sarcasm. You should work on your customer service skills. You're forgetting that the customer is always right, and believe me when I say, you're way off about my love life."

Delphinium ignored him. "White jasmine means friendship."

His mouth made a flat line. "Sounds bland. Are you going to sprinkle in some of your pizzazz? Because I don't want her to see me as her *buddy*."

"Friendship should come before love. Getting to know someone takes one step at a time. If you want this relationship to have any value, you have to become friends first."

He sighed. "How about we skip the relationship advice and concentrate on the flowers?"

Delphinium scanned her inventory. "How about the light pink roses that Bob just brought out? Light-colored roses stand for admiration. I'll mix in some baby's breath, which means happiness. The bouquet will convey the high esteem you hold her in and make her feel special. The beauty of the bouquet alone should make her giddy as soon as you present them to her. The arrangement will be very pretty, and then you can compliment her on how her grace and beauty surpass the elegance of the bouquet."

Mason flashed his pearly white smile. "That sounds perfect. Go work your magic."

"Why don't we make it a dozen and a half to make the presentation a bit more dramatic. Sometimes more *is* better."

"Do I get a preferred customer discount for the number of flowers I buy from you?"

"No. Magic comes at a cost."

Mason's smile disappeared. "Fine."

The bouquet was simple to put together. As she rang the flowers up, she asked him, "Can I interest you in some cute dish towels in autumn themes as fall approaches?"

Mason eyed the fresh stack of white dish towels with pumpkins and sprigs of wheat printed on them lying in a basket near the register. Each was tied with orange or brown raffia ribbon. "Fall isn't for another two months. Aren't you jumping the gun a bit?"

She shrugged. "I like being prepared. Fall is something to look forward to, and it's the most beautiful time of year."

"But isn't that being too . . . optimistic, or even in denial? I thought the shop wasn't doing well."

Delphinium's eyes narrowed. "How do you know that?"

"What? Oh, um . . ." He shifted on his feet. "I think you mentioned it the first time I was in here. Plus, it's not hard to assume things aren't going that great if you're using Moonberry's most frail and vulnerable population to help drum up business."

Delphinium frowned so her bottom lip stuck out. "Again, I'm not abusing the seniors. And my business doesn't concern you. Do you want the dish towels or not?"

"Ah, no thanks." He reached out to stroke the top one. "But I'll give you credit on the presentation. I've never seen dish towels looks so nice."

"Thanks. Helen irons and folds them for me and Gurdy ties the raffia."

Mason let out an aggravated breath and rubbed his forehead as if her words were evoking a migraine. "You're killing me," he said while shaking his head.

"What?"

"Nothing." He paid for the expensive bouquet in cash. "I'll never understand your commitment to those people, or your obsession, whichever it is. I wish you and your senior sweatshop the best of luck."

"Luck for what?"

"Nothing," he grumbled. "I'll see you soon, Delphinium. Thanks for the flowers. Tell Henry I stopped by, and we'll talk in a few days."

As she watched him leave, it occurred to her that there had been a shift in her luck. The work of the seniors had actually made a difference in the number of people who came into her shop that week. Even if it was out of curiosity from having these unexpected people handing out flowers, she got individuals into the shop who hadn't been inside before. Some bought flowers, but some preferred the selection of little gift items.

She had sold three fairy houses, five candles, and the seasonal dish towels were a hit. They really did look great. Helen was meticulous about her job and came in every day to see if she could do more. She was also no longer grouchy but scooted her walker inch by inch with a sweet smile. She'd go to the back corner and turn the walker around so that it was secure against the wall, and then she sat down on the built-in seat. The others pushed the table up to her, and she would iron and fold to her heart's delight. When she ran out of dish towels, she folded the cleaning rags.

Things were slowly turning around for the shop. It buzzed with the activity of a beehive when the seniors were there. Delphinium also felt a shift inside her. There were days that she didn't even feel Annie's absence like she usually did. The seniors made her laugh and were generous with their love, like a cadre of foster grandparents. Perhaps it was a sign that things were going to be okay.

For the first time in months, she had a spark of hope that the shop might survive. Although it was only a small flicker, she held on to it, wishing with all her might that she wouldn't lose her beloved home.

Nine

I t was the second week of July, and the farmers' market on
Saturday morning was a highlight of everyone's weekend in
Moonberry Lake. Local farmers, merchants, and artists from
the area came and set up tables and tents in the parking lot of
the huge Catholic church only a couple blocks from Main Street.
Delphinium typically had a small display and sold a scattering of
bouquets and succulent arrangements but decided to take this
weekend off since her inventory was still low after the hard work
she put into the Fourth of July parade last weekend.

It was a treat to browse the stalls as a customer and buy her
produce for the week.

Her bag was heavy with a couple jars of honey, some tomatoes,
zucchini, and onions. It was inevitable she would run into friends
and customers shopping, but she was pleasantly surprised when
she spotted her new favorite couple in town—Ben Walker and
Cora Matthews.

The town was buzzing with excitement over the match since
Ben had been the most eligible bachelor for some time. Ben was
a dentist in town. Cora had moved to the area the previous year
and seemed more reclusive since she lived on the outskirts of town
while she renovated a big lodge on one of the neighboring lakes.

Although she hadn't been able to get to know Cora as much as she would like, Delphinium learned everything she needed to know from the light in Ben's eyes and the perpetual smile on his face. Anytime someone could make another so happy, it was a good thing. Also, the minute she had picked up Cora's scent of pink camellia, she knew Cora was a perfect match to Ben's scent of zinnia. Pink camellia represented longing, while zinnia indicated long-lasting affection. The goodness and enduring friendship of Ben was exactly what Cora was seeking, and she would respond with adoration, another trait of camellias.

Delphinium knew some people might dismiss the correlation between the attributes of the floral scents and a person's character as silly, but she had never found her gifted conclusions to be far from the truth. An individual's scent was like an arrow pointing to the center mark of their strongest characteristic. And when it came to love matches, when the scents complemented each other, Delphinium could see how the two people's strengths and weaknesses harmonized and brought out the best in each other.

The couple strolled up to Delphinium hand in hand, both grinning from ear to ear. Ben was in cargo shorts, a worn baseball cap, and a T-shirt with his office logo printed on the back. Cora was dressed in shorts with a pretty summer blouse tied at the waist, and she had her long brown hair pulled up into a ponytail. The gossip mill was right. They were cute together.

"Hey, Delphinium," Ben said in greeting.

"Hi, you two. It's nice to see you again, Cora. We don't seem to run into each other in town much."

Cora rolled her eyes. "That's because I'm either at the lodge or the hardware store. My life is consumed with the renovation."

"Except when I steal her away," Ben added with a wink. He wrapped an arm around Cora and pulled her close, making her cheeks color and her eyes shine.

"Well then, it looks like I'm going to have to get on a list to see you."

Cora let out a laugh. "I promise I'll make the time to see you anytime you're available."

Ben looked between the two women, faking outrage. "Why am I being omitted from this future outing? Delphinium and I were friends first. And I introduced the two of you."

Delphinium grinned at the adorable pair. "Fine, we can all go out to dinner so you don't feel left out."

That made them both laugh.

"I thought of you during the Fourth of July parade," Cora told her. "The flowers everyone used were beautiful."

"Thank you. It's always a lot of work but so much fun to see the finished product." She adjusted the bulky bag on her shoulder. "The VFW float was my favorite in terms of flowers, but my heart always melts at the sight of the little kids on bikes and tricycles with crepe paper woven through the spokes of their wheels."

Cora nodded. "Mine too."

"It looks like you've already made quite the haul here at the market," Ben said, giving a nod to her bulging bag.

Delphinium opened it. "Yep. All I need are some strawberries and I'm done."

"Ooh, we just had some strawberry shortcake that the high school choir is selling for a fundraiser," Cora said. "It was delicious."

Delphinium's mouth watered. "Where is that?"

Ben pointed to the end of the market she hadn't hit yet.

"Well then, that will be my next stop."

They said their goodbyes, promising to get together soon, and Delphinium made a beeline to the stand filled with a bunch of teenagers wearing shirts with printed musical notes all over them. She saw they were selling strawberry shortcake on paper plates with a cloud of whipped cream on top. As she ordered one, a couple of the teenagers recognized her as the lady who supplied the flowers for their float, so they added so much extra whipped cream, she couldn't even see any strawberries or shortcake underneath. She loved it.

Balancing the plate in one hand, she moved off to the side and began eating it with the plastic fork they provided. She plunged her fork into the mound and only came up with whipped cream for the first few bites. When she finally hit a berry with the spongy cake, she closed her eyes and savored the taste. When she opened her eyes, she noticed Elliot Sturgis, who had been perusing the items at the next booth. For whatever reason, a little rush of panic came over her. As he peered up from the vegetables he was buying, their eyes met for a half second before she quickly spun around.

Maybe he didn't notice me, she kept repeating to herself. *Finish this and get out of here.* She quickly took three giant bites of the remaining shortcake and tossed the plate into the nearby trash can. Just as she was about to sneak between the high schoolers' booth and a table with a guy selling cartons of eggs, an unmistakable voice caused her to freeze.

"Ms. Hayes."

Her heart sped up at the sound. The guy missed his calling as a middle-school teacher. He could scare kids into submission with his tone that brooked no argument.

She turned around slowly. "Oh," she said, trying to appear surprised. "Hello." She cleared her throat. "What are you doing here?"

His thick brows arched with the same sharpness as his other facial features. "What am I doing at a farmers' market?"

Dumb question. "Um, right." She tried to chuckle, but it came out sounding like a high-pitched snicker of a cartoon hyena.

He stared at her and then answered her question. "I came to get a small bouquet of flowers for a resident who isn't doing too well. I went by your shop first, but you were closed."

She nodded. "The shop is closed Saturday mornings because I'm typically here with a small stand, but my supply was too minimal after the parade to have one."

"So you came to buy fresh produce and enjoy some strawberry shortcake?" he said, answering her explanation and asking a question at the same time.

She nodded again. Even with his attempt at small talk, she could not relax around him. He wore khakis that looked freshly ironed and a gingham button-down shirt that was still neatly tucked in. But the sleeves had been rolled up to just below his elbows. Incredibly put together for a farmers' market where most people came in workout clothes.

Elliot reached into his pocket and pulled out a pale-blue hand-kerchief. "May I?"

She looked at him quizzically.

He stepped close and gently wiped both her cheeks with the barest touch.

And there it was again.

His scent.

Violets.

Her breath caught and she stood absolutely still, not even blinking.

For a man so solid and authoritative, she was surprised by the slightest tremble in his hand. "There. You had some whipped cream on your cheeks."

"Of course I did," she said under her breath. She could only imagine how she looked with whipped cream on both sides of her mouth. "Thank you."

"Not at all."

He took a step back and stared at her, which she guessed allowed him to take inventory of their vast differences. His tidy appearance to her summer boho look. She had on a long yellow sundress with tiny daisies printed all over it. Her curly hair was down and out of control, and she hadn't put on any makeup. Her only accessory was a thin gold necklace with a small enamel flower in the same shade as her dress that nested right below the base of her throat.

"It's nice of you to give flowers to a resident who isn't feeling well," she said, trying to calm her racing nerves.

Elliot put a hand in his pocket and looked away as if he was perusing the market, but it was obvious by the way his jaw was subtly moving that he was working something out in his head. He peered back at her, meeting her gaze straight on. "Believe it or not, I am not the monster the elders who come to your shop portray me to be."

She flinched. "Oh, um, I never thought you were. I'm well aware of their unrealistic demands. They tried talking me into providing a daily charcuterie board with a selection of fancy cheeses and salamis."

His pointed look became a question mark again. "What did you do?"

"I gave them a block of cheddar cheese, a box of crackers, and bought one of those giant cookie cakes with the word *Behave* written on it in frosting. They got the message."

Elliot chuckled. The hardness of his face softened, giving him a more relaxed and kinder look. "That was very creative. I may consult you the next time I need a solution on how to handle them."

Delphinium smiled, enjoying what felt like an inside joke between the two of them. "They are a wily bunch. If they have this much spirit in them now, can you imagine how they were at our age?"

Elliot shook his head. "No. I don't even want to try to imagine that because there is no way I could've kept up with them. They have me running circles now." It tickled her how genuinely puzzled he looked. "Are you cooking something special?" he asked, peering at her bag of groceries.

"Um, not really. I'm just picking up the basics. And I was running low on honey."

He nodded and they stood staring at each other.

The seconds of silence stretched into awkwardness again.

"Um, do you cook?" Delphinium asked to fill in the empty space. She wasn't sure how to exit the conversation gracefully. Part of her wanted to get away, but part of her—a tiny part—didn't.

"Yes, it relaxes me. I find the precision of following the formula within a recipe calming."

Delphinium stared at him and realized he wasn't joking. "I . . . I've never thought of cooking that way. I typically throw a bunch of things together and keep tweaking until it tastes good. I'm a master at creating messy cuisine that tastes decent if you don't look at it."

A grin played at the corners of Elliot's mouth.

She shifted and looked around. "I should get going. I have to get some broccoli and then need to get on with my day."

"What a coincidence. I was going to buy some broccoli as well." He motioned with an open palm in the opposite direction they were facing. "Shall we?"

The panicky feeling in her stomach returned. He made her nervous, or maybe excited? It unnerved her that she couldn't tell which.

They ended up stopping at four tables for her to buy more vegetables and then strolled up and down the last couple aisles before reaching the end. They talked about what was being sold and sometimes didn't talk at all but simply walked side by side. It felt oddly comfortable.

Delphinium purchased more than she intended. She carried her first bag of produce, which was nearly overflowing, and Elliot insisted on carrying her second bag. When she tried to take it from him to walk to her car, he again insisted on continuing to hold it and escort her.

Once she placed the bags in her trunk, she gave Elliot the broccoli he had purchased. His small bag looked a bit ridiculous compared to her haul. He could have left right after he got the one broccoli head but accompanied her, making the outing feel strangely like a couple's shopping trip—which she surprisingly enjoyed. It may have even led to her buying more groceries to elongate their time together.

"Thank you for your help. I went overboard in my shopping, but at least I won't have to go grocery shopping for a few days."

She again looked at his small bag of broccoli.

"I feel as though you are leaving rather empty-handed. You didn't even get your honey or flowers." She frowned.

"No worries. I still got what I was looking for," he said, staring at her intently.

She gulped.

"It was nice seeing you, Ms. Hayes." With that, he turned and walked away.

Delphinium got in her car feeling flushed.

What. Was. That?

Ten

Early Monday morning, Mason came bursting into the shop with such force that the door remained stuck open. Delphinium had just turned over the Open sign and the seniors hadn't yet arrived. He breezed by her, not waiting for her to come back to the counter. "I've come up with a plan," he announced, bouncing and fidgeting.

His high energy was too much for this time of day. She hadn't even had coffee yet. "Well, good morning to you too."

"I'm going to set up a meeting with a representative from The Gardens and you're coming with me," he said, pacing back and forth in front of the counter.

She made a face. "What?"

"A meeting. You, me, and the director of The Gardens. We need this issue of them using your flower shop as their rec center resolved so we can get them out of here."

Her brow furrowed. "Why do you even care where they hang out? And why the sudden urgency?"

"Just because." He flailed his hands as if he didn't have time to explain his reasoning.

"Okay. But why do *I* have to go with you to this meeting? Why can't you do it alone? You're the lawyer. You're the one who volunteered to represent them."

101

Mason pounded a fist on the counter, knuckles down, making a hard knock. "Because you have a personal relationship with every one of those seniors. You've befriended them and have an emotional stake in the outcome of this case. You know them better than anyone else, so you're also the key to getting them out of here. Trust me, it'll look better if you're there. We need to play up what an empathetic soul you are toward their petition for ice cream."

"Sorbet," she corrected.

"Whatever." He waved away her comment. "The point is"—he began pacing again—"we need someone who appears *sane* to convince The Gardens' management to implement changes that will make the residents happier and stop them from coming here anymore."

Delphinium's eyes narrowed. "Are you implying you don't think these elderly people are sane?" She gritted her teeth and glowered at him. "Because if you are, we have a problem. Those people have decades of education and life experience over you, including going to war to fight for this country. Don't you dare put them down. Ever."

Mason threw his hands in the air in surrender. "Sorry. Okay. But it does look weird that they come to play strip poker in a florist's cooler."

Delphinium sighed. It was too early for his cheeky tone. "It's not strip poker. I would never allow that. The guys just get overheated. They like to hang out in their undershirts when the summer heat is too much, and it also gives them a sense of empowerment. You know that's how they behaved when they lived in homes of their own. I think they do it simply to feel something familiar and free. The Gardens has them buttoned-up tight even to eat breakfast."

"Whatever. I wouldn't care if they paraded around in their pajamas. I just need to stop them from handing out flowers to everyone in sight. They're attracting too much attention."

Delphinium's impatience grew as Mason's responses became saltier. "I don't understand why this matters to you. As I told you before, they love the work, and it gives them some exercise. I don't exhaust them. I'm simply giving them a short activity that moves their bodies and gets them interacting with people. By their own choice. It's all good."

Mason blew out a breath while smoothing his forehead with a hand. "We'll use that, then. You can explain things from your perspective on how Henry and his friends have thrived here. Give the director ideas on how to improve and replicate what you've done. It can only help our case."

Delphinium gathered her hair into a messy bun. She didn't like him spouting orders before she had her morning coffee. "Why aren't you at work like the rest of us? Don't you have a real job?"

He shot her a patronizing look. "You asked for my help. Remember?"

"Actually, Henry did. I had no part in it."

He acted as if he didn't hear her. "I know you don't want to go to any meeting. And I don't really want to take on this preposterous plea for frozen dessert and full-size muffins. But you're not the only one with a soft spot." He looked down. "I was pretty much raised by my grandmother," he said in a quiet voice. "My parents were busy and rarely around. Most of the time it felt like she was all I had. I'm all business until it comes to elderly people. They're my Achilles' heel."

Delphinium studied him. He still wasn't making eye contact with her. He shifted his weight from one foot to another, appearing both embarrassed and vulnerable by what he had revealed.

"May I ask what your parents were doing while you were being raised by your grandmother?" she asked.

Mason shrugged. "Traveling, working, golfing, whatever they wanted to do. They weren't into the whole parental thing."

Delphinium sensed that she should not push or tease him on this subject. "My grandmother was very special to me too," she said finally. "She was my best friend and the only one who has ever understood me."

A momentary silence fell between them.

Mason squared his shoulders. "So we both have a grandma story, and we both share a weakness for old people. That's fine. Lots of kids are raised by their grandparents. It's the only reason I agreed to go along with this harebrained case." He looked her up and down. "Speaking of *hair*, isn't there some gel or spray you could put on yours to better control it? I think it would look more . . . professional."

Delphinium leveled him with her glare. "Seriously, why aren't you at work? Don't you have a boss or real work you need to do?"

He went back to walking around the shop floor, but at a much slower pace this time. "I have certain liberties at my work that allow me to come and go. I set my own hours. The benefit of becoming a partner at my father's firm right out of law school. This case with The Gardens might seem absurd. I admit, at first I was only amused by it, but now I see its importance. If we don't speak up for these people, who will? This is a matter of human rights."

"*Human rights?*" she scoffed. "Are you serious? Their most recent demand is for a selection of lime, orange, *and* raspberry sorbet because they're tired of vanilla and chocolate ice cream! The list gets only more ridiculous by the day. They are currently working on the idea of having a barbeque festival on the front lawn and making it a community potluck."

"That's actually not a bad idea," he said. "It'd be good PR for the facility's image."

She was watching him analyze her displays when the phone rang.

Clearing her throat, she put on her singsong voice before answering. "Delphinium's Flora Emporium. How can I help you?"

Mason turned and wandered over to the fairy village display.

"Hello, Ms. Hayes, this is Elliot Sturgis."

She gulped. "Oh, hello, Ell— Mr. Sturgis. What can I do for you?" She glanced at Mason, who was still perusing her store, oblivious to her conversation.

"I was hoping we could meet to discuss the matter at hand. Things are getting more out of control."

"You want to meet?" she asked, her voice rising at the end.

"Yes. I need to discuss the seniors' most recent demands, which include a trip to New York and the creation of a miniature golf course."

Delphinium grimaced. Where did they come up with these pie-in-the-sky ideas? The last thing she wanted to do was meet alone with Elliot. He raised too many conflicting feelings. But if anything was going to be resolved with the seniors, she supposed she had to. She cleared her throat. "What did you have in mind?"

"How about something more informal, like getting a cup of coffee?"

"Coffee? As in outside of The Gardens and my shop?"

There was a brief silence on the other end. "Yes."

"I'm sorry. It's hard for me to leave the shop during the day, and I don't feel comfortable leaving it in the hands of all your residents."

Mason had emerged from his reverie and cocked his head attentively.

"You close the shop at six o'clock, correct?"

"Yes."

"Then how about dinner? We could meet at my favorite Italian restaurant, Mama's. Are you familiar with it? It's on North Shore Street."

"Yes, I'm familiar." She didn't want to go to any meeting, and she certainly didn't want to go out for dinner where she would be stuck as he guilted her for indulging the whims of the seniors. It was bound to be an uncomfortable meal. Elliot was so serious and uptight, and she was, well . . . her. Surrounded by the chaos of the flower shop or the distraction of the farmers' market was one thing. Sitting alone with him at a cozy restaurant was another.

"We need to come to a resolution, Ms. Hayes."

She turned away from Mason's penetrating gaze.

"You know, we could simply discuss this over the phone." Her voice sounded small at the cop-out.

"It will be easier in person. Could we meet after you close? You have to eat either way."

"I suppose I do."

"Excellent. I'll make reservations for seven."

"All right, then. Seven o'clock. See you there. Goodbye."

After she hung up, Delphinium and Mason stared at each other for a few seconds before he broke out in a huge grin. "Was that who I think it was?"

She nodded.

"The director asked you out on a *date*?"

He didn't have to sound so amazed. "It's not a date. I can't meet to discuss the senior boycott during the day so he suggested dinner. Apparently, their list of demands is growing and becoming more preposterous."

"You don't have to tell me," Mason said. "The latest request they shared with me is for an in-house *masseuse* and communal mud bath after the facility agreed to cucumber water in the reception area. It sounds as if they're trying to turn the place into a spa."

Delphinium furrowed her brow. "A meeting has to take place no matter the time or location. You can come with me and negotiate details."

"Oh, no. He asked *you* and only you to meet him for a candlelit dinner. This is actually perfect." Mason rubbed his hands together, grinning. "It will definitely put the odds in our favor. Best to wine and dine the enemy. Make them think we're working with them. Just play along until we get what we want."

Delphinium made a face. "Don't act like a jerk. This isn't a game of chess where you strategize or, in your case, manipulate your next move to get what you want. We are talking about the lives of people and their happiness."

Mason shook his head and stared at her as if she was the most naive person in the world. "Everything is a game, Delphinium. Everything."

There was a reason Delphinium didn't play poker. As soon as the seniors arrived that day, Henry took one look at her face and knew something was up.

"All right, fess up," he said to her. "What aren't you telling me?"

Unfortunately, there were numerous seniors within earshot who picked up the question since most of them were wearing hearing aids with the batteries she bought. They all stopped and stared at her. Delphinium couldn't fib if she wanted to.

"I'm having dinner with Elliot Sturgis tonight," she confessed. "He called and asked me to meet him at Mama's Italian Restaurant to discuss the ruckus you all have created, and I said yes. I think it would be good to talk to him at a neutral place. I'm going on your behalf to resolve the hunger strike."

While the men grumbled about this news, the women surprised her by responding with shrieks and clapping. They were clearly not as invested in the war on The Gardens as the guys if the idea of a dinner date thrilled them so much. They acted like a bunch of schoolgirls talking about who liked who.

"It's not like that," Delphinium insisted, but they all ignored her.

Henry scowled. "I set you up with a perfectly nice guy—"

Delphinium rolled her eyes. "I don't know how many times I have to tell you that it isn't that way with Mason and me. You've got to give that up."

Henry continued talking as if she hadn't interrupted him. "And now you've decided to become Benedict Arnold and woo the enemy with your feminine wiles."

"I'm not *wooing* anyone. And please don't say 'feminine wiles' to me ever again. It sounds creepy coming from you." Delphinium cringed. "I'm simply talking to him while we share a meal because it's happening at the end of the workday for both of us and we'll be hungry. It's business. If it makes you feel better, he asked me to coffee first, but I said I couldn't leave the shop midday."

Henry crossed his arms over his chest and pouted. "I wouldn't put it past him to offer that just to look innocent. He set you up because he knew you'd say no. It's pretty crafty of him. Come to think of it, I haven't ever seen him drink coffee."

"Give it a rest, Henry. Pick a different battle," Delphinium said.

George raised his hand. "I've seen him with tea. I know this because I asked if I could have a cup with him but to make mine a hot toddy and the scoundrel refused."

"He was never going to add liquor to your tea, George. That's an unreasonable request," Delphinium said, turning her focus back to Henry. "I thought you said I was the Benedict Arnold pursuing him, not the other way around."

"I'm confused which side either of you are on," Bob said, moving past them to the back room. "I only know that I want donut holes with my coffee."

Exasperated, Delphinium rubbed her forehead. "All of you, go to the back and leave me be." She waved them away. The men moved on, but the ladies stayed to chat. They were still giddy.

Joanna and Arlene insisted, in no uncertain terms, that they were capable of watching the store for the last couple hours, which were typically slow anyway, so she could go upstairs and get ready. She politely refused and they spent all afternoon drilling her on what she was going to wear and what she was going to say. Out of sheer exhaustion from all the discussion, Delphinium caved in and let them babysit the place. She did want to run up to her apartment to wash her hair and attempt to tame it. She spent extra time on her makeup and choosing what to wear. When nervousness wrestled and won over every other emotion, she chalked it up to how rarely she got dressed up and went out. *It's been a long time. I'm just out of practice. It's just business.*

After an hour and a half, she entered the shop wearing a strapless white dress with a bold cherry blossom print, a solid pink cardigan in the same shade as the blossoms on the dress, and heels. All the seniors were gathered near the front counter since the small bus from The Gardens would be out front in a few minutes.

The bus had arrived one day the previous week, right as she was heading out to get the first round of seniors. It had been coming ever since, dropping them off and picking them up at the same time every day. She was thrilled with the time it saved her transporting them. When she had mentioned how nice that was of the nursing home, the men all said it was a conspiracy to keep tabs on them.

George let out a low whistle when he saw her outfit. "Va-va-voom! Talk about getting dolled up!"

"Yep, you're a looker all right," Charlie said.

Joanna clapped her hands together. "Oh, honey, you look beautiful!"

"I'd say more like a million bucks," Bob added.

"You're as lovely as a summer day," Gurdy gushed.

"So, so pretty," Arlene said. "You're going to take his breath away."

"Definitely as regal as the queen of hearts," Patsy nodded. "You could turn heads in a casino—you're pretty enough to be mistaken for the entertainment."

"Thank you for all the compliments," Delphinium said, "unusual as some of them may be." She felt the heat from her face reach her toes. "Tell me the truth. Is it too much? I was going for summer night dress flair with the common sense of a cardigan. Mason said I need to look professional."

The grumpy look on Henry's face was replaced with something soft and proud. "You look perfect," Henry assured her. "The finest Cabernet there is."

"You could pass for my granddaughter. She's a rare beauty too," Gurdy said, smiling.

Helen pushed her way through the crowd using her walker as a plow and approached Delphinium. She took her hands off her walker long enough to slide off a stretchy bracelet of beads that were the same color as Delphinium's hair. "Here, put this on for luck."

"Oh, no. I can't."

"Hush now, I insist. Don't argue with this old lady. You'll never win."

Delphinium held out her hand as Helen slipped the bracelet over her wrist.

"These are carnelian stones. They will bring you luck and give you courage. I wore them when I met my husband." The woman gave her a wink. "Knock him dead, sweetheart."

Delphinium placed her hand over Helen's before the woman pulled away. "Thank you. I'll return the bracelet to you tomorrow."

"Bus is here," Patsy's deep, smoker voice croaked.

All the seniors began to move like a stampede of buffalo spooked by a noise. Delphinium wasn't sure if Charlie was trying to get to the bus first or simply trying to free himself from the group, but he hurried ahead, shuffling rapidly.

He was going too fast.

It was because the others were blocking her that she couldn't reach out and stop him from falling. She could only watch, as if in slow motion, as he crashed to the floor.

Hard.

There was a collective gasp as his cry of pain pierced the air.

Eleven

Sitting bent over with her head in her hands, Delphinium stared at the hospital floor. A pair of perfectly polished black wingtip shoes stepped up and stopped in her line of vision. She peered up. Elliot Sturgis held out a Styrofoam cup of coffee to her.

"You look like you need this."

"Thanks." She took it and held it in her hands, comforted by the warmth.

Elliot took a seat in the chair next to her. He was dressed in a dark, tailored suit and a crisp white shirt, looking neat as a pin.

"I'm so sorry," she whispered.

He frowned. "For what? Charlie falling?"

She nodded.

He exhaled loudly. "It wasn't your fault. It was an accident. One that was bound to happen at some point, I'm afraid. Charlie has had a bad hip for years and has become increasingly unsteady. Which is why we've encouraged and asked him to use a walker, though he's stubbornly refused. Unfortunately, I see this quite often. It could have been prevented only if someone had been at his side, or better yet, someone on *each* side, insisting on holding onto him as he walked, which he wouldn't have allowed. The saying 'pride goes before the fall' rings true just about every time in old age."

Delphinium continued to hold the coffee cup without taking a sip. She kept her gaze straight ahead as she thought of Charlie at the flower shop. He was always trying to flirt with the ladies like George and seemed so happy to be included in the group. She had watched him go from quiet as a mouse to full of vitality. She hadn't taken enough notice of his limp when he walked. Guilt weighed on her chest and tears stung her eyes as she replayed the image of him lying on the floor—the groaning and grimace of agony on his face as the paramedics carried him away.

"May I offer you this?" Elliot asked.

Delphinium looked down at his hand that held a small packet of disposable tissues. She hadn't realized that she'd been crying but now felt the wetness on her cheeks and her stuffy nose. She placed the cup of coffee on the empty seat to her other side and took the tissues. As she took a couple and wiped her nose, she grew aware of his pervading scent.

"Thank you." She sniffled.

"I always keep a packet on me. They're useful to have in a nursing home setting."

She took another tissue and dabbed under her eyes to wipe away her smeared makeup. Even though they were disposable, the tissues had been in the breast pocket of his suit and smelled like him.

She inhaled deeply, the calming scent comforting her. "These smell like violets."

He gave a questioning look.

"I mean, they smell like *you*. You give off the scent of violets."

His brow creased. "I-I don't wear cologne."

"It's your natural scent." She smiled shyly, then hurried to explain. "Don't worry. Nobody else would smell it but me. I pick up on people's natural scent, and yours is violets."

He stared at her.

"The aroma is truly lovely. Only the faintest baby powder base note is emitted from violets. However, I personally believe the potency of a scent is accentuated by the strength of the attribute that goes along with it. The fact that you smell so intensely of violets tells me how loyal and devoted you are to your life's passions. With the powerfulness of your fragrance, I'd say that faithfulness is one of your fiercest and most admirable characteristics. Am I correct?" She knew she was babbling and couldn't stop herself.

He gave a hesitant nod, watching her. "I like to believe I am a man of faith."

"There is faith and then faithfulness. Which is it?"

He stared at her again, unblinking as if not wanting to miss what she would say next. "I like to believe I possess both. The faith I hold, or rather, which holds me, causes me to react with faithfulness."

The corner of Delphinium's mouth turned up at his response and the character it bared. "Well, it must be very strong in your life. It's just a theory, but I'm usually correct. I've always been able to pick up scents that others typically cannot detect."

Elliot studied her the same way she memorized the most intricate details of the patterns, textures, and color ranges within flower petals. Whenever she revealed a person's aroma, they usually looked at her like she had antennas coming out of her head. Her parents always gave a sympathetic look, somewhere between sad and disturbed, which she interpreted as them being disappointed that she was as eccentric as Annie. She'd since stopped telling people their fragrance, but it just slipped out with Elliot.

Growing uncomfortable, she set her gaze back on the floor.

"That's . . . an unusual perception," he said.

She dismissed his comment with a low chuckle. "My parents always thought it was peculiar. I've had the ability since I was a kid. As I grew, I was able to train my olfactory sense to an even greater heightened acuity. It gives me a sneak peek into who people are, like an intuition or the deepest gut feeling. But I suppose you're right. It's more of a perception."

"I think it's extraordinary."

The sincerity in his voice made her lift her eyes to his. The look on his face as he held her gaze told her that he was telling the truth. She'd never met anyone who was so unapologetic about staring. It didn't hurt that he had beautiful eyes.

"You should work for a perfume company. Imagine the wonderful scent combinations you would be able to create."

She shook her head. "It would never work. I pick up scents that are too faint for the average person." She paused. "My grandmother had a special ability too. She saw colors for every letter in the alphabet and could taste flavors for different shades of color." She blurted out the admission like it was a dark secret set free.

"Synesthesia."

"Yes! You've heard of it?"

Elliot nodded.

"My grandmother was my best friend. She's the one who encouraged me to go into the flower business." She hesitated. "Annie died last year." Delphinium didn't know why she told him that last part, but it felt good saying it out loud. She sensed that the reality of the statement wouldn't come back to hit her hard but would find a gentle resting place with him.

She was right.

He gave her no typical platitudes. "You must miss her greatly."

Delphinium nodded, feeling a couple tears escape and run down her cheeks. She wiped them away with the crumpled tissue in her hand. "She was an amazing woman."

"You must take after her."

Delphinium looked at him curiously.

"You're a very interesting woman, Ms. Hayes. I'm sorry our date was interrupted." His voice was softer and not so businesslike.

Her head jolted back a bit. "Date?"

"I mean, dinner meeting. I'm sorry," he quickly corrected.

Delphinium didn't miss the blush that tinted his cheeks and how he looked down to straighten his glasses to hide it.

Elliot took a sip of his coffee. "What you said back at your shop gave me a glimpse into who you are and why all my residents are flocking to you. You gave me a lot to think about and made quite the impression."

Silence.

A nervous excitement fluttered in her stomach.

Elliot straightened his posture and touched the knot of his tie as if making sure it was still tight at his throat. He licked his lips. "I was going to propose at dinner, er, I mean . . ." He shook his head at the slip of words. "I was hoping to run an idea past you that I came up with on how to make The Gardens feel more like home for those who live there."

She nodded, encouraging him on.

"I'd like to build a garden for the residents to work in and then sit and enjoy. They can have different jobs like planting, weeding, and watering. Or they can simply sit and enjoy the natural beauty if that's all they are physically capable of doing. If vegetables are planted, we will incorporate them into their meals. For the flowers that bloom, the residents can use them to make small bouquets for their rooms."

"That's a brilliant idea. I love it."

He exhaled in relief. "I'm glad you like it because I was hoping that you would help establish it."

Her eyes widened. "Um, I'm sorry, but I don't have the time to devote to such a large project. I would love to, but things in my life are complicated right now. I have to put all my effort and energy into my shop."

Elliot repositioned himself on the chair, although he was already sitting as straight as one could. He was clearly not ready to give up. "Which is why you would have many, many helpers. I'm not asking you to take ownership of it but rather oversee it and give your professional input. Perhaps give suggestions on what to plant and how to care for things? You've shown me what the seniors are capable of physically and how much they like to work. And as compensation for your time, you could take a large portion of the flowers and use them for your business."

"I buy flowers wholesale to make my arrangements. I don't actually grow them myself."

"Yes, but something tells me you would be excellent at this. You've organized the seniors into a small army. They do whatever you ask of them—and happily, I might add. The garden would be about taking ownership of something and beautifying the space inside and out."

She would never consider such an undertaking if he hadn't hit her soft spot. It would give the seniors work, a purpose, a community project, all of which would make them feel part of a home. Not a nursing home but a real one. Henry could be the lead consultant, which he'd love.

She took a big breath. This would solve so many issues. If it meant working on it after she finished at the shop, she'd find the energy. "How big of a garden are we talking about?"

"Big."

She had to admit that it would be nice to get some free flowers as well. "It would be only a short seasonal thing because of the weather here."

"At first," he added. "If it's as successful as I believe it will be under your supervision, I will propose to the board that we build a year-round greenhouse, where the residents could plant seedlings in small containers at raised tables so they wouldn't have to bend over. We would also have a table for those in wheelchairs. Then in the spring we could sell the sprouted plants to the community to cover some of the cost. During the winter months, we could have succulents and plants inside the residence that the seniors could care for. And even start a project of giving holiday bulbs of amaryllis away to family members when they come visit. I've read all about them."

Now it was Delphinium's turn to stare. She couldn't find the words. Buried deep in the reservoir of this man was a bubbling brook of ideas and empathy. "You've really thought this through."

He looked pleased by her shock. "Your shop gave me some inspiration." The tenderness in his eyes and his shy smile were melting every defense she had. "What do you say?"

"You know the seniors don't actually come to my shop to work with flowers, right?"

Before he could respond, they were interrupted by a doctor. Elliot stood and introduced himself as the director of The Gardens. He shared that the family had been notified and would be arriving shortly and that he was very familiar with Charlie's medical history. The doctor explained that the break in Charlie's hip was going to require surgery. After being assured that Charlie was being heavily medicated to alleviate any discomfort, and that the surgery wouldn't take place until the morning when the surgeon arrived, they both thanked the doctor for letting them know. Delphinium gathered her purse.

"Did you drive here?" Elliot asked.

She shook her head. "I rode in the ambulance. I promised the others that I'd look after Charlie if they went back to The Gardens. I'll call for a ride and then give Henry the news."

"Let me give you a ride home."

"You don't have to do that."

"I insist." Elliot placed his hand on the small of her back as he accompanied her out of the waiting room. She felt comforted by his touch. He was like a strong retaining wall holding back the storm of emotions trying to push her down. She loved the feel of his hand supporting her. Even after he removed it, the warmth lingered.

They walked to his car without talking. He opened the door for her, and she didn't realize how tired she was until she sank into the plush leather seat. They drove in a comfortable silence. When she told him that he could drop her off at the shop because she lived right above it, she didn't miss how his eyebrows raised.

He didn't talk the rest of the ride. Tired from the long day, she didn't mind not having to create conversation. As a matter of fact, she very much liked that he wasn't a chitchatty sort of guy. Elliot seemed the type who only spoke when he had something to say. She kept telling herself that they didn't have anything but the seniors in common, but it felt like a lie as soon as she thought it. The fact that she was so at ease with him when she was typically so tongue-tied and awkward with men proved it. Elliot Sturgis was like the thick winter sweater in the back of the closet or the knitted blanket in the hope chest for cold nights—having it around made you feel better.

Delphinium found forced conversation and pleasantries more awkward than silence, and by how relaxed Elliot looked, she gathered he probably agreed. He pulled up beside the front of the shop and quickly got out to go open her door again.

"Thank you for the ride," she said, getting out of the car and giving him a small smile. She noticed him standing next to the car watching her walk to the door of the shop, which was less than fifteen feet away. As she reached for the handle, he spoke up.

"Ms. Hayes."

She turned.

"Again, I'm sorry our dinner was interrupted." He hesitated while straightening his shoulders. "You look beautiful tonight."

Her breath caught at the unexpected statement. "Um, thank you." She took in his polished appearance. "You look very . . . handsome as well." He really did. "I think I would've enjoyed having dinner with you."

She wasn't sure if she imagined it, but his chest rose slightly at the comment.

"I'm sure you'll hear about Charlie's recovery from the others, but I'll contact you in a couple days to schedule a time when we can discuss the details of crafting a gardening program."

She chuckled. "That's rather brazen of you considering that I haven't fully agreed to do it."

His disarming smile made her feel weak in the knees. "When have you ever said no to anything that had to do with the seniors?"

She couldn't hold back a smile. "So, you're going for my true weakness in convincing me?"

He tried to keep from smiling but failed. "Good night, Ms. Hayes."

She knew he was being too formal but had to admit that she liked the sound of her name when he said it. Or maybe it was how he looked when he said it. "Good night, Mr. Sturgis."

After making sure everything was in order at the shop, she went up to her apartment. A note was taped to the door, and she recognized Henry's handwriting telling her to call him.

After getting into her apartment, she fell into an overstuffed chair and took off her heels while she called him. It was late, but he picked up on the first ring.

"Hey, Henry. I just got back from the hospital. Charlie has a broken hip and is going to have replacement surgery tomorrow."

"I know. Arlene posed as his wife on the phone."

"His family is arriving—"

"Delphi," he interrupted her. "The shop received an envelope today as I was closing up. It was hand-delivered by a carrier and required a signature. I opened it for you."

"Of course."

"It was from the bank."

Silence.

"Why didn't you tell me about defaulting on the loan?"

Her chest tightened. "I'm sorry. I thought I could handle it. I thought the shop would do better."

"I would have talked you out of signing this horrible agreement. You took on an insurmountable mountain of debt."

"I didn't know you well when I signed it. I was setting up the business. I had to risk taking a bigger loan to buy out the previous owners."

She heard him sigh heavily.

"How bad is it?" she whispered, knowing the answer.

"You need to pay the full amount of the missed payments plus the current payment due by August 15 or the bank will foreclose and you'll be locked out."

"I know."

"Sweetheart, there is no way to pay off the mortgage in time.

When the bank is through, there won't be enough money to open another shop at a different location. You're going to lose everything."

Silence.

Henry saying her worst fear aloud made it all too real. This was happening. It couldn't be avoided or wished away.

"Is there any other way to pull me out of this mess?"

Henry sighed. "You're in too deep. The shop is a tremendous loss, but you have to be realistic and also start looking for another place to live. I'm pretty sure you don't meet the age requirement for The Gardens or I'd take you. We'll talk more tomorrow. You know I won't abandon you and I'll try to stop you from losing it all. I'll work until they put the chains on the door. But you need to plan for the worst-case scenario so you're prepared. The best way to face something scary is with your eyes wide open, kiddo."

Delphinium felt sick to her stomach. "Thanks, Henry." And with the truthful and hard words spoken aloud, the tears began to flow.

"You're also going to have to start thinking about canceling flower orders and liquidating."

"Uh-huh" was the only thing she could get out without fully releasing a sob over the phone.

"I'll try to come up with a solution, but it's hard to deny the facts in black and white. I love you, kid."

Her teary voice came out in a squeak. "Love you too, Henry."

After he hung up, the stifled sob from her chest released.

What an absolutely rotten ending to a rotten day.

All except . . .

Perhaps not . . .

Maybe not . . .

Elliot.

That part wasn't rotten.

That part was kind of lovely.

Twelve

Delphinium lost the battle in trying to appear professional the next day. She was a blubbering mess when Lindsey cheerfully walked in carrying a bag.

Her happy face fell. "What's wrong?"

Delphinium wiped her red, puffy eyes with a tissue. "I thought I could manage my mortgage but fell behind the last few months. I owe so much in back payments now that I'm going to default on the loan and lose everything."

Lindsey's mouth dropped open. "Both the shop and the apartment?"

Delphinium sniffled. "The whole building."

"Have you told Henry? Maybe he can find a way out."

Delphinium wiped her nose with a tissue. "He told me to prepare myself for the worst."

Lindsey set down her bag and wrapped Delphinium in a hug. "I'm so sorry. You know that you can always come live with me."

Delphinium gave a wobbly smile. "Thanks. I'll probably need to take you up on that offer until I figure out what I'm going to do for a job."

"You're a florist."

"I need to find a career that pays more money."

"How about a botanist?"

"That's more plants and biology stuff, and you need a degree. Plus, when was the last time you heard of someone in dire need of a botanist?"

Lindsey slumped against the counter. "I wish there was something I could do, but you know I'm still paying off student loans. Even though more clients have signed up for my boot camps, I'm not exactly flush with income."

Delphinium shook her head. "I would never take money from you. It's my fault for having a lousy business sense. I was overly enthusiastic and unrealistically optimistic about the future when I bought the shop." She wiped her eyes.

Lindsey sulked. "There's so much history here, so much—"

"—of Annie," Delphinium finished.

Lindsey nodded. "The spirit of your grandmother is imprinted in that apartment."

"It's my home," Delphinium said, wiping away more tears. "I can't imagine having a shop anywhere else."

Lindsey frowned. "The thought of this place closing makes me sick to my stomach."

Neither said anything as sadness passed between them.

"On the upside," Delphinium said, "you don't look sick to your stomach. You look . . . all rosy and glowie, as a matter of fact."

Lindsey laughed. "*Glowie?*"

"Yeah." She stared at her more closely. "You look so pretty and happy. Did you do your makeup differently? Are you drinking more ginger-turmeric shots?"

Lindsey waved her off. "We can talk another time."

Delphinium reached out and grasped her friend's hand. "No, I want to know. I need a good distraction. What's going on?"

Lindsey smiled coyly. "I met a guy."

Delphinium gaped at her. "What? And you didn't tell me?"

"He's been coming to my morning boot camp. We've only gone out on a couple dates. He's super sweet and romantic. And *very* charming. You would approve. He brings me flowers."

Delphinium's mouth dropped open. "There are flowers involved and you didn't tell me! This is serious."

Lindsey bit her bottom lip to rein in her grin, but the sheer glee on her face could not be concealed. "It's still in the early stage, but I really like this guy."

"Who is he?"

"No way." Her friend shook her head. "My lips are sealed." She brought her fingers across her lips as if zipping them shut. "I don't want to jinx it."

Delphinium arched an eyebrow. "Afraid my bad luck with men and pretty much life will rub off on you?"

"No. I just want to go out a couple more times before I give you all the info. It's so good that I want to make sure this isn't some fairy tale that I'm dreaming up."

Delphinium crossed her arms over her chest. "You're seriously not going to tell me anything about him? I'm your best friend."

"Meeting him came completely out of the blue, and let me just say, it's not what I expected. *He's* not what I expected. He's not the typical kind of guy I would ever choose to go out with, but now that I've gone on a couple dates with him, I think he may be my perfect type."

"And what's your perfect type?"

"Well, he is athletic and smart, but we challenge each other in different ways. He loves to talk business and has given me ideas on how to expand and improve my business as a trainer. And I'm getting him to eat healthier and moving him away from his previous diet, which pretty much resembled that of a caveman. And he can talk for hours about his love for architecture but then happily watches all my favorite old, black-and-white movies with me."

Delphinium shook her head. "I can't believe it. You've fallen for him, and you don't fall for anyone."

"I wouldn't say *fallen*, maybe tripped or stumbled a bit. Does that count?" She giggled.

"As long as you don't end up landing on your face."

Lindsey smiled. "I'm pretty sure he'd catch me. He's that kind of guy. Very chivalrous."

"Then I already like him."

"I'll let you know how our next date goes." She lifted the bag she had brought in and placed it on the counter. "These are for the old folks. I made a triple batch of my energy balls. I've got cinnamon apple, oatmeal raisin, and carrot cake. There's lots of protein powder in them for energy, and they're high in fiber."

"I'm not sure they're going to be coming in today."

"Then I'll put them in the cooler. They'll keep for at least a week."

"You're so nice. They don't expect you to do this every time, you know."

Lindsey smiled. "I like to do it. George's charm is working on me. He calls me his third girlfriend." She laughed. "Though Charlie says that he's the real ladies' man."

At the mention of Charlie, Delphinium's face fell.

"What's wrong?" Lindsey asked.

Delphinium told her the entire story of her plan to go out with Elliot only to have Charlie fall and go to the hospital.

Lindsey put her hand to her heart. "That's awful."

"I know. I'm going to visit Charlie once he's been moved to the rehab center. It's better equipped than The Gardens with staff that know how to get him moving."

"Will you bring him some of my energy balls?"

Delphinium gave a sad smile. "Sure."

Lindsey was quiet for a moment. "You know, I'm getting attached to them all."

"You and me both."

Delphinium didn't have to freeze Lindsey's energy balls because less than an hour after her friend left, The Gardens bus pulled up to the shop. She couldn't believe they still came. As the usual gang exited the vehicle, Delphinium noticed that Henry was missing. *He must still be trying to come up with an alternative plan.*

Joanna was the first one through the door. She was wearing a hot pink jumpsuit, dangly earrings complete with a hot pink feather in them, and a white cap with rhinestones that spelled out *Glammy*.

"Hi, honey." Joanna waved.

Delphinium grinned. "Hi, Joanna. You look cute. What's a *glammy*?"

Joanna snapped the gum she was chewing. "I'm too sassy to be called grandma and too fun to be called grandmother. Glammy is the combination of *glamorous* and *granny*."

"Well, that term of endearment fits your personality perfectly. You are the epitome of a *glammy*," Delphinium said as she took in the woman's bright blue eye shadow, streak of rouge across her cheeks, and fuchsia lipstick.

As Bob came up behind Joanna, he made a face at Delphinium. "You look like you've been through basic training and didn't fare too well."

Gurdy gave him a slap on the arm. "She's going through a hard time. Leave her alone." She turned to Delphinium. "I hope you don't think what happened yesterday was your fault. This happens to people our age all the time. We all take a tumble at some point."

"Yeah, most of us go down like Lindbergh's *Spirit of St. Louis*," Bob said. "Usually it's a complete crash." He made the sound of a bomb exploding with his fingers splayed out.

George wormed his way to the front. "We just replace the broken parts with new ones. I've got so many robot pieces in me that my grandkids call me *bionic*." He winked. "And the higher tech the replacement is, the cooler the kids think it is. I know a fella that has a pacemaker that's adjusted simply by putting his phone to his chest. The doctor does it *remotely* with a computer far away." George shook his head. "It's remarkable. Pretty soon, we're all going to be like Ironman. That's what my grandson tells me. Wanna give my knees a knock? They're both new."

"No thanks," Delphinium replied.

Patsy nodded. "Age requires a giddyap-and-go attitude, or you're a goner. If it's broken, you fix it and then get on with your life."

"I'm content with my walker," Helen said. "Especially now that I got it in this racy red color. Same as the flashy sports cars."

They all became quiet, staring at her with their magnified, watery eyes.

"What?" Delphinium asked, looking from face to face.

Gurdy reached up and put her little arms around Delphinium's waist. It felt like hugging a child. "Henry told us about your shop, sweetie."

"Oh." Delphinium patted the small-framed woman on the back.

"Honey, we're so sorry. This cute place deserves to be here, and you've been so kind to us," Arlene said.

"Well, I still plan on fighting," George said.

"That's right. Do not retreat from the battle," Bob added, making a fist in the air. "You fight to the death! Charge ahead and sacrifice your body for the greater good."

Delphinium rolled her eyes. "No, Bob. We are not doing anything *to the death*. You need to settle down on your war analogies. They're too extreme."

"I'm a passionate man! The fire in me hasn't tamed with age. I've still got it. I burn inside." He gave a pound on his chest like he was Tarzan. "I'm ready for the hardship of battle. Glory is my destiny!"

"Okay, Mr. Passion, let's take a breath and lower that burn to a simmer. How much coffee did you drink this morning? Go have your snack to soak up some of that caffeine."

The others didn't seem fazed by his rant. Delphinium figured they must be accustomed to it.

"Honey, what Bob is trying to say for all of us is that we're not ready to give up," Joanna piped in. "We'll all work harder to get the word out. I wore my fancy watch that keeps track of my steps. I'm ready to hand out flowers! My goal is two thousand steps today."

"I'm ready to work the street!" cheered Patsy.

"First of all, please don't any of you ever say that you are *working the street* for me," Delphinium said. "Second, you're all incredibly kind to want to help, but you don't have to work to advertise the store. The situation is pretty hopeless."

"Nonsense. You can't give up!" Gurdy gave Delphinium another squeeze. The woman was so small and light, it was like having a baby inner tube wrapped around her waist.

"You can let go of me, Gurdy, I'm okay." Delphinium smiled.

"I'm going to get started on my rag pile," Helen said. "There must be a lot to fold today." Then she shuffled her way to the back with her walker that had started to leave a little mark on the door, which Delphinium found endearing instead of annoying.

"Let's pound the pavement!" Arlene cheered. "We can get our steps in while handing out flowers."

Delphinium knew she could only appease them by letting them feel as though they were doing their part to help. So she loaded them up with all the carnations they could carry. The small army marched off with small steps, some holding on to each other for balance, proud to be on a mission.

A mission that lasted twenty minutes.

They returned, tuckered out and out of breath. Everyone sat around the worktable as Delphinium handed out glasses of water and energy balls.

"We're going to go visit Charlie. Do you think you could put together a bouquet?" Arlene asked.

"Of course." Delphinium grabbed two vases and went to work. "Henry told me the hip surgery went well. It'll be a long recovery, but I think he's going to love his new hip."

They all nodded.

"I've been thinking about getting one in titanium," Patsy said.

"Do you know how long he'll be at the rehabilitation center?" Delphinium asked as she started assembling a brightly colored mix of blooms.

"No, but I plan on visiting him all the time," George said.

"That's only because you like to fawn over the attractive nurses, you ole goat," Arlene said with a pout.

George cozied up beside her, patting her on the arm. "Aw, no beauty could take your place, darlin.'"

Arlene shook her head and let out a little giggle, failing to hide how pleased she was at his response.

"What about me?" Patsy asked.

"When I was talking to Arlene, I was thinking in the *plural*," George added quickly. "You two come as a set."

Patsy shook her head and chuckled. "You're a dog, you know that. If you weren't so old, we'd have you neutered."

Everyone laughed but George.

"I spoke with Charlie on the phone this morning," Bob said. "He was in great spirits. He's thrilled to be wearing those hospital gowns. This surgery has given him a valid excuse for his lack-of-clothing choice now."

Delphinium shook her head. She finished the bouquets and placed them in the vases. "These flowers will spiff up his hospital room and add some cheer."

"Speaking of something cheery, I'm sorry your date was inter-rupted," Gurdy said with genuine disappointment.

"An absolute shame," Helen said, pounding her little fist on the table as if she were a judge making a decree.

"Young love thwarted," Patsy said with a shake of her head. "It's like the big interference in a romance novel. Now we have to wait for you two to have your meet-up again for the story to end happily ever after."

"It wasn't a date. It was supposed to be a dinner meeting," Del-phinium clarified, but the words didn't seem truthful, even to her. Not after the way he had looked at her when he'd dropped her off. The moment when they stood staring at each other, something shifted. She could have sworn the air between them even crackled with electricity.

"That's right. It was a war meeting," Bob said, giving the tabletop a slap. "Just like the kind Roosevelt, Stalin, and Churchill had."

Delphinium gave a heavy sigh. "We're not at war, Bob. You guys and Mr. Sturgis aren't your own separate countries. We are all trying to work *together*. Remember, our goal is peace and harmony at The Gardens." She put both hands on her hips. "For goodness' sake, this started out because of poker and tapioca! Let's get some perspective."

"Well, I'm making sacrifices for the fight regardless of what you say," Bob argued. "I've begun rationing my food. As much as it pained me, I refused the Salisbury steak last night and had to sneak a candy bar up to my room. I love Salisbury steak! All this snack food we are sneaking in isn't filling me up. I want a real meal."

Delphinium shook her head. "I told you all before that the hunger strike was not the way to negotiate. You cannot go hungry and lose any strength. You all are going about this the wrong way. Let me try and help now that you've roped me into this mess. Until things are resolved in some manner, please accept the meals given to you."

"Oh, it's okay, darlin'," Joanna assured her. "My grandson just got his driver's license, and he brings me Happy Meals from Mc-Donald's." She opened her purse to reveal its secret contents. Delphinium saw a red cardboard container of french fries. "I keep fries in here as a little snack whenever I'm hungry. I don't mind them cold, and they last forever."

"I'm trying to think of our protest as a spiritual fast, so I don't mind the hunger so much," Arlene said. "Although it is messing up my medication schedule."

Delphinium threw her hands up in the air. "Do you hear yourselves? You are *paying* The Gardens for food yet choosing to starve. You have to go back to eating and let me work with Mr. Sturgis. I'm trying to help you while you are all intentionally hurting yourselves by putting your health at risk. Your families and doctors would object to this dangerous behavior. If you want to keep living, you eat. Period."

They all grumbled, committing to nothing.

"I'm serious. No more refusing food."

"The bus should be out front by now," Helen announced. "The driver told me that his schedule only allowed for a short visit today."

Delphinium filled plastic baggies with energy balls for them to take home. "And from now on, I want you all to bring tote bags so I can stuff more food into them." She grabbed a small plastic grocery bag and threw in the sandwich she was going to eat for lunch, a couple bags of chips she had on hand, and gave it to Arlene. "Eat," she commanded. "Do not screw up the timing or digestion of your medication."

The woman nodded obediently and gave her a little hug.

As they made their way to the front of the store, each person gave her either an embrace or a gentle pat on the cheek.

Joanna stopped in front of her and unzipped her fanny pack. She pulled out a tube of lipstick. "Let me add some color to your lips. You need some brightening."

"Oh, no, that's okay. I typically don't wear bright pink—"

"Nonsense," she interrupted. "This color looks fabulous on every woman."

"Even redheads?" Delphinium asked.

"Shh," Joanna commanded as she began sliding the lipstick across Delphinium's lips with her shaky hands. Delphinium could feel it going above her lip line.

After going over her mouth with three strokes, which Delphinium counted silently, Joanna smeared a little dot on each cheek. "Now, this will give you a little blush. You're terribly pale." She rubbed the pads of her soft fingertips across Delphinium's cheeks and then smiled. "There. You look healthier and bushy-tailed now."

"The expression is bright-eyed and bushy-tailed," Helen corrected.

"Well, I can't work miracles without my blue eye shadow. I left that in my room," Joanna replied. "I didn't know I was going to be doing a makeover today."

"She doesn't need all that fuss," George said. "The girl looks fine."

Bob scrunched up his face, taking a closer look when he came next in line. "That pink really makes all your freckles pop. I can see every one of them now."

"Great. Thanks, Bob."

"Have you always been so spotty?" He leaned in so that his bifocals were an inch from her face. "You're like a dalmatian up close."

"Goodbye, Bob. The bus is waiting."

Arlene, the last in line, gave him a push to move over. "Don't be glum, sweetie pie. We'll figure something out."

"It's victory or death!" Bob raised his fist in the air.

"No, Bob. It's *not* victory or death," she called after him. "You've got to stop with the war talk. No one is going to *die* over this."

Bob turned and walked back to her. Under his breath, he said, "Just so you know, the issue of tapioca was never on the table. I love the stuff. I could eat it every day—that and rice pudding. Both are delicious." And then he hurried off.

She watched as they all boarded the bus. The seniors waved through the window as it drove away. As she waved back, tears began to trickle down her face. The thought of not seeing them come to the shop was as unbearable as losing the shop itself.

When the phone rang, it took three rings before she was collected enough to answer it. "Delphinium's Flora Emporium."

A buttery-smooth masculine voice replied, "Hello, Ms. Hayes. It's Elliot Sturgis."

He was the last person she wanted to speak to, yet the sound of his velvety baritone voice also gave her a small thrill, and she immediately felt butterflies in her stomach.

"Oh, um, hello." She swallowed, then cleared her throat.

"I'm following up from our short conversation yesterday. I assume you've been updated on Charlie's condition."

He was back to speaking all businesslike. Perhaps she had imagined the feeling that passed between them when he told her she looked beautiful last night. Maybe what had zinged through her body had been one-sided.

"Yes."

"Very good. I was calling to reschedule our meeting."

"Oh." She couldn't hide her disappointment. He was definitely back to sounding like the director of The Gardens. This guy on the other end of the phone was definitely not the gentle Elliot she found endearing last night. This version made her nervous, and not in a good way. She wasn't sure what to say or what to do. She felt unsettled and everything was turned upside down since yesterday. The panic and doom of her situation flooded back, filling her chest with anxiety. This was all business, his temperament too cut-and-dry compared to hers, which rode on great waves of emotion that she could never seem to get a handle on. Talk about complete opposites.

She was also in no mood to think about adding the project he mentioned last night to her to-do list, not when her life was imploding right before her. She was sure that was the only reason he wanted to meet. However, she couldn't shake the guilt over leaving the seniors with nowhere to go. Maybe she shouldn't be so selfish about the shop and should concentrate more on them and this garden project. *Ugh.* The pull to save the shop and establish a project to help the seniors was gutting. She couldn't realistically do both well.

She knew Elliot was trying to interpret her long silence. He finally cleared his throat and said, "Is this not a good time to talk?"

"It's fine," she lied, still feeling sad and a bit sick about the seniors.

"How about tomorrow morning before you open your shop?"

She sighed. "I'll meet with you, but I need you to do something for me tonight. Actually, right now."

"And what is that?"

"The only way you're going to win this war is to make friends with the other side, and you have to view Bob as General Patton. I need someone from your staff to put a tray of last night's Salisbury steak and some tapioca in his room."

"Consider it done."

Thirteen

Delphinium was sitting on a stool at the front counter a half hour before closing, moping about what to do, when Mason walked in, whistling and looking as if he'd just stepped out of a salon. It was like a bubble protected him from humidity and sweat.

"Hello, *Delphinium.*"

It irked her the way he said her name and still found humor in it. Not having the strength to put on a happy act, she grunted in greeting. With elbows on the table and her head supported in her hands, she didn't move. "You know, you don't have to say my name like that."

"Like what?" he asked with complete innocence.

"You say it with emphasis."

"I don't say it with an emphasis. I say it with dramatic effect. There's a difference. I've perfected my intonation on key words in closing big deals," he said with haughtiness in his tone.

"Go away. I've decided I don't like you."

He flashed his pearly whites, unbothered. "Sure you do. I'm a consistent customer who values your flower expertise. As a matter of fact, I'm pretty sure the free range of creative expression I give you in addition to not questioning the price of your arrangements makes me your *favorite* customer."

133

His confidence was unbelievable. Plus, it annoyed her that she couldn't deny he was right. He never once looked at the price of the bouquets as she swiped his credit card.

She did her best to look bored by him. "What do you want?"

"You know why I'm here. How did the dinner date go last night? Did you properly seduce the director into complying with all the seniors' demands? Was he overcome by your charm so much that he agreed to an ice cream sundae bar with all the fixings?"

Delphinium closed her eyes, biting down on her bottom lip to hold back the emotions that were dangerously close to spilling out and making her ugly cry.

"Please tell me you at least got him to agree to the hot wings and the monthly chocolate fountain."

She inhaled through her nose, summoning the strength to remain even-keeled. "The negotiations didn't happen. Charlie fell as they were all leaving and broke his hip." She tried to say it as matter-of-fact as possible, but a treacherous tear snaked its way down her cheek, which she quickly swiped away.

Mason flinched, his head literally jerking back. "That's terrible. I'm so sorry. Is he okay?"

"He underwent a hip replacement surgery this morning. It'll be a long road to recovery, but he should be okay." She sniffled.

"How did he fall? Was the floor slippery?"

She scowled. "No, the floor wasn't slippery. He was in a hurry and stumbled. He should have been using a walker for stability."

"You know, he could sue you. Do you have insurance for this kind of liability? That type of lawsuit could bleed you dry."

"He's not going to sue me! Stop being such a lawyer. It wasn't the shop's fault or anyone else's. Everyone saw that it was an accident. Charlie was already considered a high risk for falling. Elliot Sturgis said so."

A sly smile that resembled more of a smirk formed on his face. "Ah, so you did end up talking to the director."

"Yes. At the hospital, in the waiting room. But we didn't talk about the hunger strike, establishing a fake casino night, hiring a mariachi band, certification classes for chair yoga, or any of the seniors' other endless demands. It was all about Charlie." *Mostly.* She wasn't going to tell Mason about how interested Elliot had been in her special perception. Or how nice he was to drive her home and that he noticed how dressed up she had gotten for the dinner that didn't happen.

With his designer sunglasses perched atop his head, Mason studied her with his eyes. His gaze stopped at her hair. "Is that why you look like you've had a late night? You're a little . . . disheveled."

She shot him her best death glare, which he didn't seem to notice. The man had the broad shoulders and resolve of Superman.

"Your hair is different. Trying a new style?"

She cocked out a hip and put a hand on it. "Yeah, it's called *wild and free.* You achieve it by putting zero time into getting ready. What do you think?"

Mason shrugged. "It's more like Animal from The Muppets, but you can pull it off. It goes with your whole vibe."

"I have a vibe?"

"Definitely. It's kind of a flower child meets a kindergarten teacher at the end of the day vibe. Though I have to say, I'm not sure that's the right shade of lipstick for you. The bright pink really brings out your freckles."

Delphinium shuddered. She'd forgotten about Joanna's makeover. She must look like a clown to him. But what did it matter? Their weird connection had always been about giving the other a hard time. Their spark wasn't fireworks as much as the quick shock coming off opposite charges on a car battery.

"Is there a reason for your visit, other than to annoy me?"

"I don't annoy you." He flashed his crooked smile. "I think you actually like my visits. I bet they are the highlight of your day after playing entertainment coordinator slash work boss to the seniors."

Delphinium's expression remained neutral. "Or is it *you* who actually likes to visit me? Perhaps you're jealous that everyone wants to hang out with me and that *I'm* the cool one."

"Yeah, the cool one among the senior population," he added. "I'm green with envy."

She narrowed her eyes and pointed a look at him in warning. "They count. Their opinions matter greatly, and they've chosen me."

He maintained a steady stare, giving nothing away. "They do matter."

It perturbed her how he got under her skin so easily. She finally sighed in surrender. "Why are you really here? It wasn't to check up on the meeting. You could've called Henry to find out if something significant had been agreed upon."

His eyes twinkled. "Maybe I come to see you, just like the old folks. We're all drawn to the flower whisperer and her superpower."

They stared at each other until he lost the unspoken contest. He was messing with her, trying to get on her good side.

He rolled his eyes at her lack of reaction. "Okay, I need you to make me two bouquets."

She blinked. "For the same woman?"

"One of them will be." One corner of his mouth curled up deviously.

Delphinium's lip curled in disgust. "Adding two-timing to your list of winning qualities?"

"What can I say, I'm a very popular man." He waggled his eyebrows.

"Does contestant number one know about contestant number two?"

Mason didn't respond but stared her down.

She didn't move her gaze.

He leaned in closer, challenging her. "You know, if you treat me nicer, I might consider setting you up with a friend."

She sat up straight on her stool. "How do you know I'm not seeing someone already?"

"Oh, I know more about you than you think," he said with an arrogant gleam in his eyes.

"How?"

"I have spies everywhere. Consider me the wizard behind the curtain." His coy grin divulged his pleasure for their tit for tat.

Delphinium guffawed. "The guy behind the curtain in *The Wizard of Oz* wasn't a wizard. He was just a man trying to appear powerful." She tapped her chin and pretended to consider her words. "Hmm, on second thought, you might be exactly that guy."

Mason's smile disappeared into a firm line. "Very funny." Delphinium couldn't get over how easy it was to spar with him. She wasn't sure when, but it had begun to feel like sparring with a big brother.

"Are you going to do the bouquets or not?"

"I suppose I can throw something together for your harem."

"There's the enthusiasm that customers come here for. The service here is outstanding."

She went over to the buckets of flowers and began imagining what she'd combine.

"You know, the recipients of all your flowers think I'm quite charming."

"Of course they do," she mumbled under her breath. "What kinds of bouquets are you wanting this time? Do you want a duplicate in case you get their names mixed up?"

He ignored the bait. "You tell me."

"What is it that you want to convey?"

Mason hesitated. "I want to make both women feel special. Something that makes a statement about their individuality and strength. I want both bouquets to possess your magic touch. When they look at it, I want them both to smile. The difference being, one woman I'm trying to woo, and the other woman . . . is my grandmother, and I'm just trying to bring happiness to her day. She's in the full-care nursing home wing at The Gardens."

The impulse to tease immediately left Delphinium. Maybe there was more to Mason than what he projected. She began reaching instinctively for the flowers she knew would be perfect. "For the first, I'd go with a huge bouquet of freesia in a variety of colors.

They are beautiful and hardy and will last awhile. It will look like an explosion of color. Bunched as a bouquet, they are breathtaking. They will look like a lot, and she'll be overwhelmed. They definitely possess the *wow* factor to help woo her."

"But what do they *mean*?"

Delphinium went over and plucked a collection of freesias out of a bucket. She went back to the counter and began bundling them. "When you give freesia to someone, you are asking them in a humble way to trust you with their friendship—that you welcome them into your life and will protect that bond. It says you're thoughtful and sweet. It's as if you are taking the person by the hand and saying, 'Here I am, come join me. You're safe with me.' The colors will always make the person smile. It's like a reminder of the best days of summer. She will look at it and think the best of you."

"What about the second bouquet?"

She kept her focus on the flowers, adding a few sprigs of greenery. "I would do a southern peach arrangement. Peach roses symbolize appreciation. I would complement them with white Asiatic lilies, peach mini carnations, and echeveria succulent with some other greenery. It's not your typical bouquet, which will make your grandmother love it even more and stare at it while feeling good. It's very unique and will definitely make her day."

He looked at her with wonder. "I've got to admit, you've got a knack for what you do."

"Thanks."

"No, I'm serious. You're good at this."

She began placing the selected flowers together. "Why are you so surprised? I love flowers. They are my passion, not to mention my namesake."

He shrugged. "I guess that makes sense."

"Well, enjoy it while you can. I don't think the shop will be open much longer."

The statement had a sobering effect on him. He became very still. "Why do you say that?"

"Financial reasons. I'll be closing or, rather, losing the shop in three weeks."

He paused. "I'm sorry." Then he cleared his throat. "Can you relocate to a new location?"

"No."

"What?" His voice raised in surprise. "Why not?"

"It's not that easy. Things are complicated. And it isn't just the shop. It's my apartment upstairs also. I'm losing my business *and* my home."

The color in his face drained, his complexion even turning a little gray. "Well, maybe I can help. Real estate is what I do and I'm excellent at it."

She shook her head. "Thanks, but I don't think so. It's nothing for you to worry about. All that you need to do is present these flowers to the two women in your life. Apparently, capturing your hyperactive attention is a superhero accomplishment that cannot be done by only one woman."

"Ha ha." Mason narrowed his eyes. "So snarky."

Delphinium couldn't hold back a giggle. He stuck around and waited patiently as she put the bouquets together, never hurrying her. He even allowed her to put them in vases with a bow on each. She smiled at the end products. Oh, how she loved doing this.

Mason handed over his credit card and took the flowers but appeared distracted as she completed the order.

"What will happen to all the seniors? This is their hangout." He looked around the shop as if with different eyes.

Delphinium was quiet as her gaze also perused the space.

"Will you stay in the flower business?"

"I don't know," she said quietly.

"What if you take me up on my offer to help you relocate? I've got a knack for finding gems. My firm has connections and influence that could also extend our reach."

"Thanks, but I don't have the money to relocate and start over."

Mason frowned, looking more disturbed.

Delphinium was surprised at how bothered he was by the news. "What does it matter to you? You'll find another florist."

"Yeah" was all he said as he put his credit card back in his wallet. "Thanks for the flowers." He began to turn but then stopped. "What are these again?" He looked pointedly to the tea towels for sale.

"They're flour sack dish towels."

"I think I'd like some." He put the two vases down, reached into the basket, and picked up a bundle of three. They had wildflowers printed on them.

Delphinium tilted her head. "Is this a pity purchase because of what I told you?"

"No, not at all," he denied, unable to make eye contact with her. "I told you the last time I was in how much I admired the presentation. They are nicely ironed and tied like a present. I'll give these with the flowers or keep them for myself. A guy can never have enough dish towels, right?" He handed over some cash.

Delphinium shook her head as she counted out his change. "What?"

"As soon as I think I have you figured out, you surprise me."

"That's good, I hope," he said, flashing a winning grin.

"I'm not sure. The jury is still out."

"Is this because I don't smell?"

"Scent," she corrected. "You don't emit a *scent*."

He leaned in toward her over the counter. "Try again."

Delphinium closed her eyes and inhaled through her nose. She tried a couple times to pick up the faintest fragrance of anything. She shook her head in frustration. "Nothing."

He looked amused. "So, what does that mean?"

"I don't know. Maybe you don't have a soul or something. Maybe you're a zombie."

He chuckled. "I suppose I set myself up for that one." He tucked the towels under one arm and picked up the bouquets. "Perhaps you're simply accustomed to really smelly people. I happen to shower frequently." He flashed another one of his killer smiles.

Delphinium bit the inside of her cheeks to keep from smiling. He looked so wickedly pleased with himself.

"That's a great fish face you make when you know I'm right but don't want to admit it." He winked.

"You know, eventually a fragrance will rise out of you, and I'll pick up on it, no matter how slight the note. And that will tell me everything I need to know about your true character. Then I'll make my decision about you."

He shook his head. "Just so you know, that's creepy." He headed out holding the bouquets but then glanced back while she held open the door. "You're a great florist. A bit odd, but a great florist." He winked again.

Delphinium released the grin she was holding back as soon as he was out of sight. Their banter made her feel better. Her friendship with him, if she could call it that, was unexpected—like so many other things in her life.

Fourteen

There was no reason to feel anxious, but as soon as Delphinium stepped into the sprawling facility of The Gardens the next morning, she felt intimidated. The place was huge and resembled a bizarre kind of hotel where the staff were buzzing about in scrubs, and the lobby was full of people sitting in wheelchairs. Two elderly men sunk down in their wheelchairs at the entrance eyed her up and down before giving a nod of permission to go on as if they were the security.

After she introduced herself at the front desk, a woman made a call, and Elliot appeared within a minute. He was dressed again in a navy suit and crisp white shirt. However, he was wearing a colorful tie that seemed out of character. As he got closer, she noticed tiny flowers made up the design.

Hmm. She wondered about the coincidence but then dismissed the thought. *No, he wouldn't have done that for me.*

"Good morning. Thank you for coming, Ms. Hayes." He reached out and shook her hand. "It's a beautiful morning. How about we take a short walk?"

"Sure." His formality didn't put her at ease, but she followed obediently. She caught herself repeatedly smoothing the front of her dress. It was floral print, of course. She wore one of her better sundresses, one she'd never wear to work in the shop. It was a tropical palette against ivory. A bit garish compared to the subdued environment around her. She caught the attention of everyone as they passed by silently. For a moment, she wished she'd worn something plain but then remembered the only thing in her closet that came close to plain was what she wore to Annie's funeral.

Although she was somewhat familiar with the place after visiting Henry's room numerous times, she was completely lost now. They were going in the opposite direction of the individual little apartments. Elliot walked like a soldier, efficient and with purpose, instead of casually like she preferred. It unnerved her how he didn't talk as they walked. Just as she was going to comment about the weather out of desperation, they arrived at a side door, and he held it open for her. She slipped through. She vaguely remembered the modest courtyard and patio that looked out to a huge lawn, but she'd only ever observed it from Henry's window.

"Your dress is lovely."

She was so jarred by his compliment, she could only say "Oh."

He watched her reaction.

"Um." She cleared her throat. "Thank you."

"Do you always wear clothes that have flowers on them?"

"Kind of." She looked down and smoothed her dress again. "I guess it's my thing."

He smiled. "I like it. It's uniquely you and fits your personality. I can't imagine you in anything plain. You're meant to stand out."

Her breath caught at the sincerity in his gaze, and she could only stare. This time she knew she wasn't imagining it. Something was going on between them. A feeling of excitement bubbled up inside her. "I'm normally covered in a long apron during the day, so no one really notices."

"I notice," he said with a seriousness that made her gulp.

Completely frazzled, she looked around for a distraction and blurted out, "This is lovely. I haven't been out here before. The space is impressive."

He shifted his gaze to the courtyard. "Impressive but wasteful.

No one comes out here. It's barely used. We encourage residents to sit outside on beautiful days, but the lawn isn't used for any activities and costs quite a lot to maintain."

Delphinium looked out to the very green, perfectly manicured space. It had to be a few acres. "It's not eco-friendly to water this much lawn. It's also rather ironic that the name of the facility is The Gardens, yet the only real gardens are the flower beds at the front of the building and the small circular patch that holds the facilities sign."

"Precisely." Elliot stood next to her. "I've been doing more research on creating a garden program here."

She raised her eyebrow. "You *researched*?"

He looked away briefly, seeming embarrassed. "That's what I do. I like to research things and find a way to make them work proficiently. I couldn't get the idea of a gardening program out of my head since I saw how much the residents love your shop."

Delphinium wanted to mention again that it wasn't the flowers drawing them in, but that was for another discussion. He had good intentions, even if he was a bit obtuse when it came to the seniors' real wishes.

"In my research," he went on, "I discovered that other nursing homes have tried such programs but on a much smaller scale. We have what most other facilities lack—space. This project could be any size we choose to make it. We could start out small and have a vision for it to grow larger, or we could take the bull by the horns and go big from the beginning. It could be hands-on or simply enjoyed in viewing. I spoke with a physical therapist who works with many of our residents, and she thinks certain tasks in the garden could be wonderful exercise. Not to mention a garden would offer physical as well as emotional and psychological benefits." He cast a shy glance at her. "Henry and his friends have thrived in helping you, and I want to replicate that. A garden would also beautify the facility, bringing a truthful meaning to our name while providing flowers for arrangements throughout the facility. It would make us stand out from competitors, and I know the residents would take pride in the outcome."

Delphinium knew where this was going. His intention to entice her with the possibility of what *could be* was too obvious. Although designing a garden of this magnitude would be wonderful, it would not solve the problem the seniors had with the place. She couldn't believe that Elliot was so naive to think it was this simple.

But looking out at the space that held so much potential, she could only swallow down her disappointment in not being able to help shape his vision. It would be so much fun to help orchestrate the program while working with the seniors. However, it felt too overwhelming. The task would turn into a full-time job. And then there was the issue of her shop. If there was a thread of hope to save it, she had to try. If she lost it, she wasn't sure this would ever be her next step. What would it be like to have Elliot as her boss?

"Everything you say is true," she began. "I'm thrilled that you came up with this possibility and what it would mean to all the residents. But as I told you before, I do not have the time to devote to an undertaking this size."

He was quick to interject. "Neither does the nursing home, or more specifically, the landscape crew, but what we do have are many volunteer groups who can put in the time, work, and even donated resources for a project like this. We could finally optimize all the students who beg for volunteer hours. And there are generous donors in Moonberry Lake who would back this completely with supplies and equipment."

Delphinium opened her mouth to say something, but he continued speaking to delay, or rather stop, her refusal. He reiterated the plan he'd first shared in the hospital, emphasizing the accessible flower beds, the seedlings for transplanting, and the vegetable garden they could harvest from.

Delphinium didn't say anything. She could see it in her mind. The vast space was perfect for all kinds of beautiful plants. What a dream it would be to grow and sell her own flowers. It was as if Elliot had plucked a dream out of the deepest and most secret parts of her heart and found a way to make it come true. The sunny space in front of her could be transformed into something magical and life-giving.

"Ms. Hayes?"

She became lost in her daydream of unfettered possibilities.

"Ms. Hayes?" Elliot repeated. Worry etched his face. "Ms. Hayes?"

She shook her head. The daydream was too real. "Um, Delphinium. Please call me Delphinium, or even Delphi. Everyone does. There's truly no need to be formal."

"Delphinium," Elliot repeated, but in the same way she did when practicing how a new name sounded on her tongue—slowly and deliciously.

She felt her chest fill with emotion at the prospect of it all. Excitement for the potential of what could be and sadness for what could never be—not if she was going to lose everything. Not if the shop was gone. It was as if the solution to occupying the seniors and filling her shop with flowers was being waved in front of her, and she couldn't reach far enough to snatch it up. What joy it would be to create this space. She inhaled deeply and felt herself being swept away with the prospect of the idea. She looked down to hide the tears stinging her eyes.

"You've thought this through," she said, not making eye contact with him.

"As you are aware, some of our most active residents choose to spend a considerable amount of time in your shop. We could get them working in an actual garden. From a marketing standpoint, this could also be listed under one of the activities the residents can choose from in recruiting future residents. Pictures of people gardening would be amazing for our website and pamphlets."

Delphinium cringed at his line of thought. She hated how Elliot saw the project from a business point of view, but then, maybe if she had thought more cunningly about image, she wouldn't be facing bankruptcy.

"It's just—" she began, but he interrupted her again.

"All I would need from you is to organize and teach us how to maintain it. We could start out conservatively and then expand. I know the seniors would do whatever you say."

She stiffened. That was the wrong statement to make. She was not about to manipulate her friends the way he was suggesting. "Elliot—"

It was as if he didn't hear her. He kept plowing ahead without taking a breath. "The PR on developing this would be phenomenal. We'd invite the local news to do a before and after story to garner more attention. I would, of course, make sure you were highlighted as helping The Gardens organize everything. The angle we'd want to push is how The Gardens reached out to you to help us create something that would get the seniors active and help them build a home-away-from-home feeling. A human-interest story like this would be eaten up. If the outcome results in more residents, the board has already stated they would invest more into it."

The authoritative way he spoke and did not ask for any input made her grind her teeth. She felt as if she were shrouded in a cold blanket. Old feelings resurfaced about her parents. They spoke to her in the same way. Everything was cut-and-dry and logical. Elliot was like-minded. His plan sounded more like a scheme he could profit from. And it irritated her to no end how he kept interrupting her and speaking over her like she had no choice but to do this. Plus, he was reducing her livelihood, even her passion for flowers, to a marketing strategy. She'd heard enough. This whole idea was simply to make The Gardens look good—to make him look good. It had nothing to do with the seniors. Fuming, she struggled to hold down all the emotions rising in her chest. She needed to get out of there.

"You know, Elliot, you seem to have this all figured out. You should spearhead the project on your own to make sure you get those pretty pictures for your pamphlet. You don't need me, and I *certainly* don't want to be any part of this. Good day."

With that, she strode away with a couple hard steps toward the door they had come through earlier only to discover it was locked. After pulling a couple times, willing it to open, she spun around with her face flushed.

Elliot stared at her, clearly stunned, and although appearing gobsmacked, he managed to say, "All the outside doors are locked from the inside. You need a resident pass to open it." He held up a card.

Jutting her chin up, she said, "I'll walk around to the front." She took off, passing him without another look. Her walk across the lawn was more of an angry stomp.

Elliot's shock at her reaction must have finally worn off, because seconds later he hurried after her, matching her stride easily with his long legs. "Ms. Hayes, I mean Delphinium—please stop! Tell me what I've said, what I've done to upset you."

She didn't slow down, and she certainly didn't want to talk. She'd heard enough about his vision and the true intention behind it. Hating the fact that she was so close to tears, she tried to speed up, which seemed to make no difference to him in keeping pace. *What is this man, a runner?* Her strappy summer sandals were slowing her down in the grass.

"Delphinium, please talk to me." With that plea, he reached out and took hold of her arm in a firm but gentle grasp.

She stopped and looked down at where he was holding her.

"I'm sorry," he said, removing his hand immediately. "And I'm sorry for whatever I may have said that upset you. Please, tell me how I've offended you."

"There isn't enough time for me to go over all the ways you've insulted me and the residents. I've never met a man more single-minded and clueless. Your residents show up at my doorstep because I offer them love and compassion. I listen to their grumblings and let them have a sense of community. I'm not using the seniors as an angle to help my shop and would certainly never use them to profit in any way. Now if you'll excuse me, I have a business to run. I came over here on my own time and now you've made me late."

He stepped away as though she had slapped him. "Of course, the shop needs to be opened. Could I please talk to you after work? I want to make this right."

She was too angry and emotional to reply calmly. This time when she took off walking again, he did not follow.

After she opened the shop and filled a couple small orders, Delphinium kept busy by manically cleaning. She couldn't scrub hard enough.

When Henry walked through the door, she did a double take at how tired he looked. "Are you all right?"

He waved her off. "I'm old. You can't ask that. I'm supposed to look this way to remind young people to live it up while they can."

His brush-off didn't settle her worry. He'd definitely lost more weight.

"Can I bring in some lunch for you? I'll order your favorite cheese pizza with extra pepperoni and peppers. It's been a while since we've shared a meal."

"That's sweet, but I just had a protein drink, and you know how those fill me up." He looked at her. She was wearing rubber gloves, and the bucket of soapy water was just behind her. "Want to tell me what's up?"

"Why do you think anything's up?"

"Because I know you, and when you scrub the floor by hand, it's never good. Fess up or I'll call Gurdy and the rest of the girls to get it out of ya."

Delphinium shrugged. "Isn't losing the shop enough of a reason to look glum?"

"That's rubbish. You'll land on your feet no matter what happens, and I'm still working on a solution. It's something else."

She heaved a loud sigh. "I blew up at Elliot Sturgis."

"Then he had it coming to him."

His loyalty elicited a smile from her. "You don't even know what it was about, and you're going to take my side?"

He looked her straight in the eye. "Every time, darlin'. Every single time."

The love she felt for this man made her heart feel as if it expanded two times its size. He was the best step-in as both parent and grandparent, and his kindness and support felt like a sea of love surrounding her. He'd been the most nurturing figure she'd had in her life besides Annie. "You know I love you, right?"

The lopsided grin on Henry's wrinkled face looked iconic enough to be in the movies. "I'm a lovable guy. And I know you well enough to know you only get upset when it involves something or some*one* you really love. All the seniors who come here may drive you crazy, but you're protective of us and make us feel like family."

"You *are* family to me, Henry. And the others are my wacky relatives."

He nodded. "Then tell me what Elliot said that got you so fired up."

Delphinium took off her gloves and then brought out a stool from behind the counter for him to sit on. She told him about Elliot's idea and her reaction. Henry listened without interrupting, letting her get it all out about how it made her feel and how she walked away refusing to talk to him. When she was done, he continued to stare at her as if expecting more.

"What are you thinking?" she finally asked when he still hadn't said anything.

"I think," he began and then paused. "I think Elliot's plan really doesn't matter. Yeah, it's a great idea and would do some good to the place and for its people, but the thing we should be talking about is why it sparked such strong emotions in you." He leaned in closer, placing his hand over hers. "Brought back too many familiar memories with your folks, I bet."

Delphinium nodded, swallowing down the rising emotions.

"You reacted from an old wound. One that remains open and bleeding. You're a free spirit who doesn't like to be bulldozed into anything." He paused, looking at her with a small smile. "It reminds me of another special lady I knew."

At the mention of Annie, Delphinium had to press her fingers against her lips to seal in the cry wanting to escape.

"You're a tender heart, my dear, just like your grandmother. Annie would be so proud of you." He gave her hand a squeeze, looking at her with a bit of emotion in his eyes. "I'm proud of you." The way he held her gaze to give time for his words to sink in was her undoing.

She shook her head, losing the battle to hold back the tears fighting to come through. She looked down and confessed the guilt weighing on her. "I think she'd be crushed that I'm losing this place. In a way, I'm glad she's not here to see the end of the flower shop." She sniffled and got a tissue from underneath the counter.

"First of all, this is just a place. You have so many adventures ahead of you. This is only one of the many experiences you'll have in your long life. You'll learn to accept that places come and go, homes change, and new people will come forth. And while others fade into the background as you age, the only steadfastness in life is God. In every season of my life, whether it was during times of celebration or heartbreak, calmness or turmoil, God has been my companion and rock. I hope you discover that presence and comfort someday.

"Second, Annie would be proud that you have respected and lived up to your gifting. But even that barely covers the surface of who you really are. She would find you just as magnificent as I do. Beyond your creative work in this shop, Annie would be bursting with pride over how you express love in everything you do."

More tears slipped out as she gave a shaky smile. "That's kind of you to say."

"It's not kind. It's the truth. Annie's synesthesia was only a small part of who she was. She once told me that it only enhanced the full life she was already living. And I think that's what you're forgetting. She had a vivaciousness that put people in awe. Living vibrantly was an intentional choice. She sought out adventure while never leaving this small town. And you know what? She found it every day."

Delphinium thought of how Annie injected joy into everything she did. Everything Henry said was true.

"Wherever you go, whether it means staying here in this building or taking a new job and establishing roots somewhere else, stay open to the possibility of surprise. The same way Annie did. New beginnings are scary, but they also contain so much wonder."

"Well, as long as you're there with me, I know I'll be okay."

Henry looked upset by her words. "Just promise me you'll be open to what God has next for you. If you ask for guidance and keep putting one foot in front of the other, life will be so much more than what you could've planned or even imagined. Keep an open heart to be led."

Delphinium knew Henry was a man of deep but quiet faith. She didn't have the same background imbued with church and a religious upbringing, and in truth, she felt a bit shy about the topic, but she was open to it and wanted to respect his request. More than anything, the example of his character had watered and encouraged the small seed of faith in her to grow. "I promise."

"And in terms of what to do with Elliot. My advice is to extend a little grace and let him catch up to your vision and heart."

"I thought you didn't like him."

"I've decided to extend him some grace myself. You are a whirlwind of love and creativity, and he is simply trying to grab a handful of what you spin so effortlessly. He's already shown an interest in changing, so help him see the broader possibilities."

She nodded.

"You are a force, Delphi. Let him prove that he is up for the challenge. He's a good man. I believe his heart is in the right place." Henry paused. "I know all the seniors have given him a hard time for being a rule follower, but he's an excellent leader, and I also know there is a side to him that most never get to see. A more private side that is steeped in faith and sincere intention. He has been there for me in ways that I will forever appreciate. Yes, he's been a little stuck when it comes to change and has not been open to some of our suggestions, which is why we caused such a ruckus, but we also all know that he has the shoulders to take it.

"He's a decent and moral man, and I think both of you could learn something from each other. His discipline and order matched with your creativity and flexibility would be a force that could take over the world." With that said, he slid off the stool, gave her a wink and a tip of his imaginary hat, and left.

Fifteen

t the end of the day, when Delphinium went to the front door to flip over the Open sign, she noticed Elliot standing outside. Her breath hitched. He must have been waiting for this moment when she was done for the day.

As their eyes met, he began walking toward her. She opened the door and he stepped inside carrying a white box that she recognized from The Fudge Shoppe down the street.

"I thought it would be inappropriate if I brought you flowers from another florist," he said, handing her the box.

She took the gift, which had to weigh five pounds. There was *a lot* of fudge in it. "Although flowers are my favorite, this comes in as the close second. As a matter of fact, chocolate might even tie depending upon my mood." She looked down, embarrassed. "You didn't have to get me anything though. I shouldn't have left so abruptly this morning—and in such a huff."

"When you didn't return my phone message, I thought I'd wait until you were closed to see if we could talk."

She peered back up at him, still feeling uncomfortable. "I'm sorry I didn't call back."

"No apology needed. That is something I've been waiting impatiently to do all day." He looked beyond her at the two stools at the counter. "Do you have a few minutes to talk?"

She nodded and closed the door. He went over to the counter and sat where Henry had been not that long ago. She sat across from him.

He opened his mouth to speak but when she held up her hand, he immediately shut it.

"Let me begin by apologizing for storming off. A lot of feelings came rushing at me this morning. The garden is a fantastic idea. It would be a dream to work on, but when you were presenting it, you removed the heart and good intention of the project and began turning it into a PR circus. Caring for the seniors isn't about creating a gimmick, getting pretty images for a pamphlet, or making your bottom line look better. Or, at least, it shouldn't be. I realize that senior care is a big business, but it is also the last stage of life for these people, which makes it sacred."

He nodded, looking guilty. She could tell it was killing him not to respond by the way he pressed his lips together, but he was respectfully letting her say her piece.

"I also felt steamrolled by how you were assuming I'd do it. I hate being pushed into things without my voice truly being heard."

"Yes, I apologize for that. I was completely out of line."

She shook her head. "You couldn't have known that talking to me that way is a huge trigger for me from childhood. Another person may have felt complimented by your strong enthusiasm."

"I'm sorry. I won't make that mistake again." He sat back in his seat, waiting for her to go on.

Delphinium took a big breath. "I love the seniors and am very protective of them. Henry in particular is very special to me. He is my family. Whatever ends up being built or whatever programs are implemented, it should truly be about the seniors and not about selling the best image that promotes the idea of happy assisted living. The experience and feelings of these elderly people should not be an afterthought but what the entire project is centered around."

He nodded again. "I understand and I agree with everything you are saying. I'm sorry the analytical part of my brain got away from the emotional part that came up with the idea in the first place."

Delphinium leaned in, knowing that what she was going to say next would be hard for him to hear. "The seniors began coming here because they were miserable with all your rules. You can't lose sight of how all this began, and I'll tell you right now, planting a garden will not solve any of it. If you want authentic pictures capturing truly happy residents to put on the website or wherever, you first need to ask the residents what would make *them* happy and then negotiate on how that could happen. Do I think there should be gambling going on? Absolutely not. Should there be unrealistic expectations for entertainment or twenty-four-hour food service to their rooms? Never. But could you put on the occasional Hawaiian night or have a chocolate fountain once a month?" She shrugged. "Probably."

Elliot stared at her, not responding but still taking it all in.

She decided to keep going. "Is it unreasonable that they want to have dancing lessons or soft-serve swirl ice cream? It doesn't sound too outrageous to me. Helen loves to fold things. You can't tell me that it would be hard to find a way to let her continue that. Your laundry service would probably love it. If you agreed to sit down and listen to their suggestions, I think you might actually find that some of them aren't too demanding or unrealistic. Their rebellion got out of hand because they felt ignored. As you shook your head, they kept upping the stakes and became more imaginative and silly in their requests because they didn't feel they had a voice."

He nodded. "I hear everything you're saying and everything sounds reasonable."

She stared at him, not sure what else she could add.

He looked away, pressing his mouth together so tightly she could see the muscles in his jaw tic. When he looked back at her, the control he typically possessed faltered. "But what I want to know . . . what I *need* to know"—he cleared his throat—"is if *we're* okay."

Delphinium was so taken by surprise, she didn't know what to say. She blinked at his steady stare. Her mind raced as she replayed the word *we're* coming from him. He saw them as a *we*. His gaze was so intense and hopeful, she could only nod.

His relief was apparent. His shoulders relaxed, and his sigh aligned with hers, with both of their chests lowering at the same time.

"I have a tendency to act emotionally and passionately—"

"An admirable trait and one that is expressed in your floral creations," he quickly inserted.

"Yes, but I also need to work on seeing things from the other person's perspective. I reacted too harshly on impulse. I know that all you want to do is make The Gardens a wonderful and safe space."

He nodded. "Precisely."

"So I apologize for my reaction that left you clueless as to the reason behind my behavior. Henry reminded me of what a good person you are."

Elliot appeared briefly taken back, but then he settled into the compliment with the smallest of smiles. "That was very kind of him. I hold incredible respect for him as well. We've had wonderful discussions about the faith we share."

After a quiet moment where neither spoke, Delphinium popped up from her stool.

"I need to put some flowers in the cooler and close things up."

He got up just as quickly. "Would you mind if I helped you and then we could continue talking after?"

She did not see that offer coming but couldn't deny the thrill it gave her. She enjoyed his company and, even more, liked having him in close proximity to her. "Oh. Um, sure."

He helped her carry buckets of flowers into the cooler and then waited for her at the front counter as she wiped down the worktable and threw the garbage out. She did a quick sweep around the back even though it didn't really need it, to bide some time to think and get herself focused. She wanted to get the flurry of excitement and nervousness whirling inside her under control.

Twenty minutes later, after cleaning the back room, she washed her hands and combed her fingers through her hair, trying to tame it with a little wetness. As she walked to the front, Elliot was paying a delivery person at the door. He shut it and turned around holding a very full brown paper bag.

"I ordered Chinese food. I thought we could eat while we talk. I'm sure you're hungry after a long day."

Delphinium couldn't remember when or what she'd eaten that day, and her stomach gave a pull at the mention of food. Even though she was starving, she once again found herself staring at him, completely astonished. He had taken off his suit coat and tie and undone the top button of his dress shirt. He'd even rolled up his sleeves to just below his elbows. He still looked like Elliot but more . . . unwound. And *sexy*.

She felt herself tongue-tied by her attraction to him. His air of masculinity and strength, mixed with his scent, made the pull to get closer to him nearly irresistible. She sat down on the stool to keep herself planted. He was the opposite of anyone she had ever dated, or had ever been interested in. Typically, perfectly tailored suits and a reserved manner would have sent her running in the opposite direction. But Elliot's scent drew her close enough where she also saw his vulnerability, and the seriousness and responsibility he took with his job was admirable. Henry was right—there was another side to this man that most did not see. When he had handed over the five-pound box of fudge earlier, looking anxious, Delphinium saw a glimpse of that tender side he kept protected by suits.

She cleared her throat, forcing herself to say something. "Um, that actually sounds really good. I love Chinese food."

His tentative smile brightened as he let out a breath of relief. "Great. Everything should be in here—napkins, plastic utensils, and a couple plates." He began putting it all on the counter.

"This is a lot of food," she said, watching him unload the never-ending white cartons.

"I didn't know what you'd like, so I ordered a bit of everything," he confessed, casting her a sheepish look.

"I love Chinese food, and leftovers are the best."

They each piled their selections on a plate. Just as she was going to dig in, he said, "Would you mind if I said a dinner prayer?"

"Not at all."

He held out his hand, and she took it immediately as if she'd done it a million times before. As he held it gently nested inside his, he closed his eyes and said a prayer. Not the typical one she had heard her grandmother say countless times but one where he simply thanked God for the food and her company. Nothing fancy, but it was so sincere and surprising, she was glad when they began to eat and didn't talk to hide the lump in her throat. This man was a conundrum with all his many layers.

The food was delicious, and it felt easy sitting with him. She liked him being this close and casual. Without his suit coat and tie, he looked entirely different. He appeared younger, closer to her age than the decade between them, and more relaxed. The strength and authority his face projected didn't change, but his eyes softened as he looked at her, and the curve of his shy smile mesmerized her. She found herself waiting and wanting that smile, which she guessed hadn't changed since he was a little boy.

As he scooped more lo mein onto his plate, he said, "Again, I'm sorry for coming across too strongly over the garden project, but it's just because it seems like the perfect solution to everything. I wanted it to be right for the seniors but also for you. I can't see how I can ever pull it off without you."

"I don't believe that. You have the leadership to organize anything."

Elliot shook his head. "I have organizational skills. But I don't have the magic with the seniors that you do." He wiped his mouth that was already spotless and opened a new napkin to put on his lap. "I'm not as"—he paused, seeming to search for the right word—"*popular* with the residents. You seem to have an aptitude for dealing with them. If your name and presence was linked to the project, there would be no question that it would draw the residents in. If I lead it, I'm not sure anyone would show up."

Delphinium couldn't deny his statement when the two of them were being compared. Of course Henry and his posse preferred her. She loaded them up on sugar and indulged every whim and bad habit. She let them feel like the cool kids skipping school and passing notes behind the teacher's back, only it was card playing in their underwear tops and popping copious amounts of butterscotch candies and donut holes. She even allowed Bob to hold an unlit pipe in his mouth, but that was only to help him maintain a poker face. He knew she'd never permit him to actually smoke it.

Delphinium pushed some dumplings around her plate.

"They gravitate toward you naturally and would do anything that you suggested," Elliot continued. "I do not have your ability for persuasion."

Her eyebrow quirked up. "I'm persuasive?"

"Incredibly," he said, looking at her with an expression she couldn't read.

"How so?"

He gave her one of his piercing stares. "You just are. I'd do anything you said just as the seniors do. You have a charisma that makes people want to get closer. Perhaps persuasion isn't the right word, but magnetism."

"That's the word I'd use for your scent," she whispered. But he heard her and looked up, surprised.

They locked eyes for a moment before both concentrated on their plates.

As he pushed up his glasses, which she recognized as more of a nervous habit because they rested perfectly on his face, Delphinium thought back to when he first appeared in her shop and how Bob reacted toward him. For a man who exuded such power and intimidation, she saw the chinks in his armor that he tried to conceal. Could the seniors who stuck together like a pack of pound dogs be daunting to him instead of the other way around?

"We need to discuss their food requests to end this ridiculous hunger strike," she said.

"Agreed. And I think more would be accomplished if you were present and served as mediator. I've witnessed how you have no problem calling them out on unreasonable behavior."

"I can't argue with that. It's a dysfunctional relationship. I'm both nurturer, protector, and a grouchy mother bear."

He laughed. "It's obvious how much you care for them and vice versa."

She didn't just care for them. She *loved* them. Whatever happened to her shop, she wanted to make sure she still saw them regularly. Maybe working on this garden was what Henry meant about being open about the next step in her life. Not seeing them and working with them would feel like abandonment on both sides.

"It goes without saying, you could have a large percentage of flowers for your business. You would have full say on what is grown and what activities you think the seniors could do. The design of it would all be under your vision. I would simply be in the background to help launch it through funding and reporting back to the board for progress updates."

She didn't respond as she thought about the possibility. It was a gutting feeling to have a dream dangled in front of her like this when her current dream was falling apart.

When they finished eating, Elliot put all the containers, most of which were still quite full, back into the bag. "Take these for leftovers."

"No, you should take some home. There's far too much."

"Nope. You have more mouths to feed. Keep it here. I'm sure some of the seniors will help you eat them."

After she put it all in the cooler, she came back to find Elliot still seated. Without the scent of all the Chinese food as a distraction, the most prominent smell in the shop was . . . him.

She inhaled his violet essence deeply, which made her a bit woozy. He had no idea the effect he had on her. The way he looked, sounded, and smelled was unlike any combination she had ever encountered.

"Delphinium, do you think my idea could work? I'm having a hard time reading your silence."

She inhaled through her nose again.

"Delphinium?"

She jumped a little. "I'm sorry, but could you please step a few feet away and then talk to me?"

He blinked and his mouth parted but then closed. He clearly was not expecting her to say that. For the briefest of moments, she saw a flash in his eyes. He appeared crestfallen. "Oh, certainly."

She immediately regretted speaking up. Of course, he took her words the wrong way. They sounded rude even to her. He must have thought that he was making her uncomfortable by standing in such close proximity, which was the last thing she wanted to convey. Why did she always have to make things so awkward with men?

"I'm sorry, it's just your scent is so strong. You must be perspiring a little." Not wanting to embarrass him, she quickly went on, "Remember what I told you at the hospital about picking up on people's scent?"

He nodded.

"I have a weakness for violets. I've never met anyone who emits them as strongly as you. The fragrance is, well . . . heavenly. I'm having a hard time concentrating with you so close to me. It literally makes my head swim. I can't make such a big decision when all my attention is directed to the aroma."

He studied her. "So, it's a good scent to have?"

She waited before answering, deliberating on how honest she should be. "It's *intoxicating*." She couldn't help closing her eyes and inhaling the luscious smell again. "The only thing I can think to compare it to is the myths about sirens of the sea calling to sailors, hypnotizing them in a way. It's their sole focus."

"So," he said slowly, seeming to consider her words, "the only thing you can focus on is *me*."

She opened her eyes to find that Elliot had moved to the other side of the shop but had a huge smile on his face.

She felt the heat rise in her cheeks and was so mortified she couldn't look at him. "Maybe that was the wrong analogy to use, but yes, something like that. In a roomful of people, you'd still be the focus of my attention."

"I definitely like that."

Her cheeks were flaming at this point, and she was sure the redness was crawling down her neck, making her look blotchy. It was like a gift how she could keep digging herself into a deeper hole. Mason was right. She was odd. And talking about her ability probably did sound creepy. She cleared her throat. "I get distracted with you so close, and it makes it hard to make decisions when the scent is so heavy. You're definitely perspiring."

Elliot's smile remained but his eyes looked mischievous. "You mean, my scent cognitively affects you?" One of his eyebrows arched. He was enjoying this.

She rubbed her forehead. "Please don't think about this too much. I only wanted to explain because it's easier for me if you move a little distance away. I didn't want you to get the wrong idea when I asked for space. I don't mind you being close to me." As soon as the words came out of her mouth, she immediately wished the seniors were present for a huge distraction. *Yep, that's right. Make things even more awkward.* She could feel her cheeks going aflame again. *And this is why I'm alone. I just keep digging a deeper hole.*

He continued staring at her without a word, looking so pleased with everything she was saying. There was no way he missed all the emotions playing across her face, which seemed to delight him even more by his perpetual smile that was turning into a chuckle. He stood studying her with fascination, making no movement to break the moment.

It drove her crazy how cerebral he was, thinking and clearly processing every little thing she said. He remained reserved and rational while she functioned purely on emotion, which resulted in reactions that weren't always well thought out. The fact that he wasn't immediately responding only made her antsy and continue to ramble on. She couldn't stop herself.

"Really, it's a good problem to have," Delphinium added hastily. "You wouldn't want to smell like lemon verbena."

A corner of his mouth twitched. "I happen to like lemon verbena."

Of course he would. Crisp, clean, sharp—some of the attributes of his personality. "Yes, it's great when it's in cleaning products or candles, but when it's emitted from a person, I always feel sorry for them."

"Why? What does it mean?" The twinkle in his eyes gave away how entertaining he found the conversation. The man who typically appeared stoic looked downright giddy over how uncomfortable she was.

"The person is typically in some sort of crisis. It means 'please pray for me.'"

Elliot gave a look of mock concern. "Well, that's not good. I'll never look at my furniture polish the same way again. I'll be sure to switch brands. I wouldn't want the scent to rub off on me."

Delphinium narrowed her gaze. His teasing made her wish she had lied and told him that lemon verbena represented something awful. "You should feel good about having violets as your signature scent. If others smelled it on you, they would swoon. It's calming and brings to mind images of babies."

Elliot chuckled. "Or those on the other end of life. There are plenty of women at The Gardens who smell like baby powder or a similar powdery perfume."

Delphinium grinned. "I never thought of it that way, but you're right. You were destined to work with the elderly."

Elliot put his hands in his front pockets. "Now that I've changed my proximity and you are not influenced by my aroma, tell me, what do you think of my idea?"

She gave a heavy sigh. "It's wonderful, I just—" She flailed her arms in frustration.

"What?"

"It would be hard work setting it up, too hard physically for seniors. Especially if you want the end product of them harvesting and putting pretty bouquets together. We would have to rely on a team of dedicated volunteers to get it going. The seniors should only be there to reap the benefits."

He frowned. "You're right. I wasn't being realistic."

"What you want could still be done with an events coordinator that designs crafts for them based on the time of year and season. The work the seniors do at my shop, if any, is light. The conversation, community, and small chores are entertainment to them. They come to my shop to hang out and chat. Secondly, I wouldn't want you to go through all the trouble of setting up a garden when there most likely won't be a shop."

By the way his eyes widened, he clearly was not expecting that excuse.

She had to be honest with him no matter how it hurt her pride to admit her financial mistake.

"I'm losing my shop." She took a couple breaths to collect herself before moving closer to tell him the whole story.

Elliot listened without interrupting. He didn't pepper her with questions, jump in with advice, or show disappointment or judgment in her poor decisions. He was the best sounding board she'd ever met. He came and sat back down and let her talk and pause and pace around the shop without saying anything. He allowed her to vent and took in every word with his big, kind eyes.

Before she knew it, she was spilling out all her emotions about what it felt like to lose the shop and apartment, and her insecurities about what was next for her. She hadn't felt so comfortable talking to anyone since her grandmother. There was something in his demeanor that—even though he was as refined and reserved as her parents—made her feel . . . *valued*. He wanted to hear what she said. She felt remarkably safe and secure in his presence.

This realization rattled her.

Everything about him was ironic. He was a walking contradiction of characteristics. His expression could go from stone hard to soft, his voice stern to gentle, his stare piercing to compassionate, his presence distant to intimate. All of it seemed to make her lose her breath and train of thought. It was upsetting how distracting and disarming she found him.

He must have sensed her processing, because the moment that she took a step back, he straightened on his stool and leaned away. It was like he instinctively knew she needed a little space.

"It's okay," he whispered, encouraging her to go on.

Delphinium shook her head, trying to break away from the spell she fell under so easily in his presence. She looked at the time on her watch and was shocked that she had been talking for almost an hour. "I can't believe I just told you all that."

"I feel honored."

"I'm sorry to have taken up so much of your time."

"Not at all. I had no plans this evening except to try to make things right with you."

She sighed. "So you understand now that I need to spend all my energy on saving my shop, even if there's only a glimmer of hope."

He nodded, looking as much disappointed as concerned.

"It's been a long night. We both have work tomorrow. Thank you for dinner," she said, feeling strangely vulnerable at how much she had shared.

He got up quickly. "Absolutely. I'll be going."

She followed him to the door.

Just before he walked out, he turned around. "By the way, I watered the amaryllis and put it in a warm spot like you suggested. Nothing has happened yet."

"Something will in about twelve weeks. You just have to be patient."

"Well then, it's a good thing I'm a very patient man for things that matter to me." His serious stare made her all but stop breathing.

She gulped.

"And the amaryllis represents harmony, correct?" he asked, keeping their exchange flowing.

She nodded.

"And it's supposed to help me see and realize the beauty and uniqueness of others?"

Delphinium blinked. "You remembered what I said."

"I remember everything you say," he said, leaning forward a little to close the distance between them.

Her breath caught. She had no response to that. She was lost in the depth of his brown eyes. She was going to lose her mind over the intensity of this man and the effect he had on her. Her only hopeful wish was that the pinkness in her face didn't make her freckles pop like a dalmatian as Bob had mentioned.

They reached for the door handle at the same time.

"Sorry," she said, snatching her hand back.

But he didn't move.

Delphinium felt her pulse race. He was standing so close, she could swear he was leaning closer, or maybe that was her. Without thinking about it, solely operating from an automatic response, she closed her eyes, inhaling and exhaling slowly. His scent was so deliciously enchanting.

"It's happening again, isn't it?"

Her eyes snapped open. "What?"

"You're losing your focus because of my scent." His eyes were lit with amusement.

She groaned, her shoulders lowering. "You are literally my kryptonite."

He opened the door, stepped through, and then turned back. "I'll be in touch. I'll give you a call so that you can, um"—he cleared his throat—"think clearly." He looked downright elated now.

"I'm not sure your plans about the gardening project will work out," she said.

"I am."

Her brow crinkled. "How? How can you be so confident?"

"Because to make it a reality, I know the key player's kryptonite," he said, flashing her a wickedly charming smile before walking away.

As she watched him leave, she already felt a longing to be near him again. She groaned. He was complicating things. She needed to focus on the shop. She didn't have the time or headspace to think about him or the *possibility* of him.

But it was one thing to tell her brain that, and another to tell her heart.

Sixteen

The next day, Delphinium perused the morning headlines before opening the shop.

SIGHTINGS AND SATIRE

The largest "Hook in the Head" this fishing season goes to ten-year-old Joshua Collins. The emergency room doctor pulled out a three-inch hook lodged in his cranium, which required four stitches and a tetanus shot. His prize is a container of night crawlers and a free hat from the tackle shop that says "Bait me."

The town council reported the midyear audit looks very good. After surveying several lakes, it can be said with confidence from the quality of the boats, size of motors, and new pontoons, the economy of Moonberry Lake is thriving. The mayor believes everyone can afford an increase in taxes. She stated, "If you can buy those ridiculous Jet Skis, you can help redo the roads. And if I see one more new dock, we are adding new bike lanes!"

Our local dance troupe, the Twirling Tutus, has issued a formal apology to anyone who contracted food poisoning from their bake sale. The fundraiser covered the cost of the group going to their regional championship competition. Unfortunately, the dance troupe's performance did not win a ribbon. The instructor blames the girls passing out and falling over during their dance routine on dizziness and dehydration caused by severe vomiting. It was announced that they will fundraise for next year's competition by selling gift wrap.

Authorities were called to Off the Top Barbershop early Monday morning over a graffiti grievance. What troubled onlookers about the vandalism is that it contained several misspellings. The delinquent's defacement displayed a level of illiteracy that troubled Moonberry Lake educators. Fred Burns, owner of the barbershop, stated, "Being a hoodlum is one thing, but being an uneducated hoodlum truly reflects poorly on the community." He is heading up a campaign to get more books into the high school. He's called it "Decimate Delinquent Doodling with Dictionaries."

The annual Minnesota blood drive is underway. In other words, mosquito season is in full force. Get ready to give involuntarily to the little bloodsuckers. The Moonberry Lake Health Department reminds us that dusk and dawn are the worst times to be outside, and the people most at risk of being attacked are those who wear dark colors, are overweight, pregnant, or drink beer. Best prevention is to go to bed early, sleep in late, dress in Easter colors, cut out junk food, practice abstinence, and switch to sparkling water. Or, simply, apply bug spray.

Delphinium flipped over her Open sign, and a woman who she recognized immediately walked through the door seconds later.

"Hello," the guest said. "Kathryn Hughes from *The Town Times*."

"Hi, Kathryn. I remember you."

The woman placed a tall cup on the counter with a familiar coffee-shop insignia on it. "I thought you might like some tea."

"That's very nice of you. Thanks." Delphinium picked up the cup and took a sip. "Mmm. It's my favorite."

Kathryn smiled. "Yes, Joanna told me. I ran into her downtown. A woman named Patsy also handed me a flower with your card. She told me how they are trying to bring in more business. I think it's sweet how they are all trying to help you."

Delphinium raised an eyebrow. "You really are a snoop."

Kathryn's laugh was easy and light. "I like to think of myself as a thorough investigative reporter. I'm addicted to police shows, so humor me here."

"Well then, you'll be delighted to know that I did my own investigative work on you," Delphinium said. "I read yesterday's paper. I see that you write the gardening column in addition to feel-good stories about residents and happenings in Moonberry Lake. The piece about the neighborhood car wash to raise money for the animal shelter was well done."

Kathryn brightened. "I'm flattered that you read it. Most people focus on the most popular sections, 'Sightings and Satire' or 'A Moment with Martha.' I prefer to write longer human-interest pieces. You know, dig until I find something—and in a town this small, that's not hard. Gossip runs as strong as coffee, and there are always people willing to pour out their opinions and stories to a listening ear."

Delphinium liked how upfront this woman was. Kathryn knew what she wanted and kept going after it until she got it. Delphinium admired the woman's tenacity and grit—something she wished she had more of. She kept taking sips of the tea. "Go on, then. Tell me what scintillating news you've uncovered."

"I've learned from talking to all the seniors parading through town on your behalf that there's a great human-interest story here that readers will eat up. It sounds as if it could be the tug-at-your-heart kind of piece that sells the best."

Delphinium frowned. "It wouldn't be the kind of story that puts The Gardens in a positive light, I'm afraid. You can't write an article with the headline 'Elderly People Flee for Right to Play Poker and Eat Raspberry Sorbet.'" She shook her head. "As I stated before, I'm not interested in commenting."

Kathryn was quick to interject. "I wouldn't even have to mention The Gardens. This is a sweet small-town story, the kind that people love to read. Who wouldn't want to hear about a bunch of elderly people playing poker in your refrigerator, or a former schoolteacher tutoring your teenage helper?"

"You know about Gurdy?"

Kathryn nodded. "And Helen and Arlene and Bob, and, well—everyone. Patsy told me the entire story about how they're helping you while hanging out here. And how finding Helen a job to do changed her sour disposition. I'm telling you, readers would eat this up. You would come across as a good Samaritan."

Delphinium didn't need even a minute to think about it. "No thanks."

The genuine surprise on Kathryn's face was not well hidden. She was obviously not accustomed to being told no.

"What if I could promise that it would bring a lot of attention to your store, which would mean more sales for you. It would give a big push toward saving this place. Your friends told me the dire situation you're in."

The woman was indeed like a bulldog with a bone.

Delphinium took a deep breath, already regretting that she was considering it. "Go on."

Kathryn's eyes lit up. "I could write the article in a way that people wouldn't be able to resist coming in and checking out your shop to see if it's as endearing as I portray it."

"And you won't mention The Gardens?"

Kathryn shook her head. "It wouldn't really be necessary. This is where all the action is. All I would say is how you are a delightful host to some elderly people looking for an outing. Period. You and your shop would come off as having the biggest heart on Main Street. Who wouldn't want to save that?"

Delphinium couldn't deny that it was tempting. She told herself that it was the desperation she felt and not her conscience that was giving her a sick feeling in her stomach.

Taking a deep breath, Delphinium stood straighter. "Okay." She would do this one last thing to try to save the shop and prove she also had tenacity and grit. This might be her Hail Mary pass. Then she could close up the shop knowing that she had done everything she could to save it.

Kathryn gave a little clap and pulled out her phone to record her interview. "Great! I just have a few questions."

Three days later, she decided to visit Charlie and see how his first week of recovery went. After checking in with the nurses at the desk to find out which room he was in, Delphinium nudged the door open while holding one floral arrangement in a vase and one container with potted lavender in her arms. Charlie looked over and gave a big grin, switching off the TV.

"Well, you're the prettiest visitor I've had all day!"

"Careful, you're starting to sound like George."

Charlie laughed. "The nurses think I'm a hoot. You'll have to go back and tell George that *I'm* the real ladies' man."

Delphinium shook her head. "Like either of you need any more encouragement."

Charlie's wide smile made her feel better. She placed the new arrangements down and started spiffing up the other two bouquets that Arlene and Patsy had brought him, pulling out the wilted flowers and adding more water.

"This place is beginning to look like your shop. You're making the other patients on the floor jealous, especially the women."

"Then I'll stop. More female attention is the last thing you need."

Charlie roared. "Ha! You're a kick. I see why Henry loves you so much. You call it like you see it."

The room did look very bright and cheery with the array of flowers.

"I chose white daisies, which mean 'get well soon,' and lavender to help induce a feeling of calmness while you heal."

"Well, thank you very much for your kindness. If I knew falling would make so many females fawn over me, I would have done it years ago. I've been working entirely too hard wooing them the old-fashioned way."

Delphinium laughed and sat down on the chair next to his bed.

"So, how are you really doing?" she asked.

Charlie nodded. "Good, good. It was a long time coming. I'm actually in less pain than I was before. Should've replaced the ole hip years ago. This new titanium one is practically bulletproof. I'll be doing the jitterbug soon and be the envy of everyone—at least those my age."

Delphinium reached over and placed her hand on top of his. "I'm so sorry about the accident."

He waved her off. "I was chugging my caboose too fast. It was entirely my fault. Besides, I get to leave in better shape than when I entered. Not many people can say that in this place. It's all doom and gloom typically. Plus, my grandkids think it's cool. They think most of us will be half-robot in the future anyway—like that gold fella in *Star Wars*, C-3PO." He chuckled.

Delphinium grinned. "Well, C-3PO is a full droid. And I didn't think about it that way. You could become like him."

Charlie beamed like a proud grandpa. "Leave it to kids to put things into perspective."

"How is the rehab going?"

He frowned. "I don't like it. It's painful, and I'm shuffling at a snail's pace with a walker. It's humiliating looking so weak in front of the ladies. Although I think they watch for my laps down the hall just so they can catch my wink."

Delphinium rolled her eyes. "How is it that George is the one with the girlfriends?"

"I'm his right-hand man." He gave a rascally grin.

"Well, the only way you're going to get there and be the buddy you think you are is if you do your physical therapy. It's hard work, but necessary if you ever want to walk on your own again. Work through the pain now and it'll pay off later."

He scowled. "Bah." Then he waved her off.

"The gang misses you. Everyone wishes you were back at the shop playing poker."

"How is the shop? Henry told me about your predicament."

"To be honest, it's not looking good." She sat back in the chair. "I have only a couple more weeks to come up with a miracle or you guys will have to find another place to hang out and harass the owner." She tried to make her voice light, but it didn't come out that way.

Charlie pointed his finger at her. "Don't give up, you hear me? It ain't over 'til it's over."

Delphinium only offered a half smile. "I won't give up if you won't give up on your rehab. Deal?"

"Ah, I see what you did! Slipped a little guilt in there. Tricked me into a dirty deal. You came to give me a hard time about doing my exercises."

"I came to give you flowers because I care about you. The gang misses you. It's not the same with you gone. And also, I came to give you a really good incentive to get up and do the necessary hard work to be mobile again."

Charlie squinted, his eyes suspicious. "What's the incentive?"

Delphinium leaned in closer like she was revealing a big secret. "The nurses told me that once you're stronger and walking with more stability, you can go in the pool for water therapy." She lowered her voice and spoke as if the words were scandalous. "Imagine how jealous you'd make George if you got to do your exercises with a bunch of women doing water aerobics. And I hear the instructor is in her spry fifties."

Charlie's face lit up, and he waggled his eyebrows. "I like the way you think."

"It's not the way *I* think. I'm just smart enough to know you can only get an old dog to do tricks by dangling a new treat in front of them."

She got up to head out as Charlie roared with laughter, but he called out to her before she reached the door.

"Remember, don't give up!" he shouted.

She turned back. "I can't promise anything, Charlie. I'm in a great deal of debt."

"No, I wasn't talking about the shop. Don't give up on *us*. We need you, kid. You'll never know what you've given us."

His statement and the vulnerability in his eyes took her aback. The goofy, flirty Charlie was gone. The man speaking honestly to her now was dead serious, almost a little scared.

"You guys will be all right either way. I'll make sure of it."

"Just promise me that no matter what, we'll still see you. Promise me you'll come by and visit us. And always know that you're at the top of my list when I pray."

The lump in her throat made it impossible to respond, so she simply gave a nod and walked out with her eyes welling with tears.

All she could do was hope the newspaper article would bring in business and save the shop. Was it ridiculous to pray for a miracle? She justified it in her head that it wasn't selfish since it wasn't just for her but for the seniors too. She wanted things to work out for them also. But the presence of God and faith in her life felt so undeveloped and far away that a timidness came over her at the thought of praying. A part of her had always been envious of those who had a relationship with God. They appeared to have a grit and steadfastness from their belief to help them in trying times, which she secretly yearned for.

Closing her eyes, she whispered a simple "Please," hoping it would be heard. It felt too short and lacking the beauty and poetry of prayers she had heard from others, but she couldn't form or utter any other word except that.

Perhaps God would know what was in her heart rather than the insufficient words spoken by her mouth. Maybe God would feel her meaning. That is the God she hoped to get to know better.

The next morning Delphinium gasped at the sight of the front-page story of *The Town Times*. In big bold letters, the headline read "Seniors Find Freedom at Flower Shop." A thrill of excitement rose up in her when she saw her shop as the top news story. However, after reading the first few sentences, her delight turned to dismay.

As she read on, her stomach churned with nausea. Bob was quoted stating the need to go to war with The Gardens while also slipping in the fact that he was a vet who wasn't getting the respect he deserved. "I fought for this country, and The Gardens doesn't seem to honor that sacrifice. I took a bullet once, and I'm willing to take a bullet again for the shop."

Oh no.

George's quote said he and his friends were forced to seek refuge where they could play cards so their minds could stay alert. He mentioned how The Gardens was forbidding them from playing. He, of course, didn't mention anything about the gambling.

Joanna was cited begging her grandson to sneak her cold french fries so she wouldn't go hungry since The Gardens wouldn't give them food. That's where the quote ended, making it sound as if the facility was starving them.

Delphinium's mouth hung open as she read on.

Arlene and Gurdy talked about how being put to work at the shop helped them stay positive and active since all they were doing at The Gardens was sitting in their rooms waiting to die.

Delphinium groaned. *What have you guys done? What have I done?*

Patsy mentioned the severe lack of "proper entertainment" at The Gardens and the fact that they were forced to find it elsewhere. She told of her past in frequenting casinos and compared The Gardens to a mortuary home.

Helen was the only one who solely mentioned the flower shop, and even that was bad. She stated how she finally felt useful again after being assigned to fold rags.

Every word was more condemning and dreadful than the next. She was mortified to be associated with this horrible slam against The Gardens. Every quote from the seniors was exaggerated and taken out of context. Only a tenth of what she had told Kathryn had made it into the article.

There was practically nothing about the history of the building or her efforts to preserve the legacy. Nothing was said about the creativity she put into her floral arrangements or all the work and price cuts she gave for the Fourth of July parade floats, Christmas pageants at the elementary school, or Veterans Day wreaths. It didn't mention the shop in any detail other than to portray it as a place of refuge from the neglect and borderline abuse the seniors had to endure at The Gardens. The description of the facility was damaging to its reputation in every statement. Statements that were damaging enough for lawsuits.

A creeping panic built up in her chest. All the air in her lungs was leaving her.

This is bad.

This is really, really bad.

Elliot's going to kill me.

Seventeen

Delphinium had to stop and take deep breaths to keep her hyperventilation under control. The pressure in her chest felt like an indication of a heart attack. How could Kathryn have done this? She had promised the piece wouldn't paint The Gardens in a bad light.

How stupid was I to trust a stranger? I have only my own selfishness to blame for this being printed. If I had been more focused on the seniors instead of my shop, I never would've talked to Kathryn.

She couldn't believe she had agreed to the interview that would no doubt put Elliot on the defense. But it wasn't an interview. It was a list of horrible citations against the nursing home. For Elliot, who was so concerned about appropriate and positive PR for the facility, this was a death sentence.

Although the article didn't specifically name The Gardens, the statements about the "senior living facility" in Moonberry Lake made it quite clear. Any resident would be able to figure it out, and the clear link of her involvement made her feel as though she had blood on her hands. The story explained how it all began from the lack of air-conditioning and the seniors fleeing so they wouldn't die of heatstroke. Everything was covered—the rules against card playing, the hunger strike, and their plan to save the shop by walking around downtown and handing out flowers.

Delphinium reached in her bag for her phone and saw five missed calls had gone to voicemail. Her heart pounded as she listened to the first message. It was Henry telling her not to worry and that he was working on it. The second, third, and fourth calls were from Elliot, whose curt tone made her wince. He asked her repeatedly to call him back. And the fifth was from George asking her to pick up some soft peppermints and a tube of arthritis cream.

Unbelievable. They have no clue what they've done.

First, she had to call Kathryn. She had to see what she could do to rectify this before she spoke to Elliot. Luckily, the reporter picked up immediately.

"Kathryn, how could you do this?"

"Delphinium?"

"Of course it's me. I'm calling about this horrible article."

To her credit, Kathryn sounded shocked. "I don't know what you mean. I kept my word and never mentioned The Gardens."

"You didn't have to. Everyone in town knows it's The Gardens. What all the seniors said makes the place look like they're being held at Guantanamo Bay!"

"I admit that some of their statements came across as bold."

Delphinium scoffed. "*Bold?* Are you kidding me?"

"The piece wasn't as strong without the personal testimonies and quotes from the residents. What you're reading is nothing they haven't said to you in person."

"Yes, but I'm able to put it all into context and take their personalities into account. I know how stubborn and dramatic the guys can be, especially Bob with his war analogies. They tend to exaggerate the issue to get attention. They're bored and like stirring up drama, but readers don't know that about them."

"Well, I'm sorry you didn't like the article. My editor loved it so much, she insisted on putting it on the front page. It's my first front-page piece, Delphinium. I've never had the cover story before. I've only ever been stuck on the back pages. And you're not going to believe the buzz the piece is already getting. It's going to be reprinted in bigger papers. There's already talk of a follow-up story. This is hot news for our small town."

Delphinium felt a sinking feeling in her gut. "No, Kathryn. This article is going to hurt a lot of people."

"I'm sorry you feel that way. I don't know what else to say."

"Say that you'll write a retraction that paints The Gardens in a better light! Their reputation is on the line."

There was a pause. "I can't do that, but I will go to my editor and express your concerns about the reputation of The Gardens."

Delphinium hung up feeling ill and knew her next call was going to be terrible. There was nothing else it could be but horrible. Taking a deep breath, she prepared herself for the worst—an explosion of angry yelling, a tongue-thrashing of biblical proportions, or worse, a chilling low whisper of accusation and threat.

Her heart pounded as she dialed Elliot's number. It went straight to his voicemail, which somehow made her feel worse. She called again, and on the third time, she left a short message.

"Elliot. This is Delphinium. I am so sorry about the article. It's all a mistake and was taken completely out of context. I've already called the newspaper. Please call me back. I'll . . . I'll be waiting to hear from you."

Her voice started to quiver at the end, and she hung up quickly. How was he ever going to forgive her? He would see this act of betrayal for exactly what it was—a desperate Hail Mary to save her shop. It was completely self-seeking, and he would perceive her motives as conniving and selfish.

She knew deep down there was no saving the shop and her apartment. Denying reality was much easier than facing the pain of a lost dream and the sadness that accompanies disappointment. She had agreed to the article in a moment of panic rooted in denial.

What a stupid move.

What a stupid, selfish, desperate move.

Feeling sick, she sat down and put her head between her legs and tried to calm down. The feeling—no, the *knowing*—that she had lost much more than the shop left her gasping for breath. This Hail Mary pass was not going to save the game. It was a colossal failure displayed in front of everyone. She could handle looking like a failure to most people—it was looking horrible to one person that stung the most.

There was no way Elliot would forgive her for this.

Within hours, handfuls of people showed up at the shop simply out of curiosity. They kept glancing around looking for the seniors. Then there were the lookie-loos who weren't even discreet in their search for the described senior activity. Some actually asked for a tour of the back room. Very few purchases were made, and when Delphinium realized that the article did nothing to drive up interest in the shop, she didn't even care.

After she caught someone who had snuck in the back, she closed up altogether and taped a sign to the door that read "Phone orders only."

It had been two days since the article came out, and Elliot still hadn't returned her calls. She had hardly been able to eat or sleep. When she went over to The Gardens to talk to him in person, she had discovered that her name was put on a list of individuals banned from the facility. *Banned!*

Desperate, she made a phone call under a pseudonym, making up a story of how she wanted to move to the facility. It worked. She just hoped Elliot would interpret her trickery as how frantic she was to apologize.

"This is Elliot Sturgis."

She paused for a moment when she heard the curtness in his voice. The coolness of his tone intimidated her, and she was glad that they weren't face-to-face.

"Elliot, it's Delphinium. I'm sorry to trick you into answering my call, but I was desperate."

Silence.

"Elliot?"

"What is it you want, Ms. Hayes?"

She should have guessed that he would return to addressing her formally. She had broken any trust and obliterated any friendship they had. "You called me before, and I left you a voicemail."

"I changed my mind about talking with you, Ms. Hayes. I decided there would be no point to it. You've said quite enough."

This was going exactly how she thought it would. "I want to say how sorry I am. The article was never supposed to sound so awful. It was a mistake. Please believe me when I say it was not my intention to hurt you or The Gardens. I was promised the facility wouldn't specifically be mentioned, but I had no idea about the quotes from the seniors or that they would be so horrible. I truly regret it and want to make it up to you. Please accept my deepest apology."

Silence.

"You and I have nothing to discuss. I don't think you realize the lasting effects this article is going to have on The Gardens. Not to mention my reputation as director. The damage has been done and is irreversible. The people of this town will remember the words of that article long after tomorrow. There is nothing you can do to rectify the situation."

Tears prickled her eyes. "I know it seems bad, but I—"

"*Bad?*" he repeated loudly. "Do you have any idea what this article has set into motion? I am actually being questioned on whether or not I have inflicted abuse. Actual *physical* and *emotional* abuse because of the supposed hunger strike and the seniors' need to leave the facility in order to relax and have fun. Not only will I probably lose my job, but my reputation is on the cusp of being ruined to the point that I may never work as an administrator again. You've destroyed my career and my livelihood." He took a long, ragged breath. There was no question of how shook he was by this disaster she'd orchestrated.

He continued to speak in the same livid tone. "I blame myself for being so unguarded. I naively thought you cared about these people.... About ... The Gardens. The damage of this article will ruin everything that I've worked for. I've poured myself into making this a stellar retirement establishment and caring facility. I am proud of the safety record and nurturing environment we've created, which in one day, with one interview, was erased."

Delphinium couldn't hold back her sobs. "I'm so sorry. I don't know what more to say." Her words came out in a whisper, so she cleared her throat. "The reporter took the quotes out of context. I never meant to hurt your reputation or portray the nursing home in such a bad light."

"For the past two days, I have been constantly on the phone fielding angry calls and answering questions from family members who believe we are actually *harming* their loved ones and want to withdraw them. Do you know how that makes me feel? To actually be accused of hurting these vulnerable people that I have diligently watched over, always keeping their best interests in mind?"

"It was a mix-up. The reporter promised me she'd only write a story that could possibly save my shop."

"I see." The sharpness of his voice could cut glass. "Let me get this straight. In an effort to save your shop, you decided to destroy my career and reputation?"

"No!"

Silence.

"I trusted you, Ms. Hayes. That was my mistake. I thought you were on my side in wanting what was best for the seniors. I thought you ... I thought you were different, something special," he added quietly.

Her stream of tears was endless.

"I was. I am," she said, completely congested.

"In case you haven't guessed it by now, The Gardens will no longer be providing transportation to your shop, and you are no longer welcome here after you've invited such slander against this establishment. You are banned from this building."

Her voice came out as a small squeak. "I understand."

"I cannot forbid the seniors from visiting you, but I will be speaking to them and announcing that not only are you banned from this facility but the board of directors is looking into a lawsuit for defamation against the paper and you."

She couldn't speak.

The abrupt click of him hanging up made her wince.

She was wiping her eyes when Henry walked in, but the tears wouldn't stop.

"Now, now," he said, patting her back in a hug, "this will blow over. It's all a misunderstanding."

"It's not. I just got off the phone with Elliot and he's furious. He *hates* me. He'll never trust me or forgive me for this. His job is at risk because of me."

"He doesn't hate you."

"Yes, he does. You didn't hear him."

Henry continued patting her back lightly, like a parent soothing an upset child. "Take a breath."

She did.

"We've all gone to talk to him and expressed our regret in going overboard with our complaints. Even Bob apologized for comparing him to a dictator. Just let some time pass. For the majority of Moonberry Lake residents, I think people will see this as a ranting from seniors who have too much time on their hands."

Delphinium wasn't convinced as she took another ragged breath.

"Now." Henry pulled back from their embrace to look her in the eye. "We need to focus on the issue of the shop."

She gave a sad not. She knew what was coming next.

"The clock is counting down, and it doesn't look good. It's time to face the truth and prepare yourself. You're going to have to close up. You owe more on the mortgage than what the property is worth. Your only choice is to walk away. Big and small businesses have done it before. You just got in over your head. It happens."

She nodded, knowing the devastating repercussions would prevent her from being a business owner again. "I'm going to use the last week and a half to clear out inventory and pack up the apartment."

Henry gave a short nod of approval. "It's been a good run. You were a wonderful florist. Now it's time for your next adventure."

"Yeah," she said glumly.

"Do you have any idea what that might be?"

"No. What about you? What are you going to do?"

Henry tilted his head, giving her a small, sad smile. "I suppose it's time I start acting my age." He scanned the shop with a tender look of nostalgia. "I have to admit, I loved coming here. It was good to have a reason to get out of bed in the morning." He looked at her with his kind eyes and took both of her hands in his. "Thank you for giving this old goat a purpose."

"You still have a purpose, Henry. I'm still going to need you. You're my family. Whatever I do next, I want your input and presence. You're not getting rid of me."

Henry's lopsided smile wavered. "Annie would've been proud of the lovely woman you've become and how hard you've worked."

"Apparently, I didn't work hard enough."

"Nonsense. It doesn't matter how you finish in the race but how you run. And let me tell you, the beauty you created with flowers and the kindness you extended to the customers and to all of us, that matters greatly. You are indeed Annie's granddaughter, which makes you a gem. You'll find another way to work with your gifting."

Delphinium's lip trembled. "She told you that's what she called it?"

He nodded.

What she would give to have Annie with her now. "I need to go to the bank. If I'm going to lose this place, I want to do it with a little dignity and not have the locks changed on me."

"Mind if I tag along? Sometimes bad medicine is easier to choke down when you have company."

"Sure." She gave him a gentle hug, lingering for a moment to inhale the honeysuckle scent. He always had her best interests in mind and was bonded by genuine love. She couldn't imagine a more wonderful grandfather figure.

Later at the bank, her mortgage broker went over the stipulations of the foreclosure if she couldn't pay a week from Friday. Her stomach turned as the true reality of the situation sank in. Delphinium thought it was ridiculous to delay the inevitable that long and was ready to sign the necessary documents, but Henry, who sat in the chair to her left, placed his hand over hers, holding her back. He had been right. She would be walking away with nothing.

But even though that was monetarily true, she was still walking away with memories she'd cherish for the rest of her life. The shop had been an amazing experience where she had been able to fully express herself through bouquets and arrangements. And getting to know all the seniors had filled her life with happiness and rich memories that she'd always look back on and laugh.

"What is going to come of the place?" Henry asked the bank representative.

"We already have a potential sale. An individual who has expressed immediate interest in buying the property is waiting to see if you do indeed default on your loan. If you do, you will need to move out within twenty-four hours."

Delphinium frowned, fiddling with the hem of her shirt. "Well, I hope that they don't change it much. It's a wonderful historic building with a lot of character."

The woman wasn't paying attention to their sentimentality as she perused the unsigned documents.

"Do you know what the shop will be turned into?" Henry pressed.

The woman looked up from the papers. "Just a business office, I think. The buyer was interested in the property because of the prime location on Main Street. He approached us weeks ago and asked to buy as quickly as possible when it becomes available."

"What kind of business?" Henry asked.

"I can't legally reveal the other party."

"What does it matter now?" He leaned back in his chair. "It's practically a done deal. This is Moonberry Lake. Everyone's going to know in a matter of days anyway. I probably could just as easily go to the local bar and find out."

The woman sighed, clearly exhausted by their visit and wanting them to move on. "I suppose it doesn't matter if you know. I believe it's a real estate business."

Henry frowned.

"A law office is expanding and including high-end real estate offerings as well," the woman continued.

"Someone local? Anyone we know?"

The woman, looking bored with the entire conversation, picked up a piece of paper and read from it. "The McCormack Law Firm. The buyer being a man named Mason McCormack."

Delphinium froze. Henry rubbed his forehead and groaned.

"Sir, are you okay?" the woman asked, her eyes wide with concern.

"I'm fine," he answered. "Just feeling a kick to my stomach."

Delphinium popped up from her seat. "Thank you for seeing us. We won't take up any more of your time." She turned to Henry and took his hand. "Let's get you some fresh air."

They both walked out of the office in a sort of daze. Neither spoke until they got in the car and were on the road.

Delphinium kept her gaze straight. "I feel like such a chump."

"That makes two of us."

"When I think of all the times he came into the shop," she said, shaking her head. "He wasn't interested in buying flowers, he was checking the place out and trying to figure out where he'd put his furniture!"

Henry was quiet, staring out the window. "I'm sorry," he finally said. "I should have picked up on something."

"How?" she said, peering at him. "All he did was come in the shop and purchase flowers. How is that sketchy?"

"I should've done a background check on him." He tsked. "Especially since I was pushing him on you." He went back to peering out the window, distressed.

It was a short drive to The Gardens. She pulled up to the sidewalk on the side of the building.

Delphinium put the car in park. "I better not get any closer. I don't want Elliot to see me if he's out of his office."

Henry leaned over to give her a kiss on her cheek. "I'll call you later."

Delphinium went home and changed into her painting clothes. She was going to have to make large "Going Out of Business" signs for the front windows.

She gathered all the supplies, and just when she got on her hands and knees to draw letters on butcher paper that she had rolled out on the floor, a repeated knocking on the front window made her look up. She saw a familiar face pressed up against the glass, waving a white tissue frantically.

Delphinium frowned.

Kathryn Hughes.

She shook her head, but Kathryn knocked on the glass again and mouthed "*Please.*"

Delphinium got up and walked over to the door and opened it only a few inches.

"I have nothing to say to you, Kathryn. Literally *nothing*—on or off the record."

"Please, I come in peace. I have to talk to you."

"What do you want?"

"Can I please come in?"

"No. Now is not a good time."

"I want to make this up to you. All the seniors have been calling the newspaper demanding that I print another story."

"Good."

"No, it's a mess. They are telling my editor I took advantage of a situation to write a seedy exposé rather than a feel-good story and that I took advantage of them because of their age. All of them vowed to drag my name through the mud and go to another paper citing elder discrimination. Bob swore that he could convince anyone that they were not all mentally competent when I interviewed them."

Delphinium crossed her arms over her chest. "Sounds about right."

"My reputation as a reporter is going to be ruined."

"Along with a lot of other things, like the reputation of The Gardens and its director. It's called the power of the pen."

Kathryn peered down. "I know. Just give me three minutes of your time," she pleaded.

Delphinium sighed and moved to the side, allowing Kathryn to step through.

She looked down at the butcher paper and read the letters Delphinium had drawn so far. *GOING OUT OF BUSI—*

"I really thought the article would save the store," she said.

Delphinium didn't respond.

"Remember when I said I had a hunch there was a deeper story here?"

"Yeah. When you saw the seniors dancing in the back room."

Kathryn nodded. "The thing is, I don't think the story of the shop was the one that needed to be told. I think the story should have been about *you.*"

Delphinium crossed her arms over her chest again. "More investigative journalism? You're going to try to dig up dirt on me?"

Kathryn let out a nervous chuckle. "What can I say, all those episodes of *Cops* I've watched have gotten into my brain. If I have to do light editorial pieces, I like them to have a little bite."

Delphinium kept her expression neutral. "Sorry to disappoint you, but I live a pretty quiet life. You're not going to find much dirt."

"I'm not looking for dirt. I'm looking for heart, and you have it."

Delphinium stared at her.

Kathryn sighed. "Look, I'm sorry for how the article came across, but my editor is insisting on a follow-up piece that kind of smooths things over with The Gardens."

Delphinium went over to a ficus and began rubbing one of its waxy leaves between her fingers. "What's done is done."

Kathryn frowned. "I hate that saying."

"Me too."

Kathryn took a step closer to her. "So help me write an in-depth piece about you. People would love to read about the way you've engaged the seniors and got them out of their normal routines."

Delphinium stuffed her hands into the pocket of her apron. "Sorry, not interested. No comment. Now or ever."

Kathryn's shoulders fell. "I deserve that." She looked around at the empty flower containers. "It's really over for the store?"

Delphinium nodded, then went back over to the sign and started on the next letter.

"If you change your mind, will you give me a call?"

"I won't," Delphinium said flatly.

Kathryn began walking out when Delphinium spoke up. "Do everyone a favor, Kathryn, and cut down on the cop shows. There's enough ugliness in the world. You don't need to add to it."

Kathryn glanced back guiltily, then slipped out the door.

Eighteen

Delphinium answered the phone that night only because the caller ID showed Lindsey's name. "Hello?"

"Hey, I'm coming over. We've got to talk," her friend said quickly before hanging up.

Delphinium got up and unlocked the door.

Ten minutes later, her friend barged into the apartment not bothering to knock. "Have you seen this?" She waved the newspaper in her hand. "I had to finish my class or I would've been over sooner. A couple of my clients were poring over it. That's how I found out. It's officially the hottest town gossip. Forget about the saying, 'today's news is tomorrow's trash.' People are holding onto this and passing it around."

Delphinium nodded. "Yep. The tornado's been unleashed, and the harm's been done."

Lindsey sucked in through her teeth. "Yikes. That bad?"

"Worse. Elliot won't talk to me and might even lose his job."

Lindsey plunked down on the plush sofa.

"And to cap off an already rotten week, I found out who is buying this building," Delphinium said.

"Who?"

"Mason McCormack. Isn't that just the cherry on top?"

Lindsey paled.

"What's wrong?"

"I need to tell you something."

Delphinium waited.

"I . . . well, he . . ." Lindsey swallowed.

"What is it?"

"Mason is the guy I've been dating," Lindsey blurted out.

Delphinium stared at her friend. "That's not funny."

"It's true."

Delphinium balked. "What? How? Why?" She spat out each word with repulsion. "Why didn't you tell me it was *him* you were dating? We talk all the time. How could you not tell me?"

"He asked for my number after we spent the afternoon here with Henry and everybody."

"The guy is *playing* you!"

Lindsey threw her hands up. "He seemed really nice. I've only been on a few dates with him, but he brings me flowers every time."

"I know. I'm the one that put together the bouquets for each one of them!"

Her friend shrank back into the sofa. "Why are you getting so upset?"

"Because he used me to get to you! You can't trust him."

Lindsey sat up ramrod straight. "Why? Because you can't smell him?" She rolled her eyes. "Yeah, he told me, and that's exactly why I didn't say anything to you."

"It's not only that . . . There's just something about him. He's too smooth in how he ends and begins relationships."

"He's actually a really sweet guy," Lindsey defended in a calmer voice. "Or, at least, I thought he was. He never told me he was buying the shop."

"Exactly! You've just proven my point about him. The man is a wolf in sheep's clothing."

Lindsey frowned, biting down on her lower lip. "I've gotta go. I need to figure this out. I'll talk to you later." She left the apartment too quickly for Delphinium to stop her.

Delphinium slept fitfully that night, wrestling with the blankets as she pondered how her life was not turning out at all as she planned. She stared at the ceiling so long, the darkness began to lighten with morning. She wanted to cry or scream or do something to release the awful feeling inside her but was too tired to do anything. Fatigue settled over her like a thick fog. Disappointment over losing the shop had sucked out her energy to react. Plus, the sadness over what felt like a betrayal to Elliot kept her clutching the blanket tightly.

She turned onto her side and squeezed her eyes shut. She'd sleep in. She'd stay there as long as she wanted. There was no reason to get out of bed. There was no need to rush. The store didn't need to be opened on time. No new orders were going to be placed. She was going to open late on the off chance someone wanted to buy a fairy house or flower-scented candle on clearance. She'd put a display outside of all the leftover flowers and see if she could sell any at a bundle discount.

Focusing on blocking out the conversation with Elliot that kept replaying in her head, she was about to turn on some music to help drown out her regretful thoughts when she heard something.

A shout.

No.

It was more of a chant.

The voices were familiar.

She lifted her head and listened more carefully.

The chant was relentless. "Save our shop! Save our shop! Save our shop!"

Delphinium threw off the covers and ran to the window. She gasped at the image on the street below.

You've got to be kidding me! What are they doing now?

Her elderly friends were sprawled out across the sidewalk like scattered matchsticks. *Did they all fall down?* She grabbed her phone

194

to call an ambulance and took off at a sprint in her pajamas. After flying down the stairs and rushing outside, she knelt by Arlene first since she was closest to the shop door.

"Are you okay?" she asked in a winded voice. "Did you fall?"

"Oh, we're dandy, honey," Arlene replied with a big smile.

"What on earth are you guys doing?" Delphinium panted, looking at them all.

"We snuck out early this morning to come and try to save the shop one last time," Joanna responded from a few feet away. "I called my grandson and told him we needed a ride and that it was a matter of life and death. He's over there." She pointed to a bored teenager leaning against the building scrolling through his phone, completely oblivious to what was going on. He didn't seem the least bit concerned that his grandmother was lounging out on the sidewalk.

Delphinium glanced over. "He doesn't look old enough to have a license."

"He has his driver's permit." Joanna smiled proudly. "Plus, he has his fishing license as well."

Delphinium gasped. "That doesn't count when transporting you guys!"

Arlene patted her on the cheek. "Don't worry, honey. He's a smart cookie. He's the one that suggested Gurdy ride on my lap since she's the smallest."

"Oh, yeah, that's great." Delphinium rolled her eyes. "It's nice to know he's aware of the laws of the road."

Gurdy waved. She was blocking the entrance to the neighboring store. "Hi, sweetie. We're protesting like we did in the sixties!" The petite woman was lying on a yoga mat with her legs up as she did little bicycle movements in the air. She looked like a child peddling an imaginary tricycle.

"And you all had to protest from the *ground*?"

"We figured if we stood, we'd get tired too fast," Patsy yelled from farther down the sidewalk. "I've got arthritic feet."

"You look like you've all been plowed over and can't get up," Delphinium said.

"Well, that might be true," Patsy answered. "I don't think I will be able to get up without help."

Gurdy raised her arm with a fist. "We've got to keep this protest moving!"

Delphinium moved over to her. "Gurdy, why are you peddling your legs like that?"

"It keeps me from getting stiff. I'm missing my morning Zumba."

Delphinium shook her head. "You're all ridiculous, you know that? This isn't going to help the shop. You're only going to give people a scare."

"That's really not our intention, sweetie," Joanna said.

"We wanted to protest and do a sit-in like we did in the old days, but most of our bodies wouldn't allow it, so we ended up leaning back and kind of fell over," Patsy explained. "It became sort of a domino effect. The sit-in turned into a *lie-down*. But it doesn't matter. Our spirits are still in this fight, and we're going to prevent them from tearing down this place!"

Delphinium shook her head. "Oh, Patsy. The shop isn't being torn down. It's being peacefully sold to another buyer—an exchange of hands. You're not stopping any bulldozers. There's no wrecking ball."

The old woman didn't look pleased with that nugget of information. "That does put a damper on our fight." She frowned. But then she shrugged. "Well, we may have gotten that part wrong, but we still want to protest the closing of your cute shop." She cupped her hands around her mouth and yelled, "Save our shop!" Gurdy and Arlene joined in, clapping their hands. "Save our shop! Save our shop!" they shouted in unison.

A loud moan came from George. "This protest had better work, because this cement is as cold and hard as a rock."

"It's a *sidewalk*, George. What did you expect?" Delphinium crawled over to him. "None of you should have attempted to sit down. When was the last time you were even on the ground?"

"Voluntarily?" George asked. "It's been about three decades."

"Come on, let me help you up."

He swatted her hand away. "No. We are doing this whether you object or not. We screwed up by talking to that reporter and we want to fix it."

"So you are going to protest even if I don't want you to?" Delphinium asked.

George nodded. "Yes. We know what's best for you even if you don't. Don't question our wisdom. I've got nearly a half century on you, which means I'm right in any circumstance. You don't argue with an elder. Period."

Delphinium shook her head. "You're as stubborn as a mule."

"I'll take that as a compliment," George said, giving her a wink. "The mule is an underrated animal. It has stamina."

Bob groaned as if in agony. "I've been in foxholes with more cushion."

Delphinium looked around. A crowd of people was beginning to form. Strangers were crossing the street and getting out of their cars to come over.

Delphinium got up and walked to Joanna. "This is out of control! You all have to get up from the sidewalk right now. This doesn't look like a protest—it looks like some mass takeout! You're attracting the *wrong* kind of attention."

Joanna let out a little laugh. "Honey, when you reach my age, any attention is *good* attention—and it doesn't hurt to be wearing the right shade of lipstick to feel pretty." She unzipped the rhinestone-covered fanny pack strapped to her waist and pulled out a tube of her favorite fuchsia color. "Want some?"

People were approaching and asking if they needed help, to which all the seniors responded, "Yes, please buy some flowers from this shop."

All except Bob who responded to one lady, "Do you have a pillow?"

"Come on, we have to get you guys up," Delphinium said, giving her hand to Joanna. "And I'm not taking no for an answer."

"I don't think I can get back up," George said, wincing. "My back is spasming." He let out a little cry.

"Me either," Patsy whined. "I'll wait for some big, strong men. I've always had a fantasy of being carried by a firefighter." She gave Delphinium a pointed look. "Don't let anyone touch me except a fireman—a big, strong fireman. I know there are women firefighters now and that they do an excellent job, but I insist on a burly man hoisting me up into his arms."

Delphinium's jaw dropped. "For heaven's sake, Patsy, if you don't get up, the only thing you're going to be hoisted up into is an ambulance!"

"You all should have brought a yoga mat like me," Gurdy said. "I'm comfortable."

"That's because you're the weight of my granddaughter," George shouted at her. "It doesn't count because you're already close to the ground."

Gurdy giggled at his reasoning.

Delphinium carefully pulled Joanna into a sitting position. "We'll take this one step at a time. Let me know when you're ready to stand. I'll go on one side and your grandson will go on the other and we'll lift you from under your arms slowly and gently."

Joanna nodded. "Okay. But first I want to wait for the people from the newspaper to get here. I called them last night."

Delphinium dropped her forehead into her hand. "Oh, no. You didn't!"

Joanna grinned. "It's the best way to get attention for the store and get my picture in the paper at the same time. I wanted to look camera-ready so I applied some fake eyelashes. Took me nearly a half hour to get them straight."

Delphinium looked more closely at her and noticed that the row of lashes on her left eye looked like they were crawling toward her eyebrow.

Joanna shooed her away with her hand. "Now, don't ruin my chance to get in the paper. I'm hoping to make the front page. I've never been in the newspaper before, and the only other chance I'll ever get will be in the obituary section—and I won't even be around to enjoy that! Grant an old lady a wish and let me sit here and pose for a bit longer," Joanna pleaded.

"Help! My back is seizing up. I can't move," Bob yelled. "This bomber aircraft has gone down. Mayday! Mayday!"

"Stop being such a baby, Bob," Arlene shouted over his cries. "I made less noise giving birth."

Bob responded with another long melody of moans, which sounded eerily like the call of a humpback whale.

Delphinium moved over to him. "Can I help you shift onto your side and rub your back to stop the spasms?"

Bob covered his face with his arms. "It's too late. I'm a goner. Save the rest."

"Is it over yet? Are we done?" Helen yelled from behind.

Delphinium turned and found her sitting in the front of her walker under the awning of the next shop over. She hadn't noticed her before.

"Did we save the shop? Can I go inside now?" Helen asked.

"Man down! Man down!" George cried out.

A couple of people ran over and knelt at his side, asking what they could do.

"My back feels like it's breaking!" George yelled at them. "Don't touch me unless you're a trained professional, like a masseuse. Where are the woman paramedics?"

Between the folks on the ground and the good Samaritans hurrying to what looked like a horrible accident, Delphinium felt like everyone was talking or complaining at the same time. The only thing that pierced the volume of commotion was the sound of sirens.

Of course.

Two ambulances and three police cars came to a screeching halt in front of the shop. All of Moonberry Lake's first responders were being used up. Joanna was going to get her wish. This was going to be front-page news.

I'm never going to live this down. The only thing missing is a—

The unmistakable wail of a fire truck siren pierced the air.

There it is. The fire truck has arrived.

"I want the firefighters! Don't touch me. I want a firefighter!" Patsy yelled over the noise. She swatted and even tried to kick anyone who came close to her.

A medic came over to Delphinium as she was trying to put one arm under Joanna, but the old woman kept trying to shoo her away. "Not yet. I need my picture!"

Delphinium looked at the medic. "I need help getting them all up and standing."

"We need to check them for injuries first," a tall medic said.

"I was shot!" Bob called out.

Everyone gave a collective gasp. Three medics ran to his side. "Where?" they asked, scanning his body up and down.

"Vietnam."

The medics all looked at each other, then one of them said to his partner, "We're going to need more help."

Nineteen

D elphinium! Delphinium!" a voice called out.

Delphinium followed the voice and saw Kathryn running toward the scene. A college-age man was jogging alongside her with an expensive-looking camera against his chest. Kathryn had her phone out and was filming as she approached. The young man immediately started snapping pictures.

"Here! Take my picture! Take mine!" Joanna called out to him, waving her hand and lying back down, but this time, she lay on her side with one hand on her hip. She looked as relaxed and happy as if she were lounging on a warm beach.

Delphinium wanted to go and hide. The situation could not look worse.

A police officer approached her. "Ma'am, how did all of these people get on the ground?"

Delphinium decided that telling the truth was the only way to go. She swallowed and looked him straight in the eye. "I have no idea how they got down on the ground considering their condition and age. I simply found them this way."

Soon every senior had EMTs helping them sit up so they could check their vitals before boosting them to a stance.

Delphinium went over to Helen, who was still sitting on the seat of her walker. "Are you okay?" she asked.

Helen raised the small Styrofoam cup she was holding. "I wasn't about to miss out on all the excitement, but I knew there was no way I was getting on the ground. That's only going to happen when they are lowering me *into* the ground."

Delphinium noticed the little homemade sign she was holding in her other hand with "Anything helps" written in shaky scroll.

She groaned. "Helen, you can't sit here holding that sign."

"Why not?"

"Because people are going to take it the wrong way. It looks like you're living on the street and asking for money."

Helen looked inside her cup. "I thought it was too good to be true when someone gave me a ten-dollar bill. I hoped they wanted to save the shop as much as we do. It also explains why a nice woman gave me this bag of little oranges."

Delphinium looked down on the ground next to the walker and, sure enough, there was a bag of oranges and a bagel.

"Tell you what," Helen told her, "I'll eat the bagel and you take the ten dollars for your shop. We'll split the oranges."

Just as Delphinium opened her mouth to respond, someone behind her spoke in a very clipped tone.

"Ms. Hayes."

Oh, no. She'd recognize that voice anywhere. *You've got to be kidding me.*

She slowly turned around. Dressed in his perfectly tailored navy suit, looking wonderful except for the hardened scowl on his face, was Elliot. The juxtaposition between them would be laughable if it didn't look so tragic. A man standing polished and preened next to a not-yet-showered hot mess in mismatched pajamas, her hair pluming out like a peacock, looking fit for a mug shot that's shown to youth as a warning on what not to become.

She felt fury emanating from him and was unable to make herself talk. She half-expected smoke to come out of his nose and ears like a cartoon character.

His face was hard as marble as he surveyed the chaotic scene in front of him, clearly struggling to keep his composure before turning back to her. "I am at a loss for words on what to say about this, Ms. Hayes. I received a call from the police that many of my residents were found *lying* on the ground outside your shop."

"This wasn't my idea, I swear! I had no clue they were going to do something this wild."

"I have a hard time believing that."

"It's true! Ask Helen." She turned to Helen. "Tell him."

Helen raised her Styrofoam cup and spoke as a bit of bagel fell out of her mouth. "Anything helps. God bless you."

Delphinium grasped her head with both hands, feeling like it might explode. "Helen, this is Mr. Sturgis from The Gardens. Don't you recognize him? He came to see why you are all here lying on the ground like casualties."

Helen frowned, looking him up and down. "He doesn't look familiar, but it looks like he's got money by the way he's dressed." She jiggled her cup. "Spare change? Please, sir, loose coins for the poor."

Elliot's glare made Delphinium shrink a couple inches. She noticed the side of his jaw tic a couple times from how hard he was clenching his teeth. The man was going to grind his molars to dust just from knowing her. She tried letting out a nervous chuckle, but it came out more like an asthmatic wheeze.

Okay, forget Helen. She'd get one of the others to plead her innocence. She looked over and scanned the crowd for someone sound of mind.

Patsy had her arms around the neck of a firefighter and was refusing to let go.

Joanna kept changing poses and expressions as the photographer clicked away as if this was a photoshoot for *Vogue*.

Bob was being hoisted onto a stretcher and telling anyone who would listen about the war, repeating over and over, "They shot me! The enemy shot me!"

George was wrapped in a blanket, having his blood pressure

taken while talking animatedly to Kathryn, who was recording his words.

Arlene was sitting serenely in a kind of huddle, talking to strangers and getting to know them like this was some social gathering.

And Gurdy was doing some stretches and walking in place in front of some medics to prove she was unharmed. She had the medics chuckling, and they stopped her when she began doing little jumping jacks.

"The rest of them might be a little busy right now," she said to Elliot. "Where is Henry when I need him?" she hissed under her breath.

As if materializing out of thin air, Henry answered from behind her. "Here I am! I'm sorry I'm late."

He was hurrying toward her with a folded lawn chair in his arms.

"I couldn't fit in Joanna's grandson's car and had to call for a ride. Then I remembered that I forgot to bring a chair, so I stopped by the hardware store to pick one up."

Delphinium spoke slowly, punctuating her words. "Henry, please tell Mr. Sturgis that I had absolutely nothing to do with this"—she gestured toward the commotion all around them —"*protest*, or whatever you call it."

Henry scrunched his eyebrows together as he took in the spectacle. "Why are there paramedics and firefighters here? Who called the police?"

That was it.

Delphinium couldn't take it anymore.

She took a big breath and released the fire burning within her. "Because *your* pals decided to get down on the ground and then couldn't get back up!" she shouted, not caring that people stopped what they were doing and looked over at her. "Tell Elliot that I did not ask *any* of you to lie on the sidewalk like roadkill! Tell him that I never wanted any of this! Tell him that this is not my fault! Tell him that from day one, I never asked that any of you take over my shop, even though it doesn't matter now since you won't be able to come anymore."

She all but stomped her feet on the ground like a hysterical toddler, but she didn't care.

"Tell him that all this doesn't matter because I've lost the shop and my home, so this protest is a ridiculous waste of everyone's time!" Her voice broke with a ragged sob. "Tell him that my heart is breaking over disappointing you all. Tell him that everything I've worked for is gone, and all I want is for everyone to leave me alone so I can put up my 'Going Out of Business' sign and then cry for the rest of the day!"

Silence.

Absolute silence descended.

The air was so still, her last word seemed to echo.

Everyone appeared frozen as they stared at her. The seniors, the strangers, the medical crew, the police, Elliot—everyone.

She hadn't realized the full volume she had reached until the stillness that followed punctuated everything she had yelled.

Delphinium looked around at the faces of the seniors and saw expressions of shock and hurt. Shame shrouded her.

Henry stood pale and stricken, the wrinkled features on his face crumbling a bit more. Then his shoulders dropped along with his gaze, and all she could see was this very old man in front of her who she'd yelled at. She'd rebuked him for something that was only done with the intention of helping her.

The horror of lashing out at her beloved Henry hit her.

"I-I'm sorry," she apologized. "Henry . . ." She felt herself trembling. She turned to the other seniors. "I'm so sorry," she said, but it came out raspy because that was all the voice she had left. "I didn't mean to yell at you." Her voice broke, and the sobs inside her erupted.

There.

She'd done it. Her stifled cries released and there was no stopping the tears now.

She wept openly as everyone watched, unsure what to do.

Henry put a hand on her shoulder. "Delphi," he began.

But she shook her head. "Please forgive me," she managed to say in between sobs. "I know you were all just trying to help. You've been so kind, but this is entirely my fault. It's a lost cause. I lost the shop. I've lost Annie again."

Everyone continued to stare at her with sad eyes. When Joanna, Arlene, and Gurdy began crying, Delphinium's heart broke all over again.

She had never felt so exposed and raw. Everyone, strangers included, was a witness to her failure. They'd stumbled into a public screening of her emotional breakdown.

By the look of alarm on Henry's face, her outpour of emotions had clearly left him reeling. The embarrassment of her outburst and being blamed for this chaos was too much. It was as if it was all happening in slow motion. Everyone was getting a look at who she really was.

A complete disaster.

An incompetent mess who lost her business and her home.

The flower shop and her grandmother's apartment were lost, and she had nowhere to go. Her home was gone. The seniors wouldn't have another community gathering place like this to go to.

Drawing in a ragged breath, she hugged herself. Her legs felt weak, and the sadness weighing on her chest was too much to hold up. She wished she could dissolve right there into the sidewalk and not exist. She wanted, no, *needed* people to stop staring at her.

"Delphinium," Elliot said in a low voice, taking a step closer to her. His tone no longer had an edge to it but carried worry. Even softness.

He reached out to touch her arm, but she backed away. There was no mistaking the surprise and hurt that flashed across his face at her rejection. However, she knew one touch and she would crumble completely. Her knees were already locked to keep her from collapsing. She couldn't let that happen now.

She wouldn't humiliate herself any further in public.

She had to get out of there.

She wanted to run away.

She turned to the shop where she could hide from it all.

But just as she did, something caught her eye.

Something that took her last breath, leaving her staggering.

In between strangers, the police, medics, and firefighters, stood her wide-eyed parents, their mouths open.

Her parents. Who she hadn't talked to in weeks.

Delphinium couldn't move. She hadn't seen them in a year.

As any protective mother would, even one as reserved as Delphinium's, she dropped the carry-on bag draped over her shoulder and ran to her daughter. Wrapping her arms around Delphinium, she nudged her toward the shop.

"Let's get you inside," she said quietly, and Delphinium allowed her mother to usher her inside without looking back.

Twenty

Delphinium leaned against her mother, grateful for the support. The familiar scent of periwinkle, meaning intelligence and mental agility, enveloped her. Once inside the shop, her mother guided her to a stool behind the counter. Delphinium was thankful for the solid structure beneath her. She closed her eyes and rested her head in her hands.

It was over.

She was hidden away from that awful public scene. There was an actual wall separating her from the outside world and all the spectators, and that made her feel safe. Being enveloped by the peace of the shop was like being plucked out of a storm and set into the calm.

Her mother let out a loud sigh. "Let's just take a moment to catch our breath, shall we?" She kept smoothing her forehead as she paced back and forth, a habit Delphinium had seen her do all her life when she was puzzled or overwhelmed. On her third pass, she said, "That was—"

"A lot," Delphinium said, finishing the sentence.

"I was going to say *interesting*. Not quite the reception we expected." She kept pacing. "Let's keep breathing, shall we?"

Delphinium watched her mother's chest rise and fall with more loud breaths. The woman was never one for strong displays of emotion. Any act of hysteria rattled her, even when Delphinium was a child. "I had no idea all that was going to happen."

The confusion remained on her mother's face. "But all those people said they were out there for you. Isn't that correct?"

Delphinium wondered how to best answer but decided the shortest way to the truth was to simply agree. "Yes, at least the elderly ones."

Her mother's eyebrows went up. "You're telling me that all those people willingly chose to lie on the ground outside the shop?"

Delphinium nodded as a long sigh escaped her chest.

Her mother's mouth dropped open for a few seconds before she could articulate her words. "For heaven's sake, why would they do that?"

"Because they don't like the fact that I have to close the shop."

Her mother's eyes widened at that announcement. "What?! You're closing this shop? What on earth has happened since we last spoke?"

At that moment, the door swung open and her father entered the shop with the carry-on her mother had dropped on the sidewalk. He looked harried as he shut the door and turned the lock with a loud click. Once on the other side of the chaos, his shoulders dropped in relief. Apparently closing the door was symbolic of shutting out the world to both of them. The noise from the street was muted and it was just them.

Now that the three of them were away from the crowd and chaos, they all stared at each other. The reunion was so jarring, they all seemed to need a moment to recalibrate. The last time they were together was at Annie's funeral, and the goodbye had not been good. Delphinium had been distraught and needed time to process her grief alone.

Her parents looked a bit older but mostly frazzled from what they had walked in on. Her father peered at her with concern and a little fear that she hadn't seen since she broke her leg as a teenager. He was clearly perspiring from the stressful welcome by how sage filled the air. Sage indicated wisdom, but Delphinium always felt as if people could sense this about her father even if they couldn't smell what she did.

"I talked to Henry," he blurted out. "He gave me a brief summary of what happened. In addition, there was another gentleman from the nursing home who was very polite in answering my questions and appeared very concerned about your well-being. The police are clearing things up. Thank goodness they came, because it's a zoo out there. The majority of everyone is okay, with only one man needing to go to the hospital for his back, but it's nothing too severe. The others have received medical attention and are on their way back to the nursing home. Except for one woman who is insistent on riding in the fire truck."

Oh, Patsy.

He went over to her mother, took her hand, and looked at her. Without saying anything, she gave a small nod. "We haven't even had breakfast yet, but I feel as though I could use a drink," he said.

"Let's start over, shall we?" her mother said quietly.

Removed from the pandemonium, Delphinium was able to think more clearly. "What are you guys doing here?"

Her mother and father exchanged another look Delphinium couldn't read before responding.

"You haven't answered our calls in weeks," her mother finally said. "We were worried and wanted to check up on you to make sure you are okay, and from what we just saw, thank goodness we did."

"Why is everyone telling me that your shop is closing?" her dad asked.

As soon as Delphinium opened her mouth to speak, fresh tears began to roll down her cheeks in a steady stream, like a faucet unable to shut off. "Things haven't been going that well," she answered in a ragged whisper. "I've lost everything."

Her mother wrapped her arms around Delphinium. "But you love this shop. I don't understand."

Delphinium could only release another sob in response. She

felt like a little kid out of control. Her mother hadn't held her like this in years.

"Why don't we go upstairs and talk?" her father suggested, patting her on the back.

Delphinium got up and began to head toward her apartment. Her parents followed her up the back staircase and, once inside, directed Delphinium to the sofa. Her heaving sobs didn't let up for fifteen minutes. Her mother rubbed small circles on her back. Her father tried to ask what the matter was, but Delphinium couldn't articulate the words, so they sat quietly, waiting for her to speak. When her father couldn't find any tissues, he went to the bathroom and grabbed a roll of toilet paper for her to wipe her runny nose. Delphinium knew that neither of her parents were comfortable with big expressions of emotion, but to their credit, they sat with her, looking distraught.

After her cries had settled out of pure exhaustion, her head felt like it was pulsating from congestion.

"Why don't you go take a shower while we make tea?" her mother said. "We can always talk later."

Her father jumped up and headed to the kitchen, appearing relieved to have something to do.

Delphinium nodded and went to the bathroom to clean up. The hot water of her shower felt good and eased the tension in her body. She would have liked to stay there longer but knew her parents were waiting. A half hour later, Delphinium came into the kitchen dressed in yoga pants and an oversized T-shirt with her wet hair pulled into a messy bun. She found her parents sitting at the small kitchen table with their cups of tea. There was a third cup in front of the empty seat. Delphinium slid into it, took a sip of hot tea, then released a long breath.

The three of them sat there for a few minutes, absorbing the quiet. That was one thing the three of them were able to do well together, sit in comfortable silence. Only now, she felt as though they were waiting for her to talk first, perhaps afraid she'd get emotional again. After a few more minutes of sitting and sipping, her mother apparently decided to risk it.

"Start at the beginning," she said.

Delphinium didn't need any more prodding. The entire story of her financial fiasco and the senior debacle poured out of her, along with a new river of tears, but she was able to talk through it. She told them about Mason, Kathryn and the newspaper article, the seniors playing cards and hanging out in the back room, and Henry doing everything to help her keep the shop. Her parents listened without interrupting.

Two cups of tea and a sleeve of shortbread cookies later, she finished talking, and her parents stared at her, blinking. The fact that she could flummox such intelligent individuals was really something.

"Why wouldn't you have come to us earlier?" her father finally asked.

Delphinium looked down. "I wanted to fix it on my own since I'm the one that got myself into this mess. I didn't want to look like such a failure to you both."

Her father frowned. "We would never see you as a failure."

"The shop and apartment are a tremendous loss," her mother said. "Is it too late for us to help you? Perhaps we could write a check to cover—"

"Absolutely not," Delphinium interrupted. "I don't want you bailing me out of this hole. And I would never take away from the retirement you've carefully planned for, because it would require a lot of money."

The disturbed look on her mother's face remained. "Putting aside the financial debacle of the shop, the situation with the seniors from the nursing home is very . . . *unusual.*"

Her father nodded. "I agree. It's obvious you mean a great deal to them. Their passionate behavior on your behalf really shows the impact you've had on them. Their loyalty and love for you is impressive."

Delphinium sighed. "Which I've totally screwed up. I feel awful for how I screamed at Henry."

"Something tells me they have already forgiven you for your outburst," her mother said. "And Henry has always adored you."

"And what about the man who was standing next to you?" her father asked. "The younger one in the suit."

"Oh. That's Elliot Sturgis, the director of The Gardens."

Her parents exchanged glances. Her mother opened her mouth to speak and then closed it.

Delphinium knew what she was going to ask. "There's nothing going on between us. He is furious at me for ruining The Gardens' reputation in the newspaper article I mentioned. I agreed to the interview to hopefully bring in customers to save the shop last minute, but the reporter only ended up trashing The Gardens and making it look worse than prison." She fiddled with her napkin. "Elliot only came over this morning because the police called him about the seniors' protest. He hates me."

"I don't think he hates you," her father said. "As a matter of fact, he seemed rather upset himself. After your mother took you inside, he stopped me and apologized profusely."

Delphinium flinched. "For what?"

"For upsetting you. He told me to tell you he was sorry for misunderstanding the circumstances. It was obvious to everyone that you were not the mastermind behind the morning's event. There was no anger in his demeanor. He appeared very distressed and wanted to come in to see you, but I told him that your mother and I wanted to be with you alone."

Delphinium didn't know what to say to that.

"You did look a little—or a lot—disheveled." Her mother took a sip of tea. "The fact that you were still in your pajamas should have given him a hint over how unprepared you were for the protest."

Delphinium sunk lower in her chair. "I literally ran from bed when I saw the seniors sprawled on the ground. I thought they had fallen."

Her mother cleared her throat. "Well, we would like to meet your new friends."

Delphinium couldn't believe that was what she cared about the most or that she was referring to them as her *new friends*. "This isn't grade school. They're not my playmates." In truth, she knew exactly who they all were to her.

Family.

Which made her feel worse about how she had exploded at them. "I don't know when you'd meet them now that the shop's closing."

"Perhaps sooner than you think," her father said. "Your phone was dinging with one message after another while you were in the shower."

Delphinium checked her phone, and sure enough, there were seven messages. Two from Henry, one from Joanna, one from Patsy, one from Kathryn, and two from Elliot. She set it face down on the table. She couldn't deal with any of them right now.

Her father straightened his glasses. "Now that we are here, how can we help?" His default was going back to the business at hand.

"I have to focus on cleaning out the shop and packing up the apartment. I have one week before I'm locked out."

Her parents looked at each other and then back at her. "You could move out to California to be closer to us," her mother said. "It would be a fresh start."

Delphinium knew they were trying to be kind. "Thank you, but Moonberry Lake is my home. It feels right for me here, even if I don't have a place to go right now."

Her mother wiped a spot on the table with her napkin. "I know your grandmother's death was hard on you, but that is no reason to take us out of your life."

"*Hard* on me?" Delphinium choked out. "*Hard* is not the word. I literally lost my best friend. She's the only person who ever truly understood me. The only person who was excited about my gifting of flowers and scents."

Silence.

Neither of her parents responded. A smart calculation on their part since the topic ignited an explosion in her.

Her mother got up from the table. "Let's go downstairs. I want to see the shop," she said in a clear attempt to redirect the conversation.

Her father rose out of his chair as well.

Once downstairs, her parents walked around slowly.

"You've made some subtle changes," her mother commented. "There are more gift items. These dish towels are adorable." She ran her hand over a few of them.

"It's a nice shop, Del." Her father nodded, taking it all in. "What are you going to do with the leftover flowers?"

Delphinium stared at them. The sight made her sad. The flowers were from the last full shipment that she had ordered in hopes that, by some miracle, they would sell. The blooms still looked beautiful. The petals on the roses showed only the barest wilt at the ends. However, her trained eye knew their impending expiration and how they would need to be used in a hurry or they'd end up getting thrown out.

"It would be a shame to let them die," her mother said.

"Not to mention a waste of money," her father added.

Delphinium picked a single rose out of a container and twirled the stem in between her fingers. If the end was inevitable, then it would be on her terms. She would hold her head high and go out big. That was what Annie would have done. Staring at the menagerie of colors, an idea popped into her head, and she knew exactly what she wanted to do with them. "I'd like to do something nice."

"It looks as if you already have an idea," her father said.

She grabbed a bucket brimming over with yellow dahlias. "I do. But I'm going to need your help."

"You got it," her father said.

"Put us to work," her mother agreed.

Once every single bucket was placed on the floor surrounding the worktable, and every flower from the shop and cooler was brought out, Delphinium began organizing bundles on the table according to color. It would go faster if Paavo was there to help, but her parents were surprisingly teachable and followed her instructions without a word. She started to fill every vase with gorgeous bouquets. She'd get rid of every container she had.

Two and a half hours later, the back room was an explosion of color and texture with some of the most beautiful bouquets she'd ever created.

"Wow," her mother said. "To watch you is really incredible."

Her father shook his head. "I knew you were good, but the creative combinations you put together . . . I never would have thought of. You really think differently than I do."

"Me too," her mother added. "I don't have an ounce of the creativity that you possess. You're truly an artist in spirit and technique."

"Thanks." Delphinium felt almost shy about their shower of compliments. It was awkward hearing such praise from them. She was grateful they had the opportunity to watch her in her element before the store closed. She loved forming arrangements that made people smile. Whatever she did next, she never wanted to lose this part of herself.

"Where are you taking all of these?" her father asked, interrupting her thoughts.

She gave a wistful smile. "I want all of these to go to The Gardens. I want to apologize to the seniors and also give them a farewell gift. They worked hard to try to keep the shop open, and their hearts were in the right place. They deserve to have the final flowers."

"That's very kind of you," her mother said. "I am sure they will love them."

Delphinium silently counted the arrangements. "These aren't all going to fit in the van. It's going to take about three trips. I wish Paavo was here."

"Let me be your delivery boy," her father said, smiling. "We'll deliver them while you stay and clean up."

Delphinium hesitated. "Thanks. That would be wonderful. And it's probably the best idea since I'm banned from the facility."

"I doubt that."

"Oh, it's true. You don't know half of the mischief the seniors have wrangled me into. You only saw the mountain peak of their shenanigans. If you'd been here for the climb, you'd agree that I should be banned. I'd be shocked if my picture wasn't posted at the reception desk with a big X on it."

It ended up taking four trips to deliver all the flowers. Delphinium's parents gushed about the reception the bouquets received upon each return. They seemed energized by the surprise offering and enthusiastic response from The Gardens' residents. Delphinium had provided a list of all the names of the seniors who had hung out at the shop so each of them received their own bouquet for their room. Any remaining arrangements were dispersed throughout the facility.

"Mr. Sturgis was taken aback by your generosity," her father said. "He approached me again, this time asking how you were. He still seems very concerned about how you are recovering from this morning."

"I don't want to talk about Elliot," she responded, stacking the empty buckets after wiping them out.

She didn't miss how her parents exchanged glances again. The two of them had done that same form of silent communication all during her childhood. It was frustrating how they could speak to one another without actually speaking.

Her father pretended not to hear her. "We talked to him a little between deliveries. He apologized again for how it upset you. He also said that he'd like to apologize in person for being short with you."

Elliot hadn't been short with her. In truth, he had hardly spoken to her. Though he was the one who looked like he was ready to boil over, it was she who had erupted like a volcano. He was probably feeling guilty over her public meltdown. Delphinium still wanted to crawl under a rock when she thought about yelling at Henry as a huge chunk of the town watched. No doubt the story had already filtered through the coffee shops and knitting circles.

"I said I didn't want to discuss it. What's done is done." She carried a tall stack of buckets to the back door and let them drop with a loud thud. She normally never spoke to her parents in such a curt tone, but it had been an emotionally and now physically exhausting day.

Her mother sighed. "It's been a long day. Why don't we call it quits and go out to eat? We missed lunch but could go for an early dinner."

Delphinium shook her head. "I'm not in the mood to go out. You guys go get something."

Her mother began wiping down a counter where a rag had been left. "We are staying at a cute B&B in town. We reserved a room for a week."

Delphinium didn't expect that. When she first moved to Moonberry Lake, they had breezed in and out for short visits once or twice. A long weekend at most. "You're staying a *week*?"

Her mother stopped cleaning and looked over at her. "It's been so long since we've seen you. Is that okay?"

"Of course," Delphinium quickly soothed, seeing the hurt in her mother's eyes.

Her father came up and put his hand on her shoulder. "We'll give you some space now. You've had a lot to process today. We'll be back in the morning and can continue to help you clean up and close the shop. I'll see if I can get some moving boxes for the apartment. And then we need to talk about where you can stay in this transition."

Delphinium nodded. She looked around the space that was void of all flowers and plants. Without them, the shop was just that—a space. It was amazing how vacuous it felt. The room was hollow, like the life had been sucked out. The flowers had given it such beauty and energy. No, that wasn't the whole truth. It was the seniors and their commotion that had given the place life. Without them and their noise, it was just a bare room.

"You know," her father said, speaking softly, "maybe you could think of this as an opportunity for a fresh start. A chance to try something new."

More tears pricked her eyes. "I don't want a *fresh* start. This shop is the only thing I've ever wanted and I'm losing it."

"You could take your talent anywhere. You're young and could start a whole new life. It's too soon to see the silver lining in this. Give it time," her mother said in a soothing voice.

Delphinium had to grit her teeth to hold in the response she wanted to snap back.

Her mother seemed to take in her steely expression. She looked to her husband. "Let's go. I'm hungry."

They left Delphinium standing there.

Alone in the silence, the emptiness made her ache like she was coming down with a horrible flu. She shut off the lights and went upstairs. All she wanted to do was take a long bath and then sit in the living room while it was still hers. She wanted to feel Annie in the apartment and be close to those memories.

She wanted to say goodbye to it all privately.

Twenty-One

The next morning, Delphinium was sweeping the floor of the shop when she heard a persistent rapping on the front door. After checking it out, she saw some of the seniors waving to her from the other side of the door.

She turned the lock and opened it. "What are you guys doing here? There's no way Elliot would approve of this after yesterday."

"We snuck out," Joanna said, wearing big rhinestone-rimmed sunglasses and a beret. "That's why we're all dressed undercover!"

Delphinium groaned. "You guys are killing me." She eyed Joanna's outfit. "What are you wearing?"

"I don't own a trench coat, so I borrowed my neighbor's raincoat. He was taking a nap. I'll have it back in his closet before he knows it's gone," Joanna explained.

"And you thought wearing a beret with a man's raincoat over white capris and leopard flats was the best disguise?"

Joanna smiled proudly.

"You know, it's not like The Gardens is a prison. Why didn't you simply tell the front desk you were all going for coffee?"

"What's the fun in doing that?" Joanna responded as if Delphinium had asked the most absurd question.

"Breaking out of the joint is the only excitement we have," Bob said from the back.

Delphinium rolled her eyes. "You all pay way too much to refer to that beautiful facility as jail. How did you even get here? Please tell me you didn't pile in your grandson's car again."

Joanna shook her head. "Oh, no. We called Lindsey. She's picking up the others now."

Delphinium's stomach sank at the mention of her best friend. They still hadn't talked since their fight over Mason.

"We got the beautiful flowers you sent over, honey," Arlene said. She had a scarf over her head that was tied in a big bow underneath her chin.

Delphinium put a hand on her shoulder. "I'm so sorry about how things turned out yesterday." She looked at all of them. "I'm sorry I lost my temper."

They all waved away her comment.

"It's water under the bridge," Bob said. "We should have planned it better and brought lawn chairs. No matter now. We have to let it go like a dead body floating down the river."

Delphinium wrinkled her nose. "Bob, the things that come out of your mouth are really disturbing sometimes. How about keeping comments like that in your head rather than saying them out loud?"

Bob shrugged.

"There are flowers in every room of The Gardens," Arlene said with a smile on her face. "Like a page right out of *Better Homes and Gardens*. It's never looked so lovely and inviting."

"You made a lot of people happy with the beauty you brought in," Henry said with a wink. He was the only one not wearing sunglasses. He came dressed in his usual clothes. "A lot of heart went into those bouquets." He gave her one of his knowing looks. "They were some of your best."

Delphinium wrapped her arms around him in a gentle hug. "Can you forgive me?"

"Already forgotten," he answered with a gentle pat on her back. "There's a lot of emotion and memories tied to this place. Letting go is hard, especially when it was your dream."

"Did you see that I made the paper?" Joanna asked, pulling it out of her raincoat and waving the issue in front of Delphinium.

She smiled. "No. I haven't had a chance to read it yet." She took the paper from Joanna and pushed the door open wider. "Come on in."

Bob was the last through the door. He gave her a little tap on the cheek as he passed. He was sporting a baseball cap, a red bandanna around his neck, and a black winter down vest.

Delphinium could only imagine what the receptionist at The Gardens thought as they all paraded out dressed so oddly for an August stroll. She was sure the staff notified Elliot and knew exactly where they were all headed.

As they got settled in the back room, Delphinium began rummaging around for food and paper cups. The second wave of seniors came through the door a couple minutes later. Patsy walked in wearing mittens and a winter hat with a pom-pom on top. Instead of taking a seat, she stood at the head of the table as if to make an announcement. "I just want to say, although things got a little out of control yesterday and we never expected to draw that kind of attention"—everyone nodded in agreement, looking guilty—"getting to live out my fantasy with the fireman made it all worthwhile," she said with a wicked smile.

Delphinium went over to her and took off her hat and mittens. "Patsy, it's too hot for this disguise. You'll get overheated."

"Hi, honey," Gurdy greeted her, bunny-hopping through the doorway and wrapping her thin arms around Delphinium's waist.

"Hey, Gurdy," Delphinium said, gently hugging her back. "Did you get to go to your Zumba class this morning?"

"Yep." She did a little march in place as proof. "I'm thinking about getting my certification to be an instructor. There's no age limit."

That made Delphinium smile. "I think that's a fantastic idea. Can I ask how old you are?"

"Seventy-eight! But my body isn't a day over seventy-one. Zumba makes me spry." She gave a wiggle.

"The party can begin now that I'm here," George said as he entered wearing a tall green top hat and a green shirt that read "Kiss Me Anyway."

"Are we staying or leaving?" Helen piped in from behind everyone. "Because I need to sit down one way or the other."

"You heard her," Delphinium said, "keep moving forward everyone, Helen needs to get in. My parents will be back any minute. They've been wanting to meet you all."

Helen shuffled in last, pushing her walker.

Delphinium bent down to give her a hug. "How is it that you are always the caboose on this train?"

"It's because I don't speed. I'm on cruise control with this red racer." She winked.

Delphinium looked to the door and was disappointed that Lindsey didn't come through.

Everyone took their usual seats around the worktable like an expectant class waiting for their teacher.

"Has everyone recovered from yesterday?" Delphinium asked.

The seniors all muttered different versions of *yeah*.

"How's your back, Bob?"

"It's fine." He waved off her concern. "It just seized up on me there for a bit. The doctor gave me a muscle relaxer. The good kind you can only get in a hospital. I slept like a baby last night. Made me feel young again—at least, my top half. No aches or pains. They haven't come up with anything for my knees yet."

"I'm glad to hear it."

"I didn't expect the ground to be so hard. It set off the spot where I was shot in the war."

"You were shot in the forearm, you fool!" George barked. "An old war injury had nothing to do with your back locking up. You couldn't get up like the rest of us because you're *old*."

"I didn't expect that gravity would pull me down flat," Patsy said, frowning at the memory. "My core muscles aren't what they used to be. A woman's stomach is never the same after having children."

"You never gave birth," Joanna said. "You helped raise one step-child."

Patsy shrugged her shoulders. "Same thing."

"I didn't have a problem. I popped right up," Gurdy said with a smug smile.

Helen shook her head. "I said it before and I'll say it again—the only time any of us should be lying on the ground is when there is dirt on top."

"Everyone needs to stop talking so I can show her my picture," Joanna said, opening the newspaper up for the full view. "I made the front page!" She clapped. "I'm going to get as many copies as I can and send them out with my Christmas card. I'm a *celebrity*."

"It's not fair that the photo of you was the largest and most flattering," Bob grumbled. "The picture of me looks like I'm being carried off to the coroner."

"Wow. You guys really did make the front page," Delphinium said, taking in the headline, "Seniors Protest to Save Flower Shop," and the picture that captured Joanna lying in a pose with one hand on her hip and a huge smile on her face as if she truly was a model. The others were lying flat like they had been run over. Skimming the article, she saw it included the history of the shop and some more quotes from the seniors on how much they loved her. Delphinium's throat tightened at the sweet statements about how she had made such a difference in their lives.

"This is lovely" was all she could say in a hoarse voice.

"And we didn't get The Gardens in trouble this time," George said.

"You made the gossip column and are even featured in 'A Moment with Martha.' That's big stuff," Helen said, pointing at her with a crooked finger. "Turn the page."

Just as she was doing so, her parents came through the swinging door. Their faces brightened at the unexpected visitors.

"Everyone, these are my parents." Delphinium didn't need to say anything else because her parents went around and shook everyone's hands and introduced themselves individually. Then they surprised her by pulling up a couple stools to join the conversation.

"Did you read about your daughter in today's newspaper?" George asked. "Her shop made the headline, the feature, the opinion column, the gossip column, and everything in between! She's the star of Moonberry Lake."

Bob nodded. "She's something else. We're sold on her. She obviously comes from good stock."

Her parents nodded, smiling proudly. "Thank you," her mother said.

"Yep, she's a keeper," Bob added. "You wouldn't want to throw that one back into the lake."

Her father chuckled. "We couldn't agree more."

"Okay, Bob, thank you, but I'm not a fish. Let's move on," Delphinium said, unable to stop her cheeks heating from their outpouring of love. Oh, how she loved each one of them back.

"I saw that the shop made the newspaper, so I picked up a few copies," her father said, placing a stack on the table.

All the seniors reached over for their own copy.

"Delphi was just about to read 'Sightings and Satire' and 'A Moment with Martha' when you came in," Arlene said.

Everyone turned and stared at her expectantly.

"Oh, right," Delphinium said, turning to the page. She cleared her throat and read out loud.

SIGHTINGS AND SATIRE

Mayhem on Main Street! Boomers Battle over Blossoms! Grannies Grapple for Gardenias! Veterans Wage War over Wax Plants! Old Folks Fight for Ficus!

Delphinium paused and looked up from the paper to see if they thought that sounded as ridiculous as she did, but they all appeared delighted.

"Go on," Helen demanded.

Delphinium cleared her throat and continued.

> A shocking show of support by a specific set of seniors, splayed out on the sidewalk outside Delphinium's Flora Emporium, startled spectators. The devoted dissenters desperately demonstrated disapproval of the shop's demise with a disturbing display of lying down, looking deceased. The elders belted out "Save our shop," begging people to buy flowers in between their bellows for help as medics and saintly Samaritans rushed to their rescue to get them upright. The chaotic commotion curbing the closure created concern, congestion, and confusion while capturing careful consideration, all caught on camera. Shop owner Delphinium Hayes was surprised by the sit-down and seemed stunned and saddened that the seniors were in such a stricken state. Eventually the pandemonium paused, the flurry of excitement fizzled, and a pleasant public peace was restored.

Delphinium stared at the column. "That's a lot of alliteration. Try reading that again five times fast."

"I like it," said Gurdy. "They could use this as a silly example in the classroom for English class."

"Read the next one! It's about me!" shouted Patsy.

"All right, let's hear what they said about Patsy," Delphinium said.

> It's never too late to live out your dream! At least, that is what Patsy Frederickson was quoted as saying after hooting and hollering and waving wildly from the front seat of a fire truck going down Main Street. After demonstrating

earlier that morning with a group of elders where all of Moonberry Lake's emergency crews were called, the eighty-year-old refused help from anyone except the fire department. She asked if they would give her a lift back to a senior facility where she lives, and the firefighters were happy to oblige the wishes of the elderly woman since the nursing home was on their way to the station. They turned on all the lights for her and, once at the facility, one of them even carried her inside.

"That was one of the greatest moments of my life," Patsy said. "He was a hunk."

"I'm glad you got to live out your dream." Delphinium shook her head at the absurdity of that morning.

Patsy was grinning from ear to ear. "I also got the phone numbers of the firefighters. They said they would come to my next birthday party." She cackled devilishly. "And they said I can come by any time to visit when they are not out on a call." She leaned back in her chair and closed her eyes. "I can die happy now."

"I want to hear Martha! Read Martha!" Helen demanded from the end of the table.

Delphinium continued reading.

A MOMENT WITH MARTHA— A PLACE TO BELONG

When I was a child, there was a five-and-dime near where we lived. My friends and I frequented the store every day on our way home from school. It was a treat to look around, and if we were lucky enough to have some change, we bought penny candy. The store owners knew all of us by name, and we greeted them in turn as if they were an aunt or uncle.

When I think back to those times, those owners were closer to me than some of my real aunts and uncles. They not only witnessed every inch we grew but would also ask about our day at school and seemed genuinely interested. They noticed when I didn't come by because I was sick, and they sent a treat home through one of my friends when I had chicken pox. They heard all about homework woes and school drama and watched my transformation from a little girl to a young woman.

When the store closed, it felt as if a part of my life was coming to an end as well. And in a way, it did. I never found that same familiarity and sense of home in a store again. Sure, there are a couple friendly clerks at the grocery store who recognize me and offer a polite nod or smile, but they are not family.

Feeling a sense of belonging is a precious thing. When you are young and naive, it seems that finding your place in the world happens as easily as putting a penny into a gumball machine. As we age, that innocence is replaced with the harsh reality that finding your place is not only daunting but ongoing.

I mourn the loss of the sweet flower shop, Delphinium's Flora Emporium, with the rest of my elderly peers because I know that, although a new business will emerge, the heart that exists there cannot be replaced. One woman's ability to make such a difference in the lives of people who are so often overlooked cannot be measured or even fully expressed.

I am sad I took the shop for granted and did not purchase more flowers. I naively believed the shop's existence
wouldn't ever go away just as I believed as a child that the
five-and-dime would always be there. It feels tragic to lose
such a beloved thing because it not only closes a chapter on
Moonberry Lake's Main Street history but also leaves a number of seniors feeling as bereft as I did all those years ago.

The only thing any of us can do is hold on to Delphinium's
example of giving some elderly people a place to belong.

There was a hush in the room once Delphinium finished reading.

All the women, including her mother, were wiping their eyes,
and Delphinium was so overcome with emotion, she held her breath
and counted to ten to choke down the tears fighting for release. She
didn't want to weep in front of the seniors. They were distraught
enough over the shop.

Leave it to Bob to break the silence and speak the truth. "Where
are we going to go now? This shop was all we had."

"I'm all out of bran bars and arthritis cream," George com-
plained. "Who's going to get those for me?"

"I'll still get those for you when you need them, George. Just
give me a call," Delphinium said as she went around the table and
set cups of applesauce and mandarin oranges, spoons, and half a
donut from the small box her parents brought in front of each of
them. The seniors didn't even seem excited at the offering. They
all knew this would be their last time together in this space, and
nobody could muster a smile.

"Isn't there a service at The Gardens that could run these er-
rands for you?" her father finally asked.

"Or can't the bus drive you to any of these places so you can
shop for yourselves?" her mother added. "I've seen many seniors
shop in groups at the grocery store, dollar store, and pharmacy."

George frowned. "It's not the same. I like Delphinium doing it."

That made her mother raise an eyebrow and give her daughter a pointed look. To which Delphinium only smiled and whispered, "I may have spoiled them a bit."

"We're back to square one," Gurdy moped. "Nobody wants a bunch of old people hanging out at their business. Delphi was the only one who would put up with us."

Delphinium went over and put her arms around Gurdy. "I'm sure that you'll all find another spot. Maybe you can descend upon a coffee shop like a murder of crows."

"I don't even like coffee," Arlene confessed. "I enjoyed coming here and spiffing up the store. It was nice to work again."

"There isn't any place in town that will allow us to play poker and give us free food," George lamented.

"The poker was good, but I would've liked some hot snacks added to the menu," Bob said. "We should've made tater tots. I love those little spuds."

Helen waved his comment off. "You love all food. You're like a bear coming out of hibernation."

"I stash almonds in all my pockets now," Gurdy said, reaching into her pocket and taking out a few as proof. "Lindsey got me hooked on having protein snacks. Would anyone like some?"

Everyone shook their heads except for Bob, who reached out his hand for a couple.

Delphinium frowned at the mention of her best friend.

"What?" Helen asked.

Delphinium didn't respond.

Helen narrowed her eyes and pointed her crooked arthritic finger at her. "There's something you're not telling us."

Twenty-Two

All eyes focused on Delphinium.

Her shoulders drooped. "It's nothing. I found out that Lindsey has been dating Mason. He aske her out after they met here."

There was a collective gasp.

"The scoundrel!" Arlene exclaimed.

"That stinker!" Patsy chimed in. "Going after her while two-timing us."

Gurdy shook her head, clucking her tongue in disapproval.

"I don't blame him." Bob shrugged. "She's a catch."

The women glared at him.

"What? She's pretty. If we were of the same generation, I'd ask her out," he said in defense. "Especially if she offered me tater tots."

"Enough with the tater tots, Bob," Arlene said, exasperated. "You're missing the point of this entire discussion. Mason is the one getting the shop. He's the bad guy, and Lindsey is dating him. Keep up."

"There's no way the old folks' home is going to put up with us going to another place," Patsy commented, talking over Arlene. "The only reason we were able to come here so often was because Elliot has a crush on Delphi."

The seniors all nodded while her parents looked at each other.

"Whatever happened between you and Elliot?" Joanna asked, leaning in with her eyes sparkling at the prospect of gossip. "He wouldn't be looking so forlorn now if he wasn't so infatuated with you."

Delphinium's stomach clenched at the mention of his name. "There's nothing going on between us. Let's drop the subject," she said, not able to look any of them in the eyes.

"You are an odd pickle to match up," Bob interjected. "A bit too artsy-fartsy for my taste."

Delphinium didn't miss how her mother wiped her mouth with a napkin to cover up a smile. "All discussions involving my personal affairs are off-limits, Bob."

Helen tried to rap her fist on the table with a hard knock, but with her arthritic knuckles, it came out as a soft thump. "The two are perfect for each other. They complement each other as well as a salt and pepper set. Opposites not only attract but can support each other. That's the way it was with my husband. The deficit of one is the strength of the other. It makes for a winning team."

"I like that analogy," her mother said, giving Helen a smile.

"I just said we're not going to talk about anything to do with my love life," Delphinium countered.

"So, you admit, it *is* love," Joanna said, waggling her eyebrows.

Delphinium groaned, plunking down on a stool.

"We have seniority over you. *Literally*," George said. "Motion denied."

"This isn't a vote, George," Delphinium argued.

"I second to deny the motion," Arlene piped in, raising her hand.

"I third." Patsy waved her hand in the air. "Put my name in the report."

Delphinium threw her hands up. "There's no vote or report or discussion! What you all are doing isn't even a thing!" She tried putting an end to their nosiness. "There's no one taking notes, and we aren't following parliamentary procedure."

Everyone pretended as if she hadn't even spoken.

"So it is unanimously agreed upon that Delphi's love life is top priority and the main topic of discussion!" Joanna clapped her hands together. "There is nothing more interesting for us to debate, and I want to add that I've got the perfect shade of lipstick for her next date. I would also like to suggest that we put the topic of her makeup and outfit on the agenda."

"I agree." Her mother sat a little straighter, appearing proud to be part of the group. "Not about the lipstick but about her love life."

Delphinium let out an exasperated sigh. "Again, this isn't parliamentary procedure. None of you understand the rules of order, and I vehemently object to being on the agenda or being the subject of any conversation."

They simply talked over her.

"We don't have anything exciting going on, so your romance is our entertainment." Arlene winked, reaching over and giving Delphinium's hand a little pat.

"Yeah, it's like a soap opera!" Patsy added. "Or better, we are witnessing a reality show. It's like we're both the participants and audience."

Delphinium stood up. "Well, you're going to have to find some other entertainment and something else to focus on because I'm pretty sure that Elliot never wants to talk to me again."

"I wouldn't be too sure about that," Henry said.

"Me either," her father piped in, which made Delphinium's eyebrows shoot up. "He wouldn't have looked so disturbed if he didn't care about your opinion of him. And he did approach me multiple times to inquire about your well-being. That level of concern and interest says something."

"The man was downright distraught," Henry agreed. "For someone who's always put together, he was completely rattled with worry."

"I even saw him loosen his tie," Gurdy stated with emphasis, as if it was the most scandalous tidbit of information. "He was disheveled!"

"It all means that he's hot for her," Patsy added, letting out a hearty laugh.

Everyone at the table bobbed their heads in agreement. Even her parents!

Delphinium should have wished the floor would swallow her up to avoid this uncomfortable talk, but when it came from this group, it felt somewhat normal. She was accustomed to them sharing the raw truth, whether it was hard to hear or not. Age gave them the liberation of speaking their minds and not worrying about societal etiquette. She decided to let them talk it out. Eventually they would move on to another topic.

"Elliot has been holed up in his office, and when he does come out, he looks miserable," Henry said, strengthening the group's assessment.

Bob raised one finger in the air. "The man wasn't exactly cheery before, but now all he does is mope."

"He keeps staring at the floral arrangements you sent like a love-sick puppy," Joanna agreed. "You can practically feel his heartache."

Delphinium noticed her mother and father exchange looks.

"And he didn't even scold us when we got back after the protest," Gurdy said, again with a note of astonishment. "I was expecting some kind of lecture, but he just went straight to his office. Although I did hear from every one of my children," she said with a roll of her eyes. "They can be so dramatic."

"Elliot disappeared to his office until your flowers arrived," Arlene inserted. "Then he came out with big goldfish eyes." She let out a giggle. "The man was rendered speechless over all the glorious beauty you sent over."

"You made an impression, that's for sure." George nodded. "People were touched that you used the last of your flowers on us."

The corner of Delphinium's mouth turned up. "There's no one else I would've wanted them to go to."

"I'm going to press a few flowers from my bouquet and keep them in the box where I keep my most special things," Gurdy said, folding her hands in front of her and grinning. "No one has given me flowers in years. You cared enough to send me a bouquet that had all my favorites. Not many people would give the last of what they have away so freely, but you did. That is why you deserve someone special who understands your heart, not only for flowers but for people."

The sentiment made Delphinium's heart melt.

Her parents exchanged looks again.

Everyone became quiet. A cloud of sadness descended at the mention of her final bouquets.

One of the great losses that come with age is the continual goodbyes people must say to loved ones, beloved places, and things familiar to their younger life. Delphinium hated being the reason for one of those shifts in their lives. She didn't want to be a loss for her friends. And she certainly wasn't ready to say goodbye to any of them.

"I don't want to stop seeing you all. You're a part of my life now." Delphinium's voice caught on the last word as her eyes filled with tears.

Henry placed his hand on top of hers. "We will always be a part of your life. You're not getting rid of us that easily."

"You can say that again," George agreed. "We're going to stick to you like the sunspots on our skin."

A small chuckle erupted from Delphinium while she wiped her eyes with a tissue.

"Besides, the twelfth hour isn't up yet. There's still time for God to squeeze in a miracle," Henry added.

"That's right," Joanna said. "The fight is continuing at your doorstep."

Delphinium shook her head. "You guys are not going to protest anymore—which includes both sit-ins and *lie-downs* in your case. I think you broke the record for calling on every emergency service vehicle in Moonberry Lake."

"Oh, I didn't mean us," Joanna said. "I meant all the others who are actually outside your doorstep right now."

Delphinium's brow crinkled. "What are you talking about?"

"Didn't you wonder why Lindsey didn't come in with us?" Arlene asked. "She's out there waving her sign."

Delphinium bolted up and hurried to the front door. Even before opening it, she could see a crowd of people in front of the shop. Stepping outside, she saw her best friend holding a huge sign that read "Save Our Flower Shop." Two of her favorite and most faithful customers, Arielle Witherspoon and Sofia Bennet, had set up a table on the sidewalk.

When Lindsey saw her, she put down the sign and ran over to her. The two hugged and said "I'm sorry" at the same time.

"No, I'm sorry," Delphinium said. "Date whoever makes you happy and treats you as you deserve to be treated, and I'll be happy for you. I shouldn't have reacted on impulse."

"Are you kidding me? Once I confronted him about what he did to you, I dumped him! Best friend trumps lying boyfriend every time. I'm here to help save the shop."

Delphinium pulled her into another fierce hug. "This is so sweet of you, but I don't think that's possible."

"I wouldn't be too sure about that," Sofia said, approaching their little circle. As she did, Delphinium immediately caught the scent of orchid. The flower that represented love, beauty, and refinement perfectly encapsulated Sofia. The woman somehow managed to downplay her attractiveness and casual elegance with a quiet demeanor and disarming smile. "Arielle and I have not only been collecting donations but also securing advanced orders for a lot of floral arrangements." Sofia handed Delphinium a short stack of order sheets. She couldn't believe the number of them or the cost customers were willing to pay in advance.

Sofia and Lindsey both beamed at the look on her face. "This is real?" she asked.

Sofia nodded. "The orders have been pouring in since the newspaper came out. The 'A Moment with Martha' piece hit home with a lot of people. It's all the town's talking about. It was Arielle's idea to come here and set up a table to accept everyone's donations."

Delphinium glanced over at Arielle, a well-known painter and Moonberry Lake's local celebrity. Arielle gave a wave as she talked to a couple people who had stopped at the table.

Delphinium put her hand over her heart. "I-I don't know what to say. I'm so touched."

Sofia put her arm around Delphinium's shoulders. "I wish you would have let us know the predicament you are in sooner. We could've done so much in raising more money. But we're here now and we're not going down without a fight."

Delphinium watched more people cross the street and hurry over to put money into an enormous jar. "I'm sorry for believing I was so alone and didn't give you all the benefit of the doubt. Pride is a much bigger pill to swallow down than I thought."

"That's the fifth time the jug has overflowed with money. Not to mention all the donations given electronically. Our friend Cora Matthews runs it to the bank to deposit it into an account we set up to save the shop," Sofia said.

"I know Cora," Delphinium said.

Sofia hugged Delphinium. "Moonberry folks take care of each other."

Delphinium wiped her eyes. "Apparently so."

The seniors came out of the shop to observe the activity on the street.

"It looks like creating a little hoopla was all we needed," Henry said, giving her a wink.

Even as he smiled, the weariness in his face couldn't be hidden. Delphinium went and gently hugged his body, feeling the sharpness of his bones. "You need to go back home and rest."

He nodded. "Your parents offered to drive us all back in turns."

Each of the seniors lined up for a hug as they left. Delphinium stayed outside her shop, shaking hands and thanking people for their generosity, and then she opened the shop when some people asked about the fairy houses. She ended up selling all of them and the last of the dish towels.

When her parents returned, she was sweeping up her completely empty shop. The wide grin on her mother's face piqued her interest. "What?"

Her mother's eyes softened. "The way all those seniors talk about you," she said, shaking her head in amazement. "You must know how adored you are."

"I adore them just as much."

Her mother sighed. "You remind me so much of Annie. All the good that was ever in my mother is in you. I knew you two shared a special connection, but I really never saw you in your element before. You resemble her so much. And I'm in such awe of your kindness toward all those seniors. You have made such a difference in their lives."

Delphinium stared at her, confounded. "Who are you and what have you done with my mother?"

"I'm serious."

Delphinium took a few moments to take in all she had said. "Thank you," she responded softly. "That's kind of you to say. All those people have changed my life too."

"Annie would be proud of you."

Delphinium looked down as her throat tightened.

"You know," her mother continued, "it's not the shop that would have made her proud. She would have been beaming over how you gave those seniors a place to hang out. You really have a gift with them."

Delphinium was quiet as she thought about Annie. "I love them," she said. "In the short time I've known them, except for Henry, they've become like family to me. I feel responsible for them, which makes the thought of closing the shop even sadder."

Her mother took a deep breath. "I'm sorry we never appreciated you—or perhaps I should say, never made you feel valued for your wonderful uniqueness. You are so special and have gifts way beyond what your father and I or even Annie saw. The life you've made here is something to be proud of. The way the community is rallying to save this shop says everything about your character." Her mother looked down and cleared her throat before continuing. "I know that we have typically seen things differently, but I want you to know I think your talent and who you are is amazing."

Delphinium could only blink at the kind words. Never would she have imagined that such a confession would come from her mother. It strangely made her feel both redeemed and childlike by how that small part inside her that had sought her parents' approval was healing.

"Where is this all coming from, Mom? Why are you saying this now?"

"Because we've missed you terribly. And somehow not having Annie in our lives anymore has made me see things differently. It's made me see you differently." She paused. "I should have recognized your gifts, which are so unique and outside of what your father and I do, but bring such incredible value to the world."

The two stood staring at each other for a moment, and Delphinium felt a release—or maybe it was a soothing balm over an old wound that she had been needing to mend for a long time.

"Thanks, Mom." Just as she said it, her father tapped her on the shoulder.

"I think you better turn around."

Twenty-Three

Delphinium gasped at the sight before her.

As she walked outside, she saw a line of people with no end in sight.

An actual line of people took up the entire sidewalk and stretched all the way down the street. It looked as if every Moonberry Lake resident had come out to save the flower shop.

Arielle and Sofia went over to wrap their arms around Delphinium as her parents moved behind the table to thank people as they filtered past. Delphinium was overwhelmed with flower scent. Arielle was one of the most creative and imaginative people in town, and it was no surprise that the scent of iris wafted off of her heavily.

"I don't know the specifics about your mortgage, but with the amount of money flowing in, it has to make a difference at the bank," Arielle shared. "I have to say, I'm not surprised at the huge turnout. All people needed to know was how dire the situation was. Between the sizable donations and advance orders, a substantial chunk will be deposited. I think you've got a shot at saving this place."

Delphinium was too dazed to respond.

"I spoke with the people at the bank," Sofia said, "and they have been watching the support pour in all day. There have also been a couple people that have come forward—who shall remain anonymous," she said, giving Arielle a pointed look, "who have offered to cosign a new loan if need be."

Delphinium shook her head. "I'm absolutely overwhelmed."

Sofia smiled. "Moonberry isn't ready to let go of your shop without a fight."

Everything felt surreal to Delphinium. More townspeople approached her to give her a hug and say thank you for what she had done with the shop and the seniors. She'd never felt so supported and loved. It was like a tsunami of emotion washing over her. Neighbors, friends, and strangers were all rallying to save the shop.

As she worked her way down the sidewalk, shaking people's hands and thanking them, her heart all but stopped when she saw Elliot near the end. While everyone else was with a friend or family member, Elliot stood alone, looking uncomfortable and out of place in his suit. Although he appeared as formal and crisp as always, there was something equally vulnerable about him standing there quietly while everyone around him chatted.

In the August heat, he had to be sweltering, but he didn't so much as even take off his suit coat. As Delphinium studied his barely perceptible unease, it occurred to her that maybe his suits were worn more as a coat of armor, to protect a softer side of him she'd seen only glimpses of. She remembered the brief look of insecurity on his face when he first visited the shop and Bob gave him a hard time.

When Elliot caught her staring at him, everything in his demeanor went even more still.

They stood looking at each other before she finally approached him and uttered, "Hi."

He gave a shy smile. "Hello."

Just as she thought he was about to say something, he glanced at the people in front of him and behind him who were watching their interaction. Apparently, the electric charge they created in the air between the two of them was noticeable to onlookers.

Heads bobbed back and forth to see who was going to speak next because it was obvious to all *something* was going on. Delphinium knew he hated this kind of attention. So did she.

Feeling the need to rescue him, she asked, "Would you mind taking a walk with me?"

He immediately nodded and stepped forward. They went a good twenty feet before he cleared his throat and thanked her quietly.

They continued walking down the block and she turned the corner.

"Where are we going?" he asked.

"Anywhere but Main Street." *Where everyone was watching us.*

He let out another audible breath. "You read my mind. I appreciate the privacy."

Although the next street wasn't much better in terms of shopping or businesses, she knew he would feel better getting away from it all. A couple more blocks and they'd be nearing a park.

"You didn't return my phone calls."

She shook her head, keeping her gaze straight ahead. "I couldn't."

"I should have never blamed you. Jumping to the conclusion that you were responsible for the protest was unforgivable," he began, but she held up her hand to stop him.

"Can we both just agree the entire protest was *a lot*, and it was only natural to misconstrue things considering how overwhelming it was to see the seniors on the ground?"

"Absolutely," he agreed. "It was a disturbing sight."

"I literally sprinted from bed and found them like that." Delphinium let out a breath as they continued to walk. "It's something the town has never seen before, that's for sure. And I'm not sure it will be forgotten anytime soon since it was captured in the newspaper." She sighed. "Joanna will probably request a reprinting with the number of copies she is handing out with her autograph."

"It was passionate and displayed their loyalty to you and the shop, which says everything about the impact you've made in this community." Elliot shrugged off his suit coat as they walked, draping it over one arm, then he pulled at his tie until it loosened a bit.

"I haven't done anything. I simply sell flowers."

He shook his head. "No. It's not that simple. You're not that simple."

She turned her head and looked at him. He was studying her in that way that brought the butterflies back to her stomach. His warm eyes captivated her and made her swoon, so much that she hadn't noticed she'd stopped walking and was just standing there staring at him. She made the mistake of leaning in slightly and inhaling, which only put her more in a daze as she closed her eyes. The urge to fully lean in and nestle against him was nearly irresistible. She imagined what it would be like to nuzzle against his neck and kiss the side of his jaw. The sound of his chuckle startled her, and she opened her eyes.

He was smiling warmly at her. "Come on," he whispered. "Not here. It's still too public." He placed his hand on her arm, urging her in the direction of the park.

When she stole a look at him, she saw him grinning. It was obvious he loved the effect he had on her.

"You know, all the seniors snuck out again this morning," she said.

Elliot huffed. "In disguises no less. The fact that they felt the need to sneak out says a lot." He frowned. "They make me question everything about myself and my leadership style."

"It has nothing to do with your leadership style," Delphinium defended. "You care about their well-being and safety. That's obvious to anyone who knows you. Even the seniors know that, despite all their grumbling. This thing with them rebelling is more about them being bored and needing a challenge. You have to imagine them as the rowdy kids in the back of the room who drove the teacher up a wall with their antics. The Gardens facility is huge, and your sense of responsibility is even bigger. You're excellent at what you do. You are the calm within the storm, the stillness within the chaos. Your leadership doesn't drive them away. It directs them back to where they know it's safe and you'll be standing there waiting for them."

It was his turn to stop and gape at her.

She looked back at him quizzically.

He didn't give an answer. Instead, his eyes perused her hair and face. His steady gaze taking in every angle and contour as if memorizing her eyes and mouth.

"It drives me wild when you stare at me like that."

He gave her a sly smile. "You better get used to it, because I'm unable to stop. You are an anomaly in my ordered life."

She scrunched her face. "That sounds medical, like something to be studied under a microscope. An anomaly is an irregularity, like a weird mole."

He laughed. "Okay, that's definitely the wrong word. You are a . . ."

"Complication, difficulty, problem?" she interjected.

He grinned broadly, shaking his head. "I was going to say surprise. A wonderful surprise. There is something unexplainable about you that is intoxicating."

"Intoxicating." She considered that. No one had ever described her as that before. No man had ever seemed as taken with her or looked at her the way he was looking at her.

"Also . . . enchanting?"

"Enchanting?" she echoed. She realized she was just repeating everything he was saying, but his descriptions took her by surprise. He saw her differently than anyone else ever had. Well, maybe not Annie. But never someone romantically interested in her.

He peered at her intently. "You, Ms. Hayes, are bewitching. I am utterly captivated by you."

His sincerity took her breath away. She stared back at him, holding her breath.

He leaned in.

She jerked her head away and instinctively stepped back. "Whoa, what are you doing?"

His eyes widened and he stepped away as well. "Oh, I-I'm sorry."

"You were about to kiss me," she said at a volume that made it more of an exclamation than a question.

"I apologize." He was shaking his head. "I misread the situation. I'm not myself around you. I wanted to make things right between us."

"By *kissing* me?"

He adjusted his tie. "No, that wasn't a part of the plan. That was unplanned and apparently an error in my judgment that something was happening between the two of us right now."

By the flush in his face, Delphinium knew he was embarrassed for acting so spontaneously. He looked mortified. It wasn't like him to act so impulsively—she believed that completely. He was the steady to her wild, the control to her impulsiveness, the suit and tie to her dangly earrings and flower apron.

He took a deep breath and put his suit coat back on, then smoothed the front of it. "I apologize for the impropriety of acting on compulsion and attempting to do something so intimate in public where it is not at all romantic." He looked from side to side as if to verify to himself that this was the wrong place and time for such a thing.

"I can't deny that something was happening between us. Or is . . ." Her voice dropped off. Delphinium took a couple steps forward to close the distance between them, then she put her hand on his arm. "It was surprising and would have been very romantic if the timing was right. I like you and want to get to know you better." She paused. "But I think we should be on speaking terms for more than an hour before you kiss me."

He chuckled uncomfortably, still seeming embarrassed. "When you look at me like you did and then inhale, I lose all sense," he said. "And then when you say things that no one else in my life has ever said and seem to understand me and truly see me for who I am—" He broke off the sentence and shook his head. "You're different from anyone I've ever met."

Delphinium's heart broke open from the vulnerability on his face. She reached down and took his hand and gave it a small squeeze. "So you're saying that I get you, and that you are somehow fascinated by me."

His eyes lit up with amusement, and he held onto her hand. "More like intrigued, charmed, impressed, spellbound," he added.

"Okay, I get it." She laughed.

Elliot looked pleased with himself. "I just wanted to cover all the bases so you wouldn't think that you're something scientific to me ever again."

"Well, all those descriptions are a great place to start a wonderful friendship. And then there is this . . ." She motioned back and forth between them.

"The zing?" he suggested with a smirk.

She smiled, which made him smile. "Yeah, that. This *zing* that is—"

"Incredible and has been there from the start?" he said, completing her thought.

She arched an eyebrow. "Are you always going to finish—"

"Your sentences? Like you finish mine?" He chuckled. "Not if it bothers you."

Delphinium gave a wide grin. "Why don't we work backward and go to the part where we spend time with one another getting to know the other's history and personality."

"I'd like that very much."

She nodded. "Me too."

"And just to clarify, in spending time together, you mean without the seniors, correct?" he asked with an uncertain look.

"Oh, I can't always guarantee that," she teased. She took a breath, feeling nearly lightheaded from the happiness filling her. "But I think I'll be able to sneak away from them from time to time."

It was as if she had handed him the moon. "I'll take whatever I can get."

For a moment she wished that she had leaned in when he had.

His typically stern expression had relaxed into something different and inviting. She was taken aback by the richness of his brown eyes that exuded nothing but kindness and gentleness. She swallowed and then looked down at their entwined hands, thankful for the anchor he provided. He gave her hand a squeeze. The world seemed to disappear, and she didn't notice the people walking by them.

But he did.

"Come on. I'll walk you back. I've taken too much of your time. I've accepted that I'll always have to share you and all your tremendous gifts. You need to get back to your fans."

She laughed. "They're not fans. I think the newspaper simply inspired people to rally around a local small business."

"I beg to differ. You possess a magic in what you do and how you treat others."

They began walking back hand in hand, which thrilled her. His protective grasp gave no indication that he was going to let go of her.

"What were you doing in line?"

He looked at her like it was silly to even ask. "I was there to make a donation, of course. I've felt terrible over your circumstance and was relieved when I saw it written about in the newspaper. You deserve the attention and for the shop to be saved. Martha's column captured the feeling perfectly."

"That's generous of you to say after what the seniors put you through these last few months."

"First of all, it's the truth. And secondly, I've come to greatly appreciate their boycott because I wouldn't have met you otherwise. Their desire for unrestricted poker and theme days like Sushi Saturday, Tiramisu Tuesday, Wonton Wednesday, or whatever other food they can match to a day of the week got me to your shop."

She laughed. "I suppose so, but let's never tell them that."

"Agree." He winked and walked with a different disposition than the man who stood alone in line not too long ago. She was glad she brought out this side of him that she guessed not many people saw.

Being near him felt good. She walked closer to him so their

arms touched as well. She realized the effect he had on her was ridiculous, but it wasn't as if it was one-sided. He had already spilled the truth on how he felt.

Maybe she should stay grounded, even guarded, and go about things slowly, but all her senses went out the window when he was physically near her. This intangible, unexplainable, unreasonable force between them obliterated her practicality.

She knew this was more than his intoxicating scent. He was so much more. She was falling for the decency and care for others that he kept carefully concealed behind his suits.

"What are you thinking?" he asked, seeming to sense she was deep in thought.

"Um," she responded, giving her head a shake. "I was just wondering if the bank will extend my loan with all the unbelievable generous donations flooding in," she said, lying. "I don't know how much has been collected, but the act alone has renewed my faith in small-town community and fellowship."

"I can't imagine they won't be swayed. It's all extraordinary," he said with deep sincerity in his eyes and voice.

She held in a sigh. Those warm brown eyes were going to do her in. "That's how I feel about you and your commitment to the safety and happiness of the seniors," she said, making his face light up. "Most directors would have never even visited the shop or tried to replicate a feeling or activity that they love doing."

They turned onto Main Street.

"Have dinner with me tonight." He said it as a statement instead of a question.

"Okay," she said immediately.

His eyes lit up. "That was fast."

She quirked an eyebrow up. "Should I not have answered so quickly? Should I play harder to get?"

He erupted with laughter at that. "No. That's not at all what I meant. I thought you might not be able to with your parents in town."

She grew serious. "Oh, I didn't think about that. You're right."

"We could all go out so they can get to know me."

Delphinium looked at him like he'd grown two heads. "I am not taking my parents with me on our first date!"

He smiled. "It's technically not our first date. We've already gone out. I even drove you home."

Her jaw dropped. "If you're seriously counting hanging out in the hospital waiting room as our first date, your bar is entirely too low."

He grinned. "Any time that I get to be with you, I count as special, date or not. I know how high in demand you are. It's a win if I can get time with you."

She looked down, blushing.

"Plus, I know your parents won't be in town much longer. I spoke to them when they dropped off all the gorgeous bouquets you made, and I would appreciate getting to know them better under less strenuous terms."

He had a point.

Elliot cleared his throat. "This may be premature to say and may make you uncomfortable, but it's important to me that they have a good impression of me. My introduction on the street yesterday morning couldn't have been worse. I want them to think well of my character." He stared straight ahead but glanced at her, uncertain.

Delphinium didn't mean to, but she actually snorted.

Elliot startled. "Did you just snort?"

She nodded. "Sorry, yes. I couldn't help it. You are the *epitome* of a good impression. You're like a perfectly wrapped package with a big red bow. If the four of us were to stand in a line, believe me when I say, I would be the one that looked misplaced. If my parents could construct the perfect man they imagine me to date, it would look exactly like you. You couldn't be more right if you'd been designed by a computer and assembled by a 3D printer. I've always been their oddball child. If it wasn't for my grandmother, I'd think I was adopted."

He kept his eyes focused on the ground as he digested her words and then turned his head to her. "You're beautiful and were meant to stand out in any crowd. Your eccentricity and free spirit are one of the things I find so captivating about you. You live out your passion for flowers in everything you do, even by dressing in floral designs. I find it inspiring."

Delphinium blinked, nearly stumbling over her feet, but Elliot tightened his grip and kept her from going down. "That's not what the stoic and intimidating Mr. Sturgis who first entered my shop would have said."

"No, but it's what I thought upon leaving that day." He beamed at the teasing. "I'm not who you thought I would be?"

She shrugged. "You just come across . . ."

"Uptight? Intense?" he said, finishing her thought. "Yeah, I get that a lot. I've been a type A personality since birth. My family says I came into the world wanting to create a spreadsheet." Delphinium didn't miss the flash of sadness that crossed his face before he brightened. "You bring out a different side in me." His smile was shy and genuine.

As they drew closer to the shop, the line was nearly gone. Arielle, Sofia, and her parents were huddled together talking. When her mother and father looked over and saw her, their gaze zeroed in on Delphinium's fingers intertwined with Elliot's. Her parents exchanged a look and then grinned at her.

"We were wondering where you went off to," her mother said as they approached.

"We took a quick walk," Delphinium said, releasing her hand from Elliot's, immediately regretting the choice. She already missed the closeness.

"It's nice to see you again, Mr. Sturgis," her father said, putting his hand out.

Elliot was quick to take it. "Please, call me Elliot."

Her parents nodded and said at the same time, "Elliot."

Delphinium wanted to gag at how giddy her mother appeared.

It was as if the prodigal son had returned, and they were finally united with a younger carbon copy of them.

Arielle and Sofia seemed just as thrilled as they approached the group. Delphinium even caught Arielle waggling her eyebrows at her. For being a couple of her favorite customers, they were taking ownership of her happiness to a whole new level, affirming once again that in a small town like Moonberry Lake, one's personal business is everyone's business.

"We are closing up for the day," Sofia announced. "A couple more deposits were made to the account in the shop's name. I was about to put the rest of the cash we collected inside with the stack of orders next to your register. You can lock it all up."

"Please add this to the jar," Elliot said, taking an envelope from his inside pocket and handing it to her.

Delphinium opened her mouth to protest, but Elliot quickly took her hand in his and gave her a wink.

"We'll fold up the table and be on our way," Arielle said with a twinkle in her eyes.

"I can't thank you enough," Delphinium said.

Both Arielle and Sofia hugged her and left after Elliot and her father helped fold the table and brought it inside the shop.

As her mother watched, she put her arm around Delphinium's waist and pulled her close. "I like him," she whispered.

"Of course you do. He's all shiny and perfectly tailored. He resembles a Ken doll in a suit and looks as if he should be your child instead of me. But you really don't know anything about him," Delphinium whispered back. "For all you know, he could be a well-dressed serial killer. A total psycho."

Her mother's brows crinkled together. "Who also oversees the business and management of a sprawling senior living facility?"

Delphinium shrugged. "Makes for easy pickings."

Her mother rolled her eyes. "Your sense of humor is so odd."

"Like me?" Delphinium teased.

"Don't start," she warned, giving her daughter a pointed look.

"We are having a lovely visit. All I'm saying is I like how he looks at you. It's like he's mesmerized. His adoration is obvious, and that is what every parent wants, for their child."

When Elliot approached them, her mother straightened.

"I asked Delphinium to dinner and would like to extend the invitation to you both as well," he said.

"Well, that sounds—" her father began.

"Terrible," her mother finished.

Her father and Elliot stared at her, clearly taken aback.

She glanced at Delphinium for confirmation or denial that this was a good or bad idea. Delphinium really didn't want them crashing her date but remembered Elliot's feelings on making a good impression, so she shrugged.

"That sounds terribly *nice* of you," her mother rephrased. "Thank you for the invitation. We'd love to join you both."

Her father continued to look at her mother, confused, seeming afraid to add anything.

"Wonderful," Elliot said. He named the restaurant and time and said he'd come by the shop to pick everyone up.

Her parents said goodbye and then walked inside.

Elliot took the opportunity of being alone to take her hand again, drawing her closer. "Thank you for letting them tag along," he said into her ear.

"You're right. It's the nice thing to do. They're only going to be here for another couple days before they have to get back to get ready for fall semester at the university."

"I'll see you in a couple hours," he said, lifting her hand to place a kiss upon it.

The action made Delphinium inhale quickly and look at him quizzically.

"What?" he asked.

"You kissed my hand. That's like out of a fairy tale. Nobody does that anymore."

He shrugged. "I do, and maybe whatever is beginning with us

will end like a fairy tale," he responded with a wink as he turned to walk away.

She kept the bubbling desire to let out a little squeal to herself as she watched him. It was only when he glanced back and caught her staring at him that she moved. *Have mercy.* She couldn't wait to see him again.

As she was going into the shop, her cell phone rang. It was Henry.

"Henry, you're not going to believe the day I've had! Everyone in town showed up to save the shop. It was amazing."

Silence.

"Henry? Are you there? Are you okay?"

"Delphi," Henry said weakly.

"I'm here. What's wrong?"

"Delphi, I'm at the hospital. Can you come?"

Twenty-Four

I 'm not asking you out to dinner anymore if it means we get called to the hospital every time," Elliot said, walking through the entrance with her. "We'll have to make breakfast or lunch our thing."

Delphinium should have at least cracked a smile at his joke, but she was too worried about Henry to take in any humor at the moment. "I'm typically not a superstitious person, but you have to admit there is a pattern forming," she said, approaching the front desk. After getting Henry's room number, they made their way to the elevators. "Maybe it's a sign we're not supposed to be going out," she said, wringing her hands.

He scoffed. "That's illogical. I don't accept that."

"You have to admit that the coincidence of you asking me out and then something happening to one of the seniors is a little peculiar."

They stepped into an empty elevator and Elliot pushed the button for the fourth floor. "You're not taking into account the biggest flaw in your hypothesis, which is what you've already stated—the control group is *senior*. Things happen to elderly people all the time simply because of their age. Our plans for dinner are merely coincidental."

"*Both times?*"

He paused and then said, "I'm not accepting the data. I won't give you up now that I've found you."

The resolution in his words rang like a final bell.

Delphinium took a deep breath to settle her nerves. "I just want Henry to be okay. He *needs* to be okay." Nervous, she tried smoothing her hair and tucking some of the thickness behind her ears. "He's been looking so frail lately. I should have gotten him to the doctor sooner. The drama with the shop distracted me. I should have put him first."

"Henry is well aware of the priority you put on him and everyone else."

When the elevator doors opened, a new wave of panic rushed over her. They hurried down the hall to the room, and as she was about to walk through, Elliot reached for her hand and pulled her back.

"I'm going to wait here and let you have time with him."

Her brows knitted together. "Are you sure you don't want to come in with me?"

He held her gaze. "I'm here as a support for *you*," he said slowly, brushing her cheek as he tucked a wild curl behind her ear. Then he cupped his hand around the side of her face, holding her tenderly. "I'm aware of the medical state of all the residents who live at The Gardens."

He said it with such a meaningful look, Delphinium waited for him to go on, but he didn't. She figured he probably meant that he was aware of how fragile all the residents were. She supposed it was an occupational hazard to get too close. It would wear on anyone emotionally and physically to get attached to every senior in the facility and then have to say goodbye again and again. "Okay" was all she said. She shifted and turned out of his touch and began to leave when he reached for her hand again.

She looked over at him and was surprised to see worry etched in his eyes. "What is it?"

Elliot paused as if considering his words. Then he said, "If there is one thing I've learned from working in a senior home, it is that everyone's end-stage journey is different. What works for one person does not work for another, and you have to give the person space and freedom to share their wishes and then you have to accept them regardless of how you feel. The greatest dignity we can give a person is choice."

Delphinium had no idea why he was talking so cryptically. Before she could ask him anything else, he leaned in and kissed her cheek softly.

She rolled her eyes. "Seriously, you and your kisses at the most inopportune times."

His worried stare remained fixed, despite her teasing. He gently squeezed her hand. "Remember what I said."

She didn't have time to unpack his words. She wanted to get to Henry, so she gave him a quick nod and then turned and pushed open the door.

Walking in, she noticed that the room was dim. The shades were drawn, the only light coming from a fixture above the bed against the wall. It cast a glow on the machines. Henry was resting with his eyes closed, but as she walked closer, he opened them and gave her a small smile. She immediately rushed to his side and took the hand that didn't have an IV poked into it. In the low light, his gauntness seemed exaggerated. But she knew the sharpness of his cheekbones was no lie. Biting her lip to keep her emotions at bay, she forced herself to smile back.

"Hey," she greeted, rubbing the top of his hand with her thumb.

"Hey yourself."

"How are you feeling?"

Henry gave no typical wink, smile, or tip of an imaginary hat. Seriousness cloaked his demeanor. "We gotta talk, kid."

Delphinium held her breath. "Okay."

Henry paused. "I've been sick for a while and haven't told you."

She was not expecting that. Her brow crinkled. "What do you mean by *sick*?"

Henry looked up to the ceiling for a moment and then back to her. "It's not good and I didn't want to involve you—not after Annie. I wanted things to go back to normal for you and not be a burden."

Delphinium's free hand went to her heart. "Henry, you're never a burden. You can tell me anything. What is it?"

He took a breath. "I've had lymphoma for years, and it appears my system is tuckered out trying to fight it."

Her mouth dropped open. "What?" Tears pooled in her eyes. "Why wouldn't you share that with me? We're family. Why wouldn't you tell me so I could help you or at least be a support?"

"There was nothing you could do. I do a round of chemotherapy a couple times a year to keep it at bay and then I go on living my life as usual. That is, until recently when the treatments got closer together. I didn't want you to look at me differently. I liked how you saw me and let me work at the shop. You gave me a sense of normalcy and purpose. I never wanted to appear weak or sick."

"Henry, you know how much I love you. You could've told me."

He patted her hand. "I'm telling you now. Sweetheart, it's what I wanted. I wanted to be able to live my life and have fun and not have you worry. If you had known, you would have fussed over me. You would have worried too early on, and it would have taken away from your joy of living. By not telling you, I was able to share in that infectious joy."

"Well, I'm going to fuss over you now! When you get home, I'm going to spoil you rotten with food and love until your strength returns."

He looked at her with such sympathy, it all but made her crumble. "Honey, I'm not going back to The Gardens. I'm going home." He paused. "My true home."

The silence of the room made the words echo.

Delphinium inhaled sharply. "Don't say that."

"I'm at peace with it. Because of my faith, I'm actually looking forward to it. I've had a nice long life and have enjoyed every step to this point."

"There's got to be medicine that can help you."

He shook his head. "I've exhausted all resources. I'm so tired, Delphi. I'm ready to go. Hospice has been called. My organs are as tuckered out as I am. I don't have the strength to fight this any longer." The unwavering acceptance in his tone told her that he was speaking the truth and that it was as nonnegotiable as if it were written in stone. There was no denying or sugarcoating it. Even as he said the words that made her world come apart, he seemed at peace.

"I'm not ready to let you go." Her voice cracked. She couldn't look at him, so she kept smoothing the wrinkle in his blanket.

"We never are with those we love. There's a pull inside me that feels the same way about you, but don't think for a minute I won't be looking over you."

Delphinium bit down on her lower lip.

"You didn't think I was going to live forever, did you?"

"No," she managed to squeak out, still busying herself with the blanket.

"This has been a long time coming. But let me say, having you as a part of the ride has made the trip so wonderful."

It was all too much to process. Tears that had pooled in her eyes began spilling over. She didn't know what to say or do. She was losing her Henry, her rock.

"Are you in any pain?" she finally croaked out. She wiped her nose with a couple tissues from the box on his nightstand.

"No. They've given me all the painkillers I want at this point. They make me sleepy, but I prefer that over pain. That's why I wanted to talk to you now, before I start to sleep all the time."

She took a ragged breath as the tears flowed.

"Don't feel sad. It's actually very nice. I'm going to feel as though I'm floating away in a dream. I won't be in pain anymore. Remember that." He gave her a pointed look. "My end is really the beginning to something so wonderful and miraculous that we cannot even imagine. I can't wait to see a place that is literally called heaven. Think of what that entails."

Delphinium pressed a tissue hard against her mouth to keep the sob in. This couldn't be happening.

"You're going to be okay without me," he assured her.

She shook her head, unable to talk.

"I'm going to miss you and you're going to miss me, but the great thing about life is that even when you think it ends, it doesn't. And I promise to be the first one in line to greet you in heaven after you've had a very long and lovely life."

Henry opened his arms a little, and Delphinium leaned over and placed her head upon his chest. He stroked her hair. "You have loved me like a beloved grandfather, and for that I am blessed and feel so grateful. Your attention and care have been some of the greatest gifts I've ever received. All I want is for you to keep being you, then I'll know you'll have a remarkable life."

Since her reserve of tears seemed endless, Delphinium decided to simply talk through them. She straightened and pressed more tissues to her eyes and wiped her nose. "What can I do for you?"

He shook his head. "Nothing. I just want to sleep. I'm not hungry, only weary. Maybe you could come back later to visit." His droopy eyes began to close.

She nodded and gave him a kiss on the cheek. "I love you, Henry."

"That goes both ways, darlin'. Always have, always will."

He fell asleep and she watched him. She wanted to remember this moment. Time felt as fragile as his body, and she knew both would pass silently.

A half hour later, she walked out to the hall and saw Elliot sitting in a chair, ramrod straight as usual. When their eyes met, he shot up and they both crossed the distance to meet halfway.

He immediately took her into his arms, where she crumpled. "I'm so sorry," he said, guiding her off to the side for more privacy. He held her as she cried. "I wish he would have told you sooner. I can only imagine your shock."

Everything inside Delphinium went cold. She pulled out of his arms and stepped back. "Wait a minute. You *knew* Henry had cancer?"

He blinked. "Of course. I have access to the medical records of all my residents, and their charts are tagged when one of them requires transportation to a medical facility or when hospice gets involved. Henry has been having chemotherapy treatments for years, which requires someone from our staff to transport him."

Delphinium blinked. "Do you always talk robotic like that when a real person with real emotions is involved?"

He stared at her.

As the awkward silence grew between them, so did Delphinium's anger.

"This is Henry, *my* Henry," she emphasized. "How could you not fill me in on what was going on?"

He looked baffled by her response at first, and then he squared his shoulders and jaw, appearing like the Elliot she first encountered. "Because you are not officially his family. The information was to remain confidential. Any medical disclosure is restricted from nonfamily members and sometimes even family if that is the patient's wish. And Henry's wish was that you not know."

Her eyes widened. "After everything I have been through with him and all the seniors, you're still going to act like that?"

"Like what?"

"Like you're the tin man walking around without a heart. You're all business and uptight, completely lacking compassion or human feeling."

His face hardened. "That's not fair. I have great compassion for not only what Henry is going through but also for you. I don't know how you can say that when I've gone above and beyond indulging the seniors' whims regarding your shop. I even went so far as to provide transportation for them to have their fun eating donuts and playing cards at your shop."

Delphinium didn't want to hear or acknowledge the truth in what he was saying. "Considering my close relationship with Henry, I would expect you to bend the rules."

His face was like stone as he looked her straight in the eyes. "I am a professional. I don't bend the rules for anyone."

Delphinium clenched her fists to keep from shaking. "I'm not just anyone, I'm Henry's *someone*." Her voice broke, and she paused to get control again, but her tears were relentless. "And he's mine!" she shouted. "I can't believe that every time you saw me or spoke to me, you were lying to me."

Elliot looked around at the glances from the nurses passing by. "I never lied to you," he whispered sharply. "Not once. I simply withheld information that Henry asked not to be shared. That's what the word *confidential* means."

Delphinium shook her head. "You knew he was dying and you didn't tell me."

Elliot flinched as if she had struck him. "Delphinium, please," he said in a hushed tone.

She gave him an icy glare as she stepped farther back. "I need to be alone. I need to process this. Please go."

For a moment, they both stood wooden, glaring at each other— her with lightning bolts in her eyes and him with a veil of taciturn indifference over the slightest flicker of hurt.

Without a word, he swiftly left. Not in a huff, not at an emotional clip or run, which she would have done. He simply strode away. Quiet. Controlled. To any onlooker, he appeared aloof and impassive, as if it was a mistake to be on this floor. He did not draw attention like she did. He was the opposite of her, and now he was gone.

Even in her mixture of anger and sadness, she watched him to see if he would look back at her.

He didn't.

She walked numbly back to Henry's room to check on him one more time. He was in deep sleep. She figured by the time she got home and gathered some things, visiting hours would be over. She'd return tomorrow, prepared to sit vigil beside him.

After paying for a ride back to the shop, she was surprised to find her parents sitting in the living room, waiting for her.

"I made a light dinner," her mother said, getting up. "Some sandwiches. Why don't you sit down to eat and tell us how Henry is."

Delphinium slumped down on the chair. "I'm not hungry." There was no way she could keep anything down. The fight with Elliot had made her horribly nauseous. Between the ache in her chest and the pit in her stomach, she wanted to curl up in a ball. She told them about Henry's diagnosis and how he had been keeping it to himself.

Her parents quietly listened. When she mentioned how Elliot hadn't told her, they only exchanged a look. She knew what they were thinking, which only made her angrier.

"Don't tell me that you are actually siding with him over me?" she spat.

"It's not a matter of siding with anyone," her father insisted, raising his hands in surrender. "We are always on your side. I simply want or at least hope you'll take into account medical privacy, which is a very real thing. That confidentiality is taken as seriously as if it were court-ordered."

"It must have been so hard for Elliot to be in that position not to tell you," her mother added, shaking her head. "A tremendous burden to bear when he knew you'd be crestfallen."

Delphinium let out a loud sigh. "Of course you're both siding with him. He's just like you."

"Once again, no," her father stated, but more sternly and emphatically this time. "You are our daughter. We will always support you in every way, even when we don't completely agree or understand. All I'm saying is that we all know what a passionate person you are and how you can react sometimes with that same passion."

Delphinium had the sense to know it would be immature to scoff at her parents, so she held it in. She didn't want to discuss it anymore. Her head hurt as much as her heart. "It's been a long day. I have a throbbing headache and am going to go to bed. I have to go to the bank tomorrow as soon as it opens to find out the fate of the shop and then go back to the hospital."

"We'll go with you to the bank," her mother said, gathering the plates from the table.

"You don't have to do that."

"We want to," her father said. "It's a big deal either way, and we want to be there to support you. We shouldn't have let so much time pass between us. If we had known about the situation earlier, maybe we could have helped in some way."

"We'll be here early with breakfast and then all go together," her mother said.

Delphinium nodded and walked them out.

At the shop door, her father gave her a pat on the back. As her mother passed, she said, "I know that you've always seen us as different from yourself, but I hope you know those differences do not diminish our capacity to love each other." She leaned over and wrapped her arms around her daughter. "Get some rest. Things will appear better in the morning after a good night's sleep."

Delphinium wasn't sure about that, so she didn't respond.

After going to the bathroom for a couple aspirin, she swallowed them down with a gulp of water, then lumbered into her bedroom. She didn't even change clothes before she crawled into bed. Clutching her pillow, she wept herself to sleep over losing Henry. Her sweet Henry.

And . . .

Elliot.

Oh, Elliot.

The pain she felt over him was different. Losing Henry made her horribly sad, but losing the possibility of something more with Elliot made it hard to breathe. No matter how tightly she squeezed her eyes, she couldn't erase the look on his face before he walked away. Her words had wounded him. She knew that. He had been vulnerable with her and had waited outside that hospital room, knowing a piece of her world was going to break again.

She whispered his name, trying to summon a spark of the anger she felt before, but it felt hollow.

"Elliot."

His name, uttered again in the silence of her bedroom, touched the deepest part of her. The part that already felt lonely without him.

Twenty-Five

Her parents did as they promised and were at the apartment the next morning as she was getting dressed. She opened the door in her robe, and her father waved the newspaper he was holding. "I have to say, when you told us you wanted to be a florist, I never thought you'd be making the news. You're a celebrity. Have you seen this?"

She shook her head and followed him to the small kitchen table, where he laid the paper open and pointed to an article written by Kathryn Hughes. The title read "A Miracle in Moonberry."

Her jaw dropped. "Another article?"

"This town is not willing to let you go without a fight," her mother said, setting down the croissants and coffee they'd picked up on the way over.

Delphinium began to read and couldn't believe what Kathryn had written. The article was a beautiful and touching piece about the flower shop and the senior community's fight to keep it open. It wasn't a follow-up piece or retraction from the first—or the second. It took a new angle, putting an emphasis on the connection Delphinium and the seniors shared, despite the age difference. It talked about how they looked out for one another and loved each other as a little family—a *miracle* in today's culture.

Kathryn went into detail about how Delphinium gave the seniors a place to hang out while also giving them a purpose and reason to get up in the morning. How she fed them, let them play cards, and do small tasks to help run the business. There were testimonies from all the seniors on what the shop meant to them and how much they loved its owner.

Delphinium couldn't hold back the tears or laughter as she read Bob's quote: "She's like a daughter to us all. She always listened to our complaints and requests but wouldn't take any guff either. She was the best sergeant in command a soldier could ask for. When we found out the shop was in danger of closing, we were all willing to fight to the death to keep it open."

The sentiments from each of the seniors were the sweetest things anyone had ever said about her. The article ended with a photo of the line of people waiting to donate money to save the shop. It highlighted how Moonberry Lake residents show up for each other.

"Wow" was all she could say after she was done reading the article.

Her father patted the chair next to him. "Sit with me."

"I have to go get dressed."

"This will only take a minute."

As soon as she sat, her mother excused herself to the bathroom, but Delphinium suspected it was to give them privacy. Her father clearly wanted to talk to her alone.

He tapped his finger on the newspaper article. "It's quite something to have that written about you."

She nodded. "It's lovely."

He crossed his arms over his chest and looked down before speaking. She had seen this exact look a thousand times growing up, when he wanted to have a serious talk. "I've been thinking about you," he finally said.

Delphinium toyed with a lock of her hair. "And what conclusions have you come to?"

When he looked at her with absolute seriousness, she sobered.

"You remind me of the best definition I've ever heard of finding one's purpose."

When he didn't go on, she took the bait. "Okay, what is it?"

"A person's gift is what they do best with the least amount of effort."

Delphinium pondered that and frowned. "I've put a tremendous amount of effort into the flower shop."

He held up his hand. "That's not to say it doesn't require a lot of hard work. It means that somehow you feel led and compelled to do it. You put less effort into being a florist than you would an astronaut because it is your gift. Just as being an astronaut to some would come easier than being a florist." He pushed his coffee cup to the side. "Maybe it's not the best comparison, but you get my drift. I know you probably don't want to listen to what I'm going to say, but give your old man some grace and hear me out."

She remained quiet.

"What I've witnessed these past few days has really opened my eyes to who you are as a young woman. There is no question that you are a wonderful florist. It is definitely a tremendous, God-given talent. You've had this creative touch and artistic flair since you were a child. It's like you were born obsessed with art. You always wanted to get your hands dirty and make something wildly imaginative.

"Your mother and I both lack that gene, but your grandmother possessed it. We always knew you would go in some direction where you designed lovely things to share with the world. But after watching you this week, I have a new understanding about a component I never knew was so much a part of you." He leaned forward on one elbow and placed his chin on one hand while he drummed his fingers on the table with the other. Delphinium recognized the move. He did this with his students when he wanted to make it look like he was considering something but really wanted them to be the one thinking about it.

"You are excellent with the elderly. While others don't know what to say, while society diminishes them, and while our culture does its best to ignore them, you are totally comfortable immersing yourself in that age group. They love you and you love them back even more. It is a mutual fondness and respect."

Delphinium was not sure what to say. It wasn't like her father to talk this way.

"Your mother and I have been watching in awe as you interact with your senior friends. You make each one of them feel loved and seen. Maybe your gift, that comes effortlessly to you, is working with them. Maybe your purpose is bigger than this shop and this tiny apartment that Annie left you. Maybe it's just beginning to unfold because you are continuing to unfold as a vibrant, capable, compassionate woman who leads her life by intuition and heart."

She took a moment to take in his words. "Why are you saying this now?"

"Because I think it needs to be said. And whatever happens at the bank, I want you to know my thoughts because you're my daughter and I care about you." He folded his hands. "You worked hard at keeping the shop going, but you effortlessly create works of art and love people. You're living out your purpose without even realizing it. And I'm proud of you."

Delphinium stared at him, stunned. "Thank you. That means a lot."

Her father sighed. "I regret being so quiet at times while you were growing up. You are such a force of nature, it's hard to believe you don't have everything under control. You were so intimidating to your mother and me growing up."

Delphinium balked. "Me? *I* was intimidating?"

He nodded. "You were like a tornado unleashed when you got an idea in your head. Annie was the only one who seemed able to reason with you and direct you. I know that you've always believed your mother and I don't understand you, and perhaps we don't, but we've always loved you just the way you are. Even if we didn't express that well."

"Even with my wild hair and flower outfits?" she asked with a small grin.

He laughed. "All of it."

Her mother came from behind her and put her hands on Delphinium's shoulders. "Why don't you go get dressed and we'll go to the bank. Whatever the outcome, we know your future is bright."

The meeting at the bank surprised even her parents and left Delphinium completely stunned. The amount raised over the last few days was enough to get her out of the financial hole and, after refinancing, to begin again at a more realistic mortgage rate. The representative shared how many of the townspeople came into the bank asking for leniency on her behalf. Delphinium suspected the bank's gesture of goodwill was more about preserving their reputation in the small town, but she would take it. There was also the element of Mason protecting his reputation. She knew the publicity of what had happened would not put the next tenant in any sort of good light.

Even with the new loan, she wasn't totally off the hook. She would still have to work incredibly hard to stay afloat, but she was more than happy to do that if it meant keeping the shop and apartment.

Her dad surprised her by asking the bank manager for a minute of privacy with Delphinium. Her mother nodded in agreement and said they needed some time to discuss something. The woman excused herself, giving them her office to talk.

"What are you doing?" Delphinium asked as soon as they were alone.

Her father spoke in a low voice, "Just take a breath. I want you to make sure that this is what you want."

Delphinium tensed. "Of course it is. I can't believe you're even asking."

"Because this is a crossroads in your life—you have a choice to veer off to one side if you wish and go in another direction. It doesn't happen often." He leaned closer to her and spoke in a whisper. "You can continue going down the same path or you can start a new one. This is a turning point."

"Let's stop with the road analogies."

"Okay, how about this—you can begin something new without a heavy yoke of debt over you. You won't be able to get another real estate loan, but you can do something different."

"We know how much you love the shop, but it's something to consider," her mother added. "You're young and can go in any direction you want. Just think about that before you sign this. That's all we're saying."

A part of Delphinium appreciated how protective they were. From an adult perspective, she understood them wanting to caution her. "I appreciate your advice, but there is nowhere else I'd love to work than the shop. Moonberry Lake is my home, and I want to stay here. I know it may seem like a smaller life than you probably imagined for me, but I don't want a different one. I love my shop on Main Street. I want to be a part of the Moonberry community."

"And what about all the seniors?" her mother asked.

Delphinium shrugged. "Nothing will change. When I reorganize the shop, I'm going to have them over as often as they like."

Her mother nodded. "Okay. That's nice of you, but what about all the other residents at The Gardens who have read about your shop and will want to come? If anything, the attention you've drawn is only going to bring more to you, more than your shop could handle."

Delphinium hadn't thought of that but knew her mother was right. There would be seniors who wouldn't be able to come because of overcrowding. Not to mention how transportation would become a circus. Then she remembered Elliot's offer. She clasped her hands in her lap and looked down. "Elliot asked me to set up a gardening program at The Gardens so all the seniors could participate. It would involve me overseeing volunteers tending to a large greenhouse and flower field and interacting with the seniors. He even promised compensation by offering a huge portion of the flowers grown for my shop."

"That sounds right up your alley," her father said.

"You would be using all your gifts," her mother agreed.

"It would be a lot of work to do both jobs. I want to keep my shop, but I also want to continue working with the seniors."

"Well, if anyone has the creativity to figure out how to do both, it's you." Her father smiled.

"So, you're going to sign?" her mother asked, nodding to the paperwork in front of them.

Delphinium took a big breath. "I'll make it work." She smiled, feeling the bloom of hope and excitement in her chest. *I can make this work.*

Her dad waved to the bank manager through the wall of glass and she came back in. Then they all scrutinized every detail of the mortgage contract to make sure nothing like the previous crisis would ever happen again. In the end, an agreement was reached, and the bank even offered a financial consultant to reach out to Delphinium quarterly to make sure she was on track with her fiscal goals.

As they walked out of the bank, Delphinium was overwhelmed with a sense of relief and joy she hadn't felt in months. She let out a long sigh.

Her mother looped an arm around hers. "It's all going to work out. I'm excited to see what you do with the shop and your life in this new season."

Delphinium held that same sense of optimism. "Thanks."

"And it's also all going to work out with Henry," she added.

The sadness that Delphinium had been pushing aside resurfaced. "It can't. He's dying."

Her mother directed them toward a bench in the shade.

"Come sit with me for a minute."

Delphinium shook her head. "I need to get to the hospital."

"This will only take a minute," she said, repeating the exact words her husband had stated earlier that morning. She sat down and patted an empty spot on the bench.

Although Delphinium felt impatient, she sat. Her father stood off to the side, staring up at the sky and trees, trying to appear as if he was doing anything but eavesdropping.

Her mother looked at her. "Can I tell you the truth without you getting mad at me?"

Delphinium made a face. "There's no way I can promise that."

Her mother took a big breath before blurting out, "You are blaming Elliot for something he had no control over. He was bound by *law* not to say anything to you."

Delphinium stiffened and began to get up when her mother took her hand to stop her.

"You know what one of your absolute best qualities is?" her mother asked. "It's that you love with your whole heart. You hold nothing back when it's important to you. I think that is why you have such a gift with flowers. You express love with color, texture, and an eye for bringing different things together that would normally never go together. Everything you do is an outpouring of all the emotion you feel inside. You say things verbally, but you also act out your love."

Delphinium stared at her.

"Do you remember when the family dog died and you didn't talk to us for a week? You somehow blamed us for her death. You called us killers and accused us of not loving the dog as much as you did."

Delphinium nodded. "I remember thinking you brought Muffin to the vet to be put down because she was old and you wanted to get rid of her. I was devastated."

Her mother sighed with a slight shake of her head. "That dog was in so much pain, the vet told us it was the only humane thing to do. But you couldn't see it. You *wouldn't* see it." She paused. "Your passion sometimes gets ahead of you and leads you down the wrong path of assumption. You have a heart of gold, but you have to admit, there is an impulsive side to you." She raised an eyebrow. "You tend to react first and then think about things later."

Delphinium hated hearing these words but couldn't deny the glimmers of truth. Her shoulders slumped. "Yeah. I'm not you or Dad. I don't always act rationally."

Her mother chuckled, shaking her head. "No, you don't. I am me, as much as you are you. It is how God made me and it is how God made you. And as we both age, I hope we'll both continue to find more understanding and patience for each other."

Her dad put a hand on her shoulder. "We may react differently, but that doesn't change the fact that your mother and I want the best for you. All we're asking is that you consider the terrible position Elliot was placed in. His esteem for you was apparent the first time we spoke to him. He was devastated that you were upset at the protest, and I can only imagine how he must feel now."

They were right. She had overreacted in her emotions over Henry and took it out on Elliot.

She rubbed her forehead. "I don't know how Elliot will ever forgive me for the awful things I said to him."

"Then do what anyone else who has screwed up does," her mother said. "Begin with a genuine apology. All you can offer is sincere remorse, then move forward and try not to repeat past mistakes."

Delphinium inhaled and groaned. "The man always sees me at my worst."

Her father smiled. "Then imagine how dazzled he will be when he catches a glimpse of you at your best." He winked. "Because let me tell you from experience, it's astonishing."

Delphinium stared at him dazed. This trip had revealed such a different side to her parents. Maybe they had all reached the age and place in life where calling a truce and letting the past stay in the past was the best option to move forward. They hadn't changed in personality, and neither had she, but living and loving with huge differences between them felt fine. Unity in their family was never going to look like uniformity. The challenge would always be to embrace the contrast of the other, as an act of love.

"Plus," her father continued, "something tells me that Elliot knows about the fire that's inside of you and is willing to get burned sometimes in order to get near the flame."

Delphinium peered down. "We are so different."

"Which is why you complement each other," he added. "The best unions are those where the other person's strengths are your weaknesses and vice versa. I think Elliot is drawn to you because you have the enthusiasm and expression that he doesn't, while he can offer you a steadfast quietness and order to life."

"Is this leading back to you calling me an unleashed tornado?" Delphinium teased.

He grinned. "Well, if we're going with metaphors, how about you're a hurricane and Elliot is the calm eye of the storm."

"I'm not sure that's any better. You've now described me as fire, a tornado, and a hurricane. Those are a lot of natural disasters."

Her mother got up from the bench. "Come on, we'll drive you back to the shop and you can take the van to the hospital."

Back at the shop, she couldn't feel as happy as she should about staying open when she thought about Henry in the hospital. He loved the place nearly as much as she did. She knew he would be thrilled when he heard that Annie's place and the shop would remain on Main Street. The shop was so bare without the abundance of flowers and gifts that gave it a personality—it still appeared as if it was permanently closed.

As if reading her mind, her mother asked, "When are you going to reopen?"

Delphinium shrugged. "I don't know. I have to see how things go with Henry."

Her parents didn't respond.

"The place feels hollow. It's so empty." She turned around slowly. "It's going to take a lot of work. I'm going to have to call Paavo and see if he can work more hours. I could also freshen up the paint with another coat of delphinium blue."

"Your signature color." Her mother grinned. "You know Arlene would be tickled to help you out."

Delphinium brightened at the idea. "You're right. She would. She's a worker bee and her cleaning skills are unbelievable. Not to mention, she has an eye for creating displays. I'd hire her in a minute even if it was only a couple hours a week. All of the seniors are up to help if you give them a task."

"They fought so hard to keep it from closing—it seems natural that they be involved in the reopening," her father added.

"I wholeheartedly agree," Delphinium said. "But first, I need to spend time with Henry."

Her mother nodded. "There are some last-minute things I wanted to do before we leave. Call us later with an update."

"Okay."

"We'll lock up the shop for you," her father offered. "I want to spend a little more time relaxing in the apartment."

Delphinium thought that was a little odd but didn't say anything and left.

Twenty-Six

When Delphinium entered the hospital room, Henry was asleep. She went over and placed her hand over his. His eyes opened immediately. "Hey there."

"I'm sorry. I didn't think that would wake you. I just wanted to hold your hand."

"Nonsense. I was only snoozing lightly. I've been waiting for you," he said, giving her a small sleepy smile.

"Yeah?" She smiled back. "Well, I'm here now. What is it that you wanted to say?" She leaned over and gave him a kiss on the cheek. "I'm all ears."

"Elliot came by earlier and looked as if he lost his only friend."

Delphinium peered down guiltily. His words reawakened the ache in her chest.

"When I pressed him about his status with you, he glossed over an explanation. I knew something had to be wrong with the way he looked, but he wouldn't budge in protecting you. It's not a far jump for me to guess that you blame him for not telling you about my health." He waited for Delphinium to look back up at him and eventually she did. His expression was solemn. "I know Elliot is a man of his word. He didn't tell you about my condition because I asked him not to. He was honoring my request."

Delphinium's shoulders slumped. "Things were said between

Elliot and me. I may not have taken it well. And you know my feelings about lying since that's how men have hurt me in the past.
Elliot has to be honest with me about all things—even the hard
things—if he wants my trust."

"He was honest with you about his feelings. He only withheld
a piece of information that I asked him to keep to himself. So if
you're going to be mad at anyone, be mad at me."

"You know that's never going to happen."

Henry took a slow breath. "I want you to know how in love I
was with your grandmother."

A corner of Delphinium's mouth lifted. "I always knew you guys
were more than best friends."

Henry gave a weak chuckle. "She called me her 'companion.'
Said we were too old to marry. I told her how crazy I was about
her all the time. I was a broken record in my profession of love.
I wanted to marry her and even went so far as giving her a ring.
But she refused."

Delphinium frowned. "Why?"

"She was stubborn and fiercely independent."

Delphinium could not disagree with his assessment.

Henry pointed at her. "You have that same streak in you."

She opened her mouth to say something but had nothing to
rebut his words.

"Annie was private and guarded her freedom. We never came
out as a couple because she wouldn't ever make it official even
though we did everything together. I was so in love with her," he
said, looking away as if a memory was swallowing him up.

The obvious heartbreak in his voice nearly broke her.

"We were each other's best confidant," he went on, "but she
wouldn't take my love because she said we were 'cut from different cloth.' She was an artist, and I was all about accounting and
finance. Her world was full of color, and mine was full of numbers.
She said we were as mismatched as a pair of socks and it would
never work, but nevertheless, we were together all the time."

"I'm so sorry" was the only thing Delphinium could say.

"What got me through the grief of losing her was looking after you this past year. You two share the same spirit. So much so, that it's like watching history repeat itself."

"What do you mean?"

"I feel sorry for Elliot because I know there's heartbreak in his future too. You hold the same prejudice about certain people as your grandmother did."

She frowned. "That's not true."

"It's absolutely true. Your parents may have made some mistakes in understanding you, but now every type A personality who crosses your path pays for it."

Delphinium shifted uncomfortably. She couldn't believe Henry was talking to her this way. She opened her mouth to contradict his words, but Henry stopped her.

"I'm only telling you this because I love you. Elliot looks at you with the same admiration and wonder that I had for Annie. He sees the same marvelous uniqueness and artistic energy in you that I did with your grandmother, and you're going to toss it aside like it's nothing."

"I'm not tossing anything aside. As a matter of fact, I've already come to the conclusion that he's a good man."

"Is that so?"

"Yes. And my parents and I have learned some things about each other recently and have come to a sort of understanding also. They surprised me with their support, and we've had some good talks. We've each thrown up a flag of surrender and are talking again."

"Hmm." He looked at her skeptically.

"I'm telling you the truth. I see Elliot for the man he is, and I'm no longer hung up on the fact that he shares a scary resemblance to my parents. As a matter of fact, the last couple weeks have proven to me that I might benefit, and dare I say *need* a type A personality in my life for balance."

"Good. Because you may have this tremendous perception about others, but you don't have that gift when it comes to yourself. You don't see yourself the way others do, so let me tell you, I can say with absolute certainty that you are a person with a giving soul and a big heart."

"Henry—" she began, but he cut her off.

"You work hard at your job and even harder at being a good person. You are kind and trustworthy. But you hold on to past grievances like a turtle to its shell. However a man hurt you in the past does not dictate what a different man will do in the future."

Delphinium could only nod.

"And while I'm ranting, let me say that I've only met one other person in my entire life—which says a lot because I got a lot of years behind me—who had as much creative talent as you. Your grandmother was unlike anyone I've ever met. There was a real sparkle to her. The way she saw color, how she seemed to experience everything in life with a heightened sensitivity. There was a bravery about her that most people don't have."

He enveloped her hand in both of his. "Hear me when I say that she would see you as a success in every meaning of the word. You gave a bunch of old people who were bored to tears a place to go to find purpose. You brightened the day of every customer that came into the shop, and their days were even better with your flower creations. And most importantly, you followed your heart's passion and worked on something that brought you joy. There is no measure for that.

"I think the perception you've had about yourself is all wrong. You see yourself as only being able to pick up on the scent of people. But if you ask anyone, they would say you're a remarkable woman with many talents. You are a complex, multifaceted extraordinary person that I have the privilege of calling friend . . . and family."

She looked at him, teary-eyed. "Wow," she whispered. "I don't think most people get to hear that kind of praise about themselves until their funeral."

"Well, I'm telling you now. The world needs the beauty you bring to it."

She leaned over and rested her head against his shoulder. "I couldn't have gotten this far on my own. What am I going to do without you?"

"What everyone else does when they lose someone close," he said, patting her back. "Keep putting one foot in front of the other and finish your own race at whatever pace you choose to go. Then see where it leads you. When I did that, it led me to your shop."

They were both quiet. The room was still enough that the sounds from the hallway seemed amplified.

She straightened her posture. "I love you, Henry."

"Love you too, kid. Always have, always will." The words came out with effort. A veil of weariness descended. He blinked until he couldn't keep his eyes open any longer, and he fell into sleep.

Delphinium stayed by his bed the rest of the day, thinking about her life. Henry slept the entire time, and the nurses assured her that was normal. As evening came, she decided to go home. She'd return first thing in the morning.

Henry looked comfortable, not in pain, which soothed her sadness. More than anything, he simply looked tired as he started his journey home.

When Delphinium stepped into the shop that night, her jaw dropped. The place was bursting with balloons. Literally. There were so many floating and bumping around, their strings dangling down like confetti, that not even a patch of ceiling was showing. And there were bunches tied together in bundles to anything solid on the floor. Balloons upon balloons took up nearly every inch of space. She stood in the entrance, taking it all in.

Her parents came in from the back room, grinning from ear to ear. "Surprise!" they said in unison.

"What's this?" she asked, bewildered by the unexpected sight.

Her father made his way over to her, pushing aside balloons. "Your mother and I thought we could help you get ready for your reopening celebration."

Delphinium stared at the colorful sight. She was stunned by the heartfelt display. They were trying so hard to support and connect with her. "There are so many balloons, there's no room for actual flowers."

Her father waved away her concern. "We'll put some out on the sidewalk to draw attention and help make the big announcement."

"Thank you. This is so kind, but I think I'm going to wait. I don't want to miss a day with Henry. I want to focus on just that right now, because when I do officially reopen the shop, I have a stack of preorders to complete."

Her parents nodded. "We understand."

"Maybe it would be best to bring these all over to The Gardens to brighten the rooms of the seniors," her mother suggested. "We could say that it is a celebration for all their hard work in keeping the shop open."

"They would love that." Delphinium smiled at the thought of all the balloons decorating their rooms, but then she thought of how Elliot might feel with the reminder of her and her shop.

As if reading her mind, her father asked, "Have you spoken to Elliot?"

She shook her head.

Her parents exchanged looks but said nothing.

Delphinium couldn't take it. "Well? Aren't you going to say anything?"

"Letting go of your pride and humbly asking for forgiveness are always big pills to swallow. It's best to do both in one gulp," her father said.

"Or you could call him up and ask if you can talk," her mother added.

But the opportunity never came. When Delphinium went to see Henry the next morning, the nurses told her he had taken a turn for the worse and he was going quicker than anticipated. His transition toward leaving this world had begun. The morphine that he had asked for way ahead of time kept his respiration low and kept him in a deep sleep.

Delphinium didn't leave that day, and Henry gently slipped away in the middle of the night. His passing was as quiet and peaceful as he promised. A calm exit for the most tender soul. Standing alone in his room, Delphinium couldn't help but smile at the thought that he finally got to see what heaven was like. He had been so looking forward to going home.

Her parents had cleared the shop of balloons so she had the workspace to create the flower arrangements for Henry's funeral. She had ordered all of Henry's favorites.

"You know, you don't have to do the arrangements," her mother said. "You can take this time to mourn."

"I want to do it," she said, laying out groups of flowers for the service. "It's my farewell gift to Henry."

Besides the typical funeral array of roses, lilies, and carnations, Delphinium put together a couple arrangements filled with honeysuckle, Henry's signature fragrance. The entire time she was creating the bouquets, tears flowed down her face.

The funeral was packed with all the seniors from The Gardens. It had taken a couple of school buses to get them all to the church, but they were all present.

Delphinium sat up front and couldn't help but peek to the back to see if Elliot would show. He did. Sitting in a dark suit in the far back, he sat erect and by himself. For a moment, he caught her gaze but then looked away. She turned back around.

After the service, she resolved to go up and speak to him, but he had already disappeared.

Two days after the funeral, her parents had to leave.

"Let us know how things turn out," her father said.

"Yes," her mother agreed. "No matter what happens, promise us that you'll call or pick up when we call you."

Delphinium nodded.

"We support you," her father said. "Whatever direction you choose to take or wherever life may lead you. All we ask is that you include us in what's happening."

As they were hugging goodbye, the front door to the shop opened with familiar faces.

Gurdy threw her hands in the air. "We came to see you off!"

"I'd offer to drive you to the airport," Bob grumbled, "but they won't renew my license."

"Keeping you off the roads has probably saved many lives," Arlene said.

Her parents were clearly taken aback. "You all came just to say goodbye?" her mother asked.

"Of course," Joanna said. "My grandson got in trouble in school, so as punishment, he has to drive me wherever I want to go whenever I need a lift. I can have him drive you if you like."

"Thank you, but we already have transportation," her father quickly added.

"Wise choice," Patsy said from the back. "The kid drives wildly. If I wasn't so close to death already, I'd fear for my life."

Delphinium's father chuckled, covering his mouth like it was a cough. "It was lovely to meet you all. My wife and I are thankful for how you look after our daughter."

"Well, we feel as if she's the one looking after us." Gurdy winked.

Weaving his way to the front, George stuck out his hand. "Safe travels. It was good to meet you. We'll keep an eye on Delphi."

Bob outstretched his hand for her father to shake. "Yep. Don't worry. We'll keep her out of trouble."

"I think that's the other way around, Bob," Delphinium said.

Her mother and father hugged Delphinium one last time each. Then her mother whispered in her ear, "We will call you tonight when we get home."

Delphinium kissed her on the cheek, surprised at the emotion rising up in her chest. It had been a hard week, and she was so thankful they had been there for her.

As soon as final goodbyes were said and everyone waved them off, Bob spun around. "Okay, let's go in the back for our roundtable discussion."

Delphinium rolled her eyes. "As long as we are not following parliamentary procedure, you guys can talk about anything you want. What's on today's agenda?"

"We came for our instructions." Arlene saluted.

"Instructions?" Delphinium repeated.

"The battle plan," Bob clarified.

"Battle plan?" Now Delphinium was even more confused.

"Yes," Gurdy said with a little clap. "The big idea!" She out-stretched her hands in a motion that looked like fireworks.

"What are you all talking about?"

"How you're going to win Elliot back, of course," Helen said. "We want to be a part of your grandiose display."

"I told them all that, with your creativity, you'd be doing some-thing wild and imaginative," Patsy croaked in her raspy voice. "Something that really knocks his dress socks off."

"That man looks as if his dog was run over," Bob said. "He still hasn't responded to my written complaint about them not serving enough tapioca. One serving a day just isn't enough."

Delphinium slumped down on her stool. "I'm sorry to disappoint you, but I don't have a plan."

They all stared at her.

"This calls for our emergency backup plan." George nodded sharply.

"Yep, pull the cord on the parachute." Bob pumped his arm, mimicking pulling a cord.

Delphinium began shaking her head. "No, no, no. I don't want any of you to do something that involves the word *emergency*. You've already met your paramedic, police, and fire truck quota for the year, if not the decade."

"I do miss those firemen." Patsy sighed.

"We need to focus." Helen pounded her fist on the table like a judge's gavel.

"It has to be something spectacular." Joanna stretched out her arms like the former cheerleader she once was.

"What if you dressed up in one of those little sailor's outfits and then went to see him? You know, something less flowery than what you usually wear?" Bob suggested.

"How about you take a break from brainstorming, Bob," Gurdy suggested with a shake of her head, looking every bit like an exasperated middle-school teacher. "Or I'm going to go have you sit in the corner."

"I think we all need to approach Elliot," Arlene stated with a playful gleam in her eyes.

"No," Delphinium interjected. "Please stay out of it."

"We've got it handled," George said.

"No. Promise me that you all will stay out of it," Delphinium pleaded.

All the seniors exchanged stares and jointly gave a nod to each other while not looking directly at Delphinium.

Instead of planning some grandiose display, the seniors talked about the shop a little before heading out for the day.

Delphinium was too busy going through preorders and writing out the supplies she was going to need to pay much attention to the fact that the seniors never actually agreed to stay out of her personal business with Elliot. When the concern percolated up that they might go rogue on her again, she reminded herself she had asked them not to do anything.

They won't do anything.

Right?

Twenty-Seven

That evening, Delphinium walked into Lindsey's apartment, where every available table, counter, nook, and cranny held a container of purple hyacinth.

Lindsey came out from the kitchen holding two more flowerpots in her arms. "They just keep coming," she said, exasperated. "I don't know why Mason keeps sending these and only these."

Delphinium reached out and stroked one. "It's because he's asking for forgiveness."

Lindsey crinkled her brow like Delphinium was speaking a foreign language. "What?"

"The first time he came into the shop, I told him that you give someone purple hyacinth when you are asking for forgiveness. But by the amount he has sent, I would say he is more begging than asking."

Lindsey looked around the room. "Well, I'd say this is a bit of an overkill."

Delphinium stared at the field of flowers in front of her. Mason must have bought out every flower he could find. "This has cost him a fortune."

Lindsey didn't respond.

"You know, just because I don't like him doesn't mean you have to feel the same way." Delphinium crossed the room, then plopped onto the couch. "I would be petty and a bad friend to ask that of you."

Lindsey shifted the pots in her arms. "You're not asking. He lied to both of us. Date after date, he kept the truth from me." She shook her head. "It makes me wonder who I was even dating. I guess both of us have zero tolerance for lying."

Delphinium was quiet for a couple minutes before asking, "What was he like when you were dating? What drew you to him?"

Lindsey smiled despite herself. "He was so funny and always had me laughing. And he was up for anything I wanted to do. He loved to come to my boot camps and fully supported my love for health and fitness." Lindsey's smile turned wistful and a bit sad. "There was something adventurous about him, and he matched my high energy."

Now it was Delphinium who didn't have any words. She knew how charming Mason could come across from his visits to the shop.

Lindsey finally broke the awkwardness. "What should we do with all these flowers? We can't even move around with them taking up so much space."

Delphinium adjusted one of the plants that was teetering on the edge of an end table. "If you don't want them here, I would love to bring some over to Arielle, Sofia, and Cora as a thank-you for their help the other day. I think it would make them all smile, and these will last longer than most arrangements because they are in planters."

Lindsey nodded. "Let's do it."

Delphinium picked up a couple and then stopped. "I just want to say for the record that you can love whoever. Take me out of the equation when looking for love."

"How can I do that? You're my best friend and have a better perception about people than anyone I know."

She didn't want to admit the guilt gnawing at her. Mason wasn't the awful person she made him out to be. He was a businessman. Period. They hadn't even known each other long, so it wasn't like he was a dear friend. If she had learned anything from the financial debacle and going through the paperwork at the bank, it was that business transactions were black and white, completely void of emotion. "I'm not so sure about that anymore."

"Why would you say that?" Lindsey asked.

Delphinium shrugged. "Because at the core of it all, everything was my mistake. I'm the one that was going into foreclosure because of the decisions I made years ago. Mason had nothing to do with that."

Lindsey was quiet.

"I just want to make sure that you don't miss out on happiness because of my stubbornness and bias with picking up on people's scent."

"I'll think about it, if you promise to think about not missing out on your own happiness because of that stubbornness."

"Touché."

Walking down Main Street, Delphinium happened to glance inside the Shoelace Café. Mason was sitting in a small booth by himself, looking miserable. It was ten o'clock in the morning. As much as she wanted to keep on walking, she couldn't. Between remembering Lindsey's face the night before and seeing how unhappy he appeared, she couldn't keep moving her feet. Already regretting it, she went inside. He didn't notice her until she plunked her oversized bag down on the seat next to him.

"What do you want?" he mumbled.

"I saw all the purple hyacinth you sent Lindsey."

"Yeah, well, I learned from the best. Now I have to see if what you said is true and she gives me another chance."

They both stared at each other.

He broke the silence. "Congrats on saving your shop."

"How does that change your plans for moving offices?"

"There's always more real estate out there." Mason let out a heavy sigh. "My reputation, however, is in the garbage because of that article." He lifted his glass of soda. "Cheers to making me the town jerk. I am officially the most hated man in Moonberry. Everyone looks at me like I'm a pariah."

"That's a bit dramatic, don't you think?"

"I've had three clients leave me over wanting to buy your shop. They said they couldn't work with me in good conscience. And let's just say that no potential clients have called or returned my calls."

"And you're sure it's because of the article?"

His nostrils flared. "Of course! I am officially the guy that tried to kick a bunch of old people from their playground. How much more of a villain could I be? The only thing I could do worse is maybe bulldoze a beloved daycare or a historic church." He took a swig of his drink. "The downside to small-town living is the long memory that goes along with everyone who lives here. I don't know how I'm going to live this one down. I might as well go around wearing a big V for villain on the front of my shirt." He pushed his glass away from him. "The worst thing I ever did was enter your shop."

Delphinium crossed her arms over her chest. "How quickly you forget that you are the one who came to spy on me. A wolf dressed as a customer looking to buy flowers."

He took a big breath. "Okay, I admit, my intentions may not have been exactly pure the first time I came in, but then I became fascinated with the place. As soon as I got to know you and saw how the seniors loved the shop, I was hooked and felt guilty about my involvement. That's why I wanted to help you find another location. I didn't want you to stop being a florist or to leave the seniors abandoned. Then it became a mess when I met Lindsey. She had no idea about the sale. I knew that you would eventually put it all together and not want her to be with me."

Delphinium kept her arms tight around her as she continued to stew. "You trivialize my life down to simply shifting a few seniors to another location. The shop is my dream, my *life*. The building is where my grandmother lived, and some of my most treasured memories happened there." She took a moment to calm herself. "I love working there. And I'm good at what I do."

"I know," he said. "I know. That's why I wanted to somehow help you."

"It also explains why you pounced so quickly on notifying the bank that you were interested in buying it once I went into foreclosure."

"Which I feel guilty about. But let's face facts. The shop was closing. I saw an opportunity for a beautiful location for my office. You can't deny that anyone else would have grabbed that Main Street corner property in a minute. I completely agree that you have tremendous talent as a florist. You're one of the most gifted people I've ever come across. Not only with flowers but with people." He slouched a bit. "I'm sorry about Henry. I know how special he was to you. He was a good guy."

Delphinium's shoulders sank as well. Just the mention of Henry brought on a fresh wave of grief.

Mason drained the last of his drink. "Getting involved with your shop cost me my reputation and a very nice girlfriend."

Delphinium didn't have a response. She wasn't angry anymore. She held no real grudge toward him. She couldn't blame him for snooping on a potential real estate investment when that was basically his job. He may have done it more sneakily than she ever would have, but she could appreciate how things had become complicated with his guilt toward the seniors and then his attraction to Lindsey.

He had lost more than she had in the end. She still had her shop—but even if she didn't, what the protest and her parents proved to her was that she had a family and a community that didn't go away with her business.

She met his eyes. "I don't know what to say."

"Say you'll talk to Lindsey. Say you'll try to fix this. Convince her that I'm not this evil person for wanting your property when I thought it was available." He took a long breath. "She's different from anyone I've met."

"You're a player."

He ran his hands over his face. "I *used* to be a player. And then I met a woman who made me want to change and do anything to keep her." He stared intently at Delphinium. "I don't want to lose something that has the potential to be special and lasting."

His statement immediately brought Elliot to mind.

He put some cash on the table and got up to leave. As he turned and stepped in front of her, Delphinium reached out and grabbed his arm.

"Wait a minute," she said, pulling him closer to her.

She inhaled deeply.

Cyclamen.

"Not again," he mumbled.

"No. You're different. I smell cyclamen on you!"

"And what does that mean?" He pulled his arm from her grasp. "No, let me guess. It's some flower that validates I'm a jerk."

Delphinium shook her head. "On the contrary, the flower represents sincerity, as in freedom from deceit, hypocrisy, and duplicity. People who emit this are serious about their commitment to being truthful and kind."

Mason crossed his arms over his chest. "I told you I've changed. I'm trying to be more sincere and truthful in my actions."

Delphinium couldn't deny the earnestness in both his eyes and his scent. "I promise to talk to Lindsey."

Twenty-Eight

It was the day before the big reopening, and the shop was buzzing with activity. Arlene, Joanna, Gurdy, and Helen had come to help. Gurdy had taken her spot next to Paavo, where they worked with the flowers. Helen was seated at the table, folding a pile of rags right out of the dryer. Arlene and Joanna were washing the front windows and wiping off the displays before all the buckets of flowers went back on them. They insisted that the shop sparkle.

After a couple hours, they all said they needed to return to The Gardens to help with a big project the guys were working on. Delphinium didn't think anything of it and was too preoccupied to ask, so she gave them all hugs as they made their way to the little bus.

Paavo had music blasting in the back as he worked, and Delphinium felt swept away in the frantic excitement. She was afraid to pinch herself and not have this job be real. *It's a new beginning*, she thought. *I'm still here. It all worked out okay.* The only thing missing was her beloved Henry. He would have beamed with pride over how the shop looked.

When the phone rang, she was delighted to answer it. "Delphinium's Flora Emporium."

"Hey, Delphi, it's Gurdy. I left my purse in the back. Would you mind bringing it to me right away? There are some pills inside that I need to take."

"Of course. Want me to call you when I'm outside the building and you can just come out and get it?"

"No. Would you mind bringing it to the courtyard?"

"Oh."

"Just run in, honey. There's something I want to show you. Please hurry."

Before Delphinium could respond, Gurdy hung up.

Instead of going through the front door and risking being seen—or worse, being turned away—Delphinium took the long route and walked around the entire building as she had done that day with Elliot to get to the courtyard. As she rounded the corner, she gasped at the sight in front of her.

Gone was the pristine green lawn. It looked like an army of gophers had attacked it. There were hundreds of shallow holes in the ground.

"What have you guys done?" she hissed in alarm.

"We've started our own gardening program," George said, coming over with a woman's scarf tied around his head and knotted below his chin. He looked ridiculous.

"George, why are you wearing a scarf?"

"Joanna said I was starting to burn. I can't find my hat, so she gave me one of her scarves to protect my tip-top from burning to a crisp."

Mason came over dressed in old jeans and a T-shirt. He was holding a shovel. "Where should I start digging?"

"Start digging?" she asked. "Mason, who told you to do this?"

Mason stuck his shovel in the ground and leaned against it. "Bob called me. I got my firm to fund the gardening equipment."

"And Elliot told you this was okay to do?"

He shrugged. "No. I only spoke with Bob."

"And you trusted *Bob*?!"

"Delphinium!" The booming voice behind her sent shivers down her body.

She turned to see Elliot storming over toward her. "What is all this? I did not authorize this absolute chaos." He looked around, appearing as if the wind had been knocked out of him. "Look at all these holes! The flawless lawn is destroyed."

"This was their attempt to start the gardening program. I'm so sorry. I assure you, I never told them to do anything like this."

"I did," Mason said, stepping forward. "The seniors called and asked for my help, and I assumed they had prior authorization." He directed his words to Elliot. "I should have checked with you. I didn't even think about it when the guys asked me to bypass checking in at the front desk and bring the tools to the back. That should have been a red flag."

Delphinium put her hand on Elliot's arm. "He's not as experienced with the seniors' mischief making as we are."

"Apparently," Elliot responded, glancing down at her touch.

The three of them looked out to the lawn where all the seniors were sitting on chairs from the courtyard. They were bent over and digging into the lawn like kids in a sandbox.

"Unbelievable," Delphinium said. "It's like dealing with delinquents. They're always one step ahead of you."

Elliot huffed out a hard breath. "What's done is done." He turned his head to Mason. "At one point, the seniors have bested all of us. Bob played you. The man is personally responsible for leading a coup over wanting us to serve hot wings and tater tots twice a week."

Mason looked out to the lawn with a different perspective. "I'm so sorry I helped them desecrate this place."

"It's just as well." Elliot appeared resigned. "We are going to implement a gardening program. It was going to be a downsized version from the original plan, but once again, a select few seniors have taken the initiative to do things according to their plan."

They watched Gurdy, who was on all fours, hike one leg into the air in a pumping motion. Delphinium recognized the glute exercise from a Pilates class she took once. It didn't matter where or what Gurdy was doing, the woman found a way to move her body.

Delphinium saw through the entire ruse. "A plan meant to bring us here together." She looked at Elliot.

"Then why am I here if this is about you two?" Mason asked.

"I don't think they wanted only Elliot and me to talk," Delphinium said, gesturing across the lawn.

Mason's gaze went to Lindsey who was standing on the patio holding a tray of energy balls, appearing completely bewildered by the scene. When she locked eyes with Mason, she froze. Luckily, Joanna went over and took the tray from her hands and began walking around, offering the treats to the others as a self-appointed hostess.

Mason dropped his shovel and ran over to Lindsey.

Delphinium couldn't hear what he was saying, but when Lindsey glanced over at her, Delphinium nodded with a grin. She decided to take the same cue and stepped in front of Elliot. "Can we talk?"

Elliot gave a stiff nod.

"I am so sorry."

"You had no idea they were going to do this. I'm not faulting you for this disaster."

"No, I mean for how I blamed you for not telling me about Henry. I reacted before I thought through the position you were put in. For what it's worth, I am so sorry for what I said and how I hurt you."

"I know Henry was your family. A person doesn't have to be blood for you to love them deeply. He was a grandfather to you."

She nodded. "Thank you for understanding. I'm sorry I screwed up so badly and blew up at you when your hands were tied. You were in a terrible position that I refused to acknowledge." She bit down on her lip to keep it from trembling, but there was nothing she could do about the tears welling in her eyes.

Elliot took her hand, lifted it to his lips, and lightly kissed it.

Delphinium melted on the spot.

His gentleman's kiss was so automatic and so endearing and casual, it made her all but jump in his arms. Acting on that urge without thinking, she threw herself against him, holding on with all her might. "Please tell me you forgive me. I'm so sorry."

She waited, holding on.

He said nothing.

He did nothing.

Apparently he was always going to be surprised by her spontaneity.

Eventually his arms wound around her waist, and he held her firmly.

As he released a breath, she found that she could also exhale.

She didn't dare move or allow an inch of space between them. She wasn't simply holding on for his forgiveness or even friendship. She held on for the hope of what could be and what she wanted more than anything else.

"I've missed you," he whispered into her ear.

The intimate moment was so public, but she didn't care.

She felt him place a light kiss on the side of her head.

"I'm sorry," she repeated.

"I know. It was an emotional time. Let's move forward."

After lingering like that for a few more cherished moments, she began to draw back, and he followed suit. The physical separation was already impacting her. There was something about being in his arms that felt so familiar and safe. It was like stepping into home. She wanted the closeness. But more, she craved it.

Elliot reached up and tucked a stray red curl back into her tangled lion's mane. He grinned when the ringlet immediately bounced back. "I love your hair. I've wanted to touch it since I first saw you."

Delphinium watched his delight. "It's a force of nature."

"So are you."

Her breath caught. "That's not always a good thing."

He kept stroking her hair gently, oblivious to the ruckus around them. His eyes were focused on her. "You're beautiful. I love that your hair is so unruly and does what it wants. It fits your personality perfectly."

She looked down, embarrassed at his close attention.

"This insight that you get about people—"

She peered at him questioningly. "You mean the perception I get?"

"Yes," Elliot added, smiling. "Has it ever been wrong?"

Delphinium thought about that. "Only once, but even that turned out okay." She glanced over at Mason, who was talking and laughing with Lindsey.

Elliot brought a hand up to cup her face. "Your perception about me was acutely accurate. You said that my scent indicated that I was loyal and devoted to my life's passions."

"Yes."

"I am," he said resolutely. "I am devoted to my life's passions—one of which happens to be you."

His declaration made her breath catch.

He leaned in and kissed her forehead and then, with the most tender look, he moved to her mouth. But right before his lips touched hers, loud whistles rang out.

"Well, look who's trying to catch a kiss," George yelled.

"Fraternizing with the enemy," Bob grumbled.

"Give her a big smackeroo!" Joanna cheered.

"Lay one on her!" Patsy croaked.

"Kiss her like in the movies!" Arlene piped in.

"Turn so I can see!" hollered Helen from the patio.

"I can't believe he's making a move on our Delphi! They're smooching now? How much have I missed?!" Charlie looked outraged as he sat next to Helen in a wheelchair of his own.

The moment was over and both she and Elliot knew it.

"Another time," he said in a low voice.

Delphinium let out an unsteady breath and nodded. "Let's sort out this mess and get them inside. They've been in the sun too long."

"Good thinking." Elliot raised his voice to his director tone. "All right, folks, everyone inside for some refreshments. We can discuss the gardening project when you're all hydrated. Just leave your trowels on the table by the door."

The seniors began to file in, happy as could be. They patted Lindsey and Mason on the back as they passed. Delphinium noticed Mason standing right next to Lindsey, laughing alongside her.

"I suppose I have to go in and listen to their demands again and try to make something out of this," Elliot said, turning to her.

"Since I'm the executive manager of the gardening project, don't you think you should be discussing the details with me first?"

Shock played across Elliot's face before he smiled. "I would love that. So, you're really going to do it?"

"Absolutely. My shop isn't big enough to hold all the seniors that will want to participate, and nothing would make me happier than to know they have something that brings them together and entertains them. I'll get more help to divide my time. Arlene and Gurdy are great at watching over the shop when I'm in a pinch. Plus, I think the townspeople will love to see the elders working in the shop since they are the ones who saved it."

"So I'll be seeing a lot of you."

"Oh, yes. We've got our work cut out for us. It's going to take tremendous teamwork to keep this bunch under control," she said, wrapping her arms around his waist and leaning in close.

Elliot beamed. "I like the sound of that."

Her parents had surprised her by coming back to celebrate the reopening of the shop and worked eagerly alongside Paavo to get things ready. They were tickled to be a part of the crew, as they called it, and thrilled to be included in her life.

Delphinium and her mother had stayed up late unpacking fairy houses and putting up displays of new merchandise, including floral-scented lotions that she set next to the flowers. The shop looked magical with all the little lights and the many buckets bursting with fresh flowers. The air was filled with a bouquet of scents that would make customers smile and relax.

She woke at the crack of dawn to double-check everything downstairs. When it was finally time to open, there were already a few people at the door waiting to come in. As her parents stood at the counter in matching aprons, she greeted everyone with a cheery smile and invited them in to wander the shop.

The next wave of people were the seniors, who entered whooping in celebration. They each took a handful of carnations and insisted on standing outside and handing flowers to passersby.

When Delphinium caught a glimpse of the next visitor, she stopped in her tracks. Widgy McQuire, in grease-covered overalls, stomped over to her in steel-toed boots. She greeted Delphinium with a curt nod. "Glad to see you're back in business and those seniors out of the refrigerator and *alive*."

"Thanks" was all Delphinium could utter.

"I read about you in the paper when I was checkin' the obits and thought I'd bring you somethin' to make the shop look better like I said I would. A kinda reopenin' present." She reached down into a brown paper bag and pulled out a stuffed skunk.

Delphinium jumped when she saw it, putting a hand to her heart.

"Don't worry. It's not alive. At least, not anymore." Widgy ran her hand down its back. "Thought it would bring ya some good luck since you didn't have much before. I got another one just like it in my bathroom at home." She extended the animal to Delphinium.

"I-I don't think I can touch it," she said, stepping back.

Widgy shrugged. "It takes some folks a while to warm up to the art of taxidermy. But once you're hooked, you'll be lookin' at roadkill a lot differently. I'll just put it in between some of these flowers." The handywoman looked around the shop, wrinkling her nose as if she smelled something bad. "I see ya didn't listen when I told ya that the place is too flowery. And there's still no vending machine for my Dr Pepper." She shook her head. "You can lead a horse to water, but you can't make it swim." Going over to the largest display of flowers, she plunked the skunk down right on top of a fairy house.

With a sharp nod, she left.

George came up behind Delphinium. "I'd be happy to take that off your hands if you want."

"Yes, please," Delphinium said hastily.

He went over and tucked the skunk under his arm. "Charlie and I will have some fun with this one at The Gardens." He winked. "Some of the newcomers need to be initiated in."

Delphinium didn't respond or argue. She just wanted the creature out of her shop. She'd give Elliot a heads-up later.

After collecting herself, Delphinium kept busy flitting about, talking to customers, and putting together orders. Then suddenly she stilled. She smelled him before she saw him. Looking up, she found Elliot in the doorway. His eyes weren't on all the activity in the shop but focused solely on her. She inhaled through her nose.

They shared a smile that carried so many unspoken feelings.

Walking to her, he held out another white box from the fudge shop. "In celebration of your reopening, I thought I'd bring your second-favorite thing."

Delphinium took the box and placed it on the counter. "Chocolate has moved down one tier. It is now my third-favorite thing, with flowers being my second."

"What is your first, then?" he asked.

She took his hands and gave them a small squeeze. "You."

Elliot's chest expanded as his smile grew wide.

Delphinium was sure the pounding of his heart matched hers. She stood there nearly swaying from his scent and the love emitting from him. Her head was swimming. Her gaze went from his eyes to his mouth.

She could sense that his need matched hers, but she also remembered how he felt about onlookers when it came to showing affection. "It's okay," she whispered. "We can wait until the shop empties. Maybe you could come back after closing?"

With a glimmer in his eyes, Elliot moved closer. "You know what, some things can't wait." And with that he pulled her into his arms and kissed her, deeply and with longing. Delphinium was so shocked by his movement, she inhaled quickly with her mouth opening just enough to meet his perfectly.

It was spontaneous.

Uncharacteristically impulsive.

Deliciously reckless.

And so, so good.

The softness of his kiss grew firmer, and he showed no sign of letting her go anytime soon. And that was fine with her because she wanted it all—his intelligence, his tenderness, his warmth, and his lusciously evocative scent.

"Now there's the happy ending I was waiting for," Patsy belted out in her rough alto voice. "If you wait long enough, it always comes around."

Delphinium and Elliot pulled away from each other, laughing amid the cheers from all the seniors. Her father even whistled, and some of the customers joined in on the applause.

Delphinium's smile went from ear to ear over the eclectic community that made the most wonderful family. By the expression on Elliot's face, he was filled with the same amount of love and gratitude that was bursting inside her.

Delphinium held firm to Elliot's hand. "You were right," she whispered in his ear, "this is going to end like a fairy tale."

Looking at her with such joy, Elliot grinned.

And for a moment, Delphinium felt as though Henry and Annie were grinning down at her also.

She would cherish this memory forever. A snippet of time where everyone felt the blooming of love.

Then, above all the noise, Bob yelled, "We should celebrate with tapioca!"

Bob's Tapioca

Ingredients

1 egg yolk
3½ tablespoons tapioca
⅔ cup sugar, divided

2 cups whole milk
1 egg white
2 teaspoons vanilla extract

Instructions

1. In a large saucepan, combine egg yolk, tapioca, ⅓ cup sugar, and milk.
2. Stir and let rest 5 minutes.
3. In a bowl, beat the egg white with ⅓ cup sugar until fluffy.
4. Cook egg yolk mixture over medium heat until boiling and bubbly, stirring continuously.
5. Pour the egg yolk mixture into the egg white mixture, then add vanilla.
6. Stir to combine. Yum!

Lindsey's Oatmeal Raisin Energy Balls

Ingredients

1½ cups raw almonds
½ cup rolled oats, plus 2 tablespoons
½ cup pitted dates
¼ cup almond butter
2 tablespoons honey

2 tablespoons unsweetened almond milk
½ tsp vanilla extract
Pinch of salt
⅓ cup raisins*

Instructions

1. Pulse the almonds in a food processor until they are the consistency of almond meal. Add ½ cup of oats and process until combined.
2. Add dates, almond butter, honey, unsweetened almond milk, vanilla, and salt. Process for 1 to 2 minutes until a sticky mass forms. Transfer to a bowl and add 2 tablespoons of rolled oats and ⅓ cup raisins.
3. Wet hands slightly, then form little balls. Set on plate. The mixture should make around 16 balls.
4. Place balls in freezer for 30 minutes. Store in an airtight container in the refrigerator. Bring to room temperature before serving.

*For a variation, replace the raisins with ⅓ cup of chocolate chips!

LOVE
Moonberry
Lake?

Turn the page to read an excerpt from
the first book in the series!

One

Her mother knew when someone was pregnant and when someone was dying. She claimed it was a gift from God. At the briefest glance, she could determine if someone was experiencing the beginning of life or in the process of reaching the end.

She would see a woman shopping in a store, her stomach flat, and nod in her direction. "She's expecting."

A perfectly groomed man with only a hint of gray at the temples would be walking back from communion to his pew at Sunday service, and she'd whisper, "He doesn't have much time."

This powerful insight would have been challenged or mocked if it weren't for one annoying fact: she'd never got it wrong.

Not even when the premonition came about herself.

Cora Matthews thought of this as she looked down at the coffin. Her mother had saved her the hassle of choosing one by preordering and paying for it herself. The thing had been waiting for her mother's passing on a kind of death layaway plan. Ready when she was.

Just as well. It had saved Cora a lot of trouble, because this was *not* the casket she would have chosen. The glossy lacquer finish over the fire-engine red made her think of the wall of nail polish at a salon. For the briefest moment, she had the urge to smile at the thought of telling the pedicurist, "I'd like the color of my mother's coffin, please."

Cora restrained the impulse to display anything but misery. Appearing reticent wasn't difficult. She didn't want to be there. She was fulfilling her obligation as the sole child. The smallness of her family had dwindled to where she now stood alone in the world. The hollow feeling that accompanied that realization was surprisingly not all-consuming or overwhelming. She had gradually gotten accustomed to it over the years, like immersion into freezing cold water, nursed by her distant relationship with her mother. The closeness she had shared with her mother was more civil than familial. Neither ever saying what needed to be said.

Cora stood motionless, stuck in a state of graveside mourning expectation, not sure what to do next. A tiny part inside her, hidden below years of strife, imagined heaving sobs of heartache overcoming her—or, perhaps, searing grief that would squeeze all the air from her chest.

But she experienced neither.

At one moment she had even held her breath, waiting for a swell of emotion, but nothing came. Air moved freely in and out of her body, mingling with the tree overhead. She had no desire to collapse from sorrow onto the freshly mowed summer grass. She didn't need an arm to steady her. Her legs stood as wooden as chess pieces.

It shouldn't have been surprising. Loss was a companion that had become part of her long ago, like a callus on the pad of her foot that dulled sharp sensations. To anyone else, the bereavement would be tremendous. But Cora had been orphaned by family she cherished years ago.

Concentrating on the blades of grass, she tried to muster a single tear. She knew it wouldn't appear normal to all these people who once knew her mother to not see some show of emotion. This kind of loss was supposed to be deep and painful. Perhaps at a time that wasn't so public, she'd be able to summon that emotion from memories that still haunted her. However, today, she sensed the evaluation from others in penetrating gazes, whether it was real or imagined, and it only caused her to go more numb.

Making a fist with one hand over the other, she dug her fingernails into the soft flesh of her palm, hoping to elicit the slightest stinging in her eyes. *Just one tear*, she willed herself. *One stupid tear.*

She kept her eyes fixed on a flower resting on the coffin. The withering blossom had fallen away from the rest of the arrangement, bedraggled and abandoned. Its pitifulness captured her attention, and with luck, onlookers would assume she was lost in her grief and leave her alone. It worked successfully until the moment the service ended.

"Would you look at that, Henry? The poor dear is in shock."

Cora glanced to her right and met the stares of an elderly couple. Both had pearly white hair and pink scalps. With the same number of wisps as her nearly bald husband, the woman had pushed her thin hair back with a wide headband that looked more like a vise for her skull. The man inched closer to Cora, keeping the same distance a person would if peering into a lion's cage.

The woman pressed one hand to her chest, eyes crinkled with concern. "She's been as quiet as a mouse this whole time. I haven't seen her talk to a single soul or make a peep. I wonder if she's hysterical."

"She doesn't *look* hysterical." The man's volume revealed his hearing loss. Scrunching his face, he examined Cora through thick glasses.

Cora stared back at them. *Who on earth are these people?*

The woman squinted in concentration. "What if it's one of those silent hysterias? Do you think someone needs to shake her out of it?"

"*I* could shake her." The man spoke as if it were the most natural thing to say. His skin creased in folds as he studied Cora with magnified eyes.

"You most certainly will not, Henry Gustafson! You have a reputation to uphold in this community, and I will not be married to a man who shakes women."

"Now, settle down, Martha. I wouldn't shake her *hard.*"

His wife waved him away with a flick of her hand and stepped forward. "Oh, stop it. Let me handle this."

Curiosity bubbled up like ginger ale inside Cora. It wasn't every day that an elderly person offered to shake her.

"Honey, can you hear me? Are you all right?" the woman asked, articulating each word as if Cora were hard of hearing or knew no English. To answer her own question, the woman muttered, "Of course you're not all right." She tried again at full volume. "What I mean is, do you need me to shake you out of it? Maybe give you a hug and jiggle you about? I'm not that strong, but I'll try."

With the slightest curve touching the corners of her mouth, Cora took her time answering. "No . . . I don't think that will be necessary."

The man nodded to his wife, a wide, lopsided smile reconfiguring his wrinkled features as if to say, "See, she's not crazy after all."

The woman's face lit up in silent agreement.

Cora struggled not to laugh. The pair reminded her of matching salt and pepper shakers. They seemed proof that couples married a long time could begin to resemble each other. Their mannerisms, appearances, and ping-pong conversation were interchangeable.

"We're sorry, sweetie, but you haven't moved or said anything in a long time," Martha said. "I didn't even see you blink during the ceremony. It looked like you went into one of those catatonic trances."

Henry snorted. "I don't know how you could see anything when you're as blind as a bat without your glasses!"

"Hush, now. I'm talking to her." Martha reprimanded him with a stern look before focusing watery, cornflower-blue eyes back on Cora. "We were friends of your grandparents."

The words hit Cora as though she *had* been shaken, her numbness replaced by an unwelcome sensation. The cemetery began to feel cold, though it was a warm June day. She wrapped her arms around herself to combat the chill. She shifted, aware of the throbbing pain in her feet from standing in stiletto heels a half size too small. The sunlight suddenly seemed too bright but lacked the heat she craved.

Cora stepped out of her shoes and wiggled her toes in the grass, not caring how inappropriate it appeared. Her breath grew shallow, and she swallowed hard at the discomfort of it all.

"We loved them dearly and know they would've wanted us here today," Martha continued. "We're so sorry about your mother. We watched Lydia grow up."

The pastor cleared his throat to announce his approach, interrupting before Cora could respond. His eyes grew round, staring at her bare feet. After the service, he had mingled with the people who lingered, speaking to them in hushed tones. Though the pastor flitted around, pausing to shake hands with each person, nodding in sympathy, his hurried steps suggested he wanted this shindig to be over.

Unlike the pastor, Cora felt no rush to leave. She had nowhere she needed to be. She still hadn't found a place to live. Funny how breaking off an engagement two weeks before the wedding left one scrambling to figure out what to do—and where to go—next.

Everyone had blamed her change of heart about the wedding on the loss of her mother, and Cora hadn't done anything to contradict that assumption. She couldn't explain the panic rising like bile in her throat when she and Kyle spoke about the future together. Instead of filling out a gift registry, she had packed up her apartment and her mother's house and put it all into storage.

She had felt sick in the pit of her stomach at the look of shock and hurt in Kyle's eyes when she broke the news. She was screwing up his grand plan and doing something unexpected, which he hated. He reasoned with her that losing someone close could make a person do crazy things, which became his family's mantra to everyone after the breakup: "The bride had a breakdown."

Fine, they could think whatever they wanted. Her perceived irrational behavior had served its purpose. Her mother's death had provided an opportunity to escape the commitment she'd gotten herself into, and it was seen by others as socially acceptable considering the magnitude of her loss. She was able to abandon her life in one erratic swoop because she had seen it done. She had experienced it firsthand. That was the legacy her mother had left her—the propensity to cut ties and run.

The pastor cleared his throat again. "Pardon me, but I need to get going," he said, his eyes on Cora. "You will be in my prayers for your loss." His reverent voice, surely intended to be sincere and spiritual, felt perfunctory and scripted.

Cora couldn't explain the immediate dislike she felt when she met him. If anyone else had been available to do the service, she would've taken them. But she'd been told this man with his ashen face, drooping jowls, and sad eyes that mirrored an undeniable resemblance to a basset hound was the only pastor available.

She nodded, smiling politely, and he walked away. The service hadn't brought Cora comfort or even celebrated her mother's life. The pastor's gloom had made it hard for her to breathe, and she hated every moment in his presence.

An older man with dark eyes and a rugged appearance approached her, suddenly becoming animated after he had stood like a pillar throughout the service.

"Hello. I'm Sam Klevar." He took her outstretched hand, his grasp strong but gentle. Though not as old as the elderly couple that continued to observe her, Sam had as many deep wrinkles in his face. Thick, steely hair framed his wizened appearance, and he stood with the solid build and nonchalance of John Wayne. "Welcome back to Moonberry."

His apologetic tone and sympathetic manner felt soothing. Cora recognized his voice immediately from the phone call she'd made the previous week to discuss the funeral and her obligatory return to the town from which she had been taken almost two decades ago.

She mustered a weak smile. "It's nice to meet you."

"We've met before, but you were probably too young to remember. You couldn't have been more than six years old."

"Seven," she corrected him. "I was seven the last time I was here." That she knew with certainty. The last time she was here, her mother was crying and screaming at her grandparents and then she took her away. Cora was never allowed to see them again. And the ocean of tears she cried never brought them or her happy life at the lodge back. "I'm twenty-six now."

Sam frowned. "It has been a long time."

Her stomach growled loudly.

He smiled. "Can I offer you something to eat? Some folks have organized a small luncheon and would love to meet you. Besides, I need to speak with you about some business before you leave."

A handful of people milled around. Apparently, they weren't going to leave until she did. Spending time with a group of strangers was not something Cora wanted to do, but the guilt of proper etiquette weighed on her. She found it astounding that, even though her mother had been gone so many years, townspeople who had known her mother from childhood attended the funeral and gave a reception. She supposed the least she could do was show the same courtesy.

Cora nodded. "Thank you."

Sam's shoulders eased, and the lines on his face slackened.

"You can follow me in your car. The drive is short." He turned and nodded to the remaining mourners. Silently, they began to leave.

Cora lingered for a moment, taking one last look at her mother's lonely grave. It hadn't even occurred to her to bring flowers, the conventional sign of sympathy. Another indication of how removed she felt from the experience. Cora looked down at her feet with her sore red toes and the discarded heels next to them—shoes her mother would have loved and insisted Cora wear if she were here.

Cora had no flowers to leave behind. But she did have those uncomfortable shoes that more accurately represented their strained relationship.

Taking a deep breath, she let out a long sigh and left them, walking to her car barefoot.

Acknowledgments

I once heard the advice, "Invest in those who invest in you." Well, I am blessed beyond measure for the people who have invested in me. I only hope that each of these people feel the deep love and gratitude I have for them.

Thank you to the incredible team at Revell for your hard work and talent. Especially Kelsey Bowen and Robin Turici, who make everything shine. Kelsey, your considerate edits and explanations are always so kind. Robin, your skill is amazing. I would still like to see an MRI of your brilliant brain.

Tawny Johnson, thank you for always believing in my dreams and for helping them become a reality. The greatest gift in all of this was becoming your friend. I couldn't ask for better company in the apple orchard.

Steve Laube, thank you for being my HP. Your stories always make me feel better. Your guidance is so appreciated.

Wendi Lou Lee, Ann Newmann, and Rosie Makinney, you were present at the birth of this story. Thank you for falling in love with the characters and always rooting for the seniors. The fact that all of you get my weird sense of humor makes you very special to me.

Rosie, I know Delphinium holds a special place for you. Thank you for your advice.

Helen Arnold, your friendship is a gift every day. Your honesty in telling me the hard things and your out-of-the-box brainstorming is invaluable.

Rachel Dodge, you're a remarkable person with talent as big as your heart for God. Thanks for letting me sit by you and for being my hype girl.

Shelli Littleton, you'll never know the impact of your encouragement. Your generosity toward all writers is amazing. You are an angel.

Jennifer Hanley, you create such beauty in the world by simply being you. I'm thankful to have you in my life—and for the yellow daffodils.

To the readers who have reached out to me through my website or social media, thank you for being so passionate about Moonberry Lake. This journey began when I wrote these stories to distract myself. Little did I know they would become so meaningful to you. I am blown away by the Bookstagrammers, booksellers, and book club leaders who promote the Moonberry world. Thank you. I wish I could hug all of you.

My beloved family, you mean everything to me. In the very quiet life we live, you fill my soul to overflowing with happiness. I like to believe that God placed such introverted, tender souls together so we would understand and always support each other—which you all do.

My three bears, I love you. Each of you embody intelligence, beauty, and goodness.

I thank God, above all, for the life and stories He has given me. I am humbled that in His infinite love and wisdom, He knew I'd need Moonberry.

HOLLY VARNI is the author of *On Moonberry Lake*, a native Minnesotan of strong Norwegian descent, who was raised in the Lutheran Church that Garrison Keillor made a career depicting. Between the lutefisk, grumpy grandparents, and crazy neighbors who mowed their lawn wearing pajamas, the seed to  becoming a storyteller was planted. Though she, her husband, and their three sons live along the Central Coast of California, her beloved Midwest roots continue to haunt everything she writes. She hosts the *Moments from Moonberry Lake* podcast where she shares more stories of her beloved characters. Learn more at Holly Varni.com.

"Delightful! Charming! Full of characters
who take up residence in your heart."

—Lauraine Snelling, bestselling author

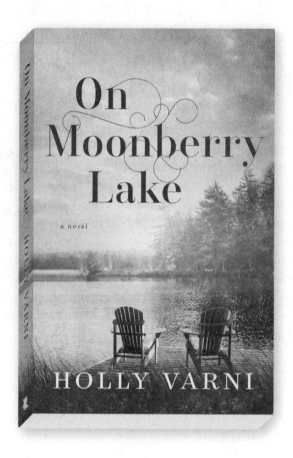

Cora Matthews returns to Moonberry Lake to settle
her mother's affairs and then get on with her life. What
she finds is a strangely enticing inheritance, including
a dilapidated lodge, eccentric neighbors, a handsome
stranger, and a whole lot of family secrets to unravel.

Ɍ Revell
a division of Baker Publishing Group
RevellBooks.com

Available wherever books and ebooks are sold.

Meet Holly

Visit Holly online at **HollyVarni.com**
to read her blog or listen to her podcast.

f HollyVarniWriter **X** HollyVarni **⊙** HollyVarni